CHRONUX

Sagar Kamath

Become
Shakespeare
.com

First published in 2017 by

Becomeshakespeare.com
Wordit Content Design & Editing Services Pvt Ltd
Unit - 26, Building A-1, Nr Wadala RTO, Wadala (East),
Mumbai 400037, India
T:+91 8080226699

©
ISBN: 978-93-86487-01-8

Acknowledgment

Writing a book as ambitious in scope as this one, brought with it innumerable challenges, and through all of it, I was incredibly fortunate to have the guidance and goodwill of all those who helped me fulfill this dream. To begin with, I would like to express my most sincere gratitude to my family, friends and all my loved ones for supporting and believing in me through this epic journey. No words on my part could ever do justice to their efforts. Special thanks must go to my mother for her 'Samsonesque' efforts in helping me proofread the manuscript and offering invaluable advice through the whole process.

For me, this journey began more than three years ago, through a stray idea that evolved and morphed into this colossus only because of a near-infinite number of conversations and discussions I had with my dear friend and colleague, Prof. Chinmay Deo. As the story developed, so did Chinmay's role in it, going from 'co-ideator' to 'devil's advocate' to 'invaluable critic'. Heartfelt thanks also to Prof. Milinda Natu, who has long been a dear friend and guide and whose support, advice and motivation has been unflinching.

Of course I could never have reached the stage of actually putting these ideas out, without the help of the rest of my colleagues at Symbiosis, who made this journey their own and whose contribution I can never ever forget. A special thanks to my Director Prof. Anupam Siddhartha for believing in me, all these years I have worked with SCMC. My thanks and highest regards to Professors Triveni Mathur, Amitabh Dasgupta, Kavitha Iyer and Ananya Mehta for their invaluable guidance and support, especially in the vital, final stages of the book.

Two people who deserve special mention are Aniket Deshmukh and Harshal Haldankar, who apart from being the best friends, one can ever have or imagine were instrumental in making this book a reality. My sincere gratitude also extends to the entire team of 'BecomeShakespear publishers', who proved wonderfully supportive in this entire venture.

No thanks would be complete without mentioning all my students, who over the years have patiently and passionately waited for this book to see the light of the day. It is unquestionably been this support that motivated me through some of the more difficult periods, to keep living this dream. I sincerely hope, the book lives up to your expectations and inspires you, the way you inspired the storyteller in me!

Dedication

I dedicate this work to my late grandfather, who first instilled the love of storytelling in me and who continued to encourage me even during his last days.

About the Author

Sagar Kamath teaches History and International Affairs at Symbiosis International University. With a Masters in History and Philosophy and over 9 years of experience in the teaching sector, he has lectured extensively on subjects ranging from global history to modern day geopolitics and specializes in issues of religion and politics.

An avid storyteller, he has spent years researching humanity's intricate interplay with the natural world, and believes that events like World War II serve to highlight the best and the worst, we as a species are capable of…something amply reflected in this work. In his free time, he loves to explore 'off-the-beaten-track' locales that have a sense of mystique about them.

Prologue

In the 4 billion year history of our planet, the human story is but an ephemeral one. Only a few hundred thousand years bear the scars of humanity's efforts at creating order, happiness and beauty on this planet. And yet, when it comes to human evolution, ours is a story without parallel! For, ever since man first learned to walk upright, a strange ability began to manifest itself...one that separated...and eventually *isolated* him from other species...by allowing him to subvert nature itself, to his calling. This remarkable ability, we now call 'Consciousness'!

As the level of this consciousness advanced, another idea began to emerge ...one that suggested we were part of a long, intangible framework, which served as a backdrop to our civilization. This belief led to a form of 'Collective Consciousness', absolutely unique, in the animal kingdom!

This 'Collective Consciousness' helped humanity perceive all events as being part of a 'Grand Design'...one whose meaning was not always clear...and *if* there was indeed a 'Grand Design'...then surely there *must* also be a 'Grand Designer'!

And thus was born the idea of 'Destiny'. The belief that certain events were *destined* to occur, *regardless of human intervention*, was a powerful motivator, in the origins of early religion!

Time

The concept of 'Time' has inspired and fascinated us, ever since we became bipedal. This is probably due to the 'promise of continuity', it carries...a sense of unchanging, non-chaotic constancy!

Great civilizations like the Sumerians, the Egyptians and the Harrapans, were greatly focused on measuring this all important phenomenon. Recording events within certain 'Temporal

Boundaries' became almost as important...as the events themselves!

This innate fascination with 'Time' stems from the fact that very early on, man realized that just as 'change' is an intrinsic part of the human experience, the ability to *comprehend* this change, requires at least a basic conceptualization of a 'dimension'...that is separate from the three, we observe around us. This understanding that there is a *hidden fourth dimension*...one, which is in *perpetual flow*, became an intrinsic part of our civilization. Mapping all human experiences against this *flow*, allowed each generation to experience a connection with the next!

In primitive tribal societies, man's relationship with the natural world was one of perfect symbiosis. This was because early man was very much a *part* of the eco-system. But with the passage of time, the ability to exploit nature became man's forte and this relationship turned *parasitic*!

A need was now felt to record these conquests and victories over nature, as precedents for the future...once again underscoring the unusual importance of 'Time'...and thus birthing the earliest attempts at establishing 'Chronology'!

Although it's impossible to ever really know how early man understood time, it is evident that he took it as something *intrinsic* to nature, best exemplified, by patterns observable in nature. Everything seemed to happen in terms of cycles. Celestial bodies — the Sun, Moon, planets, and stars provided reference points, for measuring the passage of time. Ancient civilizations relied upon the motion of these bodies, through the sky, to determine future events.

Over time, civilizations began to connect these cosmic cycles to repetitive cycles in nature. It was the Egyptians, who first realized that the 'Dog Star' in 'Canis Major', now known as 'Sirius', rose next to the sun every 365 days, around the time when the Nile began to flood. This simple observation led to one of the earliest annual calendars in human history!

These patterns were also incorporated by the Babylonians, the Aztecs, the Mayans and the ancient Indians. These early advances all led to the idea that 'Time' just like nature is cyclical i.e. events that had occurred in the past, would almost certainly occur again, and if you were adept enough at following their patterns, you could map the future!

However, with the birth of Judaism and the subsequent emergence of the other two Abrahamic religions – Christianity and Islam, this concept of time changed. All three religions put special focus on the covenant of the 'Promised Land' and 'Eternal Salvation'. As a result, the notion of time shifted from 'Cyclical' to 'Linear'. Christianity in fact, adopted this as the basis for its own doctrine, by capturing time in the form of 'birth', 'life', 'death', and in the case of Jesus Christ – 'resurrection'. This notion of time and its emphasis on a divine 'Day of Judgment' was very significant in the first millennium of the Common Era.

But even this understanding of time was destined to go through a change, in the middle ages, when the clock was born! This remarkable invention brought in the era of 'Hourly Time'. Hourly Time proved much more accurate, since it allowed us to measure time in smaller intervals. Even though this took away some of the mystique of the earlier versions, ironically, it was the Catholic Church that first adopted it, to ensure that people regularly turned up for 'Sunday Prayers'.

The subsequent invention of the bell-clock further regimented our lives. Now, all daily activities could be synchronized. Sleeping, eating, working, praying, or just spending time with family...all...determined by the 'Dreaded Bell'!

With almost all accepted theories in modern physics built around the understanding of time as a hidden *fourth dimension*, it came as a total shock to the inhabitants of 'System Gaea' – the human colonies in the inner solar system, when in the year 3067 A.D. a heretical young physicist stumbled upon the ultimate secret!!

His controversial research succeeded in isolating a single... hitherto unknown subatomic particle that travelled the cosmos at unimaginable speeds, carrying with it a 'Time Charge'...a particle that was responsible for all 'Time' experienced...since the Big Bang!

But as revolutionary as his discovery was, humanity would have to pay a terrible price for it!

Gone were the days when Time was thought of as either 'Cyclical' or 'Linear'. This was the era of comprehending Time, for what it really was... an 'Illusion'!!!

...This was the era of Chronux!!!

The Curse

The 'Mahabharata' is an ancient Indian Epic that has inspired and fascinated humanity, for millennia. With over a hundred thousand verses, over some thirteen thousand pages, it is the longest poem in the world. Debates regarding its historicity have persisted since time immemorial, but for believers, it is the true account of God's presence on Earth and an intrinsic part of Indian history!

Such debates notwithstanding, the epic's myriad interpretations have continued to fascinate students of history and anthropology, because of their stunningly elaborate descriptions of place and time. Most impressive of all are its descriptions of astronomy.

The epic describes that at the start of the 'Great War of Kurukshetra', a series of omens were observed in the sky...signs that seemed to portend the carnage to follow.

The following is a dialogue between the tragic warrior, Karna and the master strategist, Lord Krishna:

Karna: Diverse frightful visions are seen, O slayer of Madhu, and many terrible portents, and fierce disturbances also...That fierce planet of great effulgence, Sanaischara (Saturn), is afflicting the constellation called Rohini...The planet Angaraka (Mars), wheeling, O slayer of Madhu, towards the constellation Jeshthya, approacheth towards Anuradhas...O thou of Vrishni's race, the planet Mahapat afflicteth the constellation Chitra. The spot on the lunar disc hath changed its position; and Rahu also approacheth towards the sun. Meteors are falling from the sky with loud noise and trembling motion.
- MBH 5.143

Krishna: O Karna, say unto Drona and Santanu's son and Kripa that the present month is a delightful one, and that food, drink, and fuel are abundant now. All plants and herbs are vigorous now, all trees full of fruits, and flies there are none. The roads are free from mire, and the waters are of agreeable taste. The weather is neither very hot nor very cold and is, therefore, highly pleasant. Seven days after, will be the day of the new moon. Let the battle commence then, for that day, it hath been said, is presided over by Indra. - MBH 5.142

In Bhishma Parva 3:23-29, we are told that *"Two blazing planets have reduced the brightness of 'Saptarsis'. 'Brihaspathi' and 'Shani', being stationary for a year are near 'Visakha'. There is a sharp planet with the first star of 'Krittika', like a cornet. In the three stars preceding this, Budha is seen often. I know instances of 'Amavasya' falling on the fourteenth, fifteenth and sixteenth day of the fortnight, but not on the thirteenth day like now. The moon and the sun both got eclipsed in the same month, oddly in a thirteen-day interval."*

According to these verses, the following astronomical sightings were made:

1. Mars would have to be somewhere between the constellations of Scorpio and Sagittarius after having performed a retrograde motion;
2. Saturn would have to be in the constellation of Gemini, near the star named Aldebaran;
3. A lunar eclipse followed by a solar eclipse in the same month.

Curiously, these positions while rare are not arbitrary and can be narrowed down to the year 3067 B.C.E. according to the standard calendar in use today!

The epic then goes on to discuss a great war fought between two warring clans, the five 'Pandava' brothers – personifying the righteous and the hundred 'Kaurava' brothers – personifying the unjust. This battle was fought for upholding 'Dharma' or righteousness and brought out the best and worst aspects of humanity...with all rules of combat being discarded.

Untold millions die on either side and the casualties described are so great that they force even the most ardent supporters to concede that the description *might* be hyperbolic!

However, as brutal as the war is, the end is even darker! As the Kaurava army lies vanquished, one warrior, the son of a famous teacher, is unable to accept his side's defeat. Burning with anger, the young warrior named Ashwatthama, vows to avenge his father's death. He plans on assassinating the Pandava brothers...in their sleep!

Against all rules of combat, he launches a dastardly attack on the Pandava camp, in the dead of the night and carries out his bloody task. But horror of horrors...instead of beheading the Pandava brothers, he accidentally ends up killing their sons and grandsons!!

After a long search, the Pandavas find Ashwatthama hiding in the jungles of North India and challenge him to a duel unto death. The battle ranges on, till both sides decide to use the ultimate weapon - a weapon called the 'Brahma Astra' or the weapon of Brahma that was said to contain the 'destructive power of the universe'!

But when these weapons are unleashed, the air itself catches fire, trees for miles are razed to the ground and birds and animals begin to run helter-skelter. The whole of humanity stands on the brink on destruction!

In a bid to save the planet, Lord Krishna demands that the combatants immediately pull back their weapons. While Arjuna, the Pandava archer, is able to do so, Ashwatthama is either unable...or unwilling to do so. Rather, the fiery hate-filled warrior, redirects it at the womb of Uttara - Arjuna's daughter-in-law, who is pregnant and carrying the last of the descendants of the Pandavas!

Enraged, Lord Krishna then curses Ashwatthama that he would be forced to roam the lands forever, with blood and puss oozing out of his injuries, and cry for death. Since he had no fear of death during war, death will refuse to meet him. He would find neither hospitality nor accommodation; He would face total isolation from mankind and society!

Thus burdened with the knowledge of his terrible mistake, the very power and immortality that Ashwatthama had craved during his life became his worst nightmare…his most horrible curse!

EPISODE ONE

CHAPTER ONE

HIMALAYAN FOOTHILLS
3067 B.C.E:-

The people of Aruhu had found the stranger deep in the forest that straddled their tiny Himalayan village. Even though there didn't seem to be any visible signs of injuries on his body, the man had appeared to be on the verge of death. This was extremely unsettling! Even more disturbing, was that those who first approached him, had noticed a mysterious glowing energy emanating from his body!!

The villagers had never encountered anything like this, in their long but simple existence.

Should they move him to safety…or…was there more to this than what met the eye? Could this strange man be an emissary of the Gods? Was he a threat?

A heated discussion had followed.

Little did the village-folk suspect that regardless of the outcome of the debate, their actions were about to change history forever!

CHAPTER TWO

In an early chapter of human history, a period we now refer to as the 'Bronze Age', civilizations emerged across the planet, primarily on the banks of great rivers. From the Sumerians, to the Egyptians and the Chinese…humanity's constant march towards riparian civilizations was remarkably consistent!

One such culture emerged in India, on the banks of a now forgotten river that flowed from the Himalayan foothills to the Arabian Sea…a River that according to legend, was a staggering twenty two kilometers wide and one that Indian epics recount as the 'Saraswati'.

While today, the legend of the Saraswati is a matter of great debate among archeologists and historians, satellite imagery has revealed an astonishing paleo-river channel through India's western desert that mirrors the descriptions in India's oldest text - the 'Rg Veda'…of just such a river!

A comparative analysis of the pre historic sites found in this region also reveals that most of them were strung along this ancient river!

CHAPTER THREE

Our story begins in one such site in the Himalayan foothills…isolated and inoculated from the rest of the world and almost entirely self-sufficient - a tiny hamlet known as 'Aruhu'.

Aruhu

With dense Himalayan forests bordering the village on three sides and the River Saraswati serving as the primary source of water, the villagers had for long, managed to carve out a simple and primitive existence centered around foraging, hunting and a little bit of agriculture. Pre-industrial and having just about mastered the use of fire, an early form of Paganism, based on the worship of the river and various forest entities had evolved over time and each member of the community was expected to pay his/her respects to these *guardian deities*, on a daily basis.

The village had no forms of writing or documentation, but some of the elders spoke of their ancestors being survivors of a cataclysmic world-ending flood. However, with no way of confirming or disproving this, the account had fallen into disuse.

Aruhu's only form of contact with the outside world was through nomads, who wandered the village outskirts and sometimes brought valuable items from abroad. While there hadn't been too many clashes between the groups, the youth growing up in the village were educated about the perils of associating with the outsiders.

Over time, the villagers had begun to militarize, keeping in mind this potential threat. Aruhu used to import Bronze in a big way and this was put to use to manufacture large quantities of swords and shields. This put the villagers miles ahead of the nomads, who used rudimentary reed based weapons and rode horses. Whether or not the village folk were preparing for an invasion was hard to say, but one could argue that even at this early stage, the idea of *the other* was getting stronger...the embers of what would eventually become India's infamous caste system were smoldering!

Nonetheless, life in Aruhu would have probably gone along the slow natural process of evolution, had a series of remarkable incidents not occurred on that fateful night of August the 15th, 3067 B.C.E...by our reckoning.

It had all begun on an ominous note, when around midnight; an unbelievably powerful explosion rocked the forest, just beyond the village, sending shockwaves in all directions. So powerful was the blast that it awoke men, women and children for miles. Birds shrieked and animals ran in all directions, as the sound of the explosion, echoed through the forest some seventeen times!

The blast was quickly followed by an eerie half-light, which even though it was well past midnight, seemed to light up the entire village. Those brave enough to venture out of their huts, claimed to have seen bright explosions that resembled a thousand suns!!

Most of the elderly and the superstitious fell to their knees in fervent prayer to placate the angry forest deity, for really, what else could it be? Mothers feverishly held their young ones close to them and prayers graced every lip. One youth even claimed to have seen a 'godlike' figure magically appear out of nowhere and then burst into flames. This was however rubbished as the fantasies of an overactive imagination...or the result of consuming too much 'Soma' - a local beverage, supposedly consumed by the gods, but as the village elders often remarked tongue in cheek, could cause one to "see" what did not exist!

The youth's insistence that he hadn't been drinking was quickly silenced by the testimony of those who said 'he had been'. It was almost as if the villagers were hoping that somehow...whatever this mysterious phenomenon was, it would soon disappear and they would be able to return to their amiable existence, come the next morning. And so it was decided that the best course of action was nonintervention in matters that were clearly far above their station. After all, what good could possibly come from interfering in the affairs of the Gods?

Nonetheless, the next morning, when some kids who had ventured into the forest came back with stories of a light skinned man in strange gold armor, muttering to himself, in a strange language and scaring the animals, it was decided that this matter *would have* to be investigated.

A band of the finest warriors, Aruhu had, was sent out to conduct a preliminary search. Not everyone had wanted to go but what other recourse was there? It was important to figure out if whatever lay in the forest was a threat. And so armed to the teeth with bronze spears and shields, they had tentatively made their way into the forest. What they would find, would change their lives...and those not yet born... *forever!*

CHAPTER FOUR

The first thing the patrol party noticed as they entered the forest was the unnatural silence. Normally, as dawn broke, the forest would resonate with the shrill cries of monkeys and the hypnotic chirping of birds, announcing the start of a new day. But on this day, there was nothing! The very air seemed to stop and take note!

Any suspicions that the explosive sounds and lights from the previous night had been mere illusions were quickly put to rest, as the group walked through the dense sub-tropical forest. With unnatural symmetry, the tops of all the trees had been scorched...but what could have caused such damage?...a powerful fire?...some kind of a weapon?

As they approached ground zero, it became clear what had frightened the kids. The village headman, who was accompanying the warriors, made the disturbing observation that even though the rest of the forest was quieter than usual, this area seemed completely devoid of life...a veritable dead zone!

And at its very center, they felt an overpowering presence. The air no longer flowed and even the act of breathing was becoming increasingly difficult. The warriors of Aruhu saw a large area of the forest floor, roughly the shape of an egg, that had been completely scorched...and then...in the dull, early morning light, they saw a strange figure lying face down in the dirt, more dead than alive!

The mysterious being seemed alien to the environment...human and at the same time...not quite...an angel fallen from the heavens?...*a demon?*

But whoever he was, it was clear that he was in urgent need of medical assistance. As the villagers gathered around him, the stranger seemed to sense their arrival and attempted to gesticulate vigorously ...Was this a warning?...an attack?

Then…even as they stared in mute terror, the stranger opened his mouth and uttered words that were completely incomprehensible… and yet, even though the language was foreign, its intent was clear…it was a dying man's desperate plea for help. Faced with this, all misgivings from the previous night were cast aside and the villagers decided to act.

Whoever or *whatever* this being was, he needed assistance of the 'medicine man'…and for that they would need to take him to the village…and since the stranger was in no state to even stand, he would have to be bodily lifted and carried. By this time of course, some of the more intrepid village youth had also reached the spot.

As these new arrivals were being briefed, one of them, an eighteen year old named Drigtha, noticed something unusual. He saw some of his more headstrong comrades fearlessly approach the stranger…and noticed that just as four well-built warriors hoisted the being to his feet and dragged him out into the clearing; an image, almost astral in quality, seemed to leap out of his body and disappear.

What in God's name was that?

It had happened so suddenly that the young warrior couldn't be certain he had actually seen it. One moment it had been there and the next…it was gone! Certainly the four who were assisting the stranger, did not seem any more perturbed than before.

Drigtha would have passed it off as an illusion, caused by the play of light and shadow, had he not turned and seen the headman's face. The village headman, a profoundly stoic man, known to keep a poker face even during the worst tragedies, had turned whiter than a slab of marble!

The gnarled roots of the alpine forest trees appeared to mock the mood of the warriors, as they wordlessly made their way back to the village. No one had dared to look back!

CHAPTER FIVE

All of this had happened a year ago.

Slowly, with proper food and rest, the stranger regained his composure and began a dialogue with his rescuers. What was unusual though was that just a couple of days after his first confrontation with the villagers, the stranger seemed to have mastered their dialect and could now address them in their own tongue, as a teacher would. Initially, this had come as a shock to the villagers, but they had soon fallen under the stranger's spell!

And so it was that every night since his mysterious arrival, the stranger had stood in front of a campfire and addressed the villagers in a calm powerful voice...speaking to them about various issues... some familiar, others otherworldly. Even though he often spoke in incoherent riddles, the villagers tried to hang on to his every word, for it was through these discourses that the stranger had taught them, new methods of cultivation and a new way of life that involved the start of an oral tradition. His very presence, it seemed was responsible for creating the notion among the village folk that there was indeed a higher purpose, beyond their simple peasant life.

The man possessed knowledge of places and events that were far away, and what was more...he seemed keen on sharing with the villagers. It was obvious that he genuinely cared for them. So much so that even though he was an outsider, he had easily superseded the village headman as the ultimate 'arbitrator' of disputes. Every time he spoke, he seemed to exude divinity. He even addressed them as 'My people'. The simple village folk had begun to trust and worship him... *irrationally!*

Along with his other sermons, this mysterious god-like figure also instilled a culture of 'star gazing' among the village folk. Every night, for an entire year, he pointed out certain specific star formations in the night sky and explained their significance...sometimes through elaborate allegorical stories...other times through words that sounded completely alien.

To the villagers, initially, these patterns seemed to make no sense whatsoever. For them the stars had always been places reserved for their worthy ancestors. The patterns of these stars and constellations had never been studied as an exact science, certainly not in Aruhu.

Yet, all that changed with the stranger's arrival. He taught his people various methods of plotting 'time' using the stars as 'landmarks' and also predicting the positions of certain specific celestial bodies. He helped the village elders form detailed 'star charts' that mirrored his stay in the village. This was no easy feat and soon the villagers realized they would have to form dedicated teams of around eight to ten individuals, if they were to avoid any errors.

The teacher insisted that this task be carried out meticulously and the villagers noticed he would get extremely disturbed, if any lacuna crept in, while recording the data. Using a fusion of his own unknown language and the local dialect, which was an early form of Sanskrit, the stranger helped the villagers create two major 'star charts'.

The first one was what he described as a conjunction of the planet, we now call 'Saturn', with 'Aldebaran' – an orange giant star located some 65 light years from Earth in the constellation of 'Taurus'. The villagers recognized it as the day of "Kartika Pornima" when "Shani" (Saturn) was seen to be near "Rohini" (Aldebaran). The exact day this phenomenon occurred was also marked by a lunar eclipse.

The second chart marked what the stranger described as a 'retrograde motion' of the planet we refer to as 'Mars', just before reaching 'Anteares', or as the villagers described it "Angaraka" (Mars) reaching " Jyeshta" (Anteares). This day was marked by a solar eclipse.

These observations came as a surprise since the villagers had never seen two eclipses within such a short interval. The fact that this seemingly unique event coincided with the arrival of their mysterious "God Teacher" seemed to strengthen their belief that this was no ordinary person.

Curiously though, throughout his year-long stay in the village, the stranger refused all attempts from the villagers to placate or worship him as a god. Even though the simple minded folk never completely understood the reason for this reluctance, they chalked it down to the strange melancholy that marked his eyes…it was symptomatic of someone who had suffered great loss!

The only time his eyes seemed to light up with passion was when he revealed his mysterious insights. Ultimately, it was that fire the villagers would remember him for. They would call him 'Ashwatthama' – the 'Fiery One'.

CHAPTER SIX

On the night marking the first anniversary of his mysterious arrival, buffeted by the pale haunting light of a campfire, the stranger made an astonishing proclamation – 'Tomorrow with the rising sun, he would leave this place and his people forever and allow them to track their own destiny'.

This statement brought forth tearful responses. For those gathered around the fire, life without their teacher seemed unthinkable. After all, hadn't he been the one who had brought order and happiness to their village? Hadn't he shown them the true scope of their existence… and thus given their lives meaning? So, how could they now go on without him? Worse still…had *THEY* somehow accidentally displeased him for him to punish them thus?

Deeply touched by their sincerity and devotion, the mysterious being, whose golden raiment shone brighter than the sun, assured them that they were in no way responsible for his decision…rather fate had already chosen a different path for him…one he couldn't refuse!

However, as a reminder of his time spent with them, he would bestow upon his people a gift…a gift unlike anything the villagers had seen before. It was an artifact…a small crystal jewel that was shaped like an "un-blossomed flower"…and glowed mysteriously, with an inner light. The villagers of Aruhu marveled at its magnificence…it would become their most prized possession. It was indeed a fitting way to remember their 'godly mentor'.

Along with this, the stranger also gave them a seal – a series of documents made of parchment, which contained the secrets of harnessing the power of the jewel. "However" the stranger warned, "Only an individual who has attained total mastery over his 'basal human instincts', who has conquered human 'desire' and who is truly worthy of the knowledge contained in the seal, must attempt to use it."

"Harnessing the artifact's power is no simple exercise, rather it is a journey meant to be undertaken only by someone who truly understands the price at the end. Any lesser being attempting the same will doom himself/herself to eternal damnation!!!"

As more and more people from the village nervously gathered around, the stranger began to instruct them in one final lesson. In the halting voice of one who is loathe to remember the past, he told them the story of his life, of a great war he had been part of, a terrible mistake he had committed and the price he had to pay for all eternity!

This last sermon was both a revelation and a warning, but along with this the stranger had ensured something more. By deliberately garbling his message, he had ensured that the simple village life these people had led so far would be forever changed. The seeds of something truly dangerous had been sown…curiosity!!

CHAPTER SEVEN

2980 B.C.E: HIMALAYAN FOOTHILLS:

Almost a century had passed since the villagers of Aruhu had last seen their mysterious teacher, and even though their society was still made up of peasants and hunters, much had changed during this period.

Following the teacher's final sermon, the villagers had gone on to establish a 'special group', dedicated to preserving his message for posterity. The 'star charts' the stranger had helped them create, were to be meticulously maintained, as per his wishes. To ensure this knowledge survived, each subsequent generation was taught to understand these patterns through detailed observations of the night sky.

Never once for more than a century, had the villagers questioned the purpose of these calculations or even contemplated their purpose. They had been single minded in the belief that their teacher's promise of a 'great' gift that lay at the heart of these calculations, would one day be theirs, if they were only able to decode the secrets in the charts.

Together with the 'star maps', they had also meticulously stored the sealed documents and texts, the stranger had compiled during his stay in the village. These texts contained pictures and diagrams all made by the stranger using charcoal. The bizarre shapes appeared to depict 'vehicles' or 'crafts' of some kind.

During his brief stay in the village, the stranger had often tried to explain to his people, how these devices could enable one to 'fly like birds' and give one 'God-like power'. "However", he had warned, "the lust for such power has always resulted in total ruin for man. There are some things that man was never meant to harness!" For the people of

Aruhu, the promise of unlimited power was intoxicating...even though they realized that attaining it was well beyond their capacity.

Most sacred of all, was the mysterious crystalline object that their teacher had gifted them...the 'Jewel' that was shaped like an 'un-blossomed flower' and that the village elders swore, often pulsed with an unearthly light.

Over time, the elders had created a 'secret order' of learned individuals, tasked with keeping safe these artifacts...guardians, who would remain unknown to *even* each other! Each member of this order would in-turn appoint one more member, should his own life come under threat, thus ensuring that the sacred relics were never lost.

The story of their mysterious god-like teacher evolved through time into an epic that was narrated from one generation to the next. As time went by, more and more esoteric elements were added to the recollection and the story evolved into a moral allegory meant to depict different facets of human existence. The villagers of Aruhu did not know it then but they had helped set into motion, a force that over time would prove unstoppable!

The stranger's arrival in the village and the knowledge he had shared, helped create the basis of an idyllic life for the villagers. The advances in agriculture that had become possible through his teachings meant that food was no longer a problem. Knowledge about how to harness various herbs and roots available in the forests, also ensured that disease and epidemics were now largely under control.

The understanding of astronomy through the star charts not only allowed the villagers to develop their own primitive form of writing, but mapping any visible changes occurring in the heavens helped create a basic understanding of 'Time'. The realization that though 'Time' as a concept could be 'measured' but not 'controlled' meant that the villagers were now moving towards a stage where they would begin to track their own destinies in the stars!

In short, Aruhu had been shaken out of the stupor that the rest of humanity found itself mired in and propelled towards an advanced 'Urban Utopia'. This rather unnatural state of affairs meant that the once simple village was now the source of great envy for those not part of this system. Over time, this would manifest as hostility towards its inhabitants and result in the entire region becoming increasingly aggressive.

This was the beginning of armed conflict!

CHAPTER EIGHT

It was common for the villagers to sit around a campfire and recount some of their earliest memories from their childhood...memories that were often filled with accounts of their great teacher's message, his artifact and the promise of power, it contained.

The youth who had grown up listening to their elders, would often compete with each other in a bid to decode the secrets of the 'star charts' and the texts to unlock the power of the crystal jewel. A lot of them had never experienced issues such as famine or the need to use resources selectively and so could not really understand some of the ideals their ancestors still held on to. For them, excelling amidst all this abundance *was* the real challenge!

Conservatism was clearly an obsolete idea. 'Surely' they thought, 'In a place of such abundance, one must find some way to excel even more. The Gods themselves have blessed this place so why should we shy away from enjoying the rewards?' Foremost amongst these youth, was Arhiti - the ten year old son of the village headman.

Because of his father's status, Arhiti had always enjoyed a privileged position among his own people. Even though it was not always that the son of a leader would follow his father, the idea of 'dynastic succession' was not completely unknown in Aruhu. As a result, since the time he had uttered his first garbled words, Arhiti had been groomed for a promising future. Then...as he grew older, the villagers would begin to notice that there were several signs that set the boy apart from others his age. Most noticeable was the fact that he had an intensely curious mind and a very vivid imagination.

While his companions would be found playing during the day, Arhiti would often go into contemplative trances, which would last for hours at a time. Initially, his parents and the village elders were perturbed by this behavior, as it wasn't natural for a child so young in years, to act in this fashion. Nonetheless, his father, the village headman, held out hope that this was just a passing phase and would soon pass. 'Arhiti' they remarked, 'would grow up to be an ideal citizen'.

By the time Arhiti was five; his father began to take him to the outskirts of the village to the forests that hugged the Himalayan ranges, so that the boy could get acquainted with *HIS* village and its people. This, the headman believed was important for a 'future leader' of the tribe.

Once, as his father had been busy showing him the different trees and herbs, used by the village folk, Arhiti suddenly asked him a series of questions…questions that had on the surface, seemed simple and innocent but which the headman had been unable to answer. The boy had started this conversation by asking 'if the trees and plants they saw all around them were really alive'. His father answered in the affirmative by telling him that 'we can hear the movement of animals and trees, if we listen carefully, thus proving that they do live.'

Arhiti had seemed less than convinced…but had persisted, "We can hear them because we are *in* the forest right now, but what happens when we are not there to listen? Do they still 'live' and 'make sounds'… then as well? If, a tree fell in the forest at night and there was no one to listen to it, would it still make a sound?"

For a moment the headman hadn't quite understood what his son was asking. "What do you mean boy? Of course it would make a noise…it *has* to…that is how nature works…" he replied, with a tinge of exasperation in his voice. Arhiti thought about this for a while and then asked again, "What makes you so sure father? What if all that we see and hear is merely an 'illusion' and we are not able to look past it?"

The headman had had enough. It was one thing for a five year old to be curious and ask questions but such thoughts were surely the work of the devil. This line of thinking was deeply disturbing. No good would come out of such thinking…something would have to be done to steer his son clear of such blasphemies.

"Enough son!" he replied angrily, "The plants and the trees that you see around you are the work of the supreme creator. To question that

31

is wrong. One must have faith in the divine and lead a righteous life as ordained by him."

The two had walked back to the village in silence. What had really bothered the headman was the fact that these thoughts that his five year old son had expressed, were eerily similar to the teachings and ideas their mysterious teacher had voiced nearly a century ago! Was this a portent of things to come?

Even the gentle forest breeze had seemed unusually aggressive!

CHAPTER NINE

Of all the teacher's many great ideas that had benefited Aruhu, his idea that reality was somehow just an 'illusion' was the most disturbing. Even the elders, while staying loyal to his legacy, had always shunned away from discussing such heresies. And now the headman was confronted with these exact ideas coming from the mouth of his five year old son! This simply could not be allowed to continue.

From that point on, the headman would take special efforts to ensure that his son got the best possible education, so that he would grow up to be a model of virtuosity. No effort would be spared towards this end.

Over time, young Arhiti excelled in his studies and more than proved himself an ideal son. As he diligently applied himself to his education; his father gradually stopped worrying about him. If any questions regarding 'existence' or 'reality' still plagued the boy, he kept those to himself. The headman proudly watched his son grow up to be the 'apple of the eye' of the entire village.

But as is so often the case; a new kind of trouble was lurking, just around the corner!

As Arhiti grew older, the headman began to get particularly concerned about some of the 'company' his son was keeping. Arhiti's closest companion was a boy named Bhrataha, roughly the same age…someone whom the rest of the village considered an 'outcast'. Bhrataha's mother was not from the village, but from one of the communities that stayed on the periphery and did 'odd jobs' for the village elite. However, the identity of his father was not known and as a result, there were often dark comments made about the boy's heritage. Bhrataha was often prohibited from attending the annual village celebrations and he used to be publicly derided for trying to latch on to the headman's son.

For Arhiti, none of this seemed to matter. The two of them were inseparable.

Arhiti had been only seven when an incident occurred that had created this unbreakable bond between them. It had happened on the anniversary of the Godly teacher's arrival in the village, a day that had always been celebrated with a lot of fanfare and festivities in the village and this time, everyone had been up and at it.

The headman's house was a flurry of activity with an endless stream of excited village folk streaming in and out of it, carrying food and drink.

The entire village was decked up for the occasion with fragrant plants and flowers, brought down from the forest and washed clean in the sparkling river waters, adorning each narrow street. But even though his entire family was involved in the celebrations, Arhiti was restive.

He had found himself drawn to a strange sound that seemed to emanate from the forest. It was barely audible – so soft that only the trees and the leaves of the forest seemed to respond. Completely unsupervised for the first time in his life, Arhiti had decided to explore the source of this sound...on his own!

As the headman's family was busy welcoming guests, their seven year old son was making preparations to enter the forest alone for the first time. Even the sentry positioned at the edge of the village was too caught up in the festivities and the stream of lovely young maidens with flowers in their hair, to notice a seven year old boy sneak his way out and...into the forest.

As the hypnotic sound drew him deeper and deeper into the forest, Arhiti felt his mind begin to wander back to the times he used to visit the forest with his father. He remembered asking his father the questions that had come to his mind and also his father's uncomfortable responses. Once again his mind threatened to enter a contemplative state...an experience so common in his childhood.

He lazily wandered off the beaten track, every now and then reaching out and touching the dew covered leaves of the trees...his ears still poised to pick up the slightest anomaly. The sound which had lured him so far away from the safety of his home now seemed to merge with the natural sounds of the forest...almost completely indistinguishable.

This bothered Arhiti...it had clearly not been his imagination that had drawn him so far into the forest. He tried to close his eyes and contemplate. This practice had helped him in the past. He took a deep breath and let it out slowly, trying to blot out the surroundings. Nothing happened...*the chirps of the birds and the squeals of the monkeys sounded just a little tense!* Arhiti cursed softly, under his breath. This simply wouldn't do...he knew finding the source of the sound was important...*why,* he could not say!

He decided to try once again. He took a deep breath...felt the air enter through his nostrils...felt its warm presence spread through his body...and then slowly...let it out. As he did, the sounds of the forest faded into the backdrop and again he heard the low monotone, clearly. It seemed to come from the very center of the forest – a place that Arhiti chillingly recalled, the villagers were told not to enter...the infamous 'dead zone' where nothing ever grew. It was a phenomenon that the elders attributed to the arrival of the mysterious stranger.

He felt a chill run down his spine. Should he investigate further? Go right down to the source of the sound...or should he do the sensible thing and report the occurrence to his father? The headman would surely be in a better position to handle this. On the other hand, Arhiti knew that his father would not approve of his son venturing alone into a forest that held known and unknown dangers. He would most likely be severely censured and prevented from ever leaving the village.

His reverie was suddenly broken by a sharp sound to his right. He felt a sudden pang of fear, as he realized he wasn't alone. *Something* was following him and he in his musings had *LET* it. Now truly frightened, he turned to run back to the comfort of the village and found himself face to face with an eight foot tall, powerfully built Himalayan Black Bear!!

Bears were not usually known to attack humans...but then again, so little was known about them...and this one seemed hungry! Nowhere to hide or run, he suddenly realized the full extent of his predicament.

Horror!!!! As the animal raced towards him, Arhiti could literally smell the rotten stink of the carnivore, signaling his end. But just as the bear was within inches of making a meal of him, it suddenly stopped its charge and arched back in pain. Arhiti dared not breathe... this was like a horrible nightmare, with the end deliberately prolonged.

Squinting through tear soaked eyes, he saw a couple of crudely made arrows sticking out of the animal's back! He desperately scrambled to his feet, looking around for the source of the arrows that had just saved his life. To his amazement, he saw a boy of around his age deftly holding a bow, poised to shoot.

Arhiti realized that this was the same boy his father had so often warned him about, the outcast!!!!...The one to be avoided!!!!

None of that mattered now...The arrows had only proved to be a temporary respite. The two boys were now faced with an almost impossible fight for survival, against an angry, injured carnivore!

The forest clearly had them at its mercy and Arhiti could find no one else to blame but himself for their terrible predicament. They would in all likelihood die at the hands of this beast, with no one in the village even aware of their fate. With nothing else to do, the two boys surrendered to instinct and ran as fast as they could.

Even though later, Arhiti could never really recount the exact details of how they had managed to evade the animal, one fact had become obvious as the two boys stumbled out of the forest...cut, torn and bleeding...this was a friendship that was born in blood and would require something extraordinarily tragic to break it. From that day on, the two had become inseparable.

In spite of his father's misgivings about fraternizing outside one's caste, Arhiti would spend all his time with his friend. As with other kids their age, the stories of their mysterious teacher were always a topic of discussion between the two of them. The teacher's promise of unlimited god-like power seemed intoxicating to their young minds. Trying to be the first to understand and master this secret became their prime obsession! The two would often in their own boyish imaginations, pretend to be great warriors, who led heroic crusades across the country, in the search for glory!

Even though the stranger's artifacts were kept hidden in a sacred enclosure at the center of the village, the headman's family, being the officially appointed custodians, had access to it. This meant that Arhiti and Bhrataha were often able to sneak into the 'alter room' without the knowledge of the elders, and view the relics.

Among the many items that were proof that a mysterious god-like being *had* indeed visited their ancestors, were numerous 'star charts', a series of texts that contained charcoal drawings, which Arhiti had seen hundreds of times and most important of all, the 'sacred crystal jewel' that the teacher had warned should not be tampered with. This most precious of relics, was kept in an inner vault and only the headman knew how to access it!

Every year the jewel shaped artifact would be taken out of its confines and paraded before crowds, during the annual festival commemorating the stranger's arrival.

However, being the headman's son, Arhiti knew where the keys to the vault were kept and he along with Bhrataha would often use them to open it. The boys knew that if they were ever caught, things would not end well. But the desire to view the jewel, to hold it and perhaps tap into its secrets proved irresistible. *The jewel seemed to mysteriously call out to them!*

The two would often gaze at its polished exterior for hours, trying to figure out its mysteries. They would run their fingers down its smooth surface and over and over again remark how the artifact, with its dull white hue and petal shaped outline, looked like an egg…or an 'un-blossomed lotus'! Every time they held it in their hands, there seemed to be something new about it, almost as if the artifact was somehow…ageing…changing with time!

Ever so often, the boys would meet and solemnly vow that one day they would be the ones to crack its code and harness its legendary power.

Little did the villagers of Aruhu suspect that in their centuries old bid to understand their heritage, they would soon encounter their greatest challenge and the secret they had been guarding would itself turn deadly!

CHAPTER TEN

2967 B.C.E: HIMALAYAN FOOTHILLS: - THE VILLAGE OF ARUHU

It was the end of an extended monsoon season…an unusual monsoon that had gone on well into the winter. Now, moving towards the winter solstice, the days were becoming smaller and the nights ever longer. For those residing at the foothills of the Himalayas, such seasonal variations had gone on for hundreds of generations and no longer held the mystique they once did. The advanced growing techniques the people of Aruhu had been using for over a hundred years now meant that up to two crops could be grown each year and so the winters were no longer cold and barren.

However, so close to the mountains, winters could still not be taken lightly and mothers throughout the village were encouraging their young ones to wear thick wool clothing as protection from the elements. Normally, at this time of the year, the village square would be ablaze with activity, with people flocking to get their first glimpse of the massive platforms being constructed of wood and bricks that would house the rituals, honoring the Sun God.

Using the Star Charts mastered since the time of their ancestors, the villagers were now able to predict the annual movements of the Sun across the sky and accurately predict its demise at the end of each year…for, at the winter solstice, every year, the sun having travelled south continuously for six months, would reach its lowest point in the night sky. This phase that essentially represented the 'Death' of the Sun was no small thing and rituals were conducted to ensure that the Sun

God - "Surya" was able to gather the necessary strength to once again overcome the evil darkness.

Even though this was normally a robust ritual, the preparations this year, were slightly subdued. Nobody could quite explain why this was the case. Some said it was probably because of the unusually long monsoon they had experienced, and this was encouraging most people to remain cooped up inside their homes. Others gave a more ominous explanation that this kind of listlessness was the precursor to something more sinister. Most simply went on with their business.

On the outskirts of the village, large parts of the once massive and forbidding forest had been decimated and cleared for fields and grazing pastures. Most of the peasants dwelled around their farms to guard against assaults from wild animals.

Life on the outskirts was generally even more serene than that in the interiors of Aruhu. Here, the rhythmic chirping of birds could be heard resonating through the crystal clear mountain air, surpassed only by the voice of Pana, a 30 year old mother of two, who was trying her best to get her young three year old daughter to wear a head scarf, against the cold.

As the mother's admonitions reached a crescendo and her head turned skywards in mock penance, the girl used the opportunity to dodge out the front door. The child's frenzied movements could scarcely contrast more with the picturesque surroundings and perfect morning quiet. As laughing neighbors came out to watch the unfolding scene, Pana found herself giving chase to her giggling little one, who managed to run into the fields, as fast as her tiny legs would carry her.

In spite of her outward displays of anger, Pana did not mind this too much. It was after all her daughter's first foray into the world and her father did often say that she would grow up to be a strong and determined young lady, who would give all the men of the village a run for their money. As a mother however, in a society that was increasingly headed towards patriarchy, Pana wanted her daughter to be more than just the village attraction. She hoped the girl would grow up to become an able sailor and explorer and sail past the confines of their tiny village to see the rest of the world. Who said that a woman was to be forever confined to her home?

So she let her daughter run ahead, as she pretended to give an exhausted chase, calling out to the child while feigning fatigue. She heard her little one giggle excitedly, as it entered another narrow column, cut into the fields for the purpose of irrigation. 'The joys and pleasures of being young', Pana sighed to herself as she saw the child round a corner and disappear from view. A flock of birds, which had been silently feasting on the fresh crop, suddenly took off. Now what had her little one done…Pana called out to her, but got no reply.

She was probably hiding amidst the thick stalks and leaves. Pana called again, now a little more concerned…hoping that the increased tenor in her voice would cause the young one to come out of hiding. Still nothing…Pana also noticed that the flock of birds hadn't settled down yet…which was a little unusual. Birds weren't usually much concerned with the affairs of men. She parted some of the heavy underbrush to search for her adamant daughter and suddenly saw her lying face down in the dirt.

Pana's instant reaction was to severely reproach the child for dirtying herself, so early in the morning, but something about the way her daughter was lying on the ground, stopped her in her tracks. She saw that the little girl was lying flat, with her tiny hands spread out at right angles, while a small circle of a dark fluid was spreading out from underneath her!

Pana's first instinct was to stop her daughter from drinking whatever it was that she had fallen into…and she rushed to pick her up. But as she turned her daughter around and looked into her glassy baby eyes, she saw the brutal end of an arrow sticking out from her tiny stomach!

A howl of pure agony burst out from Pana's throat, as the birds that had taken off moments ago began to caw loudly, turning towards the east, from where a strange rhythmic hum seemed to grow ever louder. A grief stricken Pana turned towards the source of this sound and saw the beautiful rising sun, suddenly darkened…by what appeared to a massive swarm of insects, rising off the horizon, seeking to swallow the sun!

Locusts...?

Pana watched the swarm reach all the way to the heavens and then slowly arch back toward the earth. It was only after it was just over a hundred feet high that Pana's grief stricken mind was able to pick out the unmistakable glint of metal from the tips of the swarm...it wasn't locust...or insects...it was a hail of arrows!

CHAPTER ELEVEN

The serene tranquility of a cold winter's day was suddenly disrupted by an unbelievable volley of arrows. Women working in the vegetable patches just adjoining their huts were the first casualties of this merciless barrage. Some of them did not even have time to comprehend what was happening and were ruthlessly cut down, right where they stood. Others, who weren't so lucky, had their limbs impaled to the ground, as human flesh offered little resistance to the downward trajectory of these weapons.

As howls of agony permeated the mid-morning air, Arhiti, the 25 year old son of the village headman, rushed out to see what was happening. In this tiny hamlet so far away from civilization, such panic was unheard of.

He saw a man run past him, screaming and clutching an arrow that had embedded itself just below his left rib. Arhiti was stunned. He struggled to imagine what sort of pain something like that might cause!

The terrifying scene jolted him into action. Whoever or *whatever* was the cause of this sudden, brutal and cowardly assault, it was *his* responsibility to protect his family from it. Nothing else mattered more.

As he rushed towards the huts at the center of the village, he saw people cowering behind rocks, stones and wooden logs…anything that might offer protection. A two year old child slipped from its mother's hands, as she desperately crawled to safety. Without a thought about his own safety, Arhiti rushed towards the fallen infant. As he grabbed the child by its tiny waist, an arrow whizzed past his ear and went straight through the infant's skull. Arhiti stood mute in shock, covered in the child's blood, as more arrows shot towards him…narrowly missing him. Never before in the history of the village, had the villagers even DREAMT of such carnage!

CHAPTER TWELVE

A tumult of emotions swept through Arhiti...foremost among them, was one overarching fear...*his father!*

Arhiti knew that as the headman, his father was tasked with the responsibility of keeping the village safe. He remembered that the village outcasts...the nomads, who stayed on the periphery and traded with far off regions, had brought back rumors of hordes of invaders on the other side of the mountains. These invaders...they had said were preparing for a massive assault on Aruhu...the reasons of which were unknown.

As was so often the case with these kinds of stories, they had been rubbished and forgotten. Arhiti had even asked his father *if* there could be more to these rumors and the only response his father had given him was a sigh followed by a glance towards their mysterious teacher's artifacts, as if to say that it was the 'Will of the Gods' that would protect them.

After all, these artifacts *had* become a source of pride for the villagers and were brought out and ceremonially worshipped only on certain select days. No one except the headman and the high priests were allowed to handle the artifacts, for fear of the 'calamity' that their mysterious teacher had warned them about.

But out of all the artifacts, the most sacred was the large crystalline jewel that shone like a star. Arhiti remembered how, as a child, he and his closest friend, Bhrataha would sneak into the sacred enclosure to look at it...*and like the soft whispers of forgotten spirits*, memories from another time, began to pour into his mind.

He remembered how on Bhrataha's insistence, he had once lifted the jewel off its stone pedestal to examine it closely. Arhiti still recalled how the jewel had felt metallic, but at the same time, extremely fragile.

As Bhrataha had tried to playfully wrest it out of his hand, something occurred, which would scar their minds, forever!

During this playful 'tug of war', extra pressure had been exerted and the jewel suddenly came alive! Both the boys felt themselves being hurled backwards, with uncanny force. The jewel then lit up with an inner light that seemed to emanate from both inside the jewel and outside! Arhiti had never ever managed to understand this.

The light then gradually began to fill the entire room that served as the sanctum sanctorum...terrifying the two boys. But even then... confronted with this strange light, their greatest fear was that if *they* were able to see this light, so might others, including the headman and then they would really be in for it. Little did they realize that things were about to get really, *really* weird!

The light emanating from the jewel then began to burn with unearthly brilliance, penetrating their very souls. Arhiti remembered watching in horror, as the walls of the rudimentary hut had suddenly disappeared and he had found himself floating in a vast ocean of nothingness. Weightless and hollow...his innermost thoughts laid bare before the world.

Terrified, he had tried calling out to his friend, Bhrataha...but no words would come out...even his thoughts seemed to have slowed down. Surely, this was death...Arhiti had felt empty inside. How would his father react to something like this? ...his only son ...the apple of his eye... the future leader of their community... dead as a result of his own petulance.

If only the two of them had listened to the warnings from the elders. If only they had not let their emotions get the better of them and experimented with this dangerous relic from a forgotten era. He had not even got the chance to say a goodbye to his family.

As tears rolled down his cheeks, Arhiti had suddenly become aware of a dull throbbing sensation in his legs and realized that he was lying flat on his back, in what appeared to be a very large forested area, with pine trees that reached the sky. The air felt acrid and harsh, as if it was on fire. Arhiti heard distant roars ring out intermittently...roars like thunder but unnatural somehow! There was also a constant dull hum, ubiquitous in its malice.

He was stunned, what kind of a place was this? Wasn't he supposed to be dead? Was this what the 'afterlife' felt like? He had dimly recounted childhood tales narrated at bedtime, by the elders about places where human beings go to, after death. None of those descriptions seemed to match what he was now experiencing - the 'afterlife' was a place meant to hold no further sufferings...physical or mental.

Yet, the thorns that were hurting his back and the blistering wind, filled with the acrid stench of burning flesh, seemed very real. He looked around and saw his brother in arms – Bhrataha lying a few meters away, equally dazed. He seemed to have trouble breathing and he was also holding on to his left leg, which appeared to be twisted at an impossible angle. Desperately, Arhiti lunged towards his friend and in doing so stumbled over something soft and wet. He went down heavily, cursing under his breath. But as he pulled himself to his feet, he found himself face to face with a bloodied corpse! ...the one he had just STEPPED ON and CRUSHED!!!

Arhiti screamed...,his mental equilibrium, threatening to snap. In total shock, he scrambled to his feet and surveyed the scene...and that's when the noise hit him. He wasn't alone!

In this hellish place, there were hundreds of out-landish figures... some running towards him and others lying sprawled on the ground... dying. There was carnage everywhere...a war zone! But what kind of a war was this?

He observed charred blackened corpses and broken limbs everywhere...he felt the bile rise in his throat. Suddenly out of nowhere, an incredible monster emerged out of the trees...toppling some of them, as it neared the clearing, he was in. As tall as three men, this creature was unlike anything Arhiti had seen in his life. Shaped like a house and sealed from all sides, the creature seemed to be made entirely of metal. Was this a chariot of some sort or a living creature? Had he completely lost his mind?

He desperately looked over to his friend Bhrataha, who was lying a few feet away and saw the same terrified expression in his eyes as well. So whatever, this creature was, his friend could see it as well!

Arhiti saw that the beast had a long funnel like nose...reed straight and made of metal that stuck out from its body. As it entered the clearing, it made a dull whining sound, then raised itself and fired a blast of brimstone straight out of its long nose! There was a tremendous roar.

Arhiti stood rooted in his place...his mind numb with horror! Then with a massive crash, the fireball the beast had fired, hit the trees just behind him and exploded with a tremendous shockwave. Arhiti heard a man behind him; scream in pain as he was literally cut in half by the blast. What kind of an insane theater was this? ...brutally violated corpses and incredible metallic monsters that belched fire!!!

Still in a state of shock, Arhiti saw a figure materialize out of thin air in front of him...more madness...was this figure also part of this war?

But as he looked on, he found there was something different about this new arrival. While it definitely had the figure of a man, it seemed to be almost 'wraith like'...translucent...not completely solid. The figure was wearing some kind of golden armor that was able to catch the brilliant rays of the sun, in all their glory...and on his head there was a jewel not dissimilar to the one the two boys had experimented with...albeit, a little smaller.

The jewel seemed to light up with an unnatural glow, as if it were alive! The tall figure looked over towards the two boys and seemed to shake his head sadly. He softly whispered under his breath. Even though Arhiti could not grasp the meaning of his words, one word seemed to sound louder than the rest... "Chronux"

Then...just as mysteriously as this apparition had appeared, it disappeared...its very substance dissipating in the environment. The two boys lay stunned on the ground, holding their breaths and waiting to see what further madness would engulf them.

They heard a dull sound, as a man emerged from within the metallic monster...the one with the long metal nose that had stopped only a few yards in front of them. This man wore a dull grey color helmet and clothes. Only the top half of his body could be seen. Whether the lower portion was inside the metallic beast...or the beast itself was the remainder, Arhiti could not tell.

As the smoke and debris began to settle, Arhiti saw the man stare across the clearing at them in total disbelief. The two boys stared back in turn. The tension and shock between both the sides was so palpable that it could have cut steel. The wind itself seemed to hold its breath, lest its presence be felt.

Finally...after what seemed like an eternity, the helmeted figure swallowed audibly and...exclaimed, "Mein Gott..."

Then just as suddenly and mysteriously as the effect had begun, it ended. Arhiti and Bhrataha had once again found themselves being surrounded by the white mist that seemed to burn their souls. As the two boys desperately tried to claw their way to safety and sanity, the mist slowly dissipated.

Silence...

Arhiti found himself once again lying against the comforting walls of his hut, sweating profusely. Terrified, he had touched his hands and legs...they felt real...if so, had he just dreamt the last few moments?... had it been a manifestation of the jewel's power?

He looked over towards his friend and found him to be in a similar state. Bhrataha was lying on his side in a fetal position, visibly trembling. Arhiti had been in no position to offer his friend any support. The two boys lay sprawled on the ground for a long time, not daring to say a word, lest the phenomenon start again. Throughout this time, the mysterious crystal jewel lay harmlessly between them on the floor...now seemingly devoid of all its energy!

After a while, their breathing had slowed and their limbs had seemed more in control. As soon as they were able to muster enough courage, both boys had raced out of the hut and into the safety and familiarity of their village.

Once in the open, the warm late afternoon sun had felt good on their faces. They threw themselves on the grass and lay there, wishing they could just hold on to the good old earth. The sounds and smells of their village, normally so mundane, now seemed absolutely precious. The boys had looked at each other and tried to put into words what they had gone through, but neither could muster the courage or the words to even discuss it.

The experience had shaken both of them so much that they had quietly agreed never to speak of it again. And although, the two had remained friends, even after this incident, they were never quite able to get back the level of comfort, they once had shared. It was almost as if the stranger's artifact had opened a crevasse too wide to bridge!

Their meetings began to get more and more infrequent. A particularly difficult period was the annual festival in commemoration of the stranger's relics…including the sacred jewel that both the boys did their best to avoid.

A year later, Bhrataha had disappeared from Aruhu. Neither his mother who used to do odd jobs around the village, nor any of the tribes living on the outskirts, were able to trace him. There were rumors that he had been kidnapped by a new band of violent nomads, who were said to patrol the northern grasslands. The villagers of course could care less about a boy, whom they did not have much of an opinion about…even at the best of times. Yet at the headman's insistence, they had searched for months, but no trace of the boy was ever found!

CHAPTER THIRTEEN

1944: WORLD WAR II

The year of 1944 saw a decisive shift in the fortunes of the forces fighting World War II. The armed forces of Nazi Germany – 'The Wehrmacht'...that had invaded Russia, after violating the 'Germano-Soviet Non-Aggression Treaty' had already suffered massive casualties between 1941 and 1943. Especially damaging had been the battle for the city of Stalingrad, where the Russian fight-back had cost Germany almost the whole of its 6th Army.

Buoyed by their successes, the Russians had kept advancing and had soon recaptured a large part of Eastern Europe from the Nazis, including German occupied Poland.

But by 1944, the tyrannical Soviet leader, Josef Stalin, wanted an absolute victory, which could only be accomplished by crossing over into Germany and destroying the Nazi power base. Throughout Russia's campaign, the Western allies including Britain and the United States had massively supported their war time effort, both in terms of money and resources. The Americans had supplied the Russians with huge number of tanks, cannons and food, while the British had provided naval support.

However, none of this was enough for Stalin. He had always maintained that the West was not doing enough in this war against Fascism and that the Soviet Union was made to bear the bulk of the offensive. He had even threatened to quit the East-West alliance that had been formed to combat Hitler. He wanted the West to share his burden, by committing to attack Germany, not later than 1944. This he insisted would result in massively straining German forces, which would have to then fight on two fronts...simultaneously!

The West eventually gave in to Stalin's demands and an enormous invasion was planned across the 'English Channel' on the beaches of France...beaches which had been occupied and fortified by the Germans.

The 'D-Day Invasion' or the 'Normandy Invasion' as it would be called, was a joint British-American effort, which planned to use a huge naval fleet, paratroopers and a massive land infantry. The supreme command for this all important mission was handed over to Gen. Dwight. D. Eisenhower.

Eisenhower, unlike his German counterparts, had been given absolute control of the operation. It was this fact, coupled with the unbelievable courage of his ground troops that allowed the allies to eventually overcome German defenses and take the beaches, thereby securing a landing ground in occupied France. Following the German reversals in Russia, the landings at Normandy proved to be a decisive moment during the Second World War.

Following a month of desperate fighting, the allies were finally able to break out from Normandy, by the end of July 1944 and begin to advance towards Germany.

It was then that they found themselves faced with several logistical issues: troops had been exhausted after weeks of continuous combat, supply lines were stretched extremely thin, and supplies were dangerously depleted. Quick decisions had to be made.

General Eisenhower and his staff chose to hold the 'Ardennes' region – a forested region near the French-Belgium border. The Allies believed that the 'Ardennes' could be defended by a handful of troops due to its terrain - a densely wooded highland with deep river valleys and a thin road network. They also had intelligence reports coming through which confirmed that the 'Wehrmacht' was known to use the area to the east across the German border as a 'rest-and-refit' area for its troops.

This was vital, since the Allied Air offensives of early 1944 had effectively grounded the 'Luftwaffe' – the German Air Force, leaving the German Army with little battlefield intelligence and no way of intercepting Allied supplies. Furthermore, the constant interception of their supplies combined with the bombing of the Romanian oil fields, had starved Germany of gasoline.

One of the few things still in favor of Germany by November 1944 was that it was no longer defending all of Western Europe. On the Western front, its front lines had been considerably shortened by the Allied offensive and as a result were much closer to the German heartland. This helped reduce Germany's supply problems, despite Allied control of the air.

The German Führer, Adolf Hitler, felt that the reserves he still had, allowed him to mount one last major offensive. Although nothing significant could be accomplished on the Eastern Front against Russia, he believed an offensive against the Western Allies, whom he considered militarily inferior to the Russians, could lead to success.

Hitler believed he could split the Allied forces and force the Americans and British to settle for a separate peace treaty, independent of the Soviet Union. Success in the west would then give Germany time to design and produce advanced weapons such as jet aircraft, new U-boats and super-heavy tanks and eventually once again target the east.

However, several senior German military officers expressed concern as to whether these goals could ever be realized. They offered alternative plans, but Hitler would not listen. His plan called for just under 45 divisions, including a dozen 'Panzer Tank' and 'Panzer–Grenadier' divisions, forming the armored spearhead and various infantry units to form a defensive line, as the battle unfolded.

At dawn on the 16th of December 1944, the Germans began the assault with a massive artillery barrage, across a 130-kilometre front, through the densely forested regions of the 'Ardennes' forests, spread over France, Belgium and Luxembourg. Heavy snowstorms engulfed most parts of the region, keeping the Allied aircraft grounded.

This surprise assault came as a total shock to the allies and it quickly became one of the costliest battles of World War II, with the Americans suffering the most casualties. Entire platoons were caught off guard and decimated. Outnumbered three-to-one, and with no air support, the Americans knew they were in a terrible jam.

For five, long and foggy days, the Wehrmacht was successful in creating a 50 mile westward bulge in the American lines, giving the battle its popular name – 'The Battle of the Bulge'. The Americans suffered massive losses, including the mass surrender of over 7000 troops on a single day and the mass execution of another 84 by the Waffen-S.S.

December 21st 1944: The Ardennes forest -

But by Thursday, the 21st of December, the German offensive had been considerably slowed down at 'Bastogne' in southern Belgium. Despite withering artillery fire, the Americans were desperate to prevent this key city from falling to the enemy. The '101st Airborne Division' had been rushed in, specifically for this.

While this battle has been immortalized for the ages in different forms of media, there is one curious episode that is known only to a very select group of combatants. During the most crucial phase of the fighting, with the German '6th Panzer Army' closing the loop around them, a small platoon of American soldiers led by Lieutenant Mark Thomas, found themselves trapped behind enemy lines.

The Germans had strategically used a gap in the American ranks and driven their forces straight through it. This was something the Americans had desperately sought to avoid. The German tactics of encirclement were already legend. They had done it several times in Russia and also right here in the Ardennes against the French, four years earlier. Yet despite their best efforts, the Americans realized that they had allowed themselves to be trapped!

Now, badly outnumbered and outgunned, Lieutenant Thomas and his men faced the grim prospect of capture, torture and death. In the bitterly cold subzero temperatures, they were down to their last few rounds of ammunition and almost all of them had suffered at least one direct hit. Medical supplies were almost nonexistent and their N.C.O had been killed. Moreover, in this terrible weather, there would be no reinforcements or Air support.

They knew, it was now only going to be a matter of time. All they could hope for was a mercifully quick death.

As they once again steeled themselves and hunkered down to try and withstand another withering round of artillery fire, the 26 year old Lieutenant's mind flooded with memories of the life he had left behind back in the U.S...his parents had been chicken farmers in Kansas, and Thomas had spent most of his early life at the farm.

Growing up, his grand uncle, who visited them quite often, had been a huge influence on him. The man had served in the 'First World War' as part of the Canadian Forces fighting under the British Flag. An idealist, the stories he told young Mark every night, about what war actually was for and how much it meant to be on the right side; had made a huge impact on the young boy. The romantic brush, with which his uncle painted the great divide between 'good and evil', had convinced Mark that his own destiny lay in safe guarding the 'Great American Dream'.

Growing up of course Mark had gone to college in the Mid-West and encountered a completely different life to the one he had been used to. He studied Political Science and learnt of all the subtleties and 'grey shades' in politics and international affairs. This contrast to his childhood idealism had disturbed him so much that he had quit his studies mid-way and returned to the farm, convinced he was meant to serve his country.

When he had discussed these plans with his parents, they had of course been less than pleased. 'A chicken farmer's place was on a farm not on the battlefield'. His father had outright forbidden him from EVEN bringing it up again. Mark had enrolled with the Army the next day!

As someone who had always thirsted for an opportunity to serve his country with distinction, he was one of those who had been deeply disappointed at America's early stance of 'neutrality' against Hitler's aggressions. For him and for so many other idealists, this was not just Europe's war to fight...but a war that every freedom loving country should fight...it was a war against 'despotism'!

After the bombings of 'Pearl Harbor' and America's renewed commitment to the struggle, Mark Thomas had felt his lifelong goals materialize. He had served with distinction at Normandy and had been specially nominated by Eisenhower to ensure that this part of the Ardennes, leading up to Bastogne was secure.

Now, all of that seemed lost…The brutal German offensive had devastated the allied offensive. Thomas felt his mind drift to the 'girl next door', back at the farm, whom he would never meet again. He had always loved her and had hoped that one day he would have a family with her and raise many healthy and brave kids, who like him, would serve the country bravely… 'Damn he should have asked her out when he had the time…but it was all over now…'

A feeling of warmth swept over him…maybe this was how death felt. But no! The sound of gunfire in the distance brought him back with a jolt. He could hear the German Panzer Tanks closing in…it was just a matter of time now. And then…all of a sudden, the approaching din stopped…deathly silence filling the air! What the…??

As Thomas opened his eyes, he saw a bright light like a tremendous explosion go off…but curiously, it made no sound whatsoever! It was almost as if the sound of the blast had been absorbed into some kind of vacuum. Was this some new kind of German Super-Weapon? … Some new horror?

He desperately scrambled to his feet and looked for his troops. They all seemed alright…certainly no worse for wear than they had been. There was a slight elevation in the forest floor creating a ridge against which the Americans had been crouching to withstand the German bombardment. He realized that this ridge was now blocking his view of what was happening. Cautiously, rifle in hand, he crawled up the ridge and peered over the top.

The scene that met his eyes was absolutely incredible. One of the lead tanks in the Panzer division had stopped dead just 20 feet away. It had the Americans dead in its sights, but surprisingly made no attempt to fire. Thomas looked across to the others, in his platoon, who had also scaled the small ridge, and saw that all of them appeared to have their eyes glued to something right in the center of the battleground.

He strained to see through the thick haze. One of his own soldiers pointed out at something and stammered, "Th…Th…There… Lieutenant…There…" He once again strained to see what the soldier was pointing at. 'Damn this thick late autumn fog!' The fog mixed with the German firepower was creating thick smog.

Slowly, as it lifted, he saw that right in front of the lead Panzer was an area approximately 10 feet in diameter, which had been scorched white by the explosion, he had just seen. Not a trace of anything... man-made or natural remained!!!

Thomas had seen numerous high powered explosions during his years in the army...he knew first-hand what a powerful explosive could do. But never before had he seen anything such as this. No residue...no sound...no debris...yet the trees, the soil and the rocks in that particular area had been vaporized. What kind of power could just 'delete' an entire region of the battlefield?

Thomas felt a chill run down his spine...he wasn't afraid of dying... it had been pretty clear to him that this battle would be his last, but if the Nazis, who just a few months ago had seemed on the brink of defeat, could now produce weapons like this, what hope was there for any army in the world?

What he suddenly noticed was that the Germans seemed just as awestruck as the Americans! Their ground forces were all standing around the area in stunned disbelief and the Panzers had all but ground to a halt. It was clear from their demeanor that they were just as shocked as the Americans. So if this technology was not German, then whom did it belong to?

As a thousand pair of eyes from both sides continued to stare in amazement at the scorched area in front of them, astonishingly, two young boys dressed in exotic but extremely primitive attire seemed to materialize out of thin air!

The boys seemed not more than 10 years of age and they were definitely not Caucasian. In fact, they looked distinctly Asiatic...tribal even...But who were they and how had they appeared in the region of the battle ground that had just moments earlier, seemed to have deleted all of its features? *How was any of this even possible?*

Thomas struggled to make sense of what was happening...when suddenly the situation became even more bizarre! Even though the fog was still thick and visibility extremely low...he could make out the rough silhouette of a *third figure* that had joined the two young boys lying on the ground. This figure appeared hazier than the other two, even though he was scarcely meters away from them...*somehow as if he wasn't completely real!!!*

He also appeared much older...a full grown man...dressed in some kind of almost futuristic golden armor that managed to catch the few trickles of sunlight that had successfully fought their way through the dense coniferous vegetation. The tall figure looked at the two boys, with a touch of sadness and...gently whispered under his breath. Lieutenant Thomas strained to hear what was being said but managed to catch only one word...it sounded like "Chronux". The tall figure then slowly disappeared, almost as if he had never been there at all!

As combatants from both sides stared in mute disbelief, Lieutenant Thomas saw the German commander emerge from inside the lead Panzer. He was wearing the distinctive German field grey helmet that covered the top of his face. But it still couldn't hide the shock and awe he was experiencing. As he took a deep breath, Lieutenant Thomas heard the German Commander do the same and exclaim..."Mein Gott"...'My God'!

CHAPTER FOURTEEN

Early morning on the 22nd of December, the fog finally lifted and hundreds of American planes took to the skies, dropping vital supplies into Bastogne, and destroying German Artillery positions. Less than a week later, the city was finally relieved as a column of General Patton's tanks broke through from the south.

Moreover, the allies were able to acquire a key tactical victory. The British were able to decipher all of the German strategies via 'Enigma', a duplicate of the Wehrmacht's top-secret cryptographic machine. They relayed each of the Führer's military directives directly to General Eisenhower.

The Battle of Ardennes proved extremely costly for the Germans, who lost over 100,000 men and 600 tanks, both of which could not be replaced at this late stage of the war. His gambit having failed, Hitler called his remaining troops home, to take up defensive positions in Western Germany.

Following the victory at the Ardennes, the Allies began to prepare for the great, final thrust into Germany. This coincided with a massive offensive launched by the Russians, far to the east. Within weeks, they would reach Berlin, thus marking the end of World War II.

However, as important as the American resistance and fight back in the Ardennes was to the eventual outcome of the war, the troops under Lieutenant Thomas, who had heroically held out just outside Bastogne shared a disturbing secret…one that would remain a mystery and one that would haunt them for the rest of their earthly days!

CHAPTER FIFTEEN

2967 B.C.E: THE HIMALAYAN FOOTHILLS:

Arhiti raced for cover, amid the barrage of arrows that was still falling. The scene around him was like something out of his worst nightmare. He heard a shrill cry cut its way through the early morning air, and turned to see a youth of around fifteen, run past him breathlessly, shouting out a warning. It was just one word…but it conveyed the full magnitude of the threat…one word that echoed with terrifying possibilities…"Huna!"

The 'Huna' were a nomadic people skilled in warfare, who were largely secretive. Growing up as a young boy, Arhiti had heard colorful stories, where the 'Huna' tribe had embarked on systematic missions of destruction and pillage, all along the Himalayan foothills. The elders in his village had always been reluctant to talk much about them.

After all, the village of Aruhu had its own set of nomads, who lived on the outskirts and traded with the villagers. And even though the more sophisticated villager folk considered the nomads savage and uncivilized, by and large the two communities had lived in peaceful co-existence. But the Huna, of course were a different breed…harsh… uncouth…*bestial* even! None of the old rules seemed to apply to them…and now the unwritten truce between the 'civilized world' and the 'barbarians', it seemed was over!

This was not completely unexpected though. After all, the lure of a better life was ubiquitous…but what WAS disturbing was the savagery these attackers were displaying…the Huna it seemed, were bent on taking revenge…*but why?*

"Arhiti run…" a voice rang out; as Arhiti turned and saw wave after wave of men riding horses, charge from all directions into the village. The dust these horses kicked up swirled around like demons from hell. The warriors brandished swords, spears and all kinds of metal weapons that betrayed the fact that this was no random assault…but a planned one.

The attackers were methodical and merciless in their approach. After the massive avalanche of arrows, they charged through the village, killing everyone and everything in their path. Those working in the fields just outside the village were cut down before they even realized what was happening.

Arhiti stood transfixed, in a state of shock and helplessness. His people were getting slaughtered and there was scarce little he could do to stop it. Tears streamed down his face, as he forced his unwilling legs to react and move past the dozens of corpses already littering the streets. He would have to stay alive, if he wanted to help!

He heard a man pray to the local goddess and saw him being cut down by a hail of arrows, even as he finished. The old and the sick simply looked on in horror, as decades of peaceful co-existence with their neighbors, crumbled before their eyes. This was an unbelievable catastrophe! What had they done to deserve such a fate? What was the reason behind this senseless attack?

There was only one overarching thought in Arhiti's mind. He had to get to his shack and his family. What if the real objective of this Huna assault, was their teacher's relics? He knew that his father – the headman, would fight till his dying breath to safeguard the ancient artifacts.

Even though he had never quite understood their spiritual significance, Arhiti knew first-hand that the power of the artifacts was undeniable. And now as he ran, a desperate idea was beginning to form in his head. An idea so dangerous and terrible that Arhiti knew his father would probably die before ever condoning it!!

But maybe, just maybe if he managed to get through to the 'Sanctum Sanctorum' in one piece before the attackers, he might be able to once again harness the power of the jewel. While nobody exactly knew what the artifact was or what it did, Arhiti had experienced its legendary power. Maybe...just maybe the jewel did possess the spirit of their mysterious teacher, whom the villagers called 'Ashwatthama' - the fiery one.

If so, its power might prove sufficient in stopping this carnage. With single minded determination, he charged towards the village square, where the sacred relics were housed. One Huna warrior spied him as he dashed from house to house and screamed a challenge. While his language was unknown, his intent was clear.

Arhiti ducked blindly, as he heard a swooshing sound just over his head, only to see the feathered tip of an arrow sticking out from the walls of a hut, inches from where his head had been! It was clear the Huna wanted him 'dead or alive'...it didn't seem to matter which.

Desperate, Arhiti scanned the surroundings for any sign of his father. He knew that an attack so pre-meditated would definitely target the village headman. He saw one of his neighbors rush out to protect his daughter, only to be brutally butchered by an attacker. Time was really running out, the invaders were perhaps minutes maybe seconds away from reaching the village square. Arhiti by now had no doubts that the treasures and the relics were what they sought. Almost certainly, his father would be trying to safeguard the artifacts even now; that is if he hadn't been killed already!

As he turned the corner of the square where the village 'elite' dwelt, Arhiti was confronted by a sickening sight. In the open courtyard just outside his house, lay his eleven year old sister, with her head split open. Two other children had also been murdered. There was a woman, possibly the mother of one of them, who was inconsolable.

Before Arhiti's grief stricken mind could even begin to process this horror, a commotion from inside his house drew his attention. He saw the Huna commander, a swarthy man in his forties, swagger out clutching Arhiti's father - the village headman, by the neck and dragging his mother by her hair.

Arhiti's mind snapped. With the pent up fury of a caged tiger, he hurled himself at the invaders, blood on his mind. One of the commander's aides saw him and tried to tackle him. Though the man was huge, Arhiti's fury seemed to have taken him by surprise. Arhiti grabbed the sword from his enemy's hands and with a cry like a wounded predator, swung it with all his might. The soldier's head rolled off, obscenely bouncing twice, before coming to a halt.

The Huna's cold blooded response was staggeringly efficient. Another warrior stepped up and with a simple twist of his wrist... effortlessly knocked Arhiti down. A crude, unevenly cut dagger at the headman's throat put an end to any further retaliation.

An eerie silence now gripped the whole area, broken only by the chirping of terrified birds. Arhiti heard the Huna commander speak to his father in the local dialect. "Bring me the 'jewel of eternal life' old man and your wife will not die a widow" he barked.

When his demand was met with stoic silence, the commander simply raised an eyebrow and another one of his soldiers, sprang into action. With lightning speed, he brought his sword down, beheading one of the captives. The shocking speed and brutality of this act left no one present in doubt about the invaders' intentions. It was clear these savages would stop at nothing to get what they wanted. "Bring me the 'jewel of life' or by God almighty, I will cause the rivers to run red with the blood of this village" the commander bellowed.

"Ashwatthama the all-knowing will smite you for your sins!" the headman cursed. His attempt at defiance was greeted with sadistic laughter and another signal to kill more captives. One of the women, sick to the core by what she was seeing, rushed headlong at the guards in a desperate attempt to rescue her captive son. This sudden commotion allowed Arhiti to break free from his sentry and make a dash for the chamber, where the sacred artifacts were housed. A cry went out and the Huna once again mobilized with military precision.

With two of the warriors hot on his heels, Arhiti burst into the enclosure at the center of the village, which was dedicated to the village goddess...and their mysterious teacher! A dense grove of 'Peepal' trees surrounded this sacred spot. These trees were considered especially auspicious, since it was under them that their teacher had delivered many a sermon and as such they were revered by the villagers as their only surviving living link to those times.

Now this came in extreme handy as, Arhiti managed to lose his pursuers in the dense vegetation. A thousand thoughts raced through his mind. Somehow, the Huna had become aware of the jewel that their teacher had left behind, almost a century ago. How this was possible, Arhiti couldn't say. While the legends of their divine teacher were known far and wide, the exact nature of his relics had always remained a closely guarded secret. What was even scarier was that the Huna seemed to be acutely aware of the jewel's power, something only Arhiti knew...Arhiti and his childhood friend...Bhrataha!!!

As Arhiti entered the sacred room that housed the altar and the other artifacts, a movement to his left distracted him. He saw a figure silently go through the many artifacts stored in the room. Someone else was already here! ...was he friend or foe? ...the silhouette certainly looked a little different from the other Huna warriors. Slowly the figure turned and smiled...a hollow, ruthless smile. Arhiti's eyes met those of the one person he had never expected to see again in a thousand years. "Bhrataha...!"

Arhiti screamed in horror, "Betrayer...liar...murderer..." his fury knew no bounds, as years of pent up emotions suddenly burst to the surface. His grief and helplessness at the carnage he had witnessed was surpassed only by the rage he felt at being betrayed by someone whom he had once considered a 'brother'!

Desperately, his mind searched for an alternate explanation for the treachery that had cost him his family. Surely, it couldn't be what it looked like...surely Bhrataha would never attempt such a terrible crime. He looked across at his long lost friend, hoping to find some solace...some explanation in HIS eyes for what had happened.

For a moment, Arhiti could have sworn he saw something akin to regret flare up in Bhrataha's eyes, but that moment soon passed and the eyes once again took on their cold, deathlike stare. Steeling himself, Arhiti launched himself at his friend, intent on avenging the terrible destruction of his village. As he raced towards his friend, his eyes caught the glint of a large dagger that suddenly appeared in Bhrataha's hand.

With cold efficiency, Bhrataha plunged the dagger straight through Arhiti's left shoulder. The viciousness of the attack was such that Arhiti was hurled back across the room, before coming to a painful stop. As he struggled to his feet, the two Huna soldiers whom he had earlier escaped, broke into the sacred room. They made a mark of respect towards Bhrataha and proceeded to restrain Arhiti.

Now in tears and in shackles, Arhiti could do nothing except look on, as his old friend proceeded to desecrate the holy enclosure.

Within moments Bhrataha found his prize. The mysterious stranger's shining jewel, whose very existence had been kept absolutely secret so far, was now his. As a child, he and Arhiti had witnessed its power and he knew that the legend of it being a source of eternal life was more than just a fable.

He felt absolutely euphoric! All those years of living as an outcast amongst the nomadic Huna people, earning their trust, learning their form of warfare...their way of life, and eventually becoming their supreme leader, had finally paid off.

But as he basked in his own glory, his moment of triumph was abruptly interrupted as he heard the anguished voice of his childhood friend cry out to him. "How could you of all people, do this to us?" Arhiti screamed. "For years we thought you were no more. We searched everywhere for you...and you come back and do this? ...to us? ...to ME? How many of your own brothers and friends have you murdered today, just so that you could get this worthless bauble...how many women have you widowed...how many children have you orphaned..."

For a moment Bhrataha's face again displayed the slightest trace of emotion. He took a moment, before replying, "Oh you poor, deluded fool...I thought that at least you of all people, would not be so quick to dismiss this treasure as worthless. After all, wasn't it the two of us who once accidentally tried out its power? You have been living under the protective cocoon of your family for far too long. Your father feeds you lies and your mother mollycoddles you. Your stupid precious village folk, whom you adore so much and who once treated me with such disdain, prevent you from achieving your true potential. You have grown soft and weak, a pale shadow of the courageous warrior, I knew as a boy. I could never have taken you so easily...imagine the son of the headman himself...supposedly 'trained' to protect his village...look at yourself now...cowering like a fool! All these years you had access to this jewel and you never once tried to understand its power...to master it! ...even after actually witnessing its power. I was forever ostracized by your people, yet I kept up my studies, from the outside. I became the 'unknown'...You thought I disappeared...died...but all these years, I was living alongside you in the forest...gathering resources and allies. Many were the nights, when I have sneaked in through all of your so called 'protection' and studied the jewel. I could have stolen it whenever I wanted."

"Liar" screamed Arhiti, "If you were here all these years, you would have taken what you wanted rather than stage this cowardly attack."

His friend smiled cruelly, "Maybe, the attack wasn't only to get my hands on the jewel...maybe it was also a bit of payback for years of misery. This 'worthless bauble' as you call it, is the source of unlimited power over all there is. I know from my studies that the stranger's message and warnings are true. The person, who harnesses the power of this jewel, cracks the code of eternal life."

"What is 'eternal' life for one such as you...who slaughters your own brothers and sisters...you have killed so many...how can you even live with yourself now?" Arhiti wailed.

"You have no idea what I have gone through...escaping the confines of our village, when I was but a child...living among these savages...the beatings and the tortures I have endured, so that I might prove myself worthy of being a warrior...you see a few of your family members die and it brings you to your knees...I have seen entire villages burn!"

"You disgust me Arhiti. I will stop at nothing to get what I have always wanted. I will have it all now and I will not be denied my destiny. That time when we accidentally accessed the power of the jewel, we were both naïve and innocent. Scarcely did we know that we were just scratching the surface. But now...I will unlock the jewel in its entirety and unleash its awesome power on this miserable village, once and for all wiping it from existence!!"

"Don't do it Bhrataha..." Arhiti pleaded, "For the sake of the friendship that we once shared, do not use the jewel. It's incredibly dangerous. You do not even understand how it works...the strange places it takes us to...full of metallic monsters...surely even in your bloodlust, you realize that this is no blessing, but a curse."

"Silence" Bhrataha cut him off. "From now on, you will speak only when spoken to. I will do as I see fit...any opposition from you...and the massacre of everyone still alive in the village will be on your conscience."

As if to underscore this point, a Huna warrior ruthlessly wrenched a child out of its mother's hand and proceeded to hurl it upon the ground in front of Arhiti. A stunned Arhiti and the screaming mother of the infant were then unceremoniously dragged out of the sacred enclosure and into the village square, where the other captives were being held.

Bhrataha's sudden re-appearance after so many years, and the realization that he had been the one responsible for this horrible carnage, had benumbed the villagers and especially Arhiti's father, the ageing village headman. Seeing the massacre of so many of his own people and realizing that he had failed in his appointed duty, the headman felt his heart give out and silently collapsed, blood pouring from his mouth.

But even as the few remaining survivors rushed to his side, the headman was already gone. For Arhiti this was horror without end!

CHAPTER SIXTEEN

"People of Aruhu..." Bhrataha screamed, "You who have always shunned me and treated me with contempt, shall now face my wrath! Indeed, Life does come full circle. I was once treated as an outcast and forced to flee; now I return as your retribution. Your artifacts, your treasures and your secrets are now mine!"

Arhiti's uncle, who had been mutely watching this spectacle, spoke out, "Liar...we always treated you as one of our own, yet you come here and wreck havoc...we took you in when you were actually an outcast and this is how you repay us?...my nephew was your closest companion...but you did not think twice before massacring our family...eternal damnation will be your punishment!"

Bhrataha threw back his head haughtily and laughed, "You lie to comfort yourself old man...you never really thought I was a fit companion for your nephew...I was never given the respect, I deserved...the trials and tribulations that I have gone through, to attain this status for myself will remain a testament to my success. All these years you lived in fear and awe of the teacher's mysterious heritage. You suppressed free thought in your own nephew, fearing the teacher's warning, never once allowing him or anyone else to embrace the power of the artifact. By your actions alone...you have shown yourself to be unworthy of the jewel. I have seen its legendary power...felt it...reached out to it...even now, it calls out to me! I will do whatever it takes to harness its power...and once I master it, I will call forth supernatural armies and weapons from distant realms. The petty illusions of your lives will crumble before your eyes!" As the stunned captives looked on, he triumphantly raised their teacher's jewel shaped relic... the primary cause of all this carnage!

The villagers gasped...stunned to see their most sacred treasure bandied thus. Bhrataha held it tight...his brow furrowed...his eyes closed...he seemed to be trying to concentrate...trying to recall how it worked!

And then with a knowing smile...he squeezed down on it!!!

For a moment nothing happened...the aggressors and their victims collectively held their breath. Of all those present, only Arhiti and Bhrataha actually knew what the jewel did...the rest had only the legends and their teacher's words to fall back on. An old man looked up to the heavens and began to recite a prayer...women held their children closer to them and waited...still nothing!

One by one, the captives began to break down and weep. Bhrataha was furious. He looked at Arhiti with venom, and screamed, "You traitor...you deliberately messed with the jewel's power. Tell me now... what you have done, you weak fool, correct your wrongs now!"

For the first time since this carnage began, Arhiti was calm. He looked his childhood friend in the eye and said, "You are the only one over here who has betrayed anyone. In your lust for power and your insane thirst for vengeance, you have allowed yourself to be manipulated by the intoxicating power of this artifact. The magic of the jewel still works...already; we begin to feel the effects of it... I for one can no longer remember certain events in my life...I am sure everyone over here is also feeling the same. The cursed jewel still functions...and like a warm, wet blanket, its dark shadow slowly creeps over all of us!"

"In unleashing it, you have fallen for the ultimate trap...You think of me as weak, because I never tried to harness the jewel's power...but I too have been studying its secrets, all these years...and I can say with conviction that I am the only one who has come close to understanding its true nature. You see, my brother, the jewel was never meant to be harnessed on its own the way we once did...and the way you have done now. There are sacred texts that our divine teacher left us, which need to be deciphered and studied...texts that contain the secrets of the jewel...secrets so frightening, they are enough to drive any man insane!"

"You never knew about these texts and so your knowledge of the artifact is limited and one-dimensional. I am the only one who has dared to open the stranger's seal and uncover its secrets. The artifact is not just some trinket to be bandied about by the likes of someone like you. You look at it and think only of its power in bringing together armies and weapons from different realms, but it actually does much more than that. It affects the normal 'flow of time' around itself and around those who use it…it is this that has earned it the name – 'The Jewel of Life'. And even now, as we speak, it affects us…look around you…look at those whom you attacked us with and look at those whom you attacked."

Bhrataha looked around, half suspecting a trick…and then suddenly gasped…the whole area was still the same and yet…somehow subtly different. The town square itself *felt* different…but why?

He looked across at his Huna commander; a swarthy man in his forties, powerfully built and heavily armed, and noticed something wrong…horribly, horribly wrong! The commander was bent almost in half, with his armor loosely hanging over his arms. He seemed to be gasping for breath, almost as if the weight of the weapons was too much for him! Bhrataha called out to him…and with a herculean effort; the man raised his head and looked up.

Bhrataha reeled in shock…the commander looked old…very, very old…he looked like someone in his 80s!!!…A cold sweat broke out across Bhrataha's body and he looked around at the others. A couple of the captives, old men from the village, were lying on the ground… as long dead whitened skeletons, while the Huna warriors, who had been his vanguard, also appeared near death. The swords and armor no longer glistened, but looked rusted and broken. How was this possible? He looked at Arhiti dumbfounded.

With tears in his eyes, Arhiti spoke, "You feel you have only just completed your vicious attack against our village…but look around you…it has been 40 years since you attacked the village! …The two of us, who have been touched by the jewel once before, have been spared this horror…but most of the village elders have now died. The ones, who have survived, have had their youth, their hopes and their loved ones taken away from them. You have disregarded the teacher's warning and fallen prey to your own hubris. You, who tried to gain everything there is; have cost us everything we have!"

Bhrataha remembered stories from his childhood...stories where the elders would quote the stranger's dire warning, *"Man has always and will always try to outdo his creator. Human curiosity and greed will force man to attempt the impossible - absolute control over all there is... some might say an ambitious enterprise...but it is also these exact qualities that prevent us from truly appreciating the irony that the price of attaining 'Everything' is 'Everything'. Human desire will keep pushing man to ever greater glory and material satisfaction."*

"This artifact that I leave in your care, allows one to do just that... attain the impossible...it will allow man to free himself from the cold shackles of time and walk the heavens as a god and achieve all that he desires. But what happens when man finally realizes that there is nothing left to desire...What does he desire for then?...I come from just such a place where desire and curiosity have been totally satisfied...all 'wants', totally satiated...and I can tell you that I still felt the 'need to desire'... That was my blessing...and my curse!"

"No no no..." Bhrataha screamed hysterically, "Victory will still be mine...I will possess the power of the jewel because I am worthy of it...and I will march my otherworldly armies across the face of this world."

With his once formidable army now old and senile, he looked around desperately for a way to continue the onslaught. His mind, already stretched to breaking point, seemed to snap, as he once again turned to the jewel. Arhiti sensing the moment was right leaped at his friend, intent on grabbing hold of the artifact.

Flying through the air, Arhiti tackled his childhood friend around the waist and tried to wrest the jewel from his grasp. Even though the impact of the tackle was enough to topple Bhrataha to the ground, Arhiti wasn't able to loosen his friend's death grip on the device.

As the two frantically clawed for control of the now active artifact, it seemed to take on a life of its own. From within, sprang beams of cascading light, so bright that the onlookers had to shield their eyes. The light changed from blue to red and finally turned white. It seemed to touch everything...spread everywhere!

CHAPTER SEVENTEEN

Of the hundred or so individuals still alive in the village, only two had experienced this magnificent white light before. And now, along with it, a translucent cloud seemed to envelop the village causing the very air to bristle with unearthly energy. Even as the onlookers stared in shock and awe, the familiar skyline of the Himalayan foothills slowly began to change!

Gone were the imposing peaks that had stood majestically since the dawn of time and that were so clearly visible from the village square… gone also was the dense protective canopy of conifers at the edge of the village that had kept it secluded for so long…but most of all gone was the fresh mountain air – unpolluted and so typical to the village of Aruhu.

It was now being replaced with an ominous vacuum that seemed impenetrable. Arhiti had no idea how the others were reacting to it, but he knew that those still alive and able to respond, were terrified.

The power of the artifact was such that even though it somehow manipulated the flow of time, it also seemed strongly connected to different periods of 'war' and 'conflict', throughout human history. The one time he and Bhrataha had unleashed it accidentally as kids, they had been hurled into some far flung 'future' that was steeped in war. Even though at that time the incident had seemed surreal and the boys had never spoken about it, that much Arhiti had figured out for himself…and as had now become clear…so had Bhrataha!

In his insane thirst for vengeance, Bhrataha had now unleashed the power of the artifact not once but twice in a very short span of time! The first phase had proved catastrophic for the entire village, suddenly ageing it by decades. Arhiti was quite sure; the second phase would prove no different. Worse, if Bhrataha was successful in channelizing this power, they could once again end up amidst 'war torn' lands.

Even though he could no longer see anything in this all imposing mist, Arhiti knew that he simply *had* to recover the artifact. Desperately, he tried to reach for it through the haze, as a series of ethereal images began to take shape before him. As the mist gradually lifted, he was able to discern ghostly images of men, women and children, wearing long and colorful full-length garments that seemed absolutely foreign!

The surrounding area seemed to be a magnificent city built against a deep harbor. Arhiti gasped...this definitely wasn't the village of Aruhu...even one that had been 'accelerated decades into the future... their village certainly had no harbor and it was miles from any coastline. No...this clearly wasn't their village!

Nonetheless, he found it impossible to take his eyes off this spectacle. The city he now saw seemed divine and unearthly! There were cobbled streets laid out in geometric precision that far exceeded what he had seen in his own village. Palm trees in specially constructed terraces, neatly dotted the side of each road. A small group of children played happily in the streets even as adults seemed to magically move between places, whilst sitting inside strange 'closed compartments', which had four wheels attached to them and which made a peculiar sound, as they ran along the streets.

Was this actually Earth? The denizens of this strange paradise certainly looked human enough, and there also wasn't any sign of conflict or war going on. These seemed to be very much a people at peace.

This wasn't what Arhiti has expected, when he had seen the jewel being activated. Where was the acrid, burnt and desolate battleground they had encountered the first time? Where was the war from another world, full of metallic monsters that belched fire and helmeted men who emerged from them? This landscape and the city were anything but that...an ethereal paradise if ever there was one! Had the jewel somehow changed? Was this the real gift that it could bestow? Had Bhrataha for all his faults, been somehow judged worthy by the jewel?

As Arhiti looked on, the thing that caught his eye the most was the attire the men and women wore. The fabric itself seemed delicate and perfect, unlike the course, rough cloth that he was so familiar with. So perfectly covered was each costume, with intricately painted images of flowers that it seemed to merge with its surroundings. The women, beautiful and demure, each wore a long flowing gown with a sash around the midriff and gracefully carried an umbrella over their head, in the manner of royalty. The entire scene was reminiscent of a magical paradise!

At the very center, stood a glistening white building at least two storeys tall, with a large cross shaped motif, dominating the landscape. Arhiti noticed a steady stream of demurely dressed men and women entering it, with their heads lowered in respect. It didn't seem like a place of residence. Was this a place of worship of some sort? Much like the shrine they had back in the village? A large statue of a bearded man with his arms spread out against a cross, that stood above the place, seemed to be the object of their piety.

What was this strange ghostly place and where had the jewel's power transported them this time?

In all his years of studying their mysterious teacher's legacy, Arhiti had come to view the jewel as an object that bestowed great power, but also one that could corrupt the user, if he wasn't careful. Their teacher's documents had suggested that specific star patterns were somehow significant to the jewel's power...almost as if the jewel somehow was harnessing the energy of these heavenly bodies. But the most disturbing aspect was how the jewel seemed to be connected to periods of catastrophic warfare in different parts of the world. Arhiti and Bhrataha had of course experienced this first-hand as kids.

And yet...this place was very different...certainly *not* in the midst of war. Could it be that Bhrataha had succeeded in tapping into the jewel's real power? Had he somehow managed to bypass its curse? But if so, 'success' had come at enormous cost ...so many unnecessary deaths! Was this the price one had to pay for getting into paradise?

As his mind churned through these thoughts, Arhiti suddenly realized he could no longer see the people of his own village! He was just about able to see the vague silhouette of his village. The images from this 'magical land' now seemed to dominate the landscape of *HIS* village, as if the two places were somehow connected...and overlapping! He could even hear the voices of these strange people...a foreign tongue...very different from his own rural dialect.

What the hell was happening...!!!!

Suddenly, a child playing next to the street, appeared to look directly into Arhiti's eyes...it stared...blinked...and then broke into a smile!

Could it really see him? How was this possible? Was he somehow becoming part of this strange reality? Was this actually happening or was the jewel trying to tempt him with its power?

If it was indeed getting more real by the moment, what about the others? What about that traitor Bhrataha? What about the few remaining survivors? Could they also be seen now?

Suddenly, he heard gasps go out in all directions. The people of this strange land, all around him began to turn, screaming and shouting. It was quite apparent that they could now see the Aruhu survivors and probably even hear them!!

An old woman bent with age, bowed fervently to Arhiti and whispered, "Kami...Kami." Even though her language was unknown, the meaning of her words seemed to burn itself straight into Arhiti's mind. She was calling him a spirit...a ghost!

Why???

The realization hit Arhiti like a thunderbolt. Just as HE was witnessing this strange ghostly phenomenon, to the citizens of this mysterious magical land, *he* probably seemed just as apparitional!

Was he dead then? Was this the afterlife? Some sort of a *limbo* where the soul waits, before it crosses over?

His mind went back to the stories he had heard as a child...stories about what happens to an individual, after he or she dies. His father had told him that even though the 'material life' with all its trials and tribulations is but transient, the 'divine core', the human soul, is eternal. The actions of human beings in life, whether just or unjust, are connected to each other through the 'Karmic spirit'.

"The human body is what passes on." his father had said. *"The soul is what is immortal and eternal. By living a righteous and virtuous life, one can ensure that one's legacy can last for all time. This is true immortality!"*

As a host of questions flooded his brain, Arhiti heard a shout from one of the figures, he was seeing. He saw a man point out towards the mountains that seemed to buffer this beautiful land. As Arhiti strained to see what the man was pointing at, more eyes joined his. In the distance, was the vague outline of an object that appeared to glide down towards the city at tremendous speeds!

Definitely not a bird, the object almost looked metallic from this distance. Arhiti was sure he had never seen anything like it before. The phantom citizens however did seem to recognize the object, as terrified screams rent the air, "Dôshiyô, Dôshiyô, Dôshiyô... Amerika...Bei ..."

It was clear that the denizens of this strange land were terrified of the metallic bird, which was now almost directly over the city. Arhiti saw that the 'bird' was accompanied by two others. The closer they got, the more terrified the citizens became.

He noticed that most of the people threw themselves to the ground or rushed behind anything tall and sturdy that they could find. Were they trying to hide from it? Or were they in fact placating it? Was this a god of some kind?

A small glistening object seemed to separate from the underbelly of the 'bird' and fall towards the city. Arhiti observed that this smaller object caught the morning sun and lit up...it looked cylindrical!

Perhaps this was the deity's way of answering their prayers!

CHAPTER EIGHTEEN

The cylinder picked up speed as it got closer.

Arhiti turned around to try and locate his fellow villagers and suddenly realized that his own people were now almost inseparable from the ghostly images of this strange land, he had been seeing. The two places – his own Himalayan village and this unknown paradise were now almost completely overlapping!

He gazed in amazement, as the familiar village skyline, with its picturesque mountains and thick tropical forests merged with this unknown land. He saw some of his fellow men look equally stunned by what they were witnessing…and standing at the very center… The cause of all this…Bhrataha!

His once best friend and 'oath brother' looked just as disoriented as the others. Even though, he along with Arhiti, had witnessed the jewel's power before, this latest experience, coupled with the extremely violent assault on what had once been his own village, seemed to have unhinged Bhrataha. He stood there like a rock, hands clutching the jewel that still glowed with an inner fire.

Arhiti was about to reach out to his friend, when the cylindrical object the mysterious metal bird had dislodged, crashed into the city with a thunderous roar.

So sudden was the impact that it hurled him off his feet onto the cold, hard, unforgiving city streets. He heard a woman fearfully mutter something under her breath…and then there was silence.

A single unbroken moment of silence that seemed to go on forever…*Time itself was holding its breath!*

And then it exhaled…in an earth-shattering way…a shockingly powerful explosion! A huge cloud of smoke and fire in the shape of a giant mushroom suddenly rose up in the very center of the city.

So colossal was this plume of smoke and ash that for a while it seemed to rise up all the way to the heavens and devour the sun. Arhiti found himself struck by an unimaginable blast of heat and light!

For what seemed like an eternity, the giant cloud held its shape and then began to descend back towards the city. Arhiti felt the atmosphere change. An ominous sound like a massive roar accompanied the blast, nearly deafening him. The force was so great, that he was physically lifted off his feet and hurled back some fifteen or sixteen feet...his body eventually coming to a halt, after painfully colliding with what had just moments earlier, been an outer wall. The remainder of the wall then collapsed on him, burying him underneath!

An intense pain jolted all his senses. Whatever this was, however strange and frightening, it wasn't a dream.

As his eyes began to go dark, he noticed the sky over this strange place turn blood red in color. He saw bodies fly past him, some that barely looked human anymore. The carnage seemed to go on and on, as a massive cloud of ash and dust fell onto the city, with a theatrical finality. An acrid stench filled his nostrils and the very air seemed to be on fire!

Was it the end of the world? Was this the revenge of an angry god? Was it the jewel's cursed power again? As Arhiti gasped for breath, he saw for the first time, the grisly aftermath of this terrible explosion.

He saw a child of around six, lying against a broken door of a house. He felt a catch in his throat. It was the same child that had first seen him appear in its domain, and smiled a welcome! Half of the child's face had melted away and the tarred skin still blistered angrily. However, what haunted Arhiti the most was the smile that seemed transfixed on the child's face, even in death. *An innocent life cut down by a mad god!*

Benumbed, Arhiti saw another boy run towards what appeared to be the charred remains of his father, trapped under the debris of another collapsed structure. This was the same white washed structure he had seen before...the prayer house...with its alabaster walls and the giant, bearded figure with his arms spread out perpendicular to his body. Arhiti saw the boy desperately claw through the debris to get to his father. The statue had been dislodged from its perch and was now lying at a slight angle over the collapsed ruin. With its outstretched arms, it seemed to offer refuge to those trapped beneath!

Arhiti watched the boy try and pull his father's burnt corpse out from beneath the debris. But as he struggled, the top of his father's skull melted and crumbled in his hands. The peaceful serene expression on the face of the collapsed statue was the last thing Arhiti saw...and the anguished scream of the boy was the last thing he heard, before a sickening heat wave washed all over him.

CHAPTER NINETEEN

1945 - WORLD WAR II:

By 1945, the war in the Pacific had entered its fourth year. Even as the Nazi threat hung like a dark cloud over Europe, the U.S. had been focusing its attention primarily on Japan, its principal enemy.

For a country that had started as 'neutral' to Hitler's aggressions in Europe, the U.S. foreign policy and its commitment to the Great War had changed, following the Japanese attacks on 'Pearl Harbor'. The U.S. had found new resolve and strength and mobilized its forces throughout the different theatres of the War.

In the South Pacific, the Japanese fought with unbridled ferocity, ensuring that all American victories came at an enormous cost. Of the 1.25 million battle-field casualties incurred by the United States in World War II, nearly one million occurred in the twelve-month period from June 1944 to June 1945. In virtually every battle Japan fought, its troops fought with near suicidal obstinacy!

Japan had long followed the Samurai 'code of conduct' known as the 'Bushido'. According to this code, a samurai warrior was duty bound to fight for his land and his master till death, and surrender of any kind was forbidden. As a result, even when the Japanese fighter pilots ran out of fuel or ammunition, they would nose dive their planes into American Warships and Aircraft Carriers in the South Pacific. These "kamikaze" pilots, as the Japanese called them, were probably the world's first attempt at creating the perfect suicide bomber!

In April 1945, American forces landed on 'Okinawa', where heavy fighting continued until June. It soon became clear that the Japanese were showing scant respect for human life and were executing captured prisoners of war en masse be it soldiers or civilians. However, the Okinawa landing was extremely significant as this meant that American Bombers, taking off from this volcano island, could now hit key cities including Tokyo.

Moreover, by this point in the war, the help Japan could expect from its long term allies - Italy and Germany, was also extremely limited. The Nazis had suffered their own massive reversals, following the costly battles in Russia and the allied landings at Normandy in France. That this would be the final year of the War, was now a very real possibility.

As the Allies moved ever closer to Japan, conditions began to steadily worsen for the Japanese people. Lack of raw materials forced the economy into a steep decline after 1944, eventually reaching crisis levels by the middle of 1945. The country that had been prepared to take on the great colonial empires of the world was being slowly ravaged by malnutrition and hunger. Of course the Japanese were too proud to admit this and continued to hurl men and material in a desperate attempt at warding off the inevitable.

What they would have to accept was that U.S. industrial production was now overwhelmingly superior to Japan's. By 1943, the U.S. was producing 100,000 aircraft a year and by the summer of 1944, had almost a hundred aircraft carriers in the Pacific. In February 1945, Prince Fumimaro Konoe advised the Emperor Hirohito that defeat was inevitable, and urged him to abdicate.

Preparations to invade Japan: Operation Downfall

Even before the surrender of Nazi Germany on the 8th of May, 1945, plans were underway for the largest operation of the Pacific War, 'Operation Downfall' - the invasion of Japan.

However, the Japanese still had one major advantage. Their country's geography made this invasion plan obvious, enabling the Japanese to accurately predict the Allied invasion plans and put together a monstrous defense.

The Americans were alarmed by this buildup. They estimated that in the event of an invasion, they could come up against more than

2 million Japanese Army troops and an additional civilian militia of 28 million men and women! This would mean, U.S. battle-field casualties could be anywhere between 2 and 4 million casualties, while Japanese fatalities could cross 10 million! An alternate solution had to be designed...one that could prove so terrifying that it would shock even this most fanatical of opponents into surrendering!

With this singular objective, the United States now turned to the most dreaded of options...rather than go big, they decided to go small...by tapping into the unbridled power hidden inside an unstable atom...a Uranium atom!

Manhattan Project:

The discovery of nuclear fission by German chemists - Otto Hahn and Fritz Strassmann in 1938, and its theoretical explanation by Lise Meitner and Otto Frisch, made the development of an atomic bomb, a theoretical possibility. Using a metal called Uranium, it was now possible for scientists to split the atom and engage a process called 'nuclear fission' that would result in the release of a tremendous amount of energy, much greater than all the weapons used so far during World War II.

Since the Nazi takeover of Germany in the early 1930s, a number of German scientists and physicists had fled to the United States to avoid persecution. Among them, was the eminent physicist Albert Einstein. One of his greatest fears was that a German atomic bomb project would develop atomic weapons first. This prompted preliminary research into Uranium based weapons in the United States. Dr. J. Robert Oppenheimer was recruited to organize and head the project's 'Los Alamos Laboratory' in New Mexico, where bomb design work was carried out. This ultra-secret project was called 'Project Manhattan'.

Two types of bombs were eventually developed. 'Little Boy' was a fission weapon that used Uranium-235, a rare isotope of uranium. The other, known as 'Fat Man', was a more powerful weapon that used Plutonium.

When the first such weapon was tested near Alamogordo, New Mexico, the bomb exploded with an energy equivalent of around 20 thousand tons of TNT, leaving a crater of radioactive glass in the desert some hundreds of feet wide. The shock wave was felt over distances of over 200 miles, and a massive mushroom cloud rose some 7 miles in height!

The world now had a new weapon, one so powerful that it left even its creator Dr. Robert Oppenheimer shocked and shaken. *An uncontrollable genie had been let out of its bottle and the world was now entering a dangerous new age.*

Years later at a press conference in Japan, Dr. Oppenheimer described how he felt, when he first saw the first test explosion.

"We knew the world would not be the same. A few people laughed, a few people cried. Most people were silent. I remembered the line from the Hindu scripture, the Bhagavad Gita; Vishnu is trying to persuade the Prince Arjuna that he should do his duty and, to impress him, takes on his multi-armed form and says, '*Now I am become Death, the destroyer of worlds.*' I suppose we all thought that, one way or another."

This quote would become a matter of great debate, as the same scriptures Dr. Oppenheimer quoted, while describing his reactions, contain descriptions, which are eerily similar to an atomic bomb.

In Indian epics such as the Ramayana and the Mahabharata, the 'Brahma Astra' is a weapon created by the creator of the universe - Brahma, for the sole purpose of upholding Dharma and Satya (Truth) against the forces of evil that attempt to corrupt them.

According to the epics, the Brahma Astra when discharged had neither a counterattack nor a defense that could stop it, except another Brahma Astra! The Brahma Astra never missed its mark and had to be used with very specific intent against an individual enemy or army, as the target would face complete annihilation. It could only be obtained by meditating upon Brahma, or from a Guru, who knew the invocations.

The weapon was believed to cause severe environmental damage. The land where the weapon was used became barren and all life in and around that area ceased to exist. Following an attack, both men and women became infertile. There was also a severe decrease in rainfall with the land developing cracks.

The Mahabharata describes it as a single projectile charged with all the power of the universe. It was the ultimate weapon…a 'doomsday device'…the ultimate 'last resort'.

"Now I am become Death, the Destroyer of Worlds."

CHAPTER TWENTY

1945: In early May, an interim committee set up by the U.S. government, came up with an interesting suggestion. Since the purpose of the bomb was to coerce the Japanese into surrendering, the committee proposed giving the Japanese what would essentially be a non-combat demonstration. This meant that instead of dropping the bomb over civilian neighborhoods, the committee proposed detonating it in the air inside Japanese air space. This would be enough to prompt a Japanese surrender, as they would have witnessed first-hand what the allies were capable of...and no civilians would be killed!

As attractive as this proposal was, it was met with a lot of debate and circumspection.

Those against this idea argued that if such an 'open test' were made first and failed to bring surrender, the element of surprise would be lost forever. They insisted that the Japanese leadership be given no advance warning whatsoever!

August 6th 1945: After much deliberation, the sites for the bombs were decided. The United States was very keen on the targets being of military and strategic significance, as this would force the Japanese into surrendering. The first target was the city of Hiroshima - a minor supply and logistics base for the Japanese military, but one that had large stockpiles of military supplies. It was also a communications center, a key port for shipping and an assembly area for troops.

The city center contained several reinforced concrete buildings and some lighter structures. A few larger industrial plants lay near the outskirts of the city. The houses were constructed of timber with tile roofs, and many of the industrial buildings were also built around timber frames. The city as a whole was highly susceptible to fire damage. Yet for some reason, the Japanese had been reluctant to carry out regular bomb drills and the citizens had almost forgotten they were in the midst of a war!

Some of them occasionally even wondered why the city had been spared the fury of the American air campaign, and there were certainly some very interesting opinions that had emerged. One was that the city had a relatively large catholic population and that had probably acted as a deterrent to the Americans. Certainly, not far from the city square was the 'Church of Saint Mary', easily noticeable on account of the towering white statue of Jesus Christ, with his arms spread out offering protection for all.

Others scoffed at this suggestion. *This war was anything but holy!*

Just before dawn on August the 6th, with Hiroshima as the primary target of the first nuclear bombing mission, the 393d Bombardment Squadron B-29 'Enola Gay', piloted by Tibbets, took off from 'Tinian', about six hours' flight time from Japan. It was accompanied by two other B-29s.

After leaving Tinian, the aircraft made their way separately to the volcanic island of 'Iwo Jima', recently captured from the Japanese at enormous cost. The Japanese had fought tooth and nail, refusing to surrender the island, as its capture would mean that American planes taking off from there could directly target Japanese cities.

During the night of August 5–6, Japanese early warning radar detected the approach of numerous American aircraft headed for the southern part of Japan. However, by dawn, the all-clear was sounded in Hiroshima.

At 08:09 A.M, Tibbets started his bomb run and handed control over to his bombardier, Major Thomas Ferebee. The release at 08:15 went as planned, and 'Little Boy' containing volatile uranium-235 took just under a minute to fall from the aircraft flying at about 31,000 feet.

Due to a strong crosswind, the bomb missed the aiming point, the 'Aioi Bridge', and detonated directly over 'Shima Surgical Clinic'. It created a blast equivalent to 16 thousand tons of TNT; with a region of 1 mile suffering total destruction, and secondary fires spreading across an additional 5 square miles. Enola Gay traveled more than eleven miles before it felt the shock waves from the blast. In Hiroshima, 80,000 people died in one second.

Humanity's worst nightmare was only just beginning…an atomic age! …and yet, experts would wonder for years about why the 'Hiroshima blast' was not as devastating as they had previously estimated.

It was almost as some of its massive energy output had been diverted somewhere else!

But how could such a thing be possible…

CHAPTER TWENTY ONE

For the people of Hiroshima, the 6th of August, 1945, had begun like most other days…and most of them were up and about their business, by about 6.00 A.M. For some reason though, the cool morning air seemed especially *biting* that day and the women out for their morning chores, wrapped themselves a little tighter than usual, in their long flowing 'kimonos'. Nobody could have suspected that this day would define not just their lives but those of an entire generation!

A young girl named Aiko Hashimato was sitting in her room, at the 'Novitiate of the Society of Jesus' in Nagatsuke. The 'Novitiate' was situated approximately two kilometers from the center of Hiroshima, half-way up the sides of a broad valley, which stretched from the town at sea level into this mountainous hinterland, and through which coursed a river. During the past year, the philosophical and theological section of the 'Mission' had been evacuated to this place from Tokyo.

When the war had reached Japan, and the bombing of Tokyo forced the mission to relocate to this small township, there had been a lot of disgruntled voices within the institution. It was seen as an unsavory obstruction to the work they had started in the capital.

Aiko was one of the few who had actually loved the change. From her room, she had a wonderful view down the valley…all the way to the edge of the city. Especially early in the mornings, she loved to sit next to the window and look out at the beautiful countryside.

She had joined the mission primarily because of her love for Christianity and the teachings of Jesus, which centered on compassion for everyone and the idea that we are in some way connected to something greater than ourselves. Now, out here in the wilderness, she felt a decidedly greater connect with the natural world.

Certain mornings when it was particularly cold, she would lean out of the window and close her eyes, letting the cool mountain breeze hit her face. It was at times like these, with all her senses seemingly alive at once that she felt one with the universe!

This day however, something did not feel right. Aiko had woken up earlier than usual, with an uneasy sensation. She looked around and saw that the others were still fast asleep, so she briefly wandered through the corridors of the mission, trying to still her nerves. The empty corridors seemed to echo her fears.

She tried to calm herself down, by pouring herself a glass of cold water from the cloakroom and noticed that her hands were trembling. *This was not good*...she went back to her room and picked up her copy of the 'Holy Bible'. It felt warm and firm in her hands...offering a slight respite. She let her fingers softly trace the embossed engravings on the cover as her lips uttered a familiar prayer.

Our Father, who art in heaven,
hallowed be thy Name,
thy kingdom come,
thy will be done,
on earth as it is in heaven.
Give us this day our daily bread.
And forgive us our trespasses,
as we forgive those
who trespass against us.
And lead us not into temptation,
but deliver us from evil.
For thine is the kingdom,
and the power, and the glory,
for ever and ever.
Amen.

The trembling slowed down a little...but she still felt a nagging dread ...*like an old itch that could not be reached.*

She turned her attention towards her window and looked out at the pre-dawn skyline...the sky seemed unusually purple...the sun had yet to overcome the darkness. Normally this was her favorite time of the day...still and completely tranquil...she would sit for hours staring at the scene...and watch the sun as it made its slow journey off the horizon.

Today however, her frayed nerves seemed unable to appreciate the spectacle. She clutched her blanket tightly around her body and softly admonished herself. 'This was ridiculous...this was going to be a perfectly normal day...most of it, spent in reading and introspection... and in the service of the Lord! There was nothing at all to worry about...*no demons in the closet...or under the bed...*just stupid baseless jitters!'

She tried to still her mind, by slowing down her breathing. She had learnt this long ago in school, during the weekly yoga classes, long before joining the missionary.

'Who said religions were incompatible' she thought with a slight smirk. The only sound that could be heard was that of the river as it flowed through the mountains...almost musical in its rhythm!

Listening to the shrill, yet soothing sounds of the birds waking up, she felt her eyelids grow heavy and her mind drift into a dreamlike scenario. The soporific scene was certainly having an effect on her. In her mind, she saw the sky gradually turn pink and then red...*almost as if lit up by some divine light*...the light suddenly became a bright flash...blindingly bright...and the familiar landscape she had grown to love over the last year and a half, began to change.

Over the horizon, there appeared images of a small village...barely a hamlet...one flanked by a series of great mountains. The place appeared extremely primitive by modern standards. 'What was this place?' she wondered...she was sure she had never seen it before and yet it somehow seemed strangely familiar...A voice deep in her head tried to rationalize it... 'It is only a dream and dreams certainly have a curious habit of throwing random memories together...before filtering them out.'

But if that was the case, why did this place seem so familiar to her... she had certainly never been to any location like this...it did not even look Japanese...the houses and the layout looked almost...*Indian?*

In her dream...the flash of light that was creating these images over the horizon...seemed to intensify and then suddenly disappear... leaving behind...ghostly figures dressed in outlandish costumes.

There appeared to be a whole army of them...some of them really, really old...yet carrying primitive weapons, such as daggers and swords with them.

One man, who looked to be about eighty, was bent over with the weight of his spear and the crude leather armor that he wore. Aiko smiled softly...*where was this dream going and what was it supposed to mean*...she saw that the figures had a strange ethereal quality to them as if they somehow weren't fully 'physical'...they seemed to float in and out of reality!

An alarm suddenly went off...one that seemed oddly out of place in the midst of what she was witnessing...*what was an alarm doing in this dream?*

The sound kept rising in intensity till it reached a crescendo, jolting Aiko out of her dream like state. "What the...?" This wasn't a dream...this was the 'Air Raid Alarm'...She looked across her room at the watch perched on the wall...7.00 A.M!!! She had fallen into a deep sleep indeed...no wonder the strange dream had seemed so real.

She looked out the window again and noticed that even though the alarm was still on, most of the citizens were ignoring it. They had heard this almost every day but the Americans had steadfastly refused to bomb their city. This time it would be no different. A few planes would appear over the city and perform a routine excursion... that's all.

She sighed...who can ever explain the 'minds' that went to war... *such a senseless waste of humanity!* ...she was about to move away from the window and start her early morning chores...when something caught her attention.

She saw a child of around five or six, playing on the street, just outside its house...the mother had probably just let it out, while she cleaned the front yard. The child suddenly pointed towards something in midair and smiled.

Aiko's eyes followed what the child was smiling at...and felt her breath catch. Floating in midair, just a few feet off the ground, were the same ghostly images that she had just seen in her dream! She blinked...rubbed her eyes hard and squinted...No! It was no illusion...

the child could see it and now so could she…How was this possible? This had just been a dream!

The ghostly figures wore primitive Asiatic tunics and some of them were carrying weapons…a few of them even seemed bent with age… just like she had seen in her dream! A cold sweat broke all over Aiko… What the hell was she seeing? Was this some kind of a 'waking-state' nightmare? …A premonition?

She stared at the unfolding madness and noticed that out of the ghostly figures, two young men, who looked like they were in their twenties; seemed more 'defined' than the rest…*almost as if they were somehow 'more real' than the rest!* One of them appeared to be holding some kind of a small egg shaped object that appeared crystalline.

Aiko clearly saw the morning sun reflect off the device. This was no illusion… "Madness!!!" she thought 'Was she the only one who was going through this? Surely she must notify the others at the missionary especially Father David, even though, she knew he did not like to be disturbed so early.

But how could she ever describe any of this? …surely no one in their right mind would believe her. Nonetheless, she rose from the window to make her way to the main hall, almost stumbling over herself in her panic. Out of the corner of her eye, she saw that there were more and more people gathering on the street, close to where the child was playing, and even though they seemed completely oblivious to the air raid alarm, it was clear that something else was drawing their attention in a big way. The sounds of their murmurings could be heard clearly, through the thin morning air.

Aiko paused…were the others also seeing what she and the child had seen? …that did seem to be the case…She saw a series of gasps go off and suddenly everyone was pointing towards the apparitions. Aiko saw an old woman look directly at one of the figures and bow reverently before them while softly chanting, "Kami…Kami"

"Kami" Aiko knew what the word meant. She remembered her grandmother telling her about them, when she was still little. In Japanese mythology, particularly in the ancient 'Shinto' faith, 'Kami' were spirits or phenomena that were worshipped. They could be elements in nature, animals, creationary forces in the universe, as well as spirits of the revered deceased. Many of the Kami were considered to be the ancient ancestors of entire clans, while some ancestors were thought to become Kami, upon their deaths…if they were able to embody the values and virtues of Kami in life. Traditionally, great or charismatic leaders like the Emperor would become Kami.

Was that what these apparitions were? Never in her wildest dreams had Aiko suspected that she would actually witness them.

And yet there was something even more bizarre about all of this. The figures that the old lady had just venerated seemed just as surprised, stunned and confused as those worshipping them! Aiko saw that the young man, whom she had seen holding the egg shaped device, look the most terrified. He seemed to be trying vigorously to open whatever it was in his hand, by rubbing all over it. She saw another young man reach out desperately…almost as if trying to stop him from tampering with the object.

Aiko watched…mesmerized… 'Who were these entities? …How had they got here? …what was happening? She needed witnesses… either to confirm what she was seeing or…to at least acknowledge that she was losing her mind!'

She called out… "Father David!" …her voice catching in her throat…she called out again…desperately…knowing that father David occupied the rooms just round the corner…she was met with silence. 'Where was everyone? They should have been up by now'

In the silence, she suddenly realized that the Air Raid alarm that had been going off all this while had now been called off and the 'all clear' was being sounded. She looked at the clock surprised…it was 8 A.M. already…impossible…an entire hour had gone by since the weird apparitions had first become visible!

She looked again at the watch…it was five minutes past eight… 'What?!!!' she gasped, stunned…it was almost as if five minutes of her life had just been swallowed up…she blinked and looked again… it was ten minutes past eight! …it was true…time seemed to be jumping ahead…Aiko looked out once again…those outside were also noticing something unusual…they were looking at each other in surprise, as though they had suddenly been woken up…Aiko suddenly heard a soft, faint yet familiar voice, "Father David!"…she realized with a start that it was the echo of her own cry...from ten minutes ago!!!

'Yes...time was going wonky and whatever the ghostly apparition with the device was doing, it was having an effect. She looked out again alarmed...he would have to be stopped...whoever or whatever he was. But before she could do anything else, another cry rang out... "Dôshiyô, Dôshiyô, Dôshiyô...Amerika...Bei ..."

The Americans were coming back...Aiko looked up and saw a familiar sight...three American planes coming over the horizon into the now clear blue morning sky. There didn't seem to be any obvious need for panic...the Americans had been carrying out surveillance missions over Hiroshima for weeks now.

As the planes came closer...Aiko noticed a small silvery package detach itself from the lead aircraft and head towards the city square... probably more propaganda leaflets, Aiko sighed...the Americans had dropped millions of such leaflets, imploring the Japanese to convince their leaders to surrender. It hadn't worked...the Japanese leadership had seemed immune to the sufferings of the people. Moreover, the 'Bushido' – the Samurai code of conduct, forbade the Japanese from surrendering.

She saw the package fall with unusual velocity, catching the rays of the morning sun, as it shot downwards. When will they learn!!!!... Aiko turned her head away from the window in derision, just as the object made contact with the city. As she turned, her eyes caught the clock hanging in the wall of her room...8:15!

Suddenly, the whole valley was filled by a garish light, which resembled the magnesium light used in photography, followed by a wave of heat. Aiko jumped to the window and saw a brilliant yellow light erupt...blinding in its intensity! So bright that she was forced to pull away.

As she made her way to the door, it still didn't occur to her that the light might have something to do with the American planes. She was semi-convinced the apparitions outside had something to do with it. On the way to the door, she heard a loud explosion, which seemed to come from a distance and, at the same time, her windows burst into a million shards of glass.

Aiko found herself covered in fragments of glass. She could feel it all across her body like a million ant pricks. Excruciating pain suddenly hit all her nerve endings, as tiny rivulets of blood began pouring down her arms and legs. She bit her tongue in agony and felt glass inside her mouth as well. Arggghhhh!!!

She spat some of it out...it had an odd metallic taste...one that lingered.

She saw that the entire window frame had been forced into the room and then slowly the realization dawned upon her that a bomb had just gone off and that it had probably exploded directly over the house...or in the immediate vicinity. But how could that be? Who could have dropped it? *Surely it couldn't have been the American plane!!*

Even if the object the plane had dropped was indeed a bomb, it had been dropped over the city square...at least four or five miles away! And even though the bright light that she had just seen had come from that area...*what kind of a weapon could affect structures located miles away?*

Aiko looked around herself and found she was still bleeding from cuts, all over her body. She tried to get out of her room, but found that the door was jammed. Desperately, she tried to force an opening in the door. It seemed to resist, as though someone were holding it shut from the other end.

Aiko felt the panic rise and rise...and finally erupt in a massive scream, as she threw herself against the door. With a great groan, the ageing timber gave way and she suddenly found herself sprawled face first on the floor outside. Winded, she took a moment to compose herself...then slowly surveyed the broad hallway into which opened the other rooms. Everything was in a state of chaos. All the windows were broken and all the doors forced inwards!

The bookshelves in the hallway had tumbled down and their contents, including countless copies of Holy Scriptures, lay strewn on the floor. Her eyes searched desperately for her colleagues. She saw some of them appear in a similar state of dishevel, from their rooms. Most had been injured by fragments of glass...bleeding but not too seriously.

An elderly missionary, who lived down the hall from Aiko, was sitting on the floor clutching her worn knees, her face white from terror…mumbling incoherently…something about the 'End Times'. Aiko crossed herself with the sign of the Trinity…Father…Son and the Holy Spirit…and prayed that this wasn't really the case.

She suddenly became aware of Father David…*God bless his soul*… shouting at the top of his voice, trying to get everyone outside. This was absolutely vital…whatever it was that had attacked the building, could come again…moreover; it wasn't even clear how much damage the building itself had sustained.

This thought seemed to strike everyone at the same time and a mad rush followed, as the missionaries made a frenetic dash for the back door. As soon as everyone was out, Aiko turned around and looked at the building. It became clear right away that all of them had been extremely fortunate, since the wall outside the windows had been lacerated by long fragments of glass that stuck out at an obscene angle! …Surely this was Satan's work!

Some of the women screamed and fell to their knees after seeing this. *Who but the 'Lord God' could have saved them from something so terrible?*

Aiko was quiet…something wasn't right here. Yes the long shards of glass sticking out of the walls were indeed a reminder of how close they had all come to a gruesome end and yes the Lord had in all likelihood been unusually kind to his devout worshippers, but the real question was, where had these shards come from?

Surely they could not have come from the windows of the missionary house itself! Those windows had all been broken *inwards* by the force of the blast…Aiko had herself been witness to this. Yet all over the outside walls, were pieces of glass sticking out…as if they had been fired at great force…towards the missionary…all the way FROM THE VALLEY BELOW!

'Impossible! …*What ungodly power could do something like that???*'

She was about to voice her concerns to father David, when she heard his voice summon everyone to the front side of the house.

They all proceeded to the front of the house to see where the bomb had landed. Aiko dreaded what she would find…a bomb so destructive would have caused massive structural damage. But as they rounded the sides…astonishingly, they found no evidence of a bomb…no crater…no scorch marks…no burns…nothing!!

And yet, the southeast section of the house was severely damaged. Neither door nor window remained. One entire side wall had been completely sheared off. It became clear that the blast had penetrated the house from this end and yet the house had somehow managed to withstand it. It had originally been constructed in the conventional Japanese style, with a wooden framework, but since then had been greatly strengthened by the labor of 'Brother Thomas'…as was frequently done in most Japanese homes.

The building itself had served as a 'Shinto' temple, before its conversion into a missionary house and the parts that had been made exclusively of wood, had taken the most structural damage. A strange smell…almost like burning rubber…noxious and putrid, hung in the air. As people around her began coughing and wheezing, Aiko looked out towards the valley.

Down in the valley, perhaps one kilometer from them, she saw that several peasant homes were on fire and the woods opposite the valley, were also aflame. But what had caused all this carnage? There hadn't been any large scale bombing carried out by the Americans.

Aiko had read reports from Tokyo and knew that this kind of massacre was certainly a part of this terrible war. But this hadn't seemed like an air raid at all! Except for that strange glittering package the plane had dropped, there had been nothing else…at all! Could this be some new top secret weapon that the Americans had developed… to shower even more misery on the Japanese people?

"A few of us should go over and help control the flames." Aiko heard father David's voice echo over the ensuing chaos and people began to slowly move towards the valley. As they crossed the church, the full scale of the horror finally became apparent. The entire front side of the church had been blown away. The road leading up to it from the valley was covered with debris…human or not…it was impossible to say!

Aiko eyes welled up, as she saw the magnificent statue of Christ the Redeemer - with outstretched arms, in a gesture signifying hope for all mankind, now toppled from its pedestal on the front of the church, where it had stood so proudly, overlooking the valley. The statue now lay inclined to the floor, its base partly supported by the outer wall of the church…at an angle, almost as if it were symbolically still guarding something!

Through her tears, Aiko saw some movement amid the debris just below the collapsed statue. 'My God…there was someone trapped underneath…someone still alive'…She saw a young boy, his clothes, singed and burnt, run desperately towards the statue screaming for his father. It was his father that was trapped underneath!!! Aiko saw the boy struggle through the debris underneath the collapsed statue and half lift, half drag his father out. She felt her breath catch in her throat…and saw the father move slightly in his son's arms…the man was still alive…protected probably from the blast, by the outstretched arms of the statue!!

A wave of emotions hit Aiko! …tears of pain and relief! …even in all of this carnage, *Christ WAS the ultimate solace!* She began to gingerly walk towards them, to assist the boy in fully rescuing his father.

Suddenly, hope turned to numb grief as she saw the top half of the father's skull melt and crumble in his son's hands. Aiko felt the Earth slip from underneath her feet and the blood completely drain from her body, as she collapsed to the hard ground in total shock. The anguished ear-splitting scream of the boy, was the last thing she heard, before she lost consciousness.

Over the city, the heavens opened up and it began to rain, even as thick clouds of smoke still rose…buffeted by a few smaller explosions in the distance.

Fitting…even the Gods were weeping!

CHAPTER TWENTY TWO

Arrrrghhhhh…!!!!!…Arhiti felt like he had been screaming for an eternity. The intense heat and massive pain, coursing through his body, certainly made it seem that way.

Gasping for breath, he opened his eyes and looked around. Both he and Bhrataha seemed to be back in what looked like a desolate version of their beloved village of Aruhu…one that was utterly devoid of life. *God! What had happened here?* He struggled to get up…and found that every little movement, sent bursts of pain up and down his body. The skin on his back felt like someone was holding a burning torch against it. He beat his hands viciously against his own body, hoping to dull the pain…nothing…His eyes welled up…the pain was becoming unbearable.

He looked around desperately trying to find something that could dull this terrible agony…and saw Bhrataha lying face first in the sand. *Dead?* Arhiti couldn't say.

No…Bhrataha slowly raised his head and looked around. There was a strange look in his eyes…*one that danced dangerously close to the borders with insanity!* Arhiti couldn't blame him for this of course. He felt his own grip on sanity start to slip away. Surely, after what they had been through…the outlandish place the cursed jewel had transported them to…the strange people with their unique costumes… the arrival of the metal birds followed by the massive bursts of light and heat…and finally the utter destruction of their own village, succumbing to the seductive lure of insanity, wasn't completely unexpected!

But Arhiti noticed something more in his friend's eyes…something akin to regret. The fact that it was he who had unleashed this mayhem, was clearly weighing heavily on Bhrataha. Gone was the all conquering vengeful warrior, who had ruthlessly laid waste to his former hometown…gone were the delusions of grandeur and the thirst for unlimited power. Bhrataha now seemed a broken hollowed out shell of the man, who had attacked their village!

Needless to say, Arhiti was doing no better himself…even though he was now on his feet; the left side of his body was almost completely immobile. He tried desperately to make sense of what had happened over the last…how long had it been since Bhrataha's attack on Aruhu? *A few hours? Days? Years?* Did these terms even MEAN anything anymore? 'Time' and 'duration' no longer seemed to matter!

Arhiti had witnessed the device come alive in Bhrataha's hand, and seen with his own eyes the people of the village; age decades in mere moments, while he and Bhrataha had remained untouched by the power…so how much time had actually passed?

He once again looked to see how Bhrataha was faring. He saw him awkwardly struggle to his feet…and then collapse once again. With real concern in his voice, Arhiti called out to his childhood friend.

None of what had transpired mattered any more. In this insane new landscape, with their village stripped of its soul, the two of them were in it all alone with their backs to the wall…much like they had been in the forest all those years ago! Now was not the time for revenge and retribution. Regardless of Bhrataha's actions, Arhiti realized they would have to work together to stay alive and salvage something from this terrible mess.

As thoughts of his now dead family crossed his mind, Arhiti felt his eyes cloud over. "No!!!" he admonished himself…now wasn't the time to grieve…even *that* would have to wait…he would mourn his family and friends later…his immediate concern was to ensure that the artifact that had caused all of this, was secure. Bhrataha still possessed it and there was no telling what it would do, if he again unleashed its fury…these were clearly forces no human being was meant to understand…or tamper with!

Arhiti sensed that the real danger lay in the fact that Bhrataha seemed unhinged by what had happened. If and when he realized the full extent of the carnage he had caused, he would never forgive himself for it…With nothing to lose; he might even become suicidal, making the device a potential powder keg!

Already, Arhiti saw his friend clutch the jewel tightly in his fingers, with the same demented look in his eyes. "For God's sake Bhrataha, throw away the jewel...hasn't the disaster we just experienced, been enough for you? How much more do we need to go through, before you realize that enough is enough?"

Bhrataha looked at his friend with a dazed expression, "What does the term 'disaster' mean anymore...after what we went through... what am I supposed to do with my life now? What are WE supposed to do? Why were we spared while so many others killed?"

Arhiti sensed the panic mount in his friend's voice...*this was not good*...he needed to get the artifact away from him, before he did something untoward with it. He tried to keep a calm voice, as he dragged himself over to his friend...the paralyzed lower part of his body certainly not making progress any simpler!

Seeing him come closer, Bhrataha began to panic even more "Stay away!!!" he screamed..."You are in league with the devil himself...this is all a trick to get to my soul." He was now ranting...his slender grip on sanity, slipping away rapidly.

"Calm down brother!" Arhiti spoke, his voice trembling. "This is as terrifying to me, as it is to you...I do not understand this any more than you do...let us work together and God willing we might even be able to turn back things to the way they were...but you must stay calm!!"

"Ha ha ha you fool!" screeched Bhrataha, "There is no God...the events that just unfolded, should have shown you at least that much... there is just this power that we have been entrusted with, and it is playing a grand cosmic joke on us. But I will never allow that to happen...I will harness it and be its master." Screaming hysterically... he once again began running his palms over the device.

Thwack!!!! The device was suddenly knocked out of his hands by a viciously hurled wooden staff. It had taken the last of Arhiti's strength, to hurl. The object flew through the air in a beautiful arc and landed softly in the sands.

"Noooo..." screamed Bhrataha, as his hands frantically clawed the air, trying to recover his prize, but Arhiti pounced on it and secured it with his body. He would die before he let Bhrataha handle it again!

Sssssss...the artifact still hissed and pulsed...almost angry at being silenced! Even now, Arhiti fully expected to be stabbed in the back by his friend, but he was too exhausted to do anything about it. He lay clutching the device...waiting for the blow that never came. As his breath slowly returned to normal, he cautiously turned around.

The singed and scorched trees looked back at him, accusingly!

Bhrataha lay prostrate on the ground, more dead than alive. "Thank God..." Arhiti looked around...before his friend regained his senses; he needed to find a place where he could hide the jewel. He was quite sure that once Bhrataha regained consciousness, he would almost certainly attack him if he could, and in his own semi-paralyzed state, Arhiti would be in no condition to fight him off. Worse still, the exhaustion caused by the events he had gone through, was beginning to tell, as he felt his eyelids grow uncontrollably heavy. He needed to secure the device...*and fast!*

As his eyes scanned his surroundings, he saw for the first time the full extent of the devastation, his village had gone through. The entire area leading up to the forest that once housed the village of Aruhu, was now a jumbled ruin. The remnants of buildings and household articles lay singed and burned on the floor, barely distinguishable from their surroundings. The city square that had not so long ago, housed the sacred temple in honor of their mysterious teacher was now reduced to just the foundation stones.

Shockingly, in large areas of the village, the ground seemed to have developed an unnatural sheen, as if the sand had been superheated to form a glass-like substance!

But most disturbing of all, were the human remains that lay strewn all over the place. The corpses of the dead were charred and blackened and in some cases so disfigured that they did not even resemble human beings anymore!

Who were these people? Were they members of his own village that had been killed during Bhrataha's assault? Or were these the nomads that Bhrataha had brought along with him?

One thing was sure though. This couldn't *possibly* be the result of Bhrataha's attack on Aruhu. The nomads he had brought along possessed no weapons that could cause *such carnage*. Had he not seen it with his own eyes, Arhiti would never have believed that such complete destruction was even possible!

His mind reeled from the impact of what he had...and was witnessing, and he wondered whether he was still sane. But as horrific as the carnage was, there was an eerie sense of familiarity to it!

Arhiti's mind went back to the strange magical land that the device had transported them to. In his mind's eye, he once again recalled the feeling of shock and awe he had felt, when he first saw the strange denizens of that 'urban utopia'. *But there was something more...*

He remembered how even when they had been transported to that otherworldly place, in the background, the hills and the forests of Aruhu had been still clearly visible...almost as if the two places had temporarily *merged* into one...certainly the people of that land had also been able to see Arhiti and the others. And *they* had been just as surprised!!

So much about the teacher's artifact was still not clear...but if the village of Aruhu had indeed been somehow fused with the strange city, then the devastation that he was now witnessing had only one possible explanation...one that was too horrible to even think of...but one that could very likely *be* the answer!!

The vast mushroom shaped plume of light and heat that had caused unbelievable carnage in THAT city could have easily destroyed THEIR beloved village as well, considering how the two places seemed to have been connected!

Arhiti remembered some of the images he had seen...images of entire houses going up in smoke and of people getting incinerated... Yes! ...this could well be what had destroyed Aruhu!

By all the Gods! ...he was partly responsible for the annihilation of his village! After all, hadn't he and Bhrataha, as kids first experimented with the cursed relic? Hadn't he been the one who had remained silent all those times when Bhrataha had been ill treated by his own village folk? Hadn't all of that ultimately led to all this anger and violence?

How horribly poetic was it that now, all of those actions had ensured that it would be he and Bhrataha, who were the only ones to be spared the effects of the jewel's carnage!

Arhiti's mind was numb with grief, as he idly tried to pick up a stone lying next to his feet. He watched in horror, as it crumbled to dust under his touch. Tears filled his eyes once more...his entire village destroyed...all his friends and family killed...everything turned to dust and ash, because of this cursed relic.

To hell with securing it, he needed to destroy it as soon as possible! In a blind rage, he raised it high above his head, intent on smashing it to the ground...when suddenly; he heard a haunting voice...speak to him!

CHAPTER TWENTY THREE

Arhiti spun around, half expecting Bhrataha…but instead; saw a tall man standing in front of him…a man in glistening bright golden armor! So bright was the sheen on the armor that Arhiti was forced to squint…the rays of the afternoon sun giving it an unnatural glow! He also found it extremely difficult to look at the man's face…it felt like looking straight into the sun. And yet, there was something oddly familiar about him though…Arhiti felt he had seen him before… *maybe even known him.*

The man spoke softly…calling Arhiti by name…*how did he know him?* …It was still difficult to look at his face. Arhiti suddenly felt extremely uncomfortable. It felt like he was being stripped naked, and all his secrets were being thrown open to the world. *The man's gaze seemed to penetrate right into the very depths of his soul!*

"I know what you really want my child." The man's voice was soft and clear.

"Answers!!" shouted Arhiti… "I have lost everything! …for reasons I don't even understand…I want my village and my people back…I don't want to have anything to do with this cursed artifact…I never asked for the power."

"Oh yes you did." The man whispered softly. "I have observed you throughout your life and I know all your deepest desires."

"Lies!" screamed Arhiti, "And…what do you mean you have been observing me my entire life? I have never seen you before."

"Oh have you not now? Think carefully…and stop hiding from the truth…you will realize that our paths have crossed before!"

Arhiti was about to respond, when he suddenly felt images from a twisted, hellish landscape…a war torn landscape, flood his mind. Images full of huge metallic monsters that belched fire and men who wore strange helmets. With a gasp, he realized it was the incident from his childhood days, when he and Bhrataha had innocently tampered with their teacher's relic, and been transported to this hellish place!

Long suppressed memories began to now crawl their way back into his mind, like an insidious predator! ...he remembered lying on his back in a ditch next to Bhrataha, faced with the weird formation of metallic monsters...half expecting to be killed. That was when this same figure in gold had materialized in front of them.

"You were there with us all those years ago...on that battleground." Arhiti gasped in awe. The man softly smiled. "I have *ALWAYS* been there with you...teaching you...guiding you...you just never realized it."

"Who are you?" Arhiti asked, his voice trembling. "Are you our legendary teacher? The long lost one? ...Our savior? The one, whom the elders referred to as 'Ashwatthama'?

The man smiled, "I have been known by many names, and yes I *did* visit your ancestors long ago, to guide them towards their destiny. However, I wasn't able to complete that task and had to leave your people, abruptly. The knowledge and the artifacts that I entrusted with your ancestors have unfortunately *not* been utilized for the progress of mankind...as I had hoped for, and this has caused me deep pain! Your people in spite of having the best of intentions have never quite grasped the true significance of that which they held!"

"But you Arhiti...you showed remarkable promise...you were the one I believed in...I have reached out through 'Time' itself to guide you and your path and which is one of the reasons why you still survive today, in spite of the carnage around you."

Arhiti did not know whether to laugh or cry. He had heard so many stories of their legendary teacher, growing up in the village, from his father, his grandfather and so many others, but never in his wildest dreams had he believed he would one day have the privilege of meeting his idol!

He suddenly felt giddy...*for him to meet his icon...for this to happen on the day when he had lost everything, was devastating!* He tried to look at the teacher directly...there was still so much that he did not understand.

If, the teacher had never wanted the artifact to be used, why then had he entrusted the villagers with it so many years ago, and *if* they were supposed to harness its power, then why was its knowledge so forbidden?

Before he could voice any of these concerns, the mysterious figure spoke again, "The device you hold in your hands contains the ultimate secrets of 'Time'...secrets that will be discovered approximately 6000 years in the future... *YOUR* future, during a great war! I cannot reveal too much of the actual details, for everything that I say to you now could have a catastrophic impact on events yet to happen. All you need to know is that with this artifact in your hand, the mysteries of 'Space and Time' are yours to explore forever!"

"I do not want its power...I do not want to have anything to do with it. All I want is my family. If what you say is true...bring them back to me!" Arhiti screamed hysterically.

"What you ask is *not* within my or anyone's power to give. What *HAS* happened cannot be undone...*if* it could have been, I would have prevented myself from going down this path...no child...your village and your family have passed and there is absolutely nothing you, I or anyone else can do about it...let them be in peace...consider this the price of ultimate power...to gain everything, *you must be prepared to lose everything.*" The stranger spoke softly.

"But I did not ask for it...I never wanted this at all." Arhiti wailed.

"Oh? Did you not now? Was it not you who led your misguided friend to the device all those years ago? Was it not you who tempted him into trying to decode its mysteries? The two of you activated the device all those years ago but forgot to shut it down properly...as a result the device has been keyed onto the two of you since then... waiting for an opportunity...there is no going back now."

"Those were the innocent mistakes of children." Arhiti protested through his tears, "Surely we cannot be held responsible for actions done during our childhood."

"All actions...regardless of their intent have repercussions. You unfortunately have had to learn this the hard way. Now there is nothing else to do but to embrace what life has thrown at you and become my worthy successor!"

"Your WHAT???" Arhiti gasped..."How can I be your successor? Unless...Do you mean to say, *you* currently hold the power of the device in your hands?"

"Yes my child and I have done so for more cosmic cycles than I care to recall. I have held the power of God...the secrets and knowledge of the entire universe are mine...I am 'the Alpha and the Omega'...the beginning and the end!"

"Why would you want to give up all of that?"Arhiti quizzed suspiciously...his pain gradually receding.

The stranger looked quietly at him, "Even omnipotence has its drawbacks...one gets bored even though the entire universe is one's plaything. There is only so much one can wish for...moreover, I know my time has come...I now crave a simpler existence. But you...you can listen to your destiny call out to you...just imagine, your merest wish will instantly become reality...you will never require *another* God to placate and venerate...for you will become one yourself!"

"All you have to do is grasp the device that you hold in your hand, tightly...move the top half of it towards you and the bottom half the other way. A field of energy will then begin to form around you... let it completely surround you...do not move or try to escape...in both your previous misadventures, neither you nor your overzealous friend let the process complete and that is why disaster struck... remember, the transfer takes a little while to occur but once it's done, you shall become what I am right now...God!!"

Arhiti's mind was reeling from this deluge. Here was the figure that his entire village had worshipped for over a century, standing right in front of him and handing him the keys to unlimited powers...all in exchange for nothing?

Something did not quite add up. "If what you say is true heavenly father, then what stops you from bringing back my dead family and friends? Surely, it would be well within the scope of your powers to accomplish even this seemingly impossible feat...after all, you claim to possess the powers of God."

"You are a resolute little one aren't you?" the stranger chuckled, "I clearly chose well...it's true that while I control this device, I have within me the power of God…however, some things are best not tampered with…I already told you that your family's time on this planet has come and gone…to attempt to reverse that is to act against nature itself and moreover, I have no special need or desire to do it myself."

"How can you say that!!!" Arhiti screamed, "My entire village worshipped you…we idolized you…you were our godly teacher…my family died protecting what you left us. How can you not care about bringing them back?"

"I have already made my stance clear." The stranger said…his voice cold as ice. "All you have to do is activate the device, after that what you choose to do with unlimited power is *your* prerogative…I must say though that you are proving to be a great disappointment…I have observed you for years and I always thought you would show a little more backbone Arhiti…maybe I should have chosen your more ambitious friend Bhrataha instead! In any case, your time to make your decision grows short…soon it won't matter *what* you decide, it will prove impossible for you to receive my blessing."

"Why…?" Arhiti gasped, "Are you going to abandon me again? Just like you abandoned my ancestors all those years ago?"

"In a sense…yes! You see there is one thing that neither you nor your fellow people ever realized…the device needs certain very specific conditions to be activated…conditions that currently govern us. I taught your ancestors how to identify these conditions… astronomical abnormalities visible from Earth. Certain celestial bodies in specific formations…for instance the conjunction of the planet that we call Saturn with the giant star Aldebaran that your villagers recognized it as the day of "Kartika Pornima" when "Shani" (Saturn) was seen to be near "Rohini" (Aldebaran). Another rare combination is the retrograde motion of Mars, just before reaching Anteares, or as your villagers described it "Angaraka" (Mars) reaching " jyeshta" (Anteares)."

"The Star Charts!!" Arhiti gasped, "We preserved them all those years but never once did we suspect their purpose!!"

"Yes…but now you know." The stranger spoke softly, "All the times when you have been able to activate the device were times when these celestial bodies were in the right alignment. The device is powerless otherwise. Those self-same celestial bodies are currently *IN* alignment and have been for a while now…it is why your unhinged friend was able to harness the power of the device. He of course did it without completely understanding how it works. As a result, the device was once again only activated partially and the results as you now know were cataclysmic…the utter destruction of your family and friends. If you plan to reverse the carnage he unleashed, waste no time…grasp your destiny before the celestial alignments change…it could be decades or even centuries before these bodies line up again…harness the power…*NOW!*" the stranger's voice rose to a crescendo.

Arhiti's mind nearly snapped. A cold sweat broke all over his body. He was being confronted with a terrible choice. On one hand, if what the stranger was saying was true, he could reverse the destruction of his village…he would be able to meet his father, his brothers and his entire village again. *To hear the laughter and the voices of the children once again, as they ran carefree through the narrow streets of his village, was surely worth any price!*

On the other hand, the fact that the stranger seemed so eager and anxious to give up this power was deeply troubling. Arhiti had seen the device at work…*twice* and granted they hadn't exactly known how to use it properly, but its effects had still been devastating.

As images of his family and friends flashed in front of his eyes, Arhiti steeled himself to his terrible choice. He gripped the device in his hand tightly and ran his fingers over its smooth crystalline surface. He felt it mildly pulse in his hand as if it were alive and listening to him…egging him on to make the next move. With bloodshot eyes he looked over to the stranger and nodded his assent.

A sly smile broke over the stranger's face…a face that Arhiti suddenly realized he was able to see more clearly. No longer was the stranger radiating light…no longer was he an ethereal spirit…he now seemed very VERY human to Arhiti…*almost too human!*

"Go on my child." The being urged, "The moment is upon us… rotate the top half of the device and seize the power within…put your trust in the universe and the universe shall repay it manifold."

With a deep breath, Arhiti began the process of activating the device…whatever the outcome; he felt he had nothing to lose now. As his fingers began to twist the object under them, he felt his breath catch…all of a sudden, it was impossible to breathe…*a cold dull pain seemed to snake its way up his body.* He looked down and much to his amazement saw the razor sharp tip of a cruel metallic dagger sticking out from the front of his own chest!!!

The whole world seemed to stop spinning…the air went still…he could barely comprehend what was happening. He slowly turned around and saw a familiar figure standing right behind him with a deranged look on his face…Bhrataha!!!!

Oh God!! He had completely forgotten about him! …Somehow, during his conversation with the stranger, Bhrataha had regained his composure… enough to launch a devastating attack against his childhood companion…*he had literally stabbed Arhiti in the back!* As Arhiti's eyes began to go dark and his legs started to give, he tried to scream but instead, blood poured out of his mouth.

He fell to his knees and tried desperately to reach out to the stranger. Out of the corner of his eyes, he saw Bhrataha feverishly grab the artifact, now lying on the ground and hold it aloft triumphantly.

Arhiti felt his life breath silently slip away…Now there would be no correcting the mistakes of the recent past…now there would be no bringing back his village…no one would even know what had happened over here…no one be left to sing for the dead…Now truly, all was lost…As his eyes went completely dark, Arhiti smiled softly… at least now he would once again be with his family…*one way or the other.* His final earthly memory was hearing the stranger's voice…soft and almost condescending… "Just as *we* study the universe and make demands of it, we often forget that the universe studies *us* as well… and its demands of course simply *CANNOT* be refused!"

CHAPTER TWENTY FOUR

From the foothills of the Himalayas to the 'Rann of Kutch', stretch more than 2,000 different sites that once housed one of the world's oldest civilizations – the 'Indus Valley Civilization'.

Since its discovery in the early 1920s; there have been unconfirmed reports that some of the pre-historic sites, particularly those in the Himalayan foothills, display increased levels of radiation. 'Conspiracy theorists' have cited various reasons for this, ranging from 'Aliens visiting earth in the ancient past and using advanced nuclear based weapons in their conflicts' to -'ancient Indian Empires described in Indian Epics, using divine weapons'.

These theories are largely discounted by mainstream academicians and historians. Whatever their relative merit, the fact remains, that these outlandish claims *have* captured public imagination in a big way, especially, since the suggestions about high levels of radioactivity *do* seem to be true.

So does that mean ancient civilizations had knowledge of Nuclear Technology?

'After all', the proponents argue… *'what else could have caused this?'*

The extraordinary events that once occurred in the remote Himalayan village of Aruhu, *might* serve as a possible explanation.

CHAPTER TWENTY FIVE

"The best revenge is massive success." – **Frank Sinatra**

This is exactly how Bhrataha felt, standing in front of the legendary teacher.

He held on to the mysterious artifact, tightly. After years of humiliation, isolation, plotting and planning, he had accomplished the impossible. Absolute power was just moments away...*mere fingertips away!*

He had experienced the power of the device twice before, and he knew that he couldn't afford to take it lightly. But now with all competition out of the way, he stood alone yet triumphant, over the corpses of those, who had shunned him. Like some terrible 'Death God', his vengeance had been brutal and absolute!

He looked over to the body of his former friend, Arhiti and felt a mild sense of regret...after all, the two had shared a lifetime together... *certainly the best parts!*

'No' ...he told himself... 'Now was not the time for guilt or regret... he would mourn his friend later'...after all hadn't Arhiti died because of his own weakness?...his own lack of will? The stranger had offered him the power...it had been Arhiti who had proved *unworthy* of such a prize...and as a result doomed himself...Bhrataha had merely been the instrument of his demise!

Moreover, Bhrataha reasoned that once he did gain truly unlimited power, reversing all of this would be 'child's play'.

He looked with gleaming eyes at the stranger..."Tell me master... how do I harness the power of God? How do I accomplish that which has always been my destiny? Rest assured I will prove worthy of the task, unlike my dead friend."

"Think carefully my child…what you ask for…for once you go down this path, there is no coming back."

"I don't want to go back." Bhrataha screamed…his lust for power had by now reached a fever pitch. "Tell me master…I implore you… tell me how to activate this device." Even as he spoke, his fingers tightened around the device. The top part suddenly began to move under his hands with a dull 'humming' sound…surprising him! The sound seemed to come from all directions at once. The atmosphere suddenly changed…the dead village of Aruhu seemed to recede into the backdrop, as a thin energy field began to form around him.

"It begins…" the stranger almost laughed… "Well done my child, you have taken a decision that will alter for all time, the course of history! Let the energy field form around you…do not move and try and focus only on your goal…let no other thought enter your mind… the next few moments are the most critical."

"But I am unable to see and hear you clearly master." Bhrataha mumbled…the panic rising in his voice.

"This will happen…the power is being transferred as we speak, from me to you. Soon you will become the new 'Supreme Being' and all of the universe will be your plaything…but you need to stay *within* the field…you have already attempted it before…twice…and got it wrong both times…this is not a very forgiving power."

"Master I am scared!!…it burns…it hurts…I feel like I am being torn apart!!" Bhrataha screamed as his entire corporeal structure…his very body itself started to come apart.

"Hold on my child…you are doing brilliantly…I could not be more thankful to you…just a few more seconds and it will be over."

The energy field effect was now complete…and 'Time' seemed to have stopped flowing! The only discernable movement was the flow of unknown, alien sub-atomic particles that materialized from a rip in the fabric of space. Although too small to see with the naked eye, their constant movement was creating the illusion that *the air itself was changing shape!*

Minute ripples danced through the atmosphere in this ever changing environment…and in the center of it all…a glowing Bhrataha stood within the energy field, completely immobile…

experiencing excruciating pain, as his very atoms were being displaced!

The stranger's voice cut through his agony...like cold steel, "Embrace it my child...the pain is but temporary...a brief and passing *phantasm*...on the hope-cobbled boulevards of eternal happiness... listen to me carefully child...for, *'In Chronux lies your destiny'.*"

"Arrrghhhh..." a final, ear-piercing scream burst through what used to be Bhrataha's throat...and then...then all was quiet!

EPISODE TWO

CHAPTER ONE

Ssssssssssssssssssssssssss...

For a long time...this was all he could hear, feel or perceive...As to who he was...what it even meant to exist...no such thoughts seemed possible.

His mind seemed to travel everywhere...and nowhere at the same time... 'Space' and 'Distance' no longer had any meaning...the very terms seemed inconsequential!

So what was this? Where was this? And why was it so difficult to put together a single coherent thought? 'How much time had passed' was clearly a meaningless question as 'Time' did not seem to pass at all!

"Well done my child..." A soft, subtle voice broke through this haze. Amazingly...there did not seem to be any perceivable difference in time between the different words that made up the sentence...in that he was able to hear...all the words...at the exact same instance! ...and yet somehow, their meaning was absolutely clear!

"You have done for me what a million others have failed to...you are truly my redeemer!"

Again...all the words came to him together...but this time, they carried with them, memories of another time, another life...a life dedicated to revenge and a thirst for power...a life that had seen great 'highs' and great 'lows'...one that had been abruptly cut short...but why?

The soft, almost mocking voice continued...its meaning again delivered as a whole, "One of the undying quests of humankind has always been and shall always be – immortality! Throughout history, human beings have fought and struggled over this particular problem...how does one surpass death and live forever. Just imagine... how many of us are seekers of knowledge...seekers of power and how short a life we have, to actually achieve what we seek... *'Time forever haunts our footsteps'*. But imagine if time wasn't our worst enemy... wasn't even a determining factor...what all could one learn and what all could one gain!!"

He heard and understood what the voice was saying...slowly, ever so slightly, the memory began to take on a clearer form, a more distinct shape...of a life in a small village...a life led as an outcast...a life full of frustration and anger...guided by the precise motivation the voice had spoken of...unlimited power...eternal life...but then something had happened. That life had suddenly been cut short by a dramatic event... Here again the memory seemed to falter.

Why was it so hard to think beyond this point?

The voice continued, "You and I come from very different periods in history...different 'worlds' almost, but in life, we had one thing in common. Like you, Bhrataha, I too was obsessed by the sultry lure of unlimited power...fanatically obsessed."

Bhrataha!!!...there was that name...its sound so familiar...was it connected to the life that he was now remembering? He tried harder... there was so little to go on...was he even existing?

"I came from an era that was as close to paradise on earth as possible. If we were to use parameters from your former life as a human...you could say that I lived on planet earth, roughly 6000 years *AFTER* your era...although, based on your current state, you and I can now agree that such statements about time are meaningless!"

'Former life as a human'???? What the hell did that mean? ...what the hell had happened? ...more memories now began to flood in...memories of another person...a friend...a brother even...why did the name 'Arhiti' sound so familiar...a brother, whom he had somehow hurt...Damn... why was it so difficult to think!!!

"In this perfect society that I came from, all human desires were satisfied...every problem had a solution. Humans had outgrown Earth itself and colonized almost all the celestial bodies up to the moons of Jupiter. Petty concepts like 'nations' and 'states' did not apply any more, as most of the human population lived in artificially constructed habitats, all the way from Mars to Titan. Planet Earth was too small a name for what humanity had grown into...we called it

'System Gaea'...Mankind had accomplished its full potential...and then it happened!!"

"We faced our greatest challenge...invaders from across the stars, hell-bent on colonizing Earth and undoing all that we had accomplished. We could not allow that of course...so we fought back. The battle was easily the deadliest our system has ever witnessed. You shall soon be able to access all the information of this 'mother of all conflicts' for yourself...as soon as the transformation is complete."

Transformation?

"The destruction to our planetary system was catastrophic and yet we were able to hold the foul villains to a stalemate. I know...I was there as System Gaea's foremost scientists...the proud 'torchbearer' to an age old civilization."

System Gaea? ...Great War? These would normally seem like the rantings of a lunatic, but for the fact that just as the voice had said, he was now able to witness the cataclysmic confrontation just the way it had been described...it was real...too real...it almost felt like HE was part of it!

Was this the 'transformation' the voice had spoken of? If so, what was he transforming 'into'? And why were the memories of the life in the village once again beginning to recede?

There were no answers, but an eerie sense of calm began to envelop him...he was witnessing the 'Great Battle' the voice had just described... fought at the 'end of time' by human beings just like him, against an invading foe, from beyond the stars. The causes of the conflict were not clear...what he was able to fathom was this: sometime around the time of the 'great unification' of all the diverse peoples of earth and the 'great leap forward' made by mankind, humanity had sent a message into the stars ...one that carried with it a promise...and one that was very different from what had been sent before!!

"Yes, this message was indeed *VERY* different from what we had sent before." The voice continued, sensing his thoughts.

There was a long pause and then it went on, "Mankind has always been fascinated by the question *'Are we alone in the universe?'* and has made numerous attempts to try and answer this...least of all by sending regular radio wave based signals into the universe, on the hope that *if* they were intercepted by an intelligent civilization, they would respond …and we would finally have our answer!"

"But the universe is so massive that this has always seemed like an exercise in futility…*like trying to search for an electron sized needle in a cosmic haystack!* And so we were forced to assume for hundreds of years that either our radio signals were headed towards parts of the universe that were completely devoid of life…or that the civilizations, which did receive them were simply too primitive to respond…either way a lost cause! But a thousand years after the establishment of S.E.T.I. – 'The Search for Extra-Terrestrial Intelligence', one young physicist suddenly stumbled on the truth…the dangerous, real reason we had never made contact!"

Another pause…"We had always been sure that just like we were keen on reaching out to the universe; other intelligent life forms would also be interested in reaching out to us. This was at best a naïve and arrogant assumption. We had never once considered the situation from the perspective of the 'other'. An advanced civilization, one that was capable of inter-stellar travel, on intercepting our pathetic radio signals, would no doubt conclude that the source of such signals was a primitive species, incapable of travelling through space…and as such deem us 'unfit' and 'unworthy' of being visited!!!"

"Who knows how many advanced cultures might we have actually reached and how many ignored our pathetic 'plea for attention'! We had spent a thousand years basically broadcasting our ignorance and advertising our limitations to the cosmos…an almost irreparable damage! We thought of ourselves as an advanced race, after successfully solving most of the problems on Earth, but we had probably become the laughing stock of the wider galactic community. This was the state of affairs until the fateful day in 3066 A.D…when the controversial experiments conducted by a curious young scientist, brought Earth to a standstill and made the universe finally take notice of our insignificant little mud ball planet!"

He knew the voice was speaking the truth…he could experience each of these incidents…in the FIRST PERSON!!! Whatever was happening to him was clearly increasing his perception to unbelievable levels. No longer was he just a young man from a primitive village in India's ancient past. Words like 'past', 'present' and 'future' no longer held any sway over him.

He now felt in absolute command of all time and space…the knowledge of the universe was at his fingertips…and yet…he hesitated… hesitated from unleashing this new found 'omnipotence'. He was still growing into the role and he needed the advice and wisdom of the 'calm voice' that was speaking to him from the 'beyond'. The voice of the man, who had been venerated as the 'mysterious teacher' by the now lost village of Aruhu.

The voice continued, "The events that you are now privy to, are the same ones that changed my life forever…for *I* was that young scientist, who brought the universe to our doorstep!!!"

What??

"Yes…I was System Gaea's foremost physicist…my name and former life mean nothing right now, so it's best that we let them be, for what really shaped my destiny and the destiny of all mankind, are my actions…for which like you, I would be remembered in my time as the 'Ultimate Betrayer'."

He couldn't believe what he had just heard…yes, the elders in the village where he had come from, often would describe how their long lost teacher used to bear a look of profound grief and sorrow…but what could this man have possibly done to be branded the 'great betrayer' by the whole of mankind?

"You wonder about the paths that I must have treaded…and in some ways, they are not too dissimilar to the ones you have taken… orphaned, alone, misunderstood, judged too harshly…we are two of a kind my child and that is the reason I chose you, YOU were always going to be my prize, not your weak kneed blood brother Arhiti!!"

No…no…no…no…no!

CHAPTER TWO

He had always been the chosen one!

He, who had once been Bhrataha, was stunned. This was unbelievable...he did not WANT to believe it!

If...he had always been the chosen one, it would mean that his entire life had been manipulated...all the humiliation and the suffering he had been subjected to, had somehow been the work of the mysterious being... this teacher...but to what end? What had this 'teacher' been trying to accomplish? He felt his rage rise to uncontrollable levels!!

"Careful my friend." the voice softly whispered, "Losing your temper in your current state might not be the best recourse. The whole universe could suffer the consequences. There is still so much that you don't know and as they often say, 'knowledge is power'...Ha ha ha ha!!!"

He calmed down...barely holding back the restless energy...it would be so much simpler to just explode! To let it all go...but no, he needed answers...he needed to know why he had been manipulated thus. Once again he focused on the events that the voice had spoken of.

The teacher's voice continued, "During my scientific quest to unlock the secrets of the cosmos, I stumbled upon the same irony we spoke of, a little while ago. I understood the real reason why the intelligent cultures of the universe considered us the 'backwaters'...too primitive to waste time on...and I decided to change that."

"But to undo centuries worth of damage our naïve 'radio broadcasts' had caused, I knew we would need to 'up the ante' in a big way. We would have to reach out to the 'intelligent' universe not as mendicants, but as 'equal' partners. And I could think of only one way of accomplishing this. We would approach them by preying on a quality that is the very basis of scientific temper and one that they would almost certainly possess – Curiosity!"

Time had creaked to a halt…waiting with bated breath, to hear what came next!

"My proposal to the head of humanity's scientific delegation based on Mars, began by stating that for over a thousand years, all the messages we sent into space, had pretty much carried the same content. Each dispatch had contained complete information about our planet and its dominant species…the flora, the fauna, the topography and our universal coordinates. The assumptions behind these simple dispatches had been that firstly, most of them would be lost to empty space and secondly, those that would be intercepted, would give a complete blueprint of our planetary system!"

"I argued that a lot of these dispatches *HAD* probably been intercepted, but we never received any reply, since our messages were so primitive that it would have been clear to any receiver that we were *INCAPABLE* of space travel. Any intelligent race attempting communication with other similar races, would want to be engaging in dialogue…sharing ideas, culture etc…not just sending out messages with a 'blueprint' of their planet!"

"My reasoning was that even if we - humans were confronted with another species from earth, let's say, the apes attempting this sort of conversation with us, we would treat it as nothing more than a 'novelty', as, in the long run, there would be absolutely nothing to be gained from such a 'conversation'. Other advanced races had probably dealt with our dispatches the same way… 'a primitive backward society attempting conversation…*interesting…but ultimately not worth the effort'*. This was probably why, no one ever reached out to us…and we were relegated to our own pathetic existence!"

"As you can now observe, with your new found perception, my revelation caused quite a stir in the scientific community! After all it is no easy thing for a race that has had thousands of years of unchallenged intellectual supremacy here on earth, to suddenly come to the realization that out there, the rest of the universe probably deems it too stupid to be engaged seriously."

"After months of being ostracized, I was finally allowed to propose my alternative. At long last, with the ball in my court, I began my presentation before an audience of some 20,000 of Earth's finest. However, before I offered any solution, I had to make certain points clear. You see, the fundamental problem with inter-stellar communication is the sheer amount of time that it takes for any information to get through, even travelling at the speed of light. If we are trying to make contact with an alien civilization that is let's say a thousand light years from Earth, the communication is never going to get across in our lifetime. So, most of the scientists, who had worked for S.E.T.I. over the years, had been sending out dispatches, knowing full well that they would not receive a response in their lifetimes. S.E.T.I. however had diligently stuck to its routine of sending out the same radio waves for over a thousand years."

"I had a radical alternative. My theory was that even assuming certain civilizations *HAD* been intercepting and then deliberately ignoring our signals all these years, the regularity of the dispatches would have surely had the effect of creating a sense of comfort that all was well with our planet. For them, the daily arrival of the signals would have become something akin to the daily sound of church bells…not something you specifically take note of but something that has a reassuring sense of comfort about it."

"Moreover, since we did not quite know *who* it was that was listening to us, we had to assume that some of the races could be benevolent, while some could be malevolent. Our consistency would have served the interests of both groups. For the 'liberals', our daily 'ringing of church bells' would have served as confirmation that Earth was still too primitive to be engaged seriously, while for the 'fanatics', it would be a sign that Earth was still too weak to resist and hence 'ripe for the taking', at a time of their choosing!"

"Who knew, it was possible that certain races might have already begun preparations for a full-scale invasion. This suggestion of course got our scientific community nice and riled up. They realized that if my speculations were true, then all we had done for over a thousand years was broadcast our weaknesses to the cosmos…with amazing regularity!!"

"Suddenly my viewpoints no longer seemed like just a nice alternate hypothesis. Our very survival could depend on it!"

"With the attention of the world on me, I explained that there was only one way of finding out *if* all this was true…through a dangerous experiment! Instead of sending out 'speed of light' messages that contained information of our planet, we start sending out intermittent but irregular 'distress signals'. These sporadically sent signals would contain desperate calls for help to anyone out there that cared to listen…and then…we would suddenly stop sending them, altogether!"

"I argued that while risky, this second part was extremely crucial. If we were indeed being listened to and ignored all these years, this sudden change in content would generate massive curiosity among those races. Whatever their designs towards Earth, they would surely be tempted to investigate."

"Ultimately, who would arrive to investigate and when they arrive, would depend on where our dispatches were being intercepted. If the interceptions were taking place a hundred light years or so away, we would still have a long wait. If however, they were any closer…our wait could be much smaller! But the big gamble would be the nature of the race that chose to investigate. It was quite plausible that the virile and aggressive ones would be the first to investigate, as for them a planet's distress call, might serve as an invitation for an invasion!"

He who had once been Bhrataha said nothing…the idea was indeed shocking…the experiment…beyond dangerous! But had the world of the future actually gone ahead with this insane plan? He needed to know more.

"As you can observe for yourself, the entire scientific community was split in two, over my proposal. Some saw it as errant madness… to challenge the unknown so brazenly, they said, was suicidal! Others saw it as the only alternative to a thousand year old mistake. But even while my proposal was being hotly contested, both sides agreed that as a planetary system, we must begin preparations for *any* eventuality. Thus began the first 'arms buildup' in more than half a millennium."

Through his new found omniscience, he who had once been Bhrataha was able to witness first-hand, the panic and excitement the world of the fourth millennium A.D. had gone through. The first 'real' feeling of uncertainty that every scientist and physicist had felt in their lives…and as a 'universal entity', he was now able to experience it all, like he had personally been there. He still could not fully understand how any of this was possible!

The stranger's voice had warned him this would happen. Did this mean that the 'transformation' was now nearing completion? And when it would finally be done, would he become one with the universe? ...this was certainly not the 'omnipotence' that he had envisioned...in his fantasy, he as a human being, would gain absolute power and immortality!

If achieving this power, meant he would be in no way connected with the rest of the universe then what good was such omnipotence? What would happen to all his hopes and dreams if he remained separate from the physical world for all eternity? ...my God!! Was this the reason that the stranger had been so keen on giving up this power? Had Bhrataha been the unwitting fool, who had stumbled into his trap?

Seemingly unmoved, the voice continued, "Ever since we, as a race, overcame our basal urge to attack and kill each other in the name of one puerile cause or another...ever since we attained true world peace by overcoming the disparity in resources...and ever since we became the only active species to colonize other celestial bodies, humankind had not had a reason to go to war, or even spend time and resources in planning for one."

While this statement reeked of optimism, Bhrataha, with his new found Omni-perception, could personally verify that this was true.

What really bothered him, was the manner in which the stranger had uttered the phrase 'We as a race...' ...the 'We' in it seemed to be very much in the 'third person'...almost as if the stranger was deliberately excluding Bhrataha from the human race. This was deeply distressing.

"However, if there is one thing that humanity has always had, it is ingenuity...particularly when it comes to constructing 'weapons of mass destruction'...and now with a potential 'extra-terrestrial invasion' imminent, paranoia reached a fever pitch."

Yes...he who had once been Bhrataha was indeed able to sample some of this...*extreme paranoia*...humanity was acting as if it had already been invaded! The unique irony of this was that in what was mankind's most challenging moment, *they* finally found perfect unity. All of humanity had stood together!

'They...?' One more sign that as the new holder of the power...as the new entity...Bhrataha was becoming ever more distant from humanity. Damn...this did not bode well!

The stranger's voice went on, "The kinds of technology that we turned towards war were the stuff of legend. The 'terra-forming' devices, we had invented five centuries ago and used to colonize the Moon, Mars and the outer solar system, were now weaponized. We developed massive 'fusion generators' capable of creating miniature 'stars' on demand. We also had 'plasma' weapons; hot enough to melt iridium...but ultimately, there was no way to know if all this was going to be enough."

"For now, our primary base was going to be the research facility located in the 'South Pole Aitken Basin' on the far side of Earth's moon.

"This massive crater, one of the oldest and deepest in the solar system, has in the past, often been dismissed as an ugly scar on the Moon's alabaster surface. However, by the mid-25th century, scientists realized that its size and location made it ideal for some of Earth's largest space telescopes, as the area was naturally shielded from cosmic radiation."

"All of the facility's equipment was made of 'Sentient metals' – high tensile metal alloys, infused with Nano-bots. These microscopic machines, within the alloys, have the ability to store information and update themselves on a regular basis! Every time the equipment is used or exposed to stress of any kind, the Nano-bots register the information and ensure that natural wear and tear is substantially reduced."

"We had the largest of our three Neutrino-powered force field generators on Titan. This would be our vanguard. We speculated that if an attack were to happen, an aggressive alien race, hell-bent on conquering Earth, would try to secure 'Sol' – our Sun, as a source of unlimited energy. So it was absolutely imperative that we stop them from reaching the inner Solar System. Of course, all these preparations could not answer the most important question of all... how imminent was the threat...how long did we have before something happened?"

The entity that had once been Bhrataha, grimaced...this was like watching some grand 'soap opera' playing out in front of you...one you know was going to end in disaster and yet one you couldn't do anything to prevent from happening. The fact that the entity was able to experience every emotion, every failure, made it even worse.

"The wait was unbearable for most, including myself...I even argued that we could not remain in this perennial state of paranoia... we might have to wait a hundred years...or not at all. After all, all of this was only based on a hunch...and while the survival of our species was of utmost importance, we could not simply halt all progress and wait! The best way of testing out my theory would be to do what I had initially suggested and send out the 'distress signals'. If malevolent forces were on their way, they would intercept and respond within days or weeks."

"Of course this got everyone riled up again...for them this seemed like *sending the goat straight into the lion's den.* Such was the fear that I was even banned from partaking in any of the defense buildup."

"I was furious...it was after all my genius that had forewarned mankind of its peril and now *I* was being ostracized for humanity's weakness! But the biggest secret that I had with me...my 'ace in the hole' so to speak was that I had based my theory not on idle speculations like most people assumed, but on actual fact!"

What???

"Yes...I had already made contact!!!"

In the absolute ether of this sub-space, the very fabric of space and time seemed to simmer!!

CHAPTER THREE

"It happened when I was working with S.E.T.I. as a young analyst trying to collate data that had been gathered over the last millennia. It was a monstrous task and one that was generally shunned by all and sundry. After all, this was largely experimental data that had been gathered by hundreds of astronomers and physicists over a thousand years, as part of their training at S.E.T.I."

"Imagine my astonishment, when I discovered among these vast archives, entire streams of 'space noises' that appeared to have patterns to them... 'Intelligent patterns'...that seemed to suggest language!

I knew this data had been gathered by amateur researchers... probably trainees...a few centuries ago, during a random sweep of a region in space, near the constellation of 'Sagittarius'...a section generally believed to be empty. S.E.T.I. had probably been testing out its equipment and scanners...and what better way, than to have new trainees scan the universe for 'space sounds'. The resulting massive amounts of data, had been collected and stashed...never analyzed... never checked."

"During my first few months at S.E.T.I., I was put in charge of clearing this cache. As you can imagine, I approached this task with no great enthusiasm. But even as I was mechanically sorting through this vast collection, I found certain sound patterns, which had been recorded over the years that were noticeably different from the conventional sounds you associate with the natural universe. These were not only repetitive but also displayed a sense of symmetry!"

"This was extremely unusual...conventionally the sounds that one picks up from space, are typically 'background universal radiation', the last 'gasps' and 'burps' of supernova, if you are lucky...and a whole lot of static. These patterns are easily identifiable and rarely repetitive. But a pattern that repeats can mean only one thing...intelligent design!

And this was *NOT* our communication! …so the implications were absolutely stunning…we were not alone! I was shocked. My immediate reaction was unadulterated joy…what mankind had been searching for…for millennia…the answer to that eternal question: '*Are we alone?*'…had fallen right into my lap!!!"

"However, my ecstasy was soon tempered by my scientific instincts and natural skepticism…and I began to run every test, I could think of, to try and debunk these results…surely, this had to be an anomaly! But I quickly realized that I really *did* have something on my hands… what I was witnessing here, were streams and streams of information that seemed to suggest not just a signal of intelligent origin but communication…*conversation!*"

"I was absolutely stunned…here we had spent hundreds of years trying to initiate contact…and when it had actually happened, we had seemingly missed it! I quickly analyzed the exact 'times' when these anomalies had been recorded. This was crucial, as it would help us figure out how much time it had taken this communication to get across…this would help us figure out just how far the source of this 'intelligent communication', was from us."

"It was then that I got an even bigger shock. The communication seemed to originate from a source that was only a few hundred light years from us. But this wasn't an idle 'one way transmission', the kind we had been broadcasting for centuries, nor was this a reply to any of our transmissions…When I analyzed the patterns carefully, I found that for each individual transmission, there seemed to be a counter… one that seemed to emanate from a different source…located on the opposite side of our planetary system. The implications of this discovery hit me like a meteor…*this communication did NOT involve us at all!!!*"

"I was petrified! What I had stumbled upon, was a CONVERSATION!! …one that was taking place between two races of intelligent life forms, located on opposite sides of our system…and one that we had only *ACCIDENTALLY* tapped into. A chill ran down my spine!"

"All our research through S.E.T.I. had focused on finding traces of intelligent life in the universe. Way back in the 20th century, when

S.E.T.I. had first been set up, physicists and scientists had grappled with the primary problem we faced in making contact – 'language'. Any information beamed out from Earth into the heavens, would have to be in an Earth based language and would almost certainly prove indecipherable to even the most advanced of alien life forms."

"Moreover, with no knowledge of 'who' or *'what'* was out there, what kind of a message would prove to be the right 'conversation starter'? The physicists back then had decided on the most practical solution to both these problems. It was decided that all information sent from Earth would be in 'Binary code'...believed to be the fundamental form of information in the universe. These waves would then be beamed into the cosmos, at the speed of light. As to what the content of such communication would be, it was decided that sending out basic information about the Earth, its various species, the dominant species and its coordinates would be our best bet."

"Never in all the centuries of research, had any of us questioned this logic or prepared ourselves for the scenario, which I had now stumbled upon. We had no contingency plan for this eventuality: *multiple alien races conversing amongst themselves at a location that was in terms of inter-stellar travel, only a short trip from Earth!"*

"The alternatives in front of me were clear. The data I had stumbled upon, was from a few centuries ago...so we would have to assume that for the races involved in the conversation, a lot had changed since then. The most important thing for us was to decipher the 'content' and the 'intent' behind their conversation. Was it simply 'innocent chatter'? Or did the conversation include their designs towards Earth...and if it did; were these friendly or hostile? One thing was obvious that regardless of their intent, they almost certainly knew all about our planet. Our daily broadcasts would have ensured that much...and just like *we* had been able to tap into their conversations... so too would *they* be able to do with ours!"

"But even as I was trying to wrap my head around what I had uncovered, something about this entire scenario bothered me. *Surely*, there had been other researchers before me, who had had access to the data I had just analyzed. If so, why had no one else seen the patterns I had? I tried to find out more...by trying to lock into the unique frequencies of those transmissions."

"I knew that every bit of information sent out leaves behind its own unique energy trail that remains untraceable, unless someone actually knows what to look for. Using this approach, I was able to trace the pathways that the transmissions had taken, back and forth. It was then that I got my biggest shock yet...Hidden among the data that had been gathered and stored by the S.E.T.I. trainees centuries ago, I discovered the *real reason*, why this amazing discovery hadn't been made before. The anomalous patterns I had discovered, had been 'disguised' amidst our own signals...the same innocuous signals that S.E.T.I. had been sending out for centuries. I finally realized what was happening!"

"Not only was there communication happening across our planetary system between two intelligent races, but the conversationalists were in fact using *OUR* signals to boost the strength of their own. Each of their transmissions had been sent out in such a way that it would *'hitch a ride'* on the back of OUR daily dispatches. The aliens were using our signals to enhance and effectively disguise their conversations!!!"

"As a physicist and a proud member of 'System Gaea's scientific delegation', this revelation felt like 'kick to the groin'. This was the ultimate insult. Through their actions, the aliens had made one thing clear. Not only did they deem Earth utterly unworthy of contact, but they were using us to do all the 'donkey work' for them... *'Beasts of burden'*...that is how they probably looked at us...and if so; we were 'sitting ducks' for an invasion that could happen at any time."

"I had to act...something needed to be done...*and fast!*"

"I knew that the alien races might be planning an invasion of our planetary system and if true, they already had a head start. I was faced with the obvious decision...send out a summons to all the scientific delegations of 'System Gaea' and within a month; all our labs including the 'deep space surveillance' facilities located on the moons of Saturn would go into overdrive. Each of these facilities would be given the 'specific broadcast frequencies' that I had first identified and would be put on a 'round the clock' monitoring duty.

I would probably be made overall director of this mission. My prestige amongst the scientific community would grow to unprecedented levels over night."

"And yet, I hesitated…I cannot say why exactly and I have for long pondered over the reasons. Maybe it was my own hubris…after all I was a product of an age of unbridled progress, where all of man's wants and desires had been satiated. In such a society, it would not be unbelievable for a sense of decadence to set in."

"But I believe…and I know with your enhanced perspective, you would agree with me that the reasons for my hesitation were actually more 'cosmic'. *It was almost as if some deep hidden force…universal in its nature…was reaching out to me and prompting me towards my destiny*…a 'sentient force' that had seemingly chosen me…one that did not take 'no' for an answer…I am sure you yourself felt the same force reach out to you at different times, during your brief earthly existence."

He who had once been Bhrataha said nothing.

"Any way, whatever the reason was, I chose to keep the knowledge of my shocking discovery, a secret. I was taking a huge risk of course, as this knowledge could well be the key to mankind's salvation. But the same mysterious cosmic force that was guiding my actions, seemed to re-affirm this decision of mine."

"So the only bit that I disclosed to the scientific community was the hypothesis that our daily dispatches might be tapped into and used against us. As you can imagine, in the absence of any concrete evidence, my theories weren't taken seriously and it took me months to convince, at least some in the scientific community that I could be right."

"It was then that I suggested changing the content of the dispatches, to a distress call, so as to attract any potential 'Good Samaritans', while risking potential 'Predators'. As you yourself observed, the scientific community reacted to this suggestions with shock and fear, never suspecting that I was hiding vital information. And although they did forbid me or anyone else from actually sending out a distress signal, the paranoia I had managed to create was enough to jumpstart the System-Wide safety measures."

"I heaved a sigh of relief, knowing that at least one half of my mission was done...as even though some unknown force was manipulating my actions, I still had enough integrity left to want the survival and wellbeing of my own species. At least now, whatever was out there, we would be in a position to mount an effective defense... *if* the need arose!"

CHAPTER FOUR

It is said that 'Time' and 'Tide', wait for no one. But Time certainly was waiting...with bated breath, to uncover the results of its predecessor's actions!

The voice in the void, describing the future, went on, "Even as Earth was arming itself, I proceeded with my clandestine research into the nature of the alien conversation I had accidentally uncovered... trying desperately to decipher their intentions towards us. Now this was easier said than done. To decipher their intentions, would require deciphering their language, and while I had basic training as a code breaker and access to pretty much every possible code breaking technology available, trying to break not one but *two* alien languages, without any benchmarks for either, was an almost impossible task!"

"I had no idea if their language even used any of the same basic rules of conversations, we follow on Earth. They might have concepts for which we had no earthly synonyms. All this might seem pretty mundane to you right now with your universal awareness my dear Bhrataha, but you need to remember that I did *NOT* have the power of Chronux with me back then."

Chronux!!! Why did the name sound so familiar? The term seemed to be one of those words that carried with it a natural sense of 'déjà vu'... but you never quite remember where it came from!

"I worked day and night trying to resolve this issue...I cannot even begin to describe how often the thought of disclosing what I knew, crossed my mind, but the same eerie presence that had subtly influenced my line of thinking before, seemed to restrain me. Finally, just as I was about to give up, the answer came to me as an epiphany."

He, who had once been Bhrataha, bristled with anticipation...its sphere of influence extending every moment. Gentle shockwaves rippled out as far as the Andromeda Galaxy.

The voice continued, "I realized that trying to interpret the information I already had, was clearly futile, since I had absolutely no idea of the context. Even if I did manage a breakthrough, there was no way I could verify it."

"My only option was to *once again* 'incite' this kind of conversation, but this time in a 'controlled environment'…and then monitor it…like a lab experiment! I knew there was only one terrifying way of doing this. The aliens had made it obvious that Earth did not rank very high on their merit scale. They were using our transmissions, without bothering to even acknowledge us. So the only way to get them to respond or even start reacting to us was to suddenly change the content of our dispatches."

The distress signals!!

"Yes…my earlier proposal could prove effective after all. I knew that if I did start sending out 'distress signals', it would surely catch any one out there monitoring us, by surprise. Whatever their response, the time taken for it to reach us would enable us to figure out how far they currently were from us. This would be our first clue."

"I could then use their responses and compare them with the old data we already had. My theory was that since we were 'stimulating' the conversation this time around; their responses would almost certainly contain information in the format we had set. Thus, pre-determining the context and the format would help us crack the code of their language…and maybe…even uncover their designs towards Earth!"

Brilliant…but risky!

"True…but a good scientist is one who is brave enough to take that risk."

"Moreover, I had already taken due precautions, by getting the global community on to a state of high alert. This meant even if we were visited by a hostile race, we would have all our defenses in place. I knew however, that the rest of my scientific fraternity would never sanction my experiment. So I decided to take the fateful step and secretly go ahead with it…on my own!"

You were gambling with the fate of the whole of mankind…no single person should be able to take such a terrible decision!

"Who are you to patronize me? After all you, during your miserable earthly existence, did compromise your entire village, in the lust for power! … Either way, I don't believe morals are for people like us who dare to challenge the gods."

So you decided to risk the future of humanity, just so that you could confirm your theory!

"Yes…and seeing as how I was already in control of most of S.E.T.I.'s operations, carrying out my plan without anyone else in the world figuring it out, was not an impossible task."

"So, on the 7th of May 3066 A.D…not that the date would mean anything to you…least of all in your current state…I carried out the operation that I code named: Contact."

"Had information of what I was doing, leaked out, I would have almost certainly been given the death penalty. I carefully changed the content of the 'daily dispatches' to what resembled a desperate 'distress signal' from a dying world and set the auto transmitter to broadcast these new signals intermittently for a few months…and then stop abruptly."

"I knew that this 'break' in the dispatches, would almost certainly grab the attention of the scientific community, which would then begin an investigation to find out the reasons behind the apparent 'malfunction'. It wouldn't take them long to detect my 'fraud', but I was prepared for the consequences. I was hedging my bets on the fact that by that time, I would have gathered all the data I needed. So in a sense, the success or failure of my quest…ultimately depended on the alien races responding to my broadcasts…quickly!"

The entity that had once been Bhrataha could feel literally the full weight of history bear down on its shoulders. With its new found omniscience, it was able to witness the biggest gamble in human existence…a gamble whose costs and stakes were absolute and yet one that had actually been taken.

"For close to a year, after my 'experiment', I lived under a shadow of fear and uncertainty. I knew that at any point of time, my actions could be discovered by members of my own fraternity and that would have dire consequences. Moreover, even if my experiment was successful in attracting the attention of the alien races, their aspirations towards my own planet could well turn out to be less than friendly!"

"Every day for me, seemed like a walk down the '*aisle of death*'...a never-ending nightmare...till the fateful day of December the 19th the same year, when I found myself faced with the 'unbelievable'. The aliens were indeed interested!!!!"

"I suddenly began picking up frenzied amounts of chatter, on the exact same frequencies as the archival data...and amazingly; this conversation was purely one way...meaning it was directed towards us!!!!"

"I could not believe my eyes...I had taken on odds that were 'one in a billion'...and won...we were now being spoken to *DIRECTLY!!!*"

"Of course as this new communication was directed straight at Earth, it was also picked up by all our major Astro-labs, including the 'Advance Warning Systems', located in the outer Solar System. All of them had been on a state of high alert, following the mass hysteria my theories had caused. But no one had ever imagined that contact would be made so suddenly."

"There was even a great deal of speculation among both the 'intellectuals' and the 'laymen' about the nature of this contact and how it had been made right after the military build-up. The majority thanked their stars and offered overwhelming gratitude to me and the rest of the scientific community, for having the safety protocols in place. For them, it was a godsend that even as we neared imminent contact, we were thoroughly prepared to defend ourselves, if need be."

"But there were also more cynical views that blamed our military build-up for this contact. They believed that there was a direct causal link between our building weapons of mass destruction and potentially hostile aliens suddenly taking a more active interest in us. According to them, we would have only ourselves to blame if things went wrong from here."

"And finally there were those...a relatively small but vocal minority, who professed an even more '*esoteric*' view point. For them the key factor wasn't the military build-up, but rather my ability to seemingly prophesy the arrival of the alien visitors! After all, hadn't I been the one, who had first proposed the theory of alien races monitoring Earth? For believers, my ability to predict what would happen was confirmed by these new findings that an alien race was indeed trying to make contact with us. This group began to venerate me as a 'prophet'...one who got his answers directly from the heavens! I must say, this last bit greatly amused me, for little did they realize that my answers *HAD* indeed come from above!!!"

"But ultimately none of it mattered. My primary focus still was to try and use the most recent communication to decipher 'who' or '*what*' exactly we were dealing with. I knew that every little bit of data was important...nothing could be taken for granted."

"I went ahead with the basic assumption that *this* communication was different from the earlier ones in one important way: Unlike the previous intercepts, where we had simply overheard a conversation, this time they were actually reaching out to *us!* This meant that this latest intercept, was not just a response to our distress signal, but probably also framed in a way the aliens hoped, *we* would understand."

"This time, we *did* have context for the conversation."

"This time, we had *them* playing by *our* rules!!!"

CHAPTER FIVE

The stranger's voice resonated throughout the void, "An important fact, I had to consider, was the speed to their response…we had received their response less than six months *after* the last 'fake distress signal'…this was the time required for a two way communication… which meant that they were at a distance of roughly '3 lights months' from Earth…or to be more specific…448531919471 miles from Earth. So theoretically, we could expect actual contact the following year…and I still had no idea about any of their capabilities…or intentions!"

"I spent the next few months, analyzing their response very carefully. Certain aspects of it were pleasingly predictable and others left me with an uncomfortable feeling."

"What was consistent about their message was that when broken down into a binary sequence, it was clear that whatever this message said…it had been repeated over and over throughout the dispatch… this is exactly what one would expect, when one is trying to respond to a distress signal. Even when ships or planes on Earth send out a distress signal, the respondents are expected to keep the response as simple as possible, while giving as much hope as possible and repeating the message over and over again, so that there is no ambiguity. This is also done on the implicit assumption that a ship or plane, sending out an S.O.S, might have its broadcasting and receiving devices damaged or *compromised* in some way…the response is repeated over and over again, to ensure that the distressed vessel has the best chance of picking it up."

"However, what troubled me was that, had this been a communication between two *TERRESTRIAL* vessels, this sort of a response would be perfectly acceptable…but…here we had an *EXTRA - TERRESTRIAL* race doing what we would normally do!"

"This could only mean one of two things...One: Through some absolute and implausible quirk of fate, life beyond our planet had evolved in more or less the same fashion as that on Earth. This seemed a highly unreasonable proposition to seriously entertain. Two: The aliens had been monitoring us for so long that they knew us well; they had probably seen through our bluff and were now playing us. If true, this presented a huge problem...it meant that they could be planning something much worse than just an invasion!!!"

Damn!

"Yes...damn indeed...It took me nearly two months to achieve a breakthrough in deciphering their response. After working day and night, I reached a point, where I was fairly certain of the content of their message."

A sense of calm had settled all over the unearthly area that could only be described as 'sub-space'. It is the space that exists within space. Its boundaries are the rest of reality. Philosophers and scientists have and will continue to speculate about just such a realm, where all normal rules of nature collapse and nothing is what it seems. For mystics, this is where souls travel after leaving their temporary abode – the human body. For esoteric thinkers and dreamers...this is where all thoughts and ideas flow in and out of...and for physicists and rationalists, this is a dimension of space and time that is yet to be discovered and explored. For the entity that had once been Bhrataha, this was - Home!

The voice continued..."The distress signal that I had clandestinely sent from Earth, had been framed and worded in a way that would best enable an alien race to understand what we were saying. To make it sound like an authentic distress signal, I had broadcast it not just at the quadrant; I believed the aliens were in, but in all directions. The content of these messages was a frantic call for help, along with detailed coordinates of our planet. The entire message was in binary, using the most basic rules of grammar and language, so that it would appear universal."

"My analyses showed that their response also followed the same rules I had set. This was clearly intended to be received and read by us. This convinced me that we were dealing with a species that at the very least was capable of *modifying* its communication, to suit the circumstances."

"But as I began decoding their message, I stumbled upon something even more unsettling. The response was only five words...repeated over and over again. When translated into an Earthly language, it simply said – 'In Chronux lies your destiny."

Chronux!!!! Why did that name sound so familiar!!!

"Ha ha ha...I trust that the term set off something within you as well. Yes...you are just about getting used to your new found omniscience...with time...you will of course have no choice but to accept it...as I did for so long before you." The voice replied caustically.

"However, when I first read that term in the message I had deciphered, I couldn't be sure if I had read it correctly. I had expected the response to contain either an assurance of help or a threatening precursor to an invasion."

"This reply was anything but that. It seemed like a riddle...a puzzle...one designed to entice you...engage you and ultimately suck you in. I was intrigued...I knew I was the only one on the planet, who was in a position to decipher it...After all I was the one who had sent out the distress signal in the first place...that signal which had set the format of communication for this conversation."

"For everyone else...all the other 'great scientific minds', so oblivious to my dirty little secret, this response was simply proof that we were not alone. Deciphering it was well beyond their capacity. So they did what was most practical and began to prepare for every eventuality. All the observatories were put on high alert and were given the general coordinates for the region from which this message had arrived."

"For them the main problem was that for all they knew, this alien message could have been travelling through the cosmos for anywhere between a few months to hundreds of years. They had no way of knowing how far its source was."

"None of this seemed to bother them though...after all, this was a culmination of hundreds of years of dedicated work by S.E.T.I. which had ultimately answered the most cosmic of questions...Are we alone? I wondered what they might say if they knew that right in their midst hid a traitor…one whose treachery was potentially so damning that it could well end up compromising every single life form on Earth!"

"My mind was drawn back to the alien message. I was particularly fascinated by the term 'Chronux.' It seemed to be an intentional play on the noun 'Chronos' – a figure revered and feared in Greek mythology as the titan, who fathered the Gods. Chronos is also linked with the concept of 'Time', and I wondered if there was any connection at all to this fact. Could it be possible that the alien response was meant to be a mockery? Was it a threat? - A potentially hostile race seeing through our ruse and sending out a warning. Somehow, intuitively, I felt there was more to it than just that."

In Chronux lies your destiny – "I went over the message over and over again. I was quite sure that my interpretation was correct. So what did this message really mean and why had they sent it?"

"On one hand, if the aliens had indeed been fooled by my call for help and were actually responding, this message was anything but reassuring. Why would you respond to a dying world's cry for help, with a cryptic message of your own?"

"If on the other hand, they had seen through our ruse, and were planning an assault, why send any reply at all…wouldn't it be better to simply attack a world, you plan to enslave…without any prior intimation?"

"Surely, I was missing something! I pondered over it for weeks…till finally…out of the blue…the realization hit me like a thunder bolt. In their reply…they had used the words *'Your Destiny'!!!…destiny – SINGULAR!!! …Not destinies*…why would they do that…unless… *unless*… I rechecked my results once again if I had missed out anything…but no…it was all there… 'In Chronux lies your destiny' …A cold sweat broke out all over me. The shocking implications of this were clear at last. Disturbingly, this message *WASN'T* directed at humanity…it wasn't even meant for humanity…it was meant for *ME!!!!*"

'In Chronux lies *YOUR* destiny!!!!'

The atmosphere was charged with energy,…the stranger's voice was now at a fever pitch, "I realized that my experiment had worked beyond my wildest expectations…I had simply been trying to initiate contact with 'whatever' was out there…in return, I had received a message meant specifically for me!"

"It was of course a secret too explosive to share with anyone. From now on, I realized, I would have to go ahead with the utmost care…a single slip and the full extent of my betrayal would be out."

"I knew that the whole of mankind was gearing up for an imminent confrontation…some even thought *I* was a 'Prophet' for having correctly predicted this. However, if humanity knew my true role in all of this, I knew they would not be so charitable in their praise."

"But for now, my secret was safe. Even S.E.T.I. did not have the means of reading the alien message. *Only I did.* I even briefly considered sending out another dispatch…but I soon rejected the idea, as it was too risky. I knew that another transmission originating from Earth, would surely attract the attention of the other scientific labs, across our system…almost all of them were on high alert. Moreover, without really knowing the meaning or the intent of the first cryptic response, it was foolhardy to attempt a second contact."

"By this point of course the tensions on Earth had reached a boiling point. Preparations were taking place on a 'war footing'…Nothing was being left to chance. I was even made the overall 'in-charge' of this massive system wide operation code named: INVASION."

"Something simply had to give."

CHAPTER SIX

"In the year 3067 A.D…one year after my experiment with the distress signals, we finally made contact…and for the people of Earth, it was a catastrophic one. The date of May the 7ᵗʰ 3067 A.D. will go down in history as humanity's darkest day!"

"I remember, it was around eight in the evening and I was on the orbital space station around Mars, when we first got news that there was something wrong with our main 'Weapons Server'. The Server was located under the irradiated wasteland that had once been the mighty Pacific Ocean, and was directly linked to around 70 percent of all our computerized weapons caches around the planet, making it the 'main hub' of operations, in the event of an 'intergalactic standoff.'"

"The server hub was made of a special 'Carbon Graphite Nano tube mixture', in which each individual cell was capable of withstanding a 20 mega-ton nuclear strike. There were four layers of 'redundant defensive fields' around it that were largely self-sustaining. In addition, there were 16 divisions of titanium hulled all-terrain vehicles, manned by some 800 elite commandos, armed to the teeth. There was also a 'Dead Zone' for around 3 miles around the entire complex that generated a massive E.M.F pulse every five seconds…making all 'foreign' technology unusable."

"We also had an Advance Warning System that would alert all the orbital labs throughout System Gaea, in the event that any part of the facility was compromised. This virtually unbreakable enclosure was the very definition of a 'safe zone' and it was inconceivable that it could be threatened by an external assault. Moreover, after generations of peace on Earth, we really had no reason to expect any serious Earth-based threat."

The entity that had once been Bhrataha sighed, taking all this in.

"However, the information we were now receiving, was deeply troubling. Our security team at 'ground-zero' was reporting that an unusual 'sphere of energy' was gradually making its way through the numerous security systems, we had in place."

"I was alarmed...the reports from the team said that even with their quantum enhanced detectors; they were unable to understand this phenomenon. Most surprising of all, the energy field wasn't even *registering* on any of the security systems! This was indeed a worrying prospect...not only were we up against something, we had no idea about, but the same '*something*' wasn't even being recorded by any of our devices...*like a ghost in front of a camera!*"

"I asked my Systems-in-Charge to get me holographic visuals of the energy sphere from ground-zero...and noticed how it took a good three attempts to get my message across to him! Our entire communication system seemed rife with disturbances. *If* this was indeed the result of the strange energy sphere, we were in serious trouble!"

"After what seemed like an eternity, I received a grainy shaky visual, on my hand-held receiver. I zoomed in and tried to find out what the floating cameras at ground-zero had captured. For some reason, the normally 'high-definition' images were unusually hazy. Even then, what I saw chilled me to the bone!"

"I could just about make out, our security forces, in class 3000 full body armors, shying away from a mysterious bluish green energy sphere that was gradually making its way towards them. Unfortunately, absolutely no sound had been recorded by the cameras and this increased the sense of paranoia...an eerie silence!"

"The view was disturbing to say the least...whatever this thing was, it seemed to consume anything and everything, in its path...including our defense systems. It was like nothing I had ever seen before...ten feet thick reinforced metal plates were simply disappearing under its onslaught!"

"The 'United Planet' troops that were guarding the facility were some of the bravest soldiers I had known. But under such circumstances, there was very little even they could do but watch,

helplessly, as the base, under their protection was being destroyed...
erased from existence!"

"I stared in horror...I couldn't be sure if the energy sphere was changing shape or size...but the 'space' behind the sphere seemed be to 'bending' and 'collapsing' on itself...was I witnessing a *Space-Warp* of some kind? And just then the live feed from all the floating cameras was cut...I remember thinking how this was the worst case scenario... one that we had no contingency plan for...We had planned and strategized for almost a year and had prepped every weapon system we could, for a threat we believed would come from outer space. We had never planned for a scenario where all our safety systems would be bypassed from *WITHIN!* Oh God!!! What if the threat was already on Earth?"

"We were aboard the labs on the Mars Orbiter and our life support systems depended on a regular link with the command center. If this unknown energy sphere managed to disrupt our communications systems any further, we might find ourselves stranded...without Oxygen!"

"I knew I had to get back to Earth, as soon as possible. There was no time to take the long way back via the hydrogen fueled 'X- 104 Model 13 deep space Voyager' – the standard issue space shuttle we used, to navigate the many colonies throughout System Gaea. This journey would have to be quick...*and risky.* I just had to get back to Mother Earth...and that meant only one thing...the 'Escape Pod' - a small cylindrical one-seat vehicle that was used during emergency evacuations of scientists!"

"As I was preparing myself for the rapid descent, a slew of questions crossed my mind. 'What was it that our prime facility was experiencing? Was this an attack...or a prelude to one? Could it possibly be an unknown natural phenomenon? And whatever it was, why were none of our sensors registering it?"

"Moreover, we had been expecting an alien visitation for some time now...surely, this was in some way connected to it. This could very well be a precursor, before a full scale assault on our civilization. It certainly seemed to make sense...*take out our technology and you could effectively take us all out without as much as a whimper!"*

"With a lot on my mind, I entered the Escape Pod and readied myself for the perilous journey ahead. I knew full well that a Pod like this one wasn't designed for *ferrying* people between Mars and Earth. It was meant only for short range evacuations to 'safe zones', during emergencies and hence wasn't built to handle the kind of stress, 'Inter-Planetary' travel would exert on it. The reinforced ceramic plates on its exterior would most likely burn up, while entering Earth orbit."

"Once inside, I tried to reach the Security Team on Earth to try and get an update...nothing...not even static...I tried again...still nothing...either all lines of communication had gone dead simultaneously – *something we had believed impossible*, or something horrible had happened to the team."

"So as the situation now stood, our people at the Command Center were completely cut off from the rest of our facilities throughout System Gaea and basically at the mercy of the energy sphere!"

"I sent out a unilateral alarm to all our bases – even the forward posts, located past Jupiter. My transmission was simple yet somber – We were under attack from an unknown but undeniably powerful enemy. The attack was for now centered on our Command Center, located in the Pacific...the most vital facility in the entire network. For the future survival of our species, this threat would have to be mitigated instantly. We would also need to commit resources in making sure that this attack was not simply a lure intended to serve as a distraction, while the real one took place elsewhere!"

"Having sent out this Red-Alert, I authorized the deployment of three technical teams, equipped with the finest 'state of the art' sensors, to the site of the assault. I knew I would need to use every possible resource available, to crack this mystery."

"My final thoughts, as I launched the escape pod towards Earth, were crushingly pessimistic. I had seen first-hand the raw footage captured by our cameras, at ground zero. Nothing...absolutely nothing had stopped the advance of this strange sphere. I knew *I* had nothing better to offer in that regard."

"The real reason I was headed to the site, was on account of a dangerous hunch. My hypothesis was that the 'unreadable energy sphere' that had proved so unstoppable, was not really a weapon but a transportation device - *a space-warp* that was *folding* space around it to the point that any physical object it made contact with, wasn't really being 'destroyed' or 'consumed' as it seemed, but simply being 'folded' out of our universe…almost as if it were 'free-falling' through space!"

"That's why the sphere had proved unstoppable…anything that the troops fired at it, was simply folded out of 'normal three-dimensional space'. I also speculated that when the space-warp would reach a certain critical threshold…when enough space had been bent out of proportions…it would explode, *like a bomb*… tearing a permanent hole in space…a '*doorway*' of sorts!! What this sort of a doorway would allow into our system, it was anyone's guess."

"I knew that if my assumption was in any way true, we would be in massive trouble. We had been prepared to stop a full scale invasion from deep space. However, if it was going to happen not from outer space but 'inner' space, especially so close to our Command Center, all our safety protocols would be compromised. The invading forces would have direct access to all our technologies in one go and we would be 'sitting ducks' for whatever they had planned. Resistance would be impossible…the death count in such a scenario, would be astronomical. No!!! Something had to be done!!"

This is a terrible threat!

"Yes…but I also knew that preventing something like this was beyond my capacity…I was not even going to *attempt* that. My plan was to do the opposite…rather than try and prevent what was happening, I planned to '*feed*' the sphere, as much as possible and thereby accelerate the process…causing it to reach a critical point and explode…and thus *creating* the 'doorway' into our universe!"

What???? Why???

"I was going to make sure that I was there to receive and monitor whoever or '*whatever*' came through the gateway!"

"This, I gambled was our best shot at preventing a complete takeover. But deep down I knew, there was another…more sinister reason for doing this…These events after all, had been set in motion by my clandestine experiment…now that we were in fact so close to making contact, I knew I had to see my experiment through!"

Insanity!!

"That's the curse of curiosity…my friend and how I have regretted it since…Of course, I mentioned none of this to my colleagues…no one in their right mind would forgive me if they knew the extent of my treachery. Imagine what the population of Earth would say if they knew that not only was I responsible for all of this, but I was now working to *further* it…merely to satisfy my scientific curiosity! But I know you will understand me, my friend, after all the same curiosity is what has led you to your current state…ha ha ha ha!"

The entity did not react to this slight. Gone were any feelings of personal grudges or grievances against this person who had destroyed its former existence and entrapped it in its current state. A state of complete apathy and calm was now setting in.

Memories of its former life as a villager named Bhrataha were gradually receding to the background. But surprisingly…these events that the stranger was narrating from millennia in the future were beginning to seem more and more like a first-person's account. It was as if the entity had ITSELF gone through these events. This was very strange and disconcerting…the stranger's life was gradually being superimposed on to the entity…if it chose to now, the entity could revisit these occurrences, on its own accord…without the need for a narrator…whom it now looked upon, with a sense of pity.

CHAPTER SEVEN

The entity was able to observe the events from the year 3067 A.D. as they unfolded. This was no longer *someone else's* story…The stranger's life was now *its* life…his actions… were *its* actions! Was it because the stranger had claimed to be its predecessor?

It observed the perilous journey from the Space Center to Earth…a journey full of extreme dangers and near misses…one that had almost proved fatal. The Escape Pod had not been designed for such an extended sojourn…and such extreme environmental conditions.

The entity felt the panic and the pain of the individual trapped inside as the Pod violently came apart, after re-entering Earth's atmosphere…the desperation that the person inside had felt, knowing full well that the fate of all mankind rested on his shoulders. It experienced first-hand the last minute semi-miraculous stunt the pilot of the craft had pulled off, which had allowed the Pod to slow down as much as possible, before crashing into what had once been the mighty Pacific Ocean…the bone-crushing impact that had left the individual inside, with massive lacerations all over his body and multiple concussions.

In spite of the injuries, the man inside had managed to escape the confines of the damaged vessel, with a superhuman burst of adrenalin-fuelled strength…and made the painful journey towards the Command Center, still reeling from the mysterious attack.

The entity also experienced the terror felt by the few remaining ground troops…as they hopelessly watched the energy sphere eat away the 'empty space', leading up to them…knowing full well that they like everything before them, would soon be consumed and cease to exist.

It observed the man who claimed to be its predecessor, reach the scene of confrontation just as the last defensive shield fell under the onslaught of the sphere. He tried to get readings of it, using a hand-held device. While this did nothing to slow the sphere's progress, it did confirm at least one hypothesis...this was indeed a 'transportation device'...capable of creating gateways to other dimensions.

The sphere was folding both matter and space upon itself, thereby creating an extremely high gravitational field in a very small area... not unlike a 'Black Hole'. Moreover, since it was bending both matter and space...even the *absence* of physical structures, was in no way slowing its progress.

The entity observed its predecessor run towards the main Command Center, and begin deactivating the safety protocols one by one...this was an open invitation to an all-out attack, but since none of the counter measures had worked so far, *this* would make no difference!

Seeing this, the sphere abruptly changed directions and followed him in...Interesting! ...was it being guided by some kind of 'sentience'? The entity observed its predecessor access the main control panel that was connected to the 'Large Particle Accelerator and Neutrinos Emitter', hidden deep beneath the facility. He then proceeded to redirect its contents towards the surface.

Smart!!!! The entity thought with a sense of pride...*almost personal pride!*

Neutrinos are one of the most fundamental particles that make up the universe. Neutrinos are similar to electrons, but with one crucial difference: they do not carry electric charge and hence are not affected by the electromagnetic forces, acting on electrons. Neutrinos are affected only by a "weak" sub-atomic force of much shorter range than electromagnetism, and are therefore able to pass through great distances in matter and space, without being affected by it.

Billions of neutrinos pass through each square centimeter of area on earth, every second...unimpeded, almost at the speed of light! So difficult is it to trap one of them, that trying to capture one is equivalent to *capturing a ghost in a butterfly net.* In most cases they will just pass straight through any observation or interception device that one uses.

Over the years, many different theories had emerged to explain how this was possible...ranging from how neutrinos were merely *'phantom particles'* to how they could in fact be the evidence we needed for proving the existence of 'Dark Matter'...and the reason they were able to go almost straight through 'regular matter', was proof that they followed different rules of physics.

After centuries of trying unsuccessfully to understand their nature, S.E.T.I. had developed its own Neutrinos Emitter. This experimental apparatus would bombard highly charged bits of matter with a constant stream of neutrinos. The extremely high charge and volatility of the matter used would mean that at least one in a trillion neutrinos, faced collision. The resulting collisions though few and far between, would then be observed by ultra-sensitive equipment.

The entity now understood what its predecessor had in mind. By turning the emitter towards the energy sphere, he would bombard it with a steady stream of neutrinos...trillions upon trillions of neutrinos. Since the energy sphere consumed pretty much anything on contact, including empty space...it would prove to be the perfect vessel to receive these tiny particles.

This flood of neutrinos that normally passed unmolested through pretty much any type of matter, would now find themselves unusually restricted, resulting in a massive energy build-up, in an extremely small area. When this energy reached a critical point, the entire sphere would explode with catastrophic results...either bringing to an end the assault on the facility or...permanently ripping a hole in the fabric of space and time!

It was a dangerous gamble and the entity knew the risks its predecessor was taking were astronomical! In a grudging sort of a way, it admired his sense of adventure.

What followed was not too dissimilar to a high speed chase. Time seemed to lose all meaning, as one event flowed into the next. The entity was able to gather data from different points in time... *simultaneously!*

It observed its predecessor direct the emitter at the energy sphere and bombard it with a steady stream of the ultra-high velocity sub atomic particles. The results were instantaneous and spectacular!!

Hit by wave after unceasing wave of microscopic matter, the sphere began to convulse violently. Its entire structure began to falter and come apart...initially it seemed to lose coherence at the edges, as wisps of bluish green energy started to leak...*this was stage one*...the bombardment continued...the sphere now began to respond even more violently...it was clear that the copious amounts of neutrinos being fed into it, were having an effect. The sphere swelled like a bloated beached whale...space and time began to get more and more distorted.

The area occupied by the sphere, was now a violently swirling mix of matter and energy...bending and twisting out of shape. From its very core, even light was having a hard time escaping, *much like a black hole!* On its outer edges, images of scenes and events that had already occurred some time ago, including the hopeless resistance put up by the command center's defense forces, could be seen clearly... time was getting seriously distorted!!

The entity knew that at that moment, it was already much too late to try and save these poor wretches, who had died fighting to save the facility...even though one could distinctly see them amidst the slew of images, visible on the edges of the sphere. The men were long since gone...*these were mere phantasms, conjured by distorted time.*

As the swirling energy vortex, continued to swell...the entity sensed it was reaching a critical point...once it crossed this point, all bets would be off!!

The exact moment it occurred was almost anti-climactic...The sphere unleashed its suppressed fury, in an immensely powerful explosion, that almost immediately, ended up turning *BACK* on itself...the massive amounts of matter and energy the sphere had swallowed, began to implode...pulling back all towards a central point...one that kept getting more and more compressed...squeezed into a tiny dot so incredibly dense that it tore a hole in the fabric of space itself!!

This was the moment the entity had been waiting to witness...the moment its predecessor had worked so hard towards...now finally all questions would be answered...now that the 'gateway' between our dimension and an as yet unknown alien realm had been established, it would be possible to monitor 'who' or *'what'* came through. No longer would this impending assault go unchecked...now the defenders of Planet Earth, would be able to protect themselves against it...Surely, this was the best case scenario for Earth.

The entity experienced the same sense of relief and hope that its predecessor felt, as the reins of control seemed to move into the hands of the defenders of Earth...the tide might start to change now!

It observed the rip in space and time, grow larger...the door was opening...or *BEING opened...from the other side!!!*...no more hiding...no more ambiguity...it now was just a matter of time before the purpose of this invasion and the perpetrators, whoever they were, would be revealed...the entity watched the unfolding drama, with anticipation and a certain thrill...it felt more than a sense of kinship with its predecessor in this regard...here was a man who had been at the forefront of his profession, in an era when scientific excellence was pretty much par for the course...who had taken astonishing risks by putting everything on the line, in pursuit of knowledge and discovery...trying to accomplish that which had been denied to humanity throughout history... 'Absolute God-like power'...however flawed the character of such a man may be, the entity could not find it in itself to fault such an epic endeavor.

It shared his trepidation...this was going to be his moment of truth...it followed him, as he watched the 'doorway' through space, expand and finally open fully...*This was it!!!*

CHAPTER EIGHT

Nothing...absolutely *nothing* came through the hole in space! ...how could this be possible? After all, the energy sphere assaulting their main Command Center, was the real assault...while the transmission sent from space, was a distraction... *Wasn't it??*

Distract the Planetary System you want to invade, by sending out 'unreadable' transmissions...leading them to believe that a massive interplanetary assault was underway...and then while they were running scared, conduct your real offensive through a 'Space-Warp' that would allow the bulk of your forces to bypass their security and take out the command center, leaving the enemy completely at your mercy. The alien plan had seemed obvious enough... *Hadn't it???*

The entity knew that its predecessor's plan of getting the energy sphere to explode, while risky, was a good one, as it possibly was the only way of disrupting the alien agenda. However, it was now experiencing all of his growing anxiety and sense of dread, as the hole in space...the 'Gateway'...wasn't bringing anything through... *Why wasn't anything coming through????*

And then it happened...even as the portal continued to silently simmer...the holographic communicator located on its predecessor's wrist, suddenly came alive...sounds and images, slightly distorted by the immense energies at work in the area, appeared in a Three-Dimensional format...these were images that were being broadcast across the system...images of a full scale invasion that was on...at that very moment, beyond Saturn! ...an invasion that was targeting and ruthlessly taking out the best of Earth's defenses... *Blaaaassst!!!!!*

The implications of these visuals were devastating!!!! The Gateway... the Portal *HAD BEEN THE DISTRACTION* all along! ...the real invasion was always meant to happen from outer space!!!

By making the suicidal trip from the orbital monitoring facility to Earth, Bhrataha's predecessor had effectively denied his own people their best chance of putting up a defense! He had taken *himself* off the battle-board...the only one who could understand, interpret and actually *do* something about the invasion had allowed himself to get distracted by a sleight of hand...My God!!!! This was the ultimate disaster!!!

The entity watched its predecessor collapse in horror, at this realization...it had all begun with so much hope...so much belief... *making contact with an alien civilization would only benefit mankind...* and such contact could be accomplished only by bypassing Earth's bureaucracy that stood in the way of scientific curiosity. Taking initiative, he had gone ahead with the experiment that had ultimately led to this invasion!

He was now forced to watch in helpless horror, as hundreds and thousands of his own people on multiple orbital centers across the solar system, fell prey to the alien armada. The assault was being spearheaded by a massive alien 'Mother-Ship'...one that was almost the size of Earth's own satellite – the Moon! Such was its size, that unbelievably, it was able to generate its own gravitational pull!!!

From this Mother-Ship, emerged wave after wave of smaller vessels... 'Stealth Fighters', large 'Destroyer-class Spaceships' that were using a kind of sonic cannon to take down System Gaea's defenses, *like they didn't exist.* There were also what appeared to be individual crafts that probably carried one or at the most two personnel, which were highly maneuverable.

On its predecessor's holographic display, the entity observed the human cost of this assault. Each member of Earth's defense force had a special and unique DNA marker embedded inside of him that would allow his movements to be tracked...till the point he/she was alive. The shutting down of the tracker indicated the untimely demise of an individual.

On the display, one corner was keeping a track of the casualties... and the figures just kept climbing...exponentially! One moment, the death count was in the thousands...a few moments later...it jumped into the hundred thousand range...then into the millions!!!This was

Earth's final battle...the sheer scale of it meant that whatever the outcome, mankind would never be the same again.

The entity watched its predecessor try desperately to re-initiate contact with the rest of Earth's orbital facilities...to try and get a sense of what was happening... to try and co-ordinate some sort of a defense...but such was the scale of the assault that Earth's leaderless forces were being blown to bits.

It observed the destruction of Earth's massive 'Fusion-based Power Plants', located on the moons of Saturn. The aliens were using some kind of sophisticated 'Dark Matter' based explosives that turned all matter literally inside out...*nothing could stop them!*

The power plants had huge stores of dangerously volatile substances like hydrogen and methane. The exotic components of the weapons used by the aliens intermingled with the highly charged and ionized gases, setting off explosions that were hundreds of times greater than the largest nuclear tests conducted on Earth. So powerful were these explosions that they were directly visible all throughout Earth's Northern hemisphere!

A huge chuck of Titan, Saturn's largest moon, was blown out into space by the explosions...*dangerously destabilizing the satellite!*

The death count had by now crossed two billion and the situation was rapidly going from being an 'epic disaster' to an 'extinction level event'! The holographic display tracker was predicting the complete demise of humankind in approximately 120 minutes. The situation seemed utterly hopeless!

There were still so many questions that were unanswered...who were these invaders and what was the reason for this dastardly assault? If this assault was for territorial expansion, why wait until now to attack? After all, it was clear that they had known all about Earth and its inhabitants for centuries. *So many things just didn't add up!*

The entity experienced all of the guilt its predecessor felt...Billions dead...all his fault...he had been warned not to experiment with powers far beyond his station...but no...he had to satisfy his ego...his curiosity...he had betrayed the whole of humanity and literally spread out a 'Red Carpet' for the invaders...to say that he was doomed to hell, was a colossal understatement!

He had just gone from being one of Earth's foremost scientists to being its greatest mass murderer!!!! The shame and anger that he felt at his own actions welled up within him, like an all-consuming storm. Raising his eyes to the skies...where he knew his fellow human beings were being butchered...he screamed for answers!

It was impossible to put into words the blind grief that he felt. His mind danced dangerously, on the borders of insanity...no human mind was designed to handle such sorrow. *Where was God in all of this??? Surely, someone, somewhere was listening!!!!*...As he felt his breathing grow heavier and the corners of his eyes darken...the answer literally came to him straight from the heavens!

"In Chronux lies YOUR destiny."

Those mysterious words that had started all of this!!!...What was 'Chronux' and what did this message really mean?

Behind him...the hole in space caused by the exploding energy sphere, simmered silently.

'Chronux'...even in his current state, the word seemed to carry an odd sense of solace. He rolled it around in his mouth...repeating it... whispering it softly to himself...*like a 'sacred chant'*...all the while, feeling its calming effect.

There was definitely something strangely familiar about it...hidden... forgotten memories dredged from the sands of time...old ghosts...a haunting sense of nostalgia!

He turned around and stared at the portal behind him...an open doorway, it beckoned to him.

He looked straight at it and softly spoke the word again... "Chronux" He couldn't be certain if it was merely his imagination, but the 'doorway' seemed to pulsate just a little bit.

"Chronux!!" He said it a little louder this time...*it happened again!* The word was definitely connected to what was happening over here!

He noticed that the air around him had suddenly gone very cold and the carnage and destruction that his species was going through, suddenly seemed very far and distant. An odd sense of calm was descending upon him...almost anesthetic in nature. He had read about this...an overtaxed brain pushed past its limits, released endorphins, to sedate itself...and its own consciousness!

"No!!!" he had to fight this...his people were dying and now was not the time to give in to any delusions. He *had* to do something.

As he stared into the 'Gateway', a dim silhouette started to materialize inside the warp in space...*What???* Surely, he was hallucinating...He squinted...No...there it was again...this was no optical illusion...there was definitely an entity inside the portal...one that looked loosely humanoid!

"Who are you?" Bhrataha's predecessor screamed into the warp... "Why are you doing all of this? What have we done to deserve this?"

The reply came to him in an unknown language...unknown words, but transmitted directly into his soul... Their meaning was crystal clear.

"My child, it was *you* who reached out to me...I am merely responding to your plea."

"You have slaughtered billions of my fellow human beings and now you dare tell me that you are here for me???"

"Wars...conquest...humanity...races...these are puny and utterly trivial pursuits. You need to rise beyond all of this my child, and embrace your true destiny...you need to embrace Chronux!"

There was that word again... 'Chronux' ...every time he heard it, he felt more and more drawn towards it...*an inescapable quagmire!* He felt all the energy drain from his body...no longer was he able to stand up straight. He fell to his knees, head bowed in abject surrender.

The voice continued, "You, my child, have been chosen for a very special task, from among millions and millions of others. Yours is a rare distinction indeed my Ashwat."

He was stunned! The voice had just addressed him by his real name. The entity that had once been Bhrataha shared its predecessor's amazement.

'Ashwat'...Earth's foremost young scientist...the torchbearer of humanity...a beacon of hope for future generations...Ashwat ...the man who fell from grace...the man, whose curiosity doomed all of mankind... Ashwat ...the man who doomed himself to the terrible fate of Chronux and had come as a godly teacher to a village deep in India's forgotten past...Ashwat...the man who had been held up by those simple and innocent village folk, as an Avatar of the divine and who had preyed

upon their desires and fears to lure and tempt one of them into taking over his curse...Ashwat the deceiver, who was responsible for the state in which Bhrataha now found himself!

The heavens trembled...the entity that had once been Bhrataha, finally knew the name of its tormentor...*This was Ashwatthama – the betrayer...the destroyer...the one who was cursed to wander throughout all time, in repentance for his unspeakable crimes...this was he who had caused a terrible war, described in legend and who had made a terrible choice in his mad quest for knowledge. This was Ashwatthama the cursed, shunned by all of humanity...for all eternity!*

The entity now watched Ashwat, face his final destiny at the hands of this mysterious being from beyond!

CHAPTER NINE

The being from beyond the 'gateway'...spoke to Ashwat, directly, "Look my child...even now your fellow mortals throw themselves at forces against which they have no hope, whatsoever. Surely you will not let their sacrifice go in vain. Surely you will embrace the gift that I offer you...that 'Chronux' offers you."

"I do not want any gift...please just stop this carnage...why are you allowing all of this to happen, even when you are able to stop it? And what gift do you speak of?"

"Ha ha ha...even *now* you can barely suppress that spark of curiosity...it still burns brightly within you...I know, I chose well... long have I observed you my child, even as you tried to peer into the mysteries of the cosmos and of life and death itself...I have ever so gently probed you, coaxed you, encouraged you and never once have you disappointed me. You truly are my Worthy Successor."

"Successor??? A successor to what? ...And what do you mean you have been manipulating me!!! I may have made some terrible choices in recent times but they were mine and mine alone." Ashwat screamed hysterically.

"Yes...yes of course my child...and I now need you to make one more choice...the *FINAL one*...with the same conviction. After all it is not every day that one's destiny comes knocking at one's door!"

"What choice?? I want this invasion to stop...please save my people...my planet...I will follow you to hell itself, if you but make it happen." Ashwat wept piteously.

"In the eyes of your fellow humans, you are already damned to 'hell' many times over...the knowledge of what inspired this invasion and your treacherous role in it, is now thanks to me, wide spread across the system...right now even as we converse, you are mankind's most hated enemy...they are coming for you...Just imagine, the once favorite son of humanity, now cursed and shunned for all eternity. Living on Earth, *if Earth survives*, will not be very pleasant for you from this point on, my son. And make no mistake, I ensured all of this, even before reaching out to you…after all, I am not someone, who takes *no* for an answer!"

"How could you???…you who claim to guide me…to lead me to my destiny, have destroyed any chance of redemption that I had…in this life or the next." Ashwat screamed.

"Why would you want redemption, when you can make the universe itself dance to your tunes…*why be the 'Adam' who craved one apple and then spent an eternity repenting for it, when you can have the entire garden of paradise itself!* …Surely my son, I cannot have misjudged you so badly…show some backbone my dear. Where is the fire that prompted you to defy all orders, in the quest for forbidden knowledge?"

As if to emphasize this point, the 'being from beyond', displayed images of the invasion that was even now destroying what remained of System Gaea, laying waste to a six thousand year old culture.

With humanity refusing to give up without a fight, the alien invaders had decided to use 'Shock and Awe' tactics to cow the opposition into submission. In a scarcely believable gesture of might, the invaders dramatically altered the paths of two of humanity's most formidable outposts in the Solar System!

Using a technology known as 'Gravo-Matrices' - massive Dark Matter based engines that allowed for the temporary reversal of gravitational fields, around planet sized objects - the invaders uprooted the planets Mars and Saturn from their natural orbits around the sun. Mars was launched somewhere between the constellations of Scorpio and Sagittarius in a Retrograde motion, while Saturn suddenly found itself aligned to the constellation of Gemini, near the star Aldebaran!

These tremendous astronomical changes, visible from Earth, were supposed to act as a testament to the might of the invaders. Because of these shocking distortions to the fabric of space, planet Earth would be forced to go through a lunar and solar eclipse, in the coming month.

"Stop…please stop this genocidal madness. Who *ARE* you and how are you doing all of this? What have we ever done to you?" Ashwat moaned.

"Oh you haven't done anything to me or *FOR* me yet…but there is a lot that you can and shall do." The voice responded gleefully. "As far as who I am, that is a tougher question to answer."

"I once *did* belong to the race that currently invades your civilization…a race of war mongers and expansionists known as 'Shambhala'…we were the scourge of all the species, inhabiting this quadrant of the galaxy. But like you, there was something different about me…*something unique.* I did not simply crave mindless warfare; my motivations were far grander! Like you, I spent my life trying to understand the mysteries of life and death and why everything that lives is doomed to die. Like yourself and many others before you, I craved the impossible secret of immortality. I was denounced by the others for being too weak minded and simplistic…too naïve…but I persevered…until the day I finally found Chronux…or should I say until *Chronux found me.*"

"Chronux?" Ashwat repeated numbly.

"Yes…this is a power that makes all things possible…when one embraces it, one becomes the absolute Lord of space and time…one is forever beyond the ravages of time…immortal!!! I embraced that power and became one with it. For more years than you can count, I was the absolute last word, as far as all the events in the universe were concerned…the ultimate authority!"

"But now for reasons that you do not have the ability to grasp in your current state, I cannot continue in my role as the 'Custodian' of this awesome power…and you have been chosen as the one, who will relieve me of my charge."

"Me??"

"Yes…my choice is infallible…I have long monitored your efforts in trying to understand the mysteries of the universe, even as your fellow Earthlings stumbled around listlessly, in their man-made Utopias. It was I, who discreetly aided you, as you searched for 'Extra-terrestrial life', I, who led you to the data that had been lost for centuries, amidst the records maintained by your civilization…and it was I, who subliminally coaxed you to overstep your authority and initiate contact, using the distress signals…contacts that ultimately led to this invasion!"

"What?????" a shocked Ashwat whispered.

"Yes…from your point of view, my actions might seem desperate and selfish…but then you haven't felt pain and frustration, like I have…nobody has!"

"However, now all that is behind us…what matters right now is that you do for me that what I have picked you for, and help me bring this farce to an end. It is only fair that you help me, considering how it was *me* who responded to your fake distress call and sent you a response, even while others from my race were busy making preparations to invade your planet. I responded to YOU!!!! Imagine that…how often has GOD responded to a supplicant…*personally!*"

Stunned silence followed. Ashwat looked around himself, speechless…and observed the destruction of his world. He had never been particularly spiritual…of course, the whole concept of religion had become obsolete, after the 22nd century. And yet, he and others from the scientific community, did hold on to a notion of a *'divine creator'*…not necessarily one that you could ascribe human values to…certainly not one described by any of Earth's religions, but nonetheless, the idea of an 'intelligent designer', fit perfectly, most theories about the origins of the universe.

However, regardless of his personal beliefs, Ashwat had never dreamt he would one day come face to face with a being, *who claimed to be that entity!*

He knew he wasn't dealing with just a supernatural entity but a primordial force of nature that could not be argued with! There was no alternative but to submit, if he wanted to bring to an end this carnage.

"What do I have to do? I am ready…please tell me how I can stop all of this…what is this power that you speak of…that you have left me no choice but to accept? Tell me what to do and let's get it over with." As he spoke these words, Ashwat felt the last of the energies, drain from his body.

"Ha ha ha…this is far from the end my son; this is just the beginning of something powerful…something glorious and liberating." the being screamed in wild ecstasy, "Now open yourself to the initiation, as I *transfer* the power of Chronux onto you…once you embrace this cosmic force, the universe will *rest* within you."

"Will I be able to reverse all of what has happened to my people? Will I be able to undo my mistakes? Redeem myself?" a broken Ashwat asked pathetically.

"You still are thinking much too small, my child. With the power of Chronux within you, you will have absolute control over *ALL* space and time…not just of your miserable planet. The very invaders, whom you now view as the purest form of evil, will be your play things. All of this and more will be possible, because when Chronux rests within you, you will be finally free of Entropy's crippling tethers…no longer bound by the vagaries of time…you shall be the absolute Master of Time. Concepts like 'life' and 'death' will become meaningless for one such as you…do it my child…prepare yourself for the initiation… your *TIME* has come!"

The entity that had once been Bhrataha, watched in horror, as Ashwat, the man from the future, whom it now knew as its predecessor, bent down in submission and surrendered to the all consuming…all powerful Trap of Chronux.

What followed was oddly familiar…after all, not so long ago, the entity's former life as a human named Bhrataha, had also come to an abrupt end, when *it* had been deceitfully trapped by Ashwat …this same traitor, who now appeared so helpless.

It observed the being from beyond; partially emerge from inside the Space-Warp. Even though an energy field surrounding the being, veiled the entire area in an ethereal haze, the creature now did *not* quite seem human…there was definitely something 'alien' about it… something 'Saurian'… 'Reptilian' even. *This* was the 'Custodian' of the cosmic power of Chronux!

Bhrataha - the entity, watched the being hold its hand out in front of the kneeling Ashwat. In its open palm, was a very familiar artifact… it resembled an un-blossomed flower…a crystalline metallic flower!

It was the same relic that had once been bestowed to the people of Aruhu by their godly teacher - Ashwat…the same relic that if improperly used, could transport its bearer, to places and periods of great war and cataclysms...the same relic that Bhrataha had annihilated his entire village to get to...and the very same one that had caused him to be trapped in his current state!

Now, Bhrataha was witnessing the moment, when *his* predecessor – Ashwat, had acquired the same relic and fallen into the inescapable trap of Chronux!

It watched the being from beyond initiate Ashwat into the knowledge of Chronux and the secrets of the jewel. It saw the familiar swirling of exotic energies, encircle Ashwat and heard him scream... *as his very atoms came apart.* It felt his consciousness disperse across the cosmos...billions of light years, in a matter of seconds!

Ashwat's final scream echoed across the living universe. It was impossible not to feel moved by it! In the space between two ticks of a clock, he had gone from being a leading Astro-Physicist for Earth, in the year 3067 A.D. to becoming one of the primordial forces in the universe!

Such a transformation of course, came at a cost. *The price to be paid for 'Everything' is 'Everything'.*

Ashwat had been...from that point on...forced to be...Chronux! *At last, Bhrataha truly recognized his mysterious teacher!*

CHAPTER TEN

For the entity, the entire sequence of events had carried with it a sense of Déjà vu. Until this point, whatever traces of humanity still existed within it, had been holding on to a sense of being 'wronged'…a feeling of hatred and anger, towards its predecessor Ashwat, whom it saw as a betrayer. It had wished him nothing but harm…until now!

But curiously, after seeing Ashwat being trapped and manipulated, it felt absolutely no sense of victory…or glee…merely remorse, at the human condition!

It could no longer view Ashwat as someone, who had maliciously duped its former incarnation into accepting the power and the 'Curse of Chronux'. It realized now that his actions had been prompted by the same feeling of impossible loneliness that *it* was now experiencing. Suddenly, Ashwat no longer seemed like the deceiver. The events from this dark and tragic future of 3067 A.D. had made it clear that he was as much a victim of circumstances as Bhrataha!

For the first time the entity could empathize with another individual, whom fate had dealt the same terrible cards. It observed the final moments of the transformation that stripped its predecessor of the last vestiges of humanity, and forced him to embrace his destiny as the 'Bearer of all Time' in the universe.

The 'being from beyond'…finally free of his burden, having successfully deceived another wretched soul into shouldering it, laughed in pure ecstasy!

Slowly, bit by bit, the being's original form as a male member of the race of aliens known as 'Shambhala' began to come back together. *It was like watching an autopsy in reverse!* The individual components that made up his physical shell…so long dispersed and lost to the cosmos…began to come together. No longer was he just an illusion… his former semi-humanoid, semi-reptilian self, was visible once again.

Within moments, he stood completely reassembled and all alone, amid the ruins of the destroyed Command Center...just beyond the now rapidly diminishing Space-Warp.

The sheer joy he felt, was unparalleled. In his own lifetime, he had fallen into the deadly trap of trying to gain absolute power and been cursed with the charge of carrying the power of Chronux for all eternity. For anyone else, this would have been a 'death wish'...devoid of any second chances.

But through some extremely shrewd manipulation, he had managed to entice and entrap another fool into taking over the burden from him. Yes...it *HAD* taken the near complete annihilation of Earth and System Gaea to accomplish this...*billions had died*...but to be free of the curse of Chronux was worth any cost!!!

After all, this being from beyond knew very well...*the price of gaining 'Everything' is 'Everything'!!!*

He looked up into the cosmos that he now knew, held the essence of the Earth man known as Ashwat and screamed, "My beloved savior...you now realize the trap that you have allowed yourself to be led into...and I *do* truly regret the whole deception. But even in your current state, you must appreciate...and empathize with my desire for being free once again! The burden of immortality and the curse of Chronux is a heavy one to carry. I do deeply regret that even as I now go to live out what remains of my mortal existence...in the best way that I can, you shall forever be cut off from all those you once loved, and remain an all-powerful anomaly for all time!"

"Because of the curious nature of the power, you are now one with; you will never be able to make any real meaningful contact with the physical universe...except during certain rare moments, when certain celestial bodies align. These will vary from planet to planet, system to system of course. But here on your beloved Earth, you will be able to physically reach out to the rest of humanity, *only* when the planet Mars comes between the constellations of Scorpio and Sagittarius, having performed a retrograde motion...the planet Saturn appears in the constellation of Gemini, near the star Aldebaran...and when a lunar eclipse is followed by a solar eclipse, *in the same month!*"

"This is so because, when you were taking over the power of Chronux, and relieving me of my burden, members of my race were using a technology known as 'Gravo-Matrices', on your solar system. This weapon causes the temporary reversal of gravitational fields around entire planets."

"When this was used in the Solar System...*an unusually crowded system*...the planet that you refer to as Mars was sent into a retrograde motion between the constellations of 'Scorpio' and 'Sagittarius', while the one named Saturn was unnaturally aligned to the constellation of 'Gemini', near the star Aldebaran. You already know this, as you were able to witness these developments on your holographic tracker. These distortions will cause your planet to experience a Solar and Lunar eclipse in the same month."

"Since your transformation coincided with these developments, your new state as the cosmic entity–Chronux is now forever linked to these planetary positions. Only when these astronomical anomalies line up on their own...as they will once every few decades or so...will you be able to physically interact with the rest of the universe. Remember this well...you will be able to maintain a coherent form on your beloved Earth, *ONLY* during these alignments! As soon as the alignments change...your access to the physical universe will end and you will go back to your never changing state as Chronux."

"From then on until the next alignment, you will find that while you have the whole history of the cosmos at your fingertips...Time and Space themselves, at your beck and call...you will NOT be able to interact with them in anyway. You will forever remain a passive observer...*the eternal witness*...one who is able to access the deepest secrets of the universe, and yet never able to share them... *UNBELIEVABLY* lonely!...to simply imagine a state such as that for even a moment, is unbearable...however, you my dear Ashwat, are doomed to experience it forever. Such is the curse of Chronux."

The heavens roared with unbridled fury!

"My dear beloved savior...no words exist in any language, which can truly convey my gratitude for what you have done for me. You, who forever sought knowledge, have now *become* knowledge itself...a cosmic force that is a universal anomaly and *KNOWS* it. In sharing my knowledge of Chronux with you, my dear savior, I have completed the transfer...no longer do I have to live under the shadow of Chronux... it is now your burden to shoulder!"

"If somehow, through some unthinkable quirk of fate, you are able to master the power of Chronux, like I did and reach a point where you are able to con someone else into falling for the same trap...then and only then will there be a way for you to once again be a part of the universe. This of course won't be easy and you will have to play your cards very, very skillfully...however, if there is one thing that my time as Chronux taught me, it is that there is no dearth of fools in the cosmos. After all, the promise of absolute power and immortality is a powerful incentive for you to use, in luring another wretched soul. Or else of course, you could sit and regret the one blunder that cost you everything!"

"Whatever you choose; know full well that you have all of eternity... ha ha ha!!"

"I leave you now my dear Ashwat with these final words...they might yet come back to haunt you, but as you now know very well...

In Chronux lies YOUR destiny."

And then there was silence.

It is said that if you are absolutely still and remain very, *VERY* quiet...you can even hear the primordial whispers of the living universe...*the very voice of God!* But there is more...if you continue to listen...you will hear the faint traces of an anguished scream...one that contains enough remorse to shake the foundations of the cosmos. It is a cry born out of the realization of a mistake so colossal...so costly; that it would take all of eternity to undo...*it is the anguished scream of Chronux!*

CHAPTER ELEVEN

The entity that had once been Bhrataha finally understood its true fate! It had witnessed the events that had caused *its* predecessor to fall from grace...and in doing so, had learnt to appreciate its *own* condition better. No longer was Ashwat a betrayer of men...no longer could he be seen as a false god, who had used the naïve innocence of a primitive race, to his advantage.

The entity now saw him for who he really was...a man who had gambled everything he had, in the pursuit of knowledge and in doing so demonstrated that most human of all qualities – curiosity!

It saw a man, who had fallen into a terrible trap...one older than time itself...and had no alternative but to manipulate someone else into rescuing him. A man forced to exist as a primordial force of the universe, who in his desperation, had reached out to a people, he knew would be primitive enough to be manipulated and yet intelligent enough to act out his commands. It saw a man who had only sought to free himself and it now felt no animosity towards him...simply a deep sense of sorrow. *For the first time since the birth of the cosmos, the entity known as Chronux wept!*

"You finally know the events that led to my being trapped in the state that you now find yourself in...and know that you have my deepest regrets and also my eternal undying gratitude. Just as I – Ashwat became the savior for that unnamed 'being from beyond', you my dear Bhrataha, have become mine!"

"It is *YOU*, who shall carry the 'Curse of Chronux', for all eternity and remain the one constant factor, in this ever changing universe... you are now and forever the ultimate anomaly! By experiencing my lifetime and the events that led me to my demise, you have gained all the knowledge that once was mine. And as you now know very well, with this transfer of knowledge and information, your transformation into Chronux nears completion. I have no other words for you, but the same advice that *my* predecessor left me…try to master your current predicament and use your power to get someone *else* to take the fall for you…or live out all of eternity in your current state…the choice is yours."

"As far as my fate is concerned, I now go back to my former life in my own time. While I know history and my own people will not judge me kindly…and I will be held accountable for my part in the greatest genocide in human history, at least I have a life to go back to. I leave you my beloved savior, with these final words…*In Chronux lies YOUR destiny.*"

For the second time in as many moments, the entity that had once been Bhrataha wept…*this time at its own plight*. No longer a part of the universe…no longer classifiable into anything *but a class of its own*…truly unique…truly anomalous…gone were the last vestiges of a boy named Bhrataha…the entity finally embraced its true destiny!

Now absolute master of all of space and time, it followed the series of events on Earth around the great carnage of 3067 A.D. Free of Ashwat's manipulations, it realized for the first time that the assault had been even more diabolical than it had suspected.

The 'being from beyond', who had manipulated Ashwat, had not just taken advantage of the assault, to force Ashwat into a corner, but had in fact been its *CAUSE!!!* Originally, the warlike alien race known as 'Shambhala', had no designs on Earth.

They had known of Earth's existence for centuries and had been regularly intercepting S.E.T.I.'s transmissions. But it was only the skillful manipulation of the being from beyond that had caused them to consider Earth a threat, and thus mount their offensive…one that would of course help the being rid itself of its own burden!

Even in its current state, Chronux could not but be horrified at the enormous cost that this unnamed alien being had been willing to pay, purely for its own redemption! The total death count on Earth, following the assault had crossed 38 billion! It had only been the alien armada's inability to go through the last of Earth's defenses that had prevented complete extinction.

Even then, the damage done to Earth's culture and the impact such damage would have on the civilization, was impossible to describe in words. So horrific were these scars...so traumatic were these memories, that for the next entire millennia, the only way humanity was able to overcome this nightmare, was by refusing to document any of the events to follow...by completely shunning history, for a thousand years!

As a result of this, in the history of humanity, there is a thousand year chapter that is entirely missing...intentionally so...the chapter that would have ordinarily covered the millennia, following the 'Great War'. This was the cost Earth had to pay, over and above the death count!

Earth ceased to be a Solar System wide empire and went back to small colonies that focused mainly on subsistence living. Some even threatened to revive archaic and forgotten practices such as 'tribal wars' and 'religion'. *The fragile threads of the bewitching fabric of civilization threatened to unravel under this chaos.*

Chronux sighed...all this carnage...all this chaos...and all so that the 'being from beyond' could overcome its own curse and pass the baton on to someone else. This was narcissism and antipathy, on a cosmic scale. But then wasn't that what even Ashwat had been prepared to do? Hadn't even he tricked an ancient and primitive people into doing his bidding? Hadn't he maliciously and deliberately led them down the wrong path...a path that had ultimately caused their complete annihilation at the hands of one of their own? In the destruction of Aruhu, *Bhrataha had been but a pawn in Ashwat's grand plan!*

The 'Curse of Chronux' of course was something to be feared...an unbelievable agony that no one else in the universe could hope to understand. But did it mean that to rid itself of this curse, Chronux would now *also* have to be ready to shed the blood of entire civilizations?

Chronux had once been a human being...a young man named Bhrataha, who had been deluded and manipulated into believing that the quest for immortality was the ultimate goal...the ultimate prize! Bhrataha had then gone on to use every means available, regardless of the cost, to attain it…and now that he *had* finally overcome mortality's stifling inhibitions, he wanted nothing more than to get rid of it!

But did this new bearer of the Chronux Power have what it takes, to overcome the odds? Only 'Time' would tell…

…*even Chronux HAD to smile at the irony!*

CHAPTER TWELVE

Over what would seem like millennia for others, but what was the merest blink of an eye for the universe, a plan began to form. Yes…a trap had to be set…the fires of which would have to be skillfully stoked over decades, perhaps centuries, before it reached fruition!

Such an enterprise would require incalculable patience and skill. But most important of all, it would require the right candidate…the perfect victim…someone who possessed just the right mix of narcissism, megalomania and intelligence. Someone who would go to *any* lengths in the pursuit of what he/she believed in…and with complete access to all of history, Chronux knew the perfect time and place, to search for just such a victim!

Starting from the early years of the twentieth century, a movement had emerged in Western Europe that had begun as an ideology, meant to tide over some extremely difficult times, but had then gone on to become one of the most dominant forces to ever confront mankind… The idea of 'Nazism'. Within its myriad and perverse interpretations, lay thousands of young men and women, for whom the Fascist Hitlerite ideology would become something of a divine calling. In the late 1930s, this would go on to inspire World War II!

One of the many core beliefs this ideology was based on, was the theory that the white, blond Germanic population was descended from a race of super-humans or 'Übermensch' called the 'Aryans', who lived thousands of years ago. According to this theory, the Aryans were the true inheritors of the planet and had been kept away from their destiny, by inferior sub-human races designated – 'the Untermench.' The goal of the Aryan was supposed to be one of undying struggle against the lesser races, for *only* by overcoming them, could he gain what was rightfully his.

Such a belief system was in a sense, the perfect breeding ground for narcissism, intolerance and megalomania...perfect for what Chronux needed. A carefully chosen member from this particular belief system could be very amenable to persuasion and manipulation, *if the right stimulus was provided.*

With just the right sort of encouragement, he would crash the gates of hell itself; to get to what he thought was his! And while the Nazis were most known for starting World War II...a war that cost the lives of fifty million people, one of their most important long term goals was to unearth proof of the mythical Aryan civilization.

Starting from the early nineteen twenties till the end of World War II, the Nazis sent numerous 'scientific' explorations to all corners of the planet to bring back evidence of an Aryan Super-Culture.

This was a movement that could definitely be harnessed and manipulated. Moreover, the period around the end of the war also corresponded with the rare astronomical alignments that allowed Chronux to fully interact with the physical world. But to ensure that the trap was absolutely fool-proof, Chronux would have to get all the individual pieces in place hundreds, if not thousands of years *BEFORE* these events...somewhere in Earth's distant past...a period before recorded history...about which scarce documentation existed.

Just like its predecessor Ashwat, Chronux would have to reach out and manipulate the past.

Of course, Ashwat had taken a dangerous chance. The artifact he had left in the care of the people of Aruhu, while presenting himself as their divine teacher, he had associated with forbidden knowledge. This had prevented the inhabitants of the village from tampering with it, for over a century...all the while building on the legend of the mysterious Jewel.

This was a gamble...and one that could have very easily backfired. Had the villagers stuck to their inertia, the bait would have *never* been taken. Ashwat had correctly guessed that eventually the lure and the mystery of the artifact would become impossible to resist and some fool with delusions of grandeur *WOULD* take the bait. And that is how things had panned out...*curses!!!*

Chronux now knew that taking such a chance with the same society was *not* a viable option. It would get but one shot at this and the trap needed to be foolproof!

If certain obscure 'clues' and 'hints' were placed in Earth's distant past...relating to a lost race of super humans, over time, these 'hints' would evolve into living-breathing legends and fables! By the early years of the twentieth century, these would undoubtedly attract the attention of the Nazis, who were intent on finding evidence of just such a race. However obscure the clues were to begin with, the legend would develop to accommodate all the elements required to make them compelling enough for Nazi propaganda.

During the late nineteen thirties, the Nazis would launch a series of 'scientific explorations' into the remotest regions of Asia, including Tibet. These missions were based on the hypothesis that since the word 'Aryan' first appears in the Ancient Indian text – the 'Rg Veda', there was a possibility that traces of this lost culture could be found in Asia.

Large parts of Tibet had remained completely unexplored and unknown, especially to Europeans. The theory the Nazis would hedge their bets on was that some of these Aryans could have settled down in the mountains of Tibet, thousands of years ago and been cut off from the rest of the world. If true, it would offer the Nazis a perfect opportunity to observe and study an uncorrupted version of the 'Super Race'.

Chronux knew that if along with this, the Germans were to stumble upon something even more tantalizing...a potential treasure far beyond anything else a simple expedition to Tibet could offer; one of them might be tempted to see it through. This tantalizing 'bait' could be a lost city that was literally 'Paradise on Earth'...one that the Aryans were supposedly guarding and one that was full of technologies that could give the Germans absolute victory over the rest of mankind. Surely...this was a gamble worth taking...there was no way that the Nazis, in all their megalomania, would be able to refuse its lure!

'Hmmmmm...the legend of the lost city would of course need to be romanticized as much as possible...and for starters it needed a

name. For some reason the name '*Shambhala*' seemed just…
PERFECT!!!!

Chronux headed for Tibet…it was now just a matter of setting the trap, waiting and watching…just a matter of time…and time? …*well, that was one thing, it surely had in abundance!*

EPISODE THREE

CHAPTER ONE

Dhuk…Dhuk…Dhuk…listening to the beat of your own heart can be both exhilarating and terrifying. On one hand, the sound is steady and rhythmic…much like the precious gift of life itself; On the other, it serves to remind us of just how fragile that gift *really* is!

For Captain Friedrich Gustav, leader of the Nazi S.S. expedition to Tibet, the sound was causing all the strength in his body, to fade away. Perched precariously on the very edge of a mountainous outcrop on sacred Mount Kailasha, he was still some meters from the top…*but it might as well have been a hundred miles!*

The rock climber's icicle and the harness were the only things that were preventing him from tumbling into the 6700 meter ravine. His search for 'Paradise' amidst these icy heights, had taken a terrible toll on his body. His limbs burned with pain and fatigue, and his body begged him to let go. It would be so simple. Below, the valley seemed to lovingly beckon to him…*death lovingly beckoned*…eager to take him in its warm embrace…all the pain…physical and mental would simply go away…sweet, sweet oblivion…all encompassing…eternal… perfect. *He knew that even this way he would still get to Paradise!!!*

CHAPTER TWO

In the early years of the 20th Century, Vienna, Austria was a hot bed of esoteric ideas. Especially during the pre-World War I years, the city served as a beacon for all kinds of fringe beliefs and ideas, ranging from the 'Occult' to the 'Satanic'.

However, those who propagated such beliefs were still not terribly prominent and generally met each other in forgotten 'beer halls' and defunct cafeterias. To the rest of society, they seemed 'strange'... 'outlandish'...'anachronistic'...*those not in synch with reality!* No mainstream scholar would dare risk his reputation, by entertaining their bizarre ideas! These were discussed only among the ardent... *in hushed whispers!* And yet, little did any one suspect at the time that in just a few short decades; Hitler's 'Third Reich' would take these very ideas and make them cornerstones of Nazi philosophy.

Historians have long wondered about the source of these radical beliefs. What *was* it that had caused them to emerge in the first place?

The last time, this kind of an *ideological revolution* had taken place, was a thousand years ago, at the start of the 11th century, when secretive groups and brotherhoods like the 'Knights Templars' had taken center-stage.

Today, there are probably as many theories about the Templars' real motives as there were Templars, themselves. But one thing is clear. Apart from being the scourge of the Arab World, the Templars also served as the inspiration for a series of myths, legends and poems that centered on their alleged quest for the 'Holy Grail'. These speculations led to the formation of secret societies and esoteric groups, such as the 'Rosicrucians' and the infamous 'Priory of Sion'...*and thus giving birth to a frightening new age of heretical ideas!*

But a thousand years before even that, the 1st century city of Jerusalem, under Roman occupation and desperately awaiting its prophesied 'Messiah', found itself introduced to the teachings of a charismatic yet controversial figure named 'Yeshuah'…or 'Jesus'!

Common to both these periods was the promise of an age of enlightened ideas…*a 'Golden Age'!*

With the start of the 20ᵗʰ century heralding the end of the astronomical 'Age of Pisces', and foreshadowing the 'Age of Aquarius', the promise of a new-born savior, rebirth and a 'new Golden Age', seemed to once again gain traction in Europe!

One of the basic tenets of these occultists was a belief in 'Hyperborea-Thule', a mythical land first described in ancient Greek literature. Just as the Greek philosopher, Plato had spoken of the legendary lost island of Atlantis in his dialogues; the historian Herodotus described the legend of a continent named Hyperborea, located far to the North, with its majestic capital city – 'Thule'.

While the debate still rages on, as to what Plato's real motives were, when he wrote of Atlantis, i.e. was he simply conveying the idea of a Utopia…or describing an actual place…Herodotus' works are generally taken a little more literally.

According to him, the people of Hyperborea were an ancient race of 'Super Humans', who lived well before the advent of humanity. The Hyperboreans supposedly lived in perfect harmony with nature, were absolute strangers to the concept of disease and lived till the age of one thousand years.

Herodotus also wrote that this was a land, where the sun shone for 24 hours and where the Sun God, Apollo, travelled to and fro, once every six months, riding abreast his Golden chariot.

Interestingly, similar references also appear in another…*extremely unlikely source*…the Bible!

Job 37:22, "Out of the north he comes in golden splendor; God comes in awesome majesty."

And in Ezekiel 1:4, "I looked, and I saw a windstorm coming out of the north - an immense cloud with flashing lightning and surrounded by brilliant light. The center of the fire looked like glowing metal…"

But regardless of whether the Hyperborea legend is myth or metaphor, much like the myth of Atlantis, it ended badly, when ice destroyed this ancient land. Its people now homeless, migrated south!

Certain sources from the late middle ages, identified the Atlanteans with the Hyperboreans, and located the latter, at the North Pole.

Others spoke of how Hyperborea split into the islands of 'Thule' and 'Ultima Thule', which are identified with Iceland and Greenland!

To the occultists in the former Austro-Hungarian Empire, the idea of a race of Super-humans would have seemed absolutely fascinating. After all, this was a Germany trying to find its own identity, after its separation from the once mighty Roman Empire. The possibility that the true Germanic population could be descendants of a mythical race of super-humans was utterly intoxicating! This was also the theory that would ultimately inspire Hitler's fanatical quest for a purer race.

Friedrich Nietzsche, the German Philosopher of the late 19th century, spoke about the concept of the 'Übermensch' or 'Super-Man' in his work- 'Der Antichrist' – The Antichrist.

He began with the line, "Let us see ourselves for what we are. We are Hyperboreans. We know well enough how we are living off that track." …thus identifying the Germanic population as the torch bearers of a master race. The key principle that was supposed to inspire this master race was an exotic internal energy source called 'Vril'.

Nietzsche never actually spoke about Vril, but…in his posthumously published work, 'Der Wille zur Macht' – 'The Will to Power', he did mention an 'Internal Force', responsible for superhuman development. Nietzsche categorizes society as "the herd," meaning common persons, who strive for security, by creating morality and rules, and the 'Super-men' who have an internal force that drives them to go beyond the 'herd'. That force also drives them to lie and manipulate, so as to remain free of the "herd mentality".

This belief system, *taken seriously*, was a living, breathing recipe for megalomania!

Another powerful stimulant to the idea of 'Vril Energy' was the 'Hollow Earth' hypothesis. It was at the end of the seventeenth century that the British astronomer, Sir Edmund Halley, first suggested that the earth was hollow and made up of four concentric spheres. Over time, this theory became immensely popular, across the world, with numerous books dedicated to it, both academic and works of fiction!

The 'Hollow Earth' hypothesis certainly helped bring the concept of 'Vril' into public consciousness, through the works of several writers such as the French author Louis Jacolliot, who furthered the myth in 'Les Fils de Dieu' – 'The Sons of God' and 'Les Traditions indo-européenes' – 'The Indo-European Traditions'. He made the connection between Vril and the *subterranean* super-human people of 'Thule', who would supposedly harness this power and go on to, rule our planet!

In his 1903 book, 'The Arctic Home of the Vedas', Bal Gangadhar Tilak, a powerful advocate of Indian freedom, also helped further this hypothesis, by identifying the southern migration of the Thuleans, with the origin of the Aryan Super Race!

For the occultists living in Austria and Germany, in the early twentieth century, these writings seemed to echo, what they had always believed in - that they were the descendants of Aryan tribes, who had migrated south from Hyperborea-Thule and who were destined to become the master race through the power of Vril!

One of those was a student of literature, studying in Vienna thanks to a sponsorship secured for him, by his father…a young man named Friedrich Gustav.

Another…*was Adolf Hitler!*

Soon…heretical scholars and 'New Age' researchers were all working together…all fascinated by the same ultimate goal – The New 'Golden Age'. They would come to the conclusion that to create the conditions required for *birthing* this new age, the current world would have to be destroyed…and then re-forged! The quest was now on for the search of that one power that could both 'destroy and re-create'!

To this end, a series of underground and esoteric secret societies began to crop up, all across the region. These would remain an important bastion of occult studies, till the end of World War II and would prove loyal to Hitler and the Nazis. Many of these societies drew inspiration from the legendary Nordic kingdom of Thule, further promoting the idea of a 'Master Race'…and thereby, sowing the seeds of racism in Europe.

CHAPTER THREE

It was in the year 1917 that five people met in a café in Vienna – Café Schopenhauer. One of them was a young woman named Maria Orsitch, from Zagreb, who claimed to be a spiritual medium…another was Rudolf Freiherr Von Sebottendorf, an Occultist and Orientalist, who had recently returned from the Near-East. They spoke on a plethora of topics, such as the arrival of the 'New Age', sources of mystical powers like the 'Spear of Destiny' and the possibility of making 'astral' and 'spiritual' contact with ancient Pagan Deities!

These talks were accompanied by prophetic visions that the medium, Orsitch, claimed to receive. In any other setting, at any other time, a serious discussion on such themes would have been enough to get one branded - the 'lunatic fringe'. However, in this World War I inspired environment of fear and uncertainty, any attempt at trying to regain lost German glories, was heralded as a hero's quest!

The members of this group even fancied themselves as the characters of the famous Medieval Germanic poem – 'Percival'… where the hero undertakes a series of thrilling adventures in the quest for the 'Holy Grail'. These meetings proved to be the inspiration behind the establishment of the 'Vril Society'.

During these meetings, a young Vienna student leader named Friedrich Gustav, who worked part-time at the same café, could not help but be drawn towards them. Such was the passion and conviction that the men spoke with, that in this extremely bleak and difficult period, their words seemed to bring back lost German pride. The Austro-Hungarian Empire was by now a thing of the past, and yet, for nationalistic young men like Gustav, the prospect of their country regaining her former glory, was gold!

On one such occasion, he introduced himself to the group and poured out his desire of being a part of what he believed was an 'intellectual awakening'. The group was stunned. Eventually, after a series of lengthy talks and discussions about the occult, Gustav was deemed worthy of joining them.

For the next several years, he would strive passionately to prove his commitment to the cause, he so strongly believed in. He would immerse himself into a wide range of studies to ready himself for the challenges that he knew lay ahead. *The 'Vril Society' would have some very dedicated members indeed!*

In 1918, another member of this group, Rudolf Freiherr von Sebottendorf established the Munich branch of the 'Thule Society'. Sebottendorf had previously spent several years, working undercover, in Istanbul, Turkey, where he had formed a secret society that had tried to combine the esoteric teachings of Sufism with Freemasonry. This group claimed to be able to harness the mystical powers of an assassin creed, known as the 'Ismaili', who had flourished during the Crusades. History records that these assassins were the scourge of the crusaders and even believed to have connections with 'other-worldly' beings. So fanatical was their dedication that an earthly inspiration for it was believed impossible!

However, for Sebottendorf and his associates, trying to tap into this secretive cult, had proved a step too far. The Ismailis fiercely guarded their beliefs; especially from those they considered 'Western Infidels'. After a number of his associates were killed in mysterious circumstances, Sebottendorf had abandoned his quest and returned to Europe.

By 1919, however, the German political demography had undergone massive changes. Following the defeat and surrender of German forces in World War I, and the signing of the infamous 'Treaty of Versailles', the second great German Empire or the 'Second Reich' came to an inglorious end. The 'Kaiser' of Germany – Willham the Second, abdicated at the end of the war and power was transferred to the center-leftist, Weimar Republic.

This was also a time of great economic unrest. According to the harsh conditions imposed upon by the Treaty, Germany alone was held responsible for the war and expected to pay a massive amount as 'reparation money' to the victorious allies.

The decision of the Weimar Republic to accept these conditions further polarized the German population. Those like Hitler and Gustav considered it to be the ultimate betrayal and joined the Bavarian 'Far-Right' groups, in planning an overthrow of the government. It was then that from within the Thule Society spawned the 'German Workers' Party'.

By the year 1920, Dietrich Eckart, a member of the inner circle of the Thule Society, initiated Hitler into the group and began to train him in its pseudo-scientific methods of harnessing 'Vril'...the alleged power source behind a race of Aryan 'Super-men'. For Hitler, the mysteries of the past provided an interesting challenge. As a young man, he had occasionally dabbled in the occult, and had studied 'Theosophy', in Vienna. However, now he realized that a belief in the 'Master Race', along with German pride and Anti-Semitism, was probably the best way of galvanizing the disgruntled masses.

By the early 1920s, Hitler became the head of the German Workers' Party and soon changed the name to the 'National Socialist German Workers' Party'...the abbreviated form of which...was 'Nazi'. Hitler added the word 'Socialist' to suggest a people centric approach and hide the party's fervent 'Anti-Semitic' narrative...*at least, for a while!* It was during one of the party's clandestine beer hall meetings with the Thule Society that Gustav found himself formally introduced to the man, whom he would come to idolize – Adolf Hitler.

Another major influence on Hitler's thinking and someone who had also been part of the café meetings was Karl Haushofer, a German military advisor to the Japanese, after the 'Russo-Japanese War' of the early 20th century. Haushofer had stayed in Japan for years and thoroughly understood their culture. He was a great admirer of the sense of discipline that the Japanese 'Samurai Culture', ingrained in the youth and was particularly impressed by the concept of dedicating one's life, completely to a cause. Many believe that he was responsible for the later German-Japanese alliance...*an alliance that would prove so devastating, during World War II.*

During his time in Japan, Haushofer had made numerous visits to other parts of the Far-East, including India, and he was well versed with the greats Indian epics - the Ramayana and the Mahabharata.

Regardless of their spiritual significance, the thing that most fascinated him was the descriptions of the divine weapons that the epics contained. To someone not familiar with the age of these epics, it would seem like the descriptions were of a futuristic war!

Haushofer had studied that according to Hindu Mythology, humanity goes through four great 'Cosmic Cycles' of time known as the 'Yugas'. The first one was called the 'Satya Yuga'. It is the era, where evil simply did not exist. Over the next three cycles, namely the 'Treta Yuga', the 'Dwapar Yuga' and the 'Kali Yuga', humanity increasingly finds itself in the throes of corruption and decay! As a result, we now find ourselves in the last of these four great cycles...the most degenerate of all...the 'Kali Yuga'. The wars that the great epics describe are believed to have occurred in prior cycles where the purity of the human mind made it possible to access the 'divine power of God'!!

It was rumored that during one of his visits to India, Haushofer had stumbled upon a series of documents that would forever influence his life. A passionate scholar of ancient languages, he had taught himself the rudiments of Sanskrit and would often frequent off-beat and generally unknown archives in search of esoteric literature. And it was in just such an old and crumbling Buddhist monastery, near Sikkim that he had accidentally found a centuries-old text...titled the 'Vimanika Shastra' or the science of aeronautics!

The text, even though partially destroyed, had contained information that to Haushofer seemed to suggest that the ancient knowledge described in the epics could well be re-discovered. If what the document contained were true, the world could well be looking at the birth of a New Golden Age!

In his frenzy, Haushofer had tried to commit to memory as much of the information as possible, since the monks at the monastery did not allow the duplication of sacred texts. This partially damaged and largely illegible book was also the only surviving copy the monastery possessed and no amount of persuasion on his part could get them to part with it.

Worse still, he found that his efforts to get the monks to tell him more about the text had also met with little success. Whether the monks really had no knowledge beyond what the book said, or they were reluctant to share their secrets with a Westerner, hadn't quite been clear...but the only piece of advice they had offered him was that the source of this document lay in Tibet...*although where exactly, they couldn't say.*

During his time in the Far-East, Haushofer had made three attempts to gain access into Tibet, but had never succeeded. It seemed that neither the secretive Tibetans nor India's British rulers were keen on having a German explorer, disturb the tranquility of the place!

After serving as a general during World War I, Haushofer had returned to Germany and established the 'Vril Society' in Berlin in 1918. Its members shared the same basic beliefs as the 'Thule Society' and even served as its inner circle. They sought to make contact with supernatural beings that supposedly dwelt beneath the earth, to gain from them the powers of 'Vril'.

However, history would remember Karl Haushofer for very different reasons. He firmly believed in a Central Asian origin of the Aryan race, and developed the doctrine of 'Geopolitics', eventually becoming the director of the 'Institute for Geopolitics' at 'Ludwig-Maximilians University' in Munich. His theories advocated conquering territory to gain more living space or 'Lebensraum' for those whom he considered 'superior races', ultimately leading to the invasions of Czechoslovakia and Poland and the near complete annihilation of Eastern Europe, during World War II!

CHAPTER FOUR

By 1919, Germany was in the throes of a potential revolution. Following the humiliating defeat in World War I, Germans found themselves ostracized by the rest of Europe. Britain, France and the rest of the allies, blamed Germany, for the damages suffered during the great massacre…and on the 28th of June 1919, signed the 'Treaty of Versailles'…a treaty that put the entire burden of the War, on Germany!

This infamous treaty, which was hated by one and all in Germany, would prove to be the perfect spawning ground, for a plethora of revolutionary organizations that included the Communists, who threatened to take control of Germany, much like their counterparts had in Russia.

But even as the Communists rose to overthrow the Social Democratic Weimar Republic, the German Armed Forces, ruthlessly crushed them. Adolf Hitler, who had served as a corporal in World War I, was one of those at the forefront of this drive to crush the Communists. His dedicated anti-communist stance, earned him a lot of fame, and many noted his zeal and anti-revolutionary fervor!

Hitler's primary motive at this point was merely to keep a roof over his head, and serving in the army, was one way of doing that. For this, he would stoop to any level, and even became an informer for the Army, often denouncing his own comrades, suspected of being Communists.

Some of his superiors in the army were greatly impressed by his dedication and fanaticism towards nationalistic ideas and gave him the mission of 'politically re-educating' returning soldiers and officers. The belief was that during the War, soldiers fighting for Germany, had been exposed to a lot of anti-nationalistic ideas and become corrupted. Hitler's role was to ensure that the 'Spirit of Nationalism' was reignited among them.

It was also at this point that Hitler discovered his own extraordinary oratory skills. He found that he was able to skillfully manipulate the emotions of the masses, by escalating the tempo of his own voice and forcing the audience to think the way he did. His big moment came in 1919, when he publicly denounced the 'Treaty of Versailles' as the 'National Shame.'

Apart from imposing harsh terms on the Germans, the treaty also demanded that Germany disarm nearly her entire Armed Forces...a condition that would become central to the Nazi Party's grievances. Under the treaty, Germany lost around 13% of its territory and a tenth of its population, when the regions of Alsace-Lorraine once again became French. This added further fuel to the fire and the Right-Wing extremists began to galvanize, under the Nazis.

By 1921, they appointed Hitler, their leader, and even purchased him a car. This was significant, as it meant that he was now being looked at as the unchallenged figure-head for all the right-wing extremists. His radicalism also increased the party membership, from just over a thousand to twenty thousand!

For the myriad 'esoteric societies', proliferating across Germany, such as the 'Thule', Hitler seemed like the ideal leader...someone who could further their own racist ideologies! The funds that the 'Thule Society' provided the Nazis with, during this period, proved as important as their ideology.

These funds were generated, primarily through the sales of a newspaper named 'Völkischer Beobachter'...the 'People's Observer'. This soon became the official Nazi Party mouth-piece. The editor of this paper was Alfred Rosenberg, who would one day become one of Hitler's central theoretician and inspire most of Third Reich's megalomaniacal projects, during the 1930s.

Student leader, Rudolf Hess, another member of the Thule Society, also joined hands with the Nazis and would eventually go on to become Hitler's deputy. Another prize addition to the Nazi ranks, during this period was a much celebrated World War I fighter pilot – Herman Goring. It was this bolstering of the ranks, with important and well known personalities that convinced many in Germany that the Nazis would one day become their salvation.

In addition, most of the Generals and War Veterans in the newly demilitarized German Army, felt that the 'Treaty of Versailles' had robbed them of their rightful victory in World War I...a crime they blamed on the current Government. These veterans were willing to consider any option that promised a revival of German Nationalism... *even one as extreme as the Nazis.*

In January of 1923, an event took place that further cemented the Nazi appeal, even among ordinary Germans. Germany briefly refused to pay the 'War Reparations', expected under the Treaty of Versailles. As a result, French and Belgian troops forcibly took control of Germany's mining districts.

Helpless to resist, the German government ordered passive resistance, against this indemnity. The miners took to the streets as part of a strike against the draconian French policies...and were immediately replaced by the French. This increased the tension and exacerbated the situation...leading to the assassination of one French Army Officer. The outcry that followed the assassination resulted in further humiliation, as the body was taken through German towns and villages, with the French Army forcing Germans to take off their caps, as a mark of respect.

Hitler's response was immediate and provocative. In a series of vitriolic fuelled speeches, he denounced the weak central government – the Weimar Republic, for allowing France to treat Germany, like one of its colonies!

For the Germans though, the troubles were just beginning. Without access to their own coal, the conditions became unbearable, during the winter of 1923. Stripped of its own resources, the Weimar Republic needed to import coal from abroad and for that it required huge amounts of currency. This prompted the Mint to start printing currency, in massive amounts. The German Mark depreciated rapidly. 'Off the charts' inflation now set in, as ordinary Germans were now forced to pay up to a billion Marks, simply for a loaf of bread!

For Hitler, the fervent and turmoil caused by this catastrophic inflation was the perfect opportunity to unite all those, who were denouncing the central government under his leadership. There was now open talk of launching a 'Putsch' or 'Coup D'état', under Hitler, to overthrow the Government.

It was then that Friedrich Gustav joined the ranks of the Nazi Party, after a brief stint with the communists. Already a die-hard nationalist, Gustav energetically threw himself into what he believed, was a struggle for the redemption of German Pride. He was greatly taken in by Hitler's plan, which was to overthrow the government, by first taking Munich…and then Berlin!

Herman Goring, because of his accomplices in the army, was given the charge of procuring adequate firepower and guns for the Nazis. He chose Gustav as his protégé…a decision that would go on to change the young man's life forever. It was under Goring that Gustav began to really understand the rudiments of 'Fascism' and gradually began to get more and more indoctrinated into extremism.

But unfortunately for Hitler and the Nazis, the attempted 'Putsch' did not go according to plan. Success required that the German Army and the German Police join the 'Coup', against the government. This did not happen…the army and police remained loyal to the government and Hitler's grand dreams of a takeover were reduced to a smoldering ruin. He, along with dozens of other top Nazis, was taken into custody and imprisoned.

Awaiting trial, Hitler was initially fearful that he would be branded a traitor by the courts…a charge that carried with it the death penalty. However, he soon realized that the situation was far less trying than he had suspected. He found he had a lot of sympathy among Germans and in some cases even the Jury…*for most saw him simply as a die-hard nationalist, intent on improving the state of the Fatherland.* As a result, the verdict was far less serious than he had expected it to be. He was given a five-year prison sentence, in a relatively comfortable prison at 'Landsberg'.

His stay in prison resembled a stay in a guesthouse, where he was allowed his choice of publications to read and to meet visitors at any time of the day. These included members of the Nazi Party!

While in prison, Hitler also began work on his autobiography – 'Mein Kampf' or 'My Struggle'. Along with Rudolf Hess, who shared the neighboring cell, Hitler conceptualized his singular view of life and the German world view. In Mein Kampf, he outlined a clear strategy for the party's future and also detailed his reasons for being Anti-Semitic. Building on Nietzsche's belief in the 'Übermensch' or the 'super-men', Hitler outlined the hierarchy of all the different racial groups, and their roles in society. For him, his visceral hatred of the Jews or 'Hebrew Corruptors', as he called them, prevented him from even classifying them as part of the human race!

Most of those who read the book in those early years simply rejected it as errant madness. This would prove to be a fatal mistake… one that would ultimately cost humanity…more than fifty million lives. It was a world-view however, that the Nazis would take to heart and build on.

It was also during one of these prison meetings in the middle of 1923, that Rudolf Hess and Friedrich Gustav, themselves part of the failed Coup, brought Karl Haushofer to meet Hitler. Haushofer had acted as a mentor for the two of them, during their days as student leaders and they thought it right that he be introduced to their great leader. Haushofer quickly developed a bond with Hitler, whom he saw as the *'living incarnation of the German Reich'*.

He often visited the future Führer in prison, teaching him 'Geopolitics', in association with the ideas of the 'Thule' and 'Vril' Societies'. This understanding of imperialism and expansionism would go a long way in shaping Hitler's own world view!

During all these meetings, Hess was always there with Hitler… holding on to his every word…*literally worshipping him.* Such was his singular devotion and obsessive loyalty to Hitler that Haushofer sometimes suspected Hess wasn't right in the head.

When Hitler would eventually become chancellor in 1933, he would adopt 'Geopolitics', as his policy for the Aryan Race, to conquer Eastern Europe, Russia, and Central Asia. The key to success, would be finding the forefathers of the Aryans in Central Asia, the guardians of the secrets of 'Vril'. This would once and for all legitimize the Thule Society's claim about having descended from a Master Race!

Haushofer was also extremely influential in the early 1920s' establishment of the 'Black Sun' society, whose members were obsessed with uncovering the forgotten secrets of 'Ancient Alchemy'.

Alchemists believed that the 'Black Sun' appears, when our consciousness finds itself eclipsed and 'Time' undergoes alchemical changes. Under such conditions, light and dark get reversed – everything fades to Black - the hologram or illusion of our consciousness ceases to exist - we find ourselves once again at the same source from which our soul emerged - and the full complexity of our experience finally stands revealed!

The members of this group considered the Black Sun the ultimate secret behind limitless, untapped power…they conceptualized it as an infinite beam of light, which forever remains invisible to the naked eye. They justified its existence through the analogy that just as the Sun acts as a life-giver, its polar opposite – the mysterious 'Dark Sun' could light up the very soul of man! One of the biggest supporters of this theory was Friedrich Gustav, who considered this energy as the *'Illumination of the Divine'*, and who was now rapidly rising up the ranks of the Nazi Party!

Hitler forever interested in symbolism and the power that symbols had over society, decided to adopt another ancient symbol as the official Nazi Insignia – *'The Swastika'*. Although today, the Swastika's Nazi connections have made it infamous, this was far from a German invention. Originally, it was an ancient Indian symbol of immutable good luck and has been used by Hindus, Buddhists, and Jains for thousands of years.

In early 20th century Germany, even before the birth of Nazism, the 'Swastika' was often seen as a pre-cursor to the 'Christian Cross'. It had even become a symbol of Neo-Paganism, symbolizing a revival of Germanic culture. The Germans used to refer to it as the "Hakenkreuz", which meant a "hooked cross" and for some it signified the ultimate victory of Neo-Paganism over Christianity!

Sharing this anti-Christian sentiment, the Thule Society also adopted the 'Hakenkreuz', as part of its emblem, placing it in a circle, with a vertical German dagger superimposed on it. In 1920, following the recommendation of Dr. Friedrich Krohn, of the Thule Society, Hitler adopted the 'hooked cross', in a white circle, as the central design of the Nazi Party flag. He also used red for the background, to compete against the red flag of the rival Communist Party. This was a way of ensuring that the Nazis could get the full support of even the Socialists!

This emblem would prove to be deeply symbolic, as Haushofer, who had always maintained a deep interest in esoteric Indian and Tibetan teachings, would use the widespread presence of the Swastika in India and Tibet, as evidence to convince Hitler that this region was indeed the location of their Aryan forefathers!

Along with this, Haushofer also founded the 'Bruder des Lichts' or the 'Brothers of the Light.' This group of occultists, who also went by the name the 'Luminous Lodge' quickly rose to prominence in Germany, by uniting three major occult societies: The 'Lords of the Black Stone', The 'Black Knights of the Thule Society' and the 'Black Sun Society'. The primary focus of all these groups rested on what they believed to be the innate mystical powers of the Aryan Super Race!

The 'Luminous Lodge' aggressively pushed the outlandish theory that half a billion years ago, a race of super beings known as the 'Elders' used to inhabit the Star System of 'Aldebaran'. As their homelands became uninhabitable, they began to colonize our system, starting with a planet named 'Marduk' that allegedly existed within the asteroid belt. Interestingly, Marduk was also a primordial Babylonian deity, thus supposedly confirming this group's assertions that the ancient Near-East civilizations, such as the Sumerians and the Babylonians, were aware of this.

After Marduk, the 'Elders' were said to have colonized Mars and then Earth. The theory of 'Extra-terrestrial beings' populating Earth, was largely discounted by the mainstream scientific community of the time. This however, did little to discourage the 'Luminous Lodge'.

For them, *'the absence of evidence was not evidence of absence'*. Their bizarre claim was that the 'Elders' had brought with them a primordial power source called the 'Black Sun' that now rested at the Center of the Earth. This primal source of energy was constantly emitting invisible beams of 'Vril'. The group insisted that this source of energy had been known to the ancients, by different names such as 'Chi', 'Ojas', 'Vril' and 'Orgone.' They were convinced that a single man possessing and directing this most potent of forces, could revolutionize the face of the planet.

And for them that man had to be Adolf Hitler!

CHAPTER FIVE

The members of the 'Luminous Lodge' came from all across the Nazi Party and some, even from the S.S. – Hitler's notorious Para-military unit. Heinrich Himmler, the head of the S.S. was a fervent believer in these ideas and urged S.S. members to research and study, as much as possible about the 'Vril' power source. Himmler used to even conduct seminars, where young members of the S.S. and the S.A. Storm Troopers, could be indoctrinated into these belief systems. It was at one such seminar that Friedrich Gustav found himself being introduced to Himmler.

On first meeting the man, Gustav had experienced a feeling of great discomfort…*not dissimilar to having one's bowels threaten to violently empty their putrid contents!* This was surprising, considering Gustav had already met Hitler a few times and was under no illusions about the future leader's vision for a racially pure Germany…or his fanaticism. He knew that such a project would not come about without a cost…*an enormous one!* However, he had since made his peace with this and his own role in it, by falling back on the old adage that *'the end, indeed does justify the means'.*

However, with Himmler there was something else…something darker…more sinister. It was almost as if this was an 'evil force of nature' hiding in the garb of a man! Throughout their interaction, Gustav had felt like he was being physically dissected, under Himmler's gaze…*like a lab rat!*

His misery had fortunately been brief, and ended when Rudolf Hess had made an appearance and given a speech, in his loud and bombastic way, causing many of the members to leave. Gustav soon realized that all of this had been a deliberate ploy and the obnoxious Hess had been merely playing his part, in what was a choreographed drama! This was Himmler's way of *'separating the wheat from the chaff'.*

With only the elite of the Nazi Party left behind, Himmler, Hess and a couple of others, whom Gustav did not recognize, had one by one taken the podium and explained the 'true nature' of this gathering. These words of 'wisdom' clearly hadn't been for everyone's ears!

Hess had in fact launched into an impressive presentation with the assistance of an older man, in a grey waistcoat, who seemed like a thoroughbred academician. Gustav was quite sure that it was this man's research that Hess was banding around, with such aplomb. Nonetheless, his presentation had caused a stir and Gustav noticed that it made even the normally placid Adolf Hitler, sit up and take notice.

Hess first explained how the members of the Thule Society came from all across the Nazi party and performed different roles, be it administrative or military...and also how some of the core objectives of the 'Thule' differed significantly, from the official 'Nazi Party-line'. But the one thing that united them was the desire to bring back German pride, under what was now being called the 'Third Reich.'

Hess then went on to describe the core beliefs of the Thule Society... the theories about 'Hyperborea'...the 'Hollow-Earth' hypothesis... 'Vril' and the 'Black Sun'...Even though, Gustav himself, had heard and read most of this, these 'revelations' did come as a shock to a section of the audience. Gustav had even looked over to see Hitler's reaction to these wild speculations...but from his expression, it had been impossible to make out what the great leader truly thought of these theories.

Of course Gustav knew that in a setting like this, no one in the audience...regardless of how he/she felt about what was being said, would dare raise questions or demand evidence for these claims. Even in the early 1920s, the hierarchy within the Nazi Party was iron-clad and unbreakable!

Hess, meanwhile, keen not to disappoint, barreled through a volley of subjects that ranged from 'genuine science and history' to 'pseudo-science'...to what could only be described as 'psycho-babble'. He started off by explaining the reason why the Emblem of the 'Order of the Black Sun', was different from that of the Nazi Party's official Insignia. Instead of the 'white circle with the Swastika in it,' at the center of a red flag, the 'Black Sun Society' used a 'red flag with a colored-in black circle' at its center…representing the 'Black Sun'…an emblem, he went on to display.

At this point, a hushed silence fell across the room. Gustav could almost hear the thoughts of the others… 'Surely Hess had gone too far…this was blasphemy! To challenge Hitler's vision even in spirit, by presenting an alternate emblem to the accepted Nazi Party Insignia was risking the wrath of the Führer'. Gustav knew that Hitler had a history of backing group that he deemed loyal…and then suddenly, without any prior warning…literally tossing them under the bus, for offending him. There had been many…many groups that had lost Hitler's favor, for offending him in ways that were much more trivial than what Hess had just done!

In fact, during the first half of the 1920s, a violent rivalry had taken place among the Occult Societies and Secret Lodges in Germany. But by the time the Nazis would eventually come to power, most of these groups that hadn't been loyal to them would be completely wiped out.

Adolf Hitler was not a man to be trifled with. Even established religion was not necessarily safe from his auspices. Heavily influenced by Nietzsche's writings and the creed of the Thule Society, Hitler even believed that Christianity was a weak and corrupted religion, for at its roots lay what he called the 'infection of Jewish-thinking'. For him, Christianity, with its emphasis on the principles of 'Forgiveness' and 'Self-abnegation' was 'pathetic' and 'anti-evolutionary'! Instead, he saw *himself* as the 'Messiah', replacing God and Christ. He even envisioned ridding the world of a degenerate system and bringing about humanity's next evolutionary jump, with the 'Aryan Master Race'.

Gustav once again looked over to see how Hitler would react to Hess' claims, but try as he might; he once again found it impossible to decode the great leader's expressions. Gustav knew this was one of the things that made Hitler such a powerful and charismatic individual. The fact that he could remain extremely placid…his face betraying no emotion whatsoever, when he chose to and then go suddenly from there to an extremely passionate and *even agitated state*, when he spoke, meant that you as a listener, felt compelled to follow him…no matter what! Gustav knew that once you felt Hitler's eyes on you, it changed you as a person forever. Now however, except for slightly leaning ahead in his seat, the leader kept a poker face.

Seemingly unconcerned, Hess proceeded to give an elaborate explanation about why the 'Order of the Black Sun' had chosen this motif. He explained how the inspiration behind this had come from a secret philosophy that was thousands of years old. The academician, Hess had brought along, pulled out a series of large etchings and pictures that had been rolled up, and displayed them against the podium. Since the confines of the room did not allow these to be displayed on a screen of any kind, the ageing man had to hold them open, using both his hands and gently swing them around, so that all in the room could see.

At first, there was barely any interest in the room, and all but the most devout members, remained seated. Gustav got up from his seat to get a closer look at the pictures. The images were mostly black and white and looked very much like grainy photo-negatives that seemed to have been taken, from *inside* tombs or memorials, in extremely poor lighting. The academician tried his best to invoke interest in the audience, by repeatedly turning them, this way and that. But the utter disinterest in the room was palpable!

Gustav was able to count four, maybe five people in the room, who showed even the slightest trace of interest in what Hess was saying. Among those were Gustav himself, Haushofer, Himmler and possibly Hitler...although judging by his expressions, it was best not to conclude anything. At the back of the room the puffy and obnoxious, Herman Goring – the former ace fighter pilot from World War I, audibly yawned. Gustav held his breath...such impudence from anyone else...in the presence of Adolf Hitler, would surely have resulted in severe consequences!

In the final days of World War I, Herman Goring had received an abdominal injury that had caused him to spend long hours confined to a hospital bed. During this time, the 'larger than life' and jovial soldier had become addicted to food and some said...even morphine, causing him to gain a lot of weight. This resulted in him feeling constantly sleepy and uncomfortable, particularly during seminars. Goring considered himself a military man and a decisive leader of men…and largely above scruffy academicians, who knew nothing outside the library.

For all his faults however, Goring was a valuable ally, *if not a very charming one*…and Hitler seemed to have different goals for him. There were already rumors Gustav had heard that Goring was working with Hitler in trying to create Germany's own band of the Secret Police…the 'Gestapo', to spy on civilians, believed to be disloyal to the Nazis. The large, puffy former fighter pilot clearly enjoyed more favor than most with Hitler.

Hess, unconcerned with the soporific impact he was having on his audience, launched into even wilder theories about how ancient civilizations from Sumeria and Babylonia, venerated the 'Black Sun' as an infinite source of divine power. Sporadically he would point to the charts that the academician was still gingerly holding up, and spew out the names of ancient deities, who allegedly carried the emblem of the Black Sun. For most in the audience, the names meant nothing at all and try as they might; they found it impossible to understand what this man was trying to say. But to the few, who were well versed with the occult, like Haushofer, Himmler and possibly even Hitler, Hess' rant contained the promise of a glorious new age!

Hess pointed out to a grainy image on one of the charts the academician was unfurling, and said that the image on it was that of the Babylonian deity 'Marduk'. He explained that the enigmatic pendant the deity wore around his neck was in fact the Babylonian depiction of this 'invisible power'. The Phoenicians and the Carthaginians…two great seafaring civilizations, were also apparently aware of this philosophy and ardently worshipped the Black Sun, as a source of God's power on Earth.

Hess spoke of how the Assyrians commonly referred to the Black Sun as a 'Black Cross' and audaciously claimed that the fact that this symbol closely resembled the 'Cross of the German Knight', was proof that the Nazis were being guided to their glorious destiny on Earth, by the power of the 'Inner light of God'…the 'Black Sun'. He concluded by saying that the 'torchbearer' of this wondrous power would be none other than Adolf Hitler.

At this point, regardless of how many in the audience had really understood Hess' speech, the uncanny resemblance between the ancient depictions of the Black Sun and the German Insignia, caused everyone to leap to their feet in thunderous and spontaneous applause. Seizing the moment, Hess delivered the perfect testimony of his loyalty to his leader, with the guttural cry… 'Heil Hitler!!!'

Gustav marveled at the oratory skill of this man, who within the span of one talk had managed to turn the perception of the audience completely upside down. Rudolf Hess, in the years to come, was surely going to be a force to reckon with. But *if* what he had spoken of was in any way true, Hitler's dream of creating a thousand-year 'Reich' could one day also come true.

Even Hitler, forever a master at hiding his emotions, allowed himself a smile!

CHAPTER SIX

In the years following this briefing, Gustav met with Haushofer, Hess and Himmler regularly to further discuss these ideas. As his interest in the subject grew, he found himself gravitating more towards a life of research and adventure, than military service.

To Gustav, Karl Haushofer was a legend. He never tired of listening to the details of Haushofer's forays into India and his many ventures into the crumbling, old corners of the country, in search of the past. He spent most of his weekends either trying to read up about the myths and legends of the Far-East or pestering the much older Haushofer to educate him in these aspects. To the older stately gentleman, Gustav's enthusiasm was like a breath of fresh air and he always enjoyed the young man's presence, often inviting him over to dine, at his own Bavarian country home.

It was during one such interaction that Haushofer accidentally mentioned something about an ancient manuscript, he had found at an Indian monastery...a book titled the 'Vimanika Shastra' – the Science of Aeronautics. This slip had occurred as a result of a little too much wine on Haushofer's part. Gustav was sure that such information was ordinarily meant only for the Thule 'elite', a privilege that he did not enjoy...*yet*.

Nonetheless, with the secret now out, Haushofer had to describe the incident to his much younger protégé, after securing a promise of absolute secrecy. At numerous points during the long talks that followed, Gustav's brain threatened to explode, with the sheer deluge of information. Listening to Hess ramble on about mystical forces and ancient civilizations at the Nazi Party conference, was one thing, but to hear from a person, whom he deeply respected and who had actually come across 'tangible' proof of such powers...was absolutely intoxicating!

Delighted by the young man's palpable fascination, the paternal instincts in Haushofer had taken over what remained of his desire to keep secrets and he began to show Gustav, the memory-based drawings and writings, he had made about that text. He described how even though the monks had not allowed him to 'borrow' or 'copy' the manuscript, he had managed to commit to memory...as much of it as possible!

Gustav was amazed to find that the book contained not just descriptions of ancient Indian flying devices, called 'Vimanas' or 'Bird-like devices' but also detailed instructions on how to construct and use one!!! The book even had pictures that Haushofer had done his best to reproduce...blueprints of these 'Vimanas', right down to their powering mechanisms!

Gustav gazed in wonder, as Haushofer showed him a total of ten memory based drawings he had made with varying levels of accuracy and varying levels of detailing. The first thing that struck him, was that these 'blueprints' looked nothing like conventional aircrafts, in terms of aerodynamics. None of the images he saw had the streamlined bodies that all aircrafts need, to be able to navigate the skies effectively.

Instead, most of the crafts, in Haushofer's drawings looked like 'floating castles'...broad at the bottom and tapering ever so slightly towards the top...almost like 'minarets'. One of the images even looked a little like a large 'bell' or an 'acorn'. Nowhere in any of these pictures was there any indication of any kind of a 'wing apparatus'... something so essential to any flying craft!

Although Gustav didn't dare to voice his concerns loudly, deep down inside, he felt that these drawings were nothing more than an elaborate hoax! He was sure that Haushofer had been sincere in his depictions...but the manuscript itself could not be trusted. Why else would the monks at the monastery be so protective about the contents of a book that was, as it is, on the verge of falling apart?

Haushofer noticed Gustav's skepticism and told him how even he had harboured similar doubts, on first seeing the book. Absolutely anyone giving it a cursory read would think of it as a hoax...*so outrageous were its contents!*

However, Haushofer's association with the document hadn't been just that. He described how throughout his years in Japan, he had been greatly fascinated by the myths and legends of the Far-East and especially the two great Indian Epics – The Ramayana and the Mahabharata. Gustav did not see how this information was related to this document and his expressions seemed to betray his thoughts.

As if sensing this, Haushofer suddenly asked him point blank, "How much do you know about ancient Indian literature?"

"I don't claim to be a scholar in it, but I know enough to acknowledge that neither the Mahabharata nor the Ramayana mention this document that you saw in India. In fact, this is, I believe the first such reference of the name 'Vimanika Shastra' that I have ever come across, till date." Gustav answered cautiously.

"True...like I told you, I was equally skeptical, when I first beheld the text...so following my sojourn in India, I dedicated the next several years of my life, researching Indian history and faith traditions. It turns out that there is lot of stuff that the literature contains that is beyond the stories themselves...lot of really fascinating stuff that the British won't admit to. It has been a consistent policy of the Colonialists to demean and demonize the traditions of the sub-continent, so that their own power and moral authority remains unchallenged!"

"Like what?" Gustav's curiosity was now piqued. He had read the German versions of some of the great Indian epics, but how accurate the translations had been, he couldn't say. Moreover, as he had already admitted, he was no scholar on these things.

"I will clue you into a secret my boy...*one that I haven't discussed even with Hitler*...I want to be really sure that he *IS* the leader, we think him to be...and with Himmler's influence constantly around him, I am not quite so sure yet. Something about the way this party functions, bothers me...and I fear we have some difficult times ahead of us."

Gustav didn't say a word. Haushofer had just voiced his own deepest...*darkest* thoughts. But admitting to something like this, in such polarized times, wasn't always a good idea...sometimes it was best to keep a straight face and a sealed mouth!

It was already quite late in the evening now...and the orange hue of the setting Sun, was beginning to cast its long shadows, all across Haushofer's living room. The two of them were seated next to an indoor fireplace, into which the housekeeper had just introduced some freshly scented pieces of pine wood. As the logs burned, a wonderful aroma wafted through the air, creating the perfect setting for a revelation, *intended to invoke the ghosts of the past!*

Haushofer took a long drag from his pipe...before beginning his extraordinary account, "As I told you earlier, I spent long years researching the myths and legends of ancient India...those that are well known and those that are suppressed by foreign powers. One of the things I noticed right away was that when most people try to educate themselves in Indian tradition, they judge themselves adept enough to grasp the full extent of these traditions...on their own. This was, I realized, a monumental blunder!"

"They have a saying in India, that you can only ever truly grasp the purpose of your own life, if it is revealed to you, by a great teacher...a 'Guru'. It is why ancient Indian societies placed such a heavy emphasis on the tradition of a 'teacher-student relationship'...a tradition that was destroyed, with the arrival of the Colonialists. To the British, this glorification of a teacher or a mentor, seemed like a 'smooth' way of justifying the much maligned 'Caste System' of India...with a special privilege accorded to the Brahmins, who were responsible for educating the others. However, this System had also for centuries, ensured that the texts Hinduism considers sacred, were not studied carelessly. "

"I realized the significance of this tradition *only* when I began my studies...naively making the same assumption that many before me had...that I could acquire this knowledge...entirely on my own. But as I delved deeper into some of the literature, I found myself trapped in an absolute tangle...the more I studied, the less I understood." Haushofer sighed softly...remembering those long and confusing days; he had spent as a student of Indian literature.

"It was sometime during the fifth year of my studies that I undertook a journey to the sacred city of Allahabad in Northern India...a city known for the famous 'Tirveni Sangam' - the meeting of three great rivers: The Ganges, the Yamuna and the mythical Sarasvati."

"It was here late one evening, in a remote part of the old city, while searching for more documents that a strange bearded man…a sage or 'Sadhu' as they call them in India, suddenly appeared in front of me. I had heard a little about these Indian holy men…let me tell you… *most of it quite bad*…they were known to lure westerners, by pretending to have magical powers and then con them out of whatever they had."

"But there was something remarkable about this man and the way he appeared to me. His face seemed to have an inner light and his entire persona radiated power. And even though his smile was soft and gentle, his gaze seemed to pierce the very depths of my soul and his long flowing white beard seemed to reflect some powerful inner truth!"

"When he spoke to me, he addressed me by name, even though I had only just met him and claimed to know the full nature of my quest. I was stunned…I tried to speak…but no words came out. Unmoved, the sage asked me to follow him, as he lithely turned around and began to walk. I remember even now, how for a moment, I stood rooted to my spot…a million questions crossing my mind… Who was this man? How did he know me and what I was looking for? Was this an elaborate con…a trap? *What the hell was I getting into?*"

"I looked around and saw that a strange fog now seemed to permeate the air, cloaking everything. I was barely able to see ten feet in front of me and just about hear the sage's footsteps, from where I stood."

'Come my child, when in doubt, reach out and clutch the hand of God and in him, put your trust.'…a sudden chill in the surroundings caused me to follow him.

"To this day, I cannot remember anything about the journey… neither the route, nor the destination. I have since then tried many times to retrace the steps that I took on that fateful day, but I could never again find the sage or anyone, who knew of him! All I remember is that after what seemed like hours, but it might as well have been seconds, our journey ended at a mysterious stone monument that was shaped like a jewel…*like a newly blossoming lotus petal*. Just beyond that was a small mud brick enclosure…probably the saint's house…I couldn't be sure. There was so much of this weird fog all around that I could not make out much in any case."

"Here the sage finally stopped and turned towards me, speaking in a voice that sounded strangely familiar...not the same tone that I had earlier heard him use, but one that I felt I had heard all my life."

"Disturbed by this, I looked around me and tried to see through this thick fog that had by now completely enveloped us...and noticed something unusual. All around there was simply a dull amber hue... but the very physical structure of the place seemed to constantly ebb and flow, refusing to retain its cohesive structure...*almost as if the walls of space and time were trying to reach out to us!* In all my years on the road, I had never come across such a place...not in Allahabad... not in India. Truth be told my boy, I do not think we were actually even on Earth!"

For all his Nazi Party training and the tough military education he had received under the S.S. Gustav felt a chill run up and down his spine. Haushofer's description of his encounter with an esoteric, old Indian sage was having a powerful impact on him and the eerie half-light created by the flickering flames from the fire-place was adding to the feel of the story. Gustav could have sworn that *he* was part of the narrative!

"The sage spoke to me for a long time." Haushofer continued, his eyes now half closed, recalling the incident. "To this day I remember everything that he said to me...as if it were said, yesterday. He explained to me the significance of studying ancient Indian traditions in a proper format...one; I had scoffed at for so long. I had tried to focus exclusively on the two epics – the Ramayana and the Mahabharata, since both of them contained references to 'Vimanas' or flying machines. This had always been my primary area of interest. However, what I had never realized was that the two epics cannot be studied by themselves. They collectively form part of a much wider and immensely more detailed body of work that can together be called the 'Vedic Traditions'. The sage impressed upon me the magnitude of my blunder...*I had been focusing so much on the individual trees that I had completely missed the forest they were part of!*"

"It was then that I understood the reason behind the old Indian adage of having a 'Guru'...a mentor to *really* comprehend Indian literature. I, on the other hand, had been using the worst possible approach. All my years of research had probably been a complete waste of time! 'Disappointed' is not enough to describe how I felt at that moment. My life work was lying in shambles in front of my eyes and I had no idea how to salvage it. I found myself faced with two impossible choices...give up my quest and return to Germany or restart the whole thing and keep at it for as long as it takes!"

"Probably, the saint felt sorry for me, for he then went on to flood my mind with knowledge...a deluge that I felt absolutely privileged to receive...I was able to receive the full knowledge of the 'Vedic Traditions' in just one-sitting, rather than the years that it normally took!!"

"I cannot say precisely for how long the saint spoke...to me, time and space had lost all meaning. But so powerful were his words and so profound was his understanding, that regardless of its sheer magnitude and complexity, his words will remain forever etched in my memory."

"The Vedas are held in such high esteem in Indian faith tradition since they contain all of the wisdom of the sub-continent, condensed into four books. These are literally referred to as the 'Whispers of God'. The books are meant to serve as a guide to a way of life that is as close to establishing a perfect balance with nature as possible! The sage then spoke of the significance of Vedic rituals, including those that govern different aspects of human existence, from life till death. The human condition is seen as the pinnacle of life...*the only being that has the capacity to understand God*...and as such we have a responsibility towards others in nature. I realized then that the rituals I had naively rubbished as meaningless superstitions meant to further the Brahmin cause were actually reminders of this balance between us and the rest of the natural world!"

"The sage explained to me about the four 'Purush Arthas' or the four stages of human existence that each person must go through on his/her way to enlightenment. This principle emphasized the importance of the journey itself and not just the 'end goal'...a principle that we in the west, so often ignore. He spoke of how unlike most other stories, there were no true heroes or villains in the two epics. Their real wisdom lay in something far greater than just a triumph of Good over Evil...it was about the journey that the characters, both the protagonists and the antagonists, undertake, in realizing their ultimate destiny. The Mahabharata in fact describes how at the end of the Great War...at the end of the epic, there were no true 'winners' or 'losers'. For those in the epic, the battle of Kurukshetra was more an *internal struggle* than an *external one*...more a battle with the self...of overcoming one's own ego, than of overcoming one's opponent!"

"It was only once I had understood the real essence of Hindu thought that the sage began to describe the accounts, mentioned in the epics and the significance of some of the 'divine powers' described therein."

"What powers?" Gustav breathed softly...*Haushofer's narrative had fully lured him in.*

Haushofer smiled softly, "Do you know for example that while there are numerous references to 'Vimanas' in both the epics and also other sources of Hindu Mythologies, the essential feature of these technologies lies in the name itself – 'Vimana' meaning 'bird-like'. To the average layman, this might seem like a straight forward description of a 'flying machine', but ancient Hindu scholars were prone to describe existential truths using colorful metaphors. In this instance, the word 'Vimana' is also a reference to the *'flight of Human Consciousness'* or 'ascending' to a higher state of consciousness!!!"

CHAPTER SEVEN

'Vimanas, decked and equipped according to rule, looked like heavenly structures in the sky . . . borne away they looked like highly beautiful flights of birds'. – The Mahabharata

"You mean all these descriptions are just an elaborate hoax? ...mere metaphors? ...nothing more than that?" Gustav almost screamed... the exasperation, clear in his voice.

"No my boy...the technologies that are described in the epics are very real! The metaphor is a reference to what *POWERS* these crafts!!!"

"What?" Gustav began...and suddenly paused...his attention drawn to a stack of papers that Haushofer put in front of him. On one of these, Gustav saw penciled notes Haushofer had made years ago, while trying to collate all that he had learnt.

"Over the years...*THIS* is what research has revealed." Haushofer said simply...his face dead serious.

As Gustav began to go through the notes, he found that they weren't in any particular order...it seemed very much like they were part of Haushofer's private research...*meant only for his eyes.* But in these papers, were details about the 'Vimana' that his mentor had written down...details compiled from various sources including a few from what is widely believed to be India's oldest book- the 'Rg Veda'.

Jalayan - a vehicle designed to operate in air and water. - Rig Veda 6.58.3

Kaara - a vehicle that operates on ground and in water -Rig Veda 9.14.1

Tritala - a vehicle consisting of three levels- Rig Veda 3.14.1

Trichakra Ratha - a three-wheeled vehicle designed to operate in the air - Rig Veda 4.36.1

Vaayu Ratha - a gas or wind-powered chariot - Rig Veda 5.41.6

Vidyut Ratha - a vehicle that operates on power - Rig Veda 3.14.1

It was clear from the notes that the original term for the flying machine was "Ratha" which gave way to the term "Vimana". The 'Samarangana Sutradhara' unequivocally suggested that the design of the plane was intended to resemble a palace. It was built by certain special entities known as 'Rbhus' for the Gods.

The texts of the Rig Veda ranging from the 1st -10th 'Mandalas' referred to aerial flying machines as 'Ratha'. There were references to these vehicles also known as 'Rathas' or chariots in both the Ramayana and the Mahabharata that Haushofer had documented, after years of meticulous research. But on closer inspection, it was clear that the references spoke of no mere chariots but something far superior.

In the 'Yajur Veda' which is considered chronologically *later* than the 'Rg Veda', the name "Vimana" occurs, as a possible synonym for the 'Flying Chariot'.

These vehicles were said to appear in many different forms. In the Vedic texts however the configuration of the machines was broadly shown as triangular. The inside area, was roughly 9 feet by 9 feet...a total of 81 sq. feet, an area, large enough to accommodate 7 or 8 people.

The descriptions of the flying 'aerial cities' that Haushofer had listed out from the two epics, seemed to indicate a higher degree of scientific achievement and technical skill. The flying cities were also described as being larger in size and capable of flying much higher.

Gustav read some of these references... and although not in order, the citations made it clear that there was something really, really strange, going on in these epics...*something almost unbelievable to the modern mind!*

His eyes went over some of the descriptions, compiled from the Ramayana-

- You may go to your desired place after enticing Sita and I shall bring her to Lanka by air.
- So Ravana and Maricha boarded the Vimana, resembling a palace from that hermitage.
- Then the demons brought the 'Pushpaka' aerial vehicle and placed Sita on it, by bringing her from the 'Ashoka forest' and she was made to see the battle field with Trijata.

- This aerial vehicle marked with Swan, soared into the sky with a loud noise.

Gustav held his head with both his hands… *'Surely, this was some kind of hoax!'*

On the next page, were numerous references from the Mahabharata!

One of the most significant episodes spoke of an aerial attack on Krishna's capital city of Dwaraka by a king named Salva. There was an elaborate description of how the demon king Salva had an aerial flying machine known as 'Saubha-pura', in which he attacked the island of Dwaraka.

The text described how he began to shower hailstones and arrows from the sky. As Krishna chased him, he went and landed in the high seas. Then he came back up again and once again fought Krishna while flying at an altitude of about one Krosa - roughly about 4,000 feet in modern terms - above ground. Krishna at last hurled a powerful divine weapon, which hit the plane right in the middle and broke it into pieces. The damaged flying machine fell into the Arabian Sea.

What was most extraordinary was that these descriptions about the 'Vimana' were so *pedantic*…that it was as if the narrator was describing an 'everyday' occurrence. *Yet* they spoke of 'flying chariots' and these epics were thousands of years old!!!

Even more astonishing, was that some of the references Haushofer had put together, contained details of the weapons, these 'Vimanas' carried! So apparently, these vehicles carried their own 'arsenal' as well!

But it was the descriptions of the weapons and the impact they were said to have, which most troubled Gustav. These 'unearthly weapons were said to be 'magical' or 'divine' and their effects were truly devastating! Gustav read a few references that were supposedly from the Mahabharata.

"A single projectile charged with all the power of the Universe. An incandescent column of smoke and flame as bright as the thousand suns rose in all its splendor…

"A perpendicular explosion with its billowing smoke clouds... the cloud of smoke rising after its first explosion formed into expanding round circles like the opening of giant parasols...

"It was an unknown weapon, an iron thunderbolt, a gigantic messenger of death, which reduced to ashes...the entire race of the 'Vrishnis' and the 'Andhakas'...The corpses were so burned as to be unrecognizable. The hair and nails fell out; Pottery broke without apparent cause, and the birds turned white. After a few hours all foodstuffs were infected...to escape from this fire, the soldiers threw themselves in streams to wash themselves and their equipment."

"Dense arrows of flame, like a great shower, issued forth, encompassing the enemy... A thick gloom swiftly settled upon the hosts. All points of the compass were lost in darkness. Fierce wind began to blow upward, showering dust and gravel. Birds croaked madly... the very elements seemed disturbed. The earth shook, scorched by the terrible violent heat of this weapon. Elephants burst into flames and ran to and fro in frenzy...over a vast area, other animals crumpled to the ground and died. From all points of the compass the arrows of flame rained continuously and fiercely." 'Mausala Parva' - The Mahabharata.

And another one that was said to be from the Ramayana:-

"It was a weapon so powerful that it could destroy the earth in an instant. A great soaring sound in smoke and flames and on it, sits death..."

Gustav sat back...his mind reeling!! "This is a hoax...it MUST be... how could an ancient civilization know all this...it's impossible...if the Vedic traditions do carry the echoes of such knowledge, why is it that we don't know anything about them?"

Haushofer did not answer the question...he seemed lost to the world...still recalling the conversations, he had with the sage. He took a long drag from his pipe, allowing the tobacco to crawl deep into his lungs, soothing his insides...drawing strength from its vapors. Then, after what seemed like an eternity, he spoke softly, "These were my exact thoughts when I first found out about this. But before I answer your question, you need to grasp the level of scientific understanding that the culture, who wrote the Vedas had. One only has to look at the way these texts describe the functioning of 'Time', to understand this."

"The Vedic conception of time is fundamentally different from ours. In classical Indian tradition, universal time is divided into different periods. These periods are linked to the lifetime of one of the primordial entities in Hindu cosmology...Brahma - the Creator, who operates on a scale that is almost unfathomable to those on Earth. For instance, one day of Brahma is equivalent to 4,320,000,000 of our years on earth. Brahma's night is equally as long and there are 360 such days and nights in one year of Brahma!"

Gustav simply stared.

"Each day of Brahma is divided into one thousand cycles of four 'Yugas' or eras, namely the 'Satya-Yuga', the 'Treta-Yuga', the 'Dvapara-Yuga', and finally the 'Kali-Yuga', which is the one, we presently are in. The 'Satya-Yuga' lasts 1,728,000 years, and is an age of 'absolute purity' when all residents live extremely long lives and have tremendous mystical and spiritual powers. Some of these abilities include changing one's shape, becoming very large or microscopically small, becoming very heavy or even weightless, securing any desirable thing, becoming free of all desires, or even flying through the sky to wherever one wanted to go on one's own account. So during this Yuga the need for using mechanical flying machines was not felt."

"But as the Yugas continue, there is a downward trend in humanity's purity and values. The second Yuga – the 'Treta-Yuga' sees evil raise its ugly head for the first time and lasts 1,296,000 years. During this age, the human mind become increasingly dense, and finds it difficult to understand the higher spiritual principles, described in the Vedas. Society starts to become more ritualistic and self-centric and the ability to fly through the sky by one's own power, is lost. It is said that it is during this period that the events described in the Ramayana took place. The first of India's two great epics, describes the clash between the just God-King Rama and his arch nemesis the pious yet unjust Demon-king Ravana, who had kidnapped Rama's wife. At the end of the epic, Rama rescues his wife Sita, slays the demon king and restores law and order in the universe."

"The era that follows the 'Treta-Yuga', is known as the 'Dvapara-Yuga' and it lasts 864,000 years. This is the era, when the 'Battle of Kurukshetra', described in the Mahabharata takes place. The battle is again for restoring 'Dharma' or 'the righteous code' and is fought between two sets of cousins.

It is said that the end of the war saw so many rules of 'Dharma' or 'Righteousness' being violated that society slipped into the fourth age …the darkest of all, where evil reigns supreme…the 'Kali Yuga'…the era that we currently inhabit. The 'Kali-Yuga' lasts 432,000 years, of which 5,000 have now already passed. During this period, mankind reaches its absolute nadir as 'Dharma' the foundation of human morality is completely compromised in an era of base materialism. In the 'Kali Yuga', mankind loses almost all spiritual understanding and as a result, is unable to access any of the 'mystical abilities', described in Hindu tradition."

"At the end of the 'Kali-Yuga', the age of 'Satya-Yuga' starts again and the Yugas continue through another cycle. One thousand such cycles is one day of Brahma! This is quite extraordinary, considering that for a long time we in the West, had a hard time accepting that the Earth and the universe were older than 6000 years. One lifetime of Brahma clearly puts the number in the billions of years mark!"

"There is another very interesting thing that the sage spoke to me about. It is something that I have spent a lot of time trying to 'de-bunk' and yet as improbable as it is, I have been forced to accept it. Ancient Vedic tradition uses several units to measure distance and time. One such unit of measuring distance is called the 'Yojana' that is approximately the equivalent of 9 miles in our terms, and one such unit of time is called 'Nimisha' that is 16/75 of a second. Now the 'Rg Veda' mentions that the sun's light traverses 2,202 Yojana in half a Nimisha. If we translate this into the units we use today, we get the speed of the sun's light according to Vedic tradition as 189574 miles per second!!! This is very close to what we know the speed of light as 186000 miles per second!"

"What? How can that be possible? How the hell did they calculate something like that…in the Bronze Age?" Gustav gasped.

"Yes...keep in mind the slight variance we get, could also be because we have approximated the unit called the 'Yojana' as being roughly equal to 9 miles! Such is the knowledge to be found in this tradition that when I understood the full extent of it, I had to rethink my earlier conclusions about the document I had found. Surely, a culture that had the capacity for such scientific acumen was capable of using technology that has since been lost to history!"

CHAPTER EIGHT

Throughout the dusky firmament advancing,
Laying to rest the immortal and the mortal,
Borne in his golden chariot he cometh,
Savitar, God who looks on every creature.
A seven-named horse draws the three naved wheel,
Seven steeds draw the seven-wheeled chariot,
Wise poets have spun a seven-strand tale,
And glorified this Heavenly calf, the Sun. - The Rg Veda.

"We must find out more about this!" Gustav spoke, his voice full of passion, "If we get our hands on these ancient secrets, the future would be ours to shape...just imagine, we could bring in a new Golden Age! Perhaps that's what the legends speak of...after the 'Kali Yuga', the cycle repeats...maybe *WE* are the ones prophesied to bring in the 'Satya Yuga'!"

"All we have to do is find that text again. We can launch a joint expedition to India and re-visit the monastery, where you saw it. Between the two of us, surely we shall find some way of smuggling that book out. After all it's much too valuable to be just lying in the care of some Buddhist monks, who I am sure, don't even realize its significance."

"If only it were as simple as that..." Haushofer shook his head and sighed, "You really think I haven't considered this possibility before? Every waking moment of my life, since I met the sage, I have thought about it. Unfortunately, there have been many factors over the years that have prevented me from acting on it."

"First and foremost, we need to consider that the area of British - India, where this monastery lies, is no longer an easy place to access. The Russians have long had an influence in Tibet and by extension

Sikkim, and especially, following some bitter defeats in the recently concluded World War, the British fear that the newly formed 'Bolsheviks' in Russia, might try and expand their own territory for financial gains. If these fears prove true, then the British will have a lot on their plates, in the Indian territories bordering China. As you know quite well, the opium trade that the British have with China, is especially lucrative and they would want nothing to jeopardize it."

"But surely, *we* could get permission to visit the monastery? After all, we don't represent any of the threats that you just mentioned." Gustav argued...*unwilling to concede so easily.*

"You forget my friend, due to our role in the recently concluded War; We Germans haven't exactly endeared ourselves to the British. Two members of the Nazi Party – a party that the British Media sees as brutal and intolerant, would almost certainly be denied access to a sensitive location *INSIDE* British territory. On what grounds do you propose we get our Visas approved? Sikkim is definitely not on most tourists' agenda and we can of course never reveal the true purpose of our visit. Even those in the Nazi Party are unaware of what I have shared with you. Imagine the stir it would cause within *our* circles, if Himmler or Hess knew what I know!"

"So then why *HAVE* you kept this a secret for so long...why did you never reveal this in any of our meetings? We spent so much time discussing New Age Power Sources and concepts like the 'Vril'...yet all of those seem to pale in front of what you claim to have seen." Gustav demanded aggressively...but then...bit back on his words...he knew it had only been the alcohol that had caused Haushofer to confess all of this...and he did not want the older statesman to feel threatened and cover up, again.

"I cannot say for certain, why I have kept this secret for so long. Many are the times, I have felt like sharing what I know, especially when I see my countrymen struggling to regain their lost pride, in these difficult times. But something has always held me back. Maybe it's the feeling that we aren't quite 'ready' yet for such a revelation... 'Spiritually ready' or maybe it's something that the sage whispered to me towards the end of our dialogue."

"What?" Gustav asked in wonderment.

Haushofer took a long breath, unsure how to explain this next bit, "Well you see my boy, as I listened to the words of wisdom pouring out of the sage's mouth, I couldn't help but get the feeling that he knew far more about the nature of my quest...than he was letting on. I knew that there was something very strange going on over there. All of this information, in all its extreme complexity, was making absolute sense to me."

"Now I must confess that I have never been a very good listener, and even though I have tried hard to overcome this handicap, I have always found it hard to retain large amounts of information. And yet there I was, able to understand and retain every word the sage said, like I already knew all of it. His words were able to penetrate the very depths of my being!"

"So unusual was this that after a while, I began to suspect that the sage was able to read my innermost thoughts. I had heard legends of Hindu saints, who possessed supernatural mystical powers, but I had always rubbished them as wild superstitions. Yet here I was sitting in front of an unknown man, who knew all about me!"

"I was keen to test this out and so even as he was speaking, I mustered up some courage and asked him directly, if he knew anything about the book I had seen...the one that described the 'Vimanas'."

Gustav could barely breathe.

"I was fully convinced that the sage would rebuke me for this abrupt interruption. But instead, his eyes twinkled and his face lit up with a broad smile. He told me that he knew my reasons for being here and had been merely testing me to find out if I was indeed worthy of such knowledge."

"I was stunned. Did that mean that I would finally get the answers to my questions? The sage nodded slowly and whispered that sometimes the answers we seek are quite different from the ones we *THINK* them to be."

"What does that mean?" Gustav asked...now a little cautiously.

"Well...the sage's cryptic reference meant that there were things that he wasn't willing to share yet, and try as I might, I could not get him to elaborate. So I did the next best thing I could think of, and showed him the drawings I had made from what I had seen at the monastery."

"You mean these etchings?" Gustav questioned, picking some of them up to once again study them.

"Yes...except the ones you hold right now...contain way more details than what I showed to the saint. As I have told you before, my keen interest in Indian spiritual traditions had inspired me to equip myself with a functional knowledge of Sanskrit, to the point where I could read the script reasonably well...*if not always understand it.* Even at the monastery, while I was able to get a fair idea of what that document was about, some of the finer details had been lost on me. The only saving grace had been that the text was accompanied by illustrations...illustrations that I was able to memorize and later reproduce."

"I fully expected the sage, for all his wonderful insights and wisdom, to have no knowledge about the document, I was referring to. But much to my amazement, his face beamed with recognition when he saw my drawings. He even complimented me on my renditions, haphazard though they might have been...occasionally chuckling to himself, when he observed some of the mistakes I had made. I distinctly remember he pointed out some of my flaws, using names like 'Rukma-Vimana'...and even suggested a few corrections."

"I wrote down like mad whatever this mysterious mystic was saying, all the while trying to suppress my excitement. After my disappointment at the monastery, I had almost given up hope of ever finding out more about this extraordinary document. No matter whom I spoke to, I had never received any meaningful insights, on how to proceed with my quest. And yet, after months of unsuccessfully searching for some illumination, the answers themselves seemed to have found *me.* Here...you can look at my original papers and notice some of the changes and corrections that the sage made." So saying Haushofer handed Gustav another bundle of papers...that looked a little older, as they had been carefully rolled up.

Reverently, Gustav held out his hand and proceeded to gently unfurl them out onto a table. He noticed that these papers contained many of the same drawings he had already seen, but the main difference was that the artwork on these seemed extremely rushed and crude. This was of course because Haushofer had scribbled these out from memory, as he had left the monastery all those years ago.

Gustav was impressed. While of course there would be errors in Haushofer's renditions, the fact that in some forgotten corner of India lay a book outlining technology far beyond any that was in use today, was mouthwatering! Next to each of these images, Haushofer had scribbled various words, which in some cases had been overwritten. Gustav realized that these were probably the corrections the sage had suggested.

Haushofer had already mentioned that in the original text, there were detailed descriptions, next to each device that contained the names of that particular device and its operating procedures...almost like a rule-book. Unfortunately, as the words had been in ancient Sanskrit, he had been able to arrive at only a partial understanding of what those terms meant. Looking at these depictions though, Gustav once again felt within himself, the intense urge...the desire...of wanting to see this quest through!

But before he could voice his feelings, something written on one of the papers next to an illustrated 'Vimana', caught his attention. It was a single word in the Indian 'Devanagri' script that had been highlighted by Haushofer. But what most fascinated Gustav was that next to this word, was an arrow head...like a bullet-point. The arrow head connected the word with what appeared to be the 'fueling mechanism' of the Vimana...a primitive fuselage of sorts! Was this an indication of what powered these devices? If yes, then this was clearly the most important point in all of these diagrams!!!

"Ah you found it." Said Haushofer, his face lighting up, "I do believe that it is what you suspect it to be; the most significant aspect of this quest. That term does in fact refer to what it is that powers these devices, and therein lies our second major problem."

"What? What does the term say?"

"It's called 'Laghima.'" Haushofer said simply. "And the way the sage described it to me...it is no mere physical substance that one would normally expect to use as fuel, but a force of nature unparalleled in its efficiency!"

"What does that even mean?"

"During our conversation, the sage had made quite a few cryptic references to the 'Vimanika Shastra' being a metaphor for the *flight of human consciousnesses*. Like you, I had also been extremely distressed, on hearing this…for to me, this sounded like an elaborate hoax… some ancient writer exercising a bit of poetic license!"

"You see my friend; the key to it lies in the word 'Vimana' itself meaning - 'birdlike'. Now at first glance, someone who sees these layouts…outlandish though they might be…is likely to conclude that the book is named after these crafts…as in, the crafts themselves are the 'Vimana'."

"They aren't?" Gustav asked stunned.

"Not exactly…and that's the interesting part. While it's true that the text does claim to describe ancient esoteric flying machines, what really gives them their 'birdlike' qualities, is this mysterious energy source called 'Laghima'!"

"So you see, without the means of tapping this energy source, these layouts are of no use at all. Even if we were to somehow procure the complete document from the monastery, and reconstruct one of these crafts, we would *still* not be able to use it. The designs themselves are far from aerodynamic…and hence cannot be powered using conventional fuels!"

Gustav took a moment to take all of this in. His mind raced to find some answers, even as he kept thumbing through the drawings, made by his mentor. Looking at them now, he had to admit that these definitely did not seem like the kind of crafts you would construct, if you had conventional flight systems in mind. Most of them were shaped like 'acorns' or 'large bells'. Even though he couldn't make out all the terms Haushofer had written next to them, he realized that some of the crafts were intended to be quite large…large enough to seat 7-9 people. And of course there was the complete absence of any kind of wing mechanism or functioning engine, making it impossible for the crafts to take off and fly. If he didn't know Haushofer better, he would have suspected this to be a 'con man's hoax'.

In one of the designs, Gustav even noticed what appeared to be a series of interlocking wheels…a 'gyroscopic device', probably constructed to facilitate levitation, by vigorously spinning air in a circular fashion to the point where it creates lift...so clearly the blueprints had been created by someone, who was familiar with the basics of flight. Of course, for the gyroscope to work there would have to be some sort of a combustion process...meaning 'fuel'...and that brought one back to this mysterious energy source called 'Laghima'.

"Doesn't this energy source seem a lot like the 'Vril energy' that we in the Thule Society believe, exists in nature?" Gustav asked with some hesitation.

"Yes...I am glad that the commonalities between the two have not been lost on you. It is quite possible that the two terms actually refer to one and the same concept. And if that's indeed true, then we are looking at not just an alternative form of energy, but actually an altogether different branch of science that will most likely turn conventional physics on its head."

"What?" Gustav started.

"Let me ask you something first...during your many interactions with members of the Thule Society, has the name Victor Schauberger ever come up?"

"No...no wait...yes...I vaguely remember his name cropping up, when some offbeat researchers were being discussed. But I don't think I have heard him discussed very prominently." Gustav replied after a brief pause.

"Not surprising, since Himmler is not too fond of him or his ideas. Schauberger in fact has openly criticized the use of conventional propulsion systems that all of today's vehicles use, going so far as to call it a 'mistake'. So for most in the scientific community, he is a bit of a maverick...a 'loose end', so to speak. But let me tell you something about the man...I have met him and spoken to him at length about his beliefs and even though I have never shared with him what I have shared with you, I think he has some very interesting points, in his hypothesis."

"So what *IS* his hypothesis?"

"Well Schauberger believes that forces of nature always act in polar opposites... 'life and death', 'light and darkness', 'good and evil', 'creation and destruction'...and so on. If we accept this as true, then for each natural phenomenon, we should be able to find *its* opposite. For instance, theoretically there should be an opposite to the force of gravity as well…a force that will allow for levitation. Schauberger calls this 'Vril Levitation'. And let me tell you, even though Himmler might not think much of him, your friend Hess is quite taken in by the man."

"Rudolf Hess? But he hasn't mentioned Schauberger or any of these ideas in our conversations and we certainly do share quite a bit!"

"Oh…don't let Hess' jovial and fun loving exterior fool you. Underneath the dour academic exterior he projects, the man is a die-hard Nazi and fanatically loyal to Hitler. There is a lot about Hess that you don't know."

"But coming back to the point, the main reason Hess is so fascinated by these theories is that Schauberger speculates that among these polar opposites, it is the creative and the destructive forces that can satisfy our energy needs."

"For instance consider that all our mechanical devises have what we call a 'combustion engine' that uses the principle of 'explosion' to generate the requisite energy to fulfill our needs. This 'burning' of fuels in an explosive manner is essentially a destructive act, leaving behind waste."

"Now if you compare this with all forms of 'divine creations' such as life for instance, they have always been fueled by forces that are 'creative' and not 'destructive'. In a sense, the formation of life through any kind of reproduction is a form of 'Implosion' rather than 'Explosion'. As a result, we find that in nature, the procreation of life does not result in any kind of waste that is harmful to the environment. This has led Schauberger to conclude that any kind of technology, based on the principles of explosions and destructive forces *cannot* be in synch with the divine."

"So Schauberger believes that the energy source, we refer to as the 'Black Sun' or 'Vril', is this constructive process that is in keeping with the divine?" Gustav asked.

"Yes, and there are rumors that even as we speak, he is experimenting with a type of flying object that he claims will use 'Vril levitation'…he is even calling it the 'Mind of Man.'"

"But how could something like this work? We barely know anything about 'Vril'…it's just a theoretical energy source, at this stage. Surely Schauberger knows that getting this device to actually work will be impossible." Gustav wondered…stunned.

"If you had to know one thing about Victor Schauberger, it is that he is not a man, who will let practical limitations stand between him and his mission." Haushofer replied with a laugh. "He even has some of the key financers of the Thule Society, convinced about some of his blueprints and has been hard at work to try and make one of these 'self-levitation' crafts operational."

"But how does he plan to achieve something like this? Surely even he realizes that there is no way yet, that we can tap into an energy source like this!" Gustav said incredulously.

"Yes…but Schauberger believes that there are certain 'lines of energy' that flow just beneath the surface of the earth, all across the planet. He refers to these as 'Lay-Lines' and believes that, if one were to place a craft over one of these lines and then augment their strength with one's own inner mental strength, one could accomplish levitation! It's certainly an interesting theory and one that is not too different from its Indian counterpart, which believes that within each human being, there exists an energy source called 'Kundalini' that connects us to the divine! If activated, through the right focus of mind and body, this energy can help us accomplish the impossible. I believe this is what the Vimanika Shastra refers to as 'Laghima.'"

"So you believe Schauberger can succeed?" Gustav asked, still not fully sure of what he had just heard. "Why then don't you share your knowledge with him? Surely, if resources are already being poured into this project, we owe it to our nation to enhance any chance of success we might have."

"I have not shared these secrets with Schauberger or with anyone else so far, because I know that with or without my help, he is doomed to fail. This is an impossible venture."

"How can you give up so easily? Just because *you* were denied access into Tibet, you think that's the end of our dream? The world awaits the arrival of a New Golden Age and we Germans are responsible for ushering it in…we have spoken about it and now is the time to act."

"I do not use my words lightly. Do you think it was easy for me to accept this? Much before you ever heard of these concepts, I was dedicating my life trying to unearth their secrets. I know Schauberger's quest is a losing venture because I know something about the nature of the energy source that we are talking about. 'Vril'… 'Laghima'… 'Chi'…this brings us to the second major problem…one that is much more difficult to overcome than just getting an access into Tibet."

"Which is?"

"The sage, who had become my mentor, made it very clear that the Hindu belief in the 'Yuga' concept of Time was not metaphorical…but an actual representation of how the universe functioned. So, like we discussed a while ago, humanity has gone through a slow moral and spiritual degradation from the first era – the 'Satya Yuga' to the fourth and current era – the 'Kali Yuga'. This has resulted in mankind losing almost all its spiritually acquired powers, including the ability to understand, control and manipulate this mystical energy source…the one the Vimanika Shastra refers to as 'Laghima'. So you see the problem we face? Even if we were to reconstruct these devices using either my drawings or Schauberger's designs, we would still have absolutely no way of powering them…*we are simply born in the wrong era!*" Haushofer concluded with a sardonic chuckle.

The silence that followed this somber revelation could have dispelled a thousand demons. *So near…and yet so far! …*Gustav could not…*would not* believe his ears. The discussion had started off on such an optimistic note. Even though, there were so many unanswered questions, there had been so much hope for this new technology. Now all of that seemed to have turned to dust. It was as if the very universe was conspiring against him!

"If you knew all of this already, why tell me any of this?" Gustav moaned, "You never mentioned the futility of our plans, at any of the meetings we had at the Thule Society. You knew all along that our efforts were doomed to fail, yet you just stood by and allowed groups like the 'Black Sun' to not just come into existence, but also invest massive amounts of time and effort into this quest. By allowing our society to stumble in the dark like this, you have in fact acted *against* it!"

Haushofer looked at the distraught Gustav for a long time... pondering whether or not to tell him the next bit. The gothic style vaulted ceiling of the room, seemed to arch its eyebrows at him. The wine in the glass, he held, seemed to have lost all its taste. Finally he broke the silence and spoke again...in a monotone, "All that you have accused me of is probably true. Yes...I should have revealed all of this earlier. But I did not want the efforts of these groups to stop...I was probably holding on to one last wild hope...a slender one but a plausible one nonetheless.!"

"Call it the naïve fantasy of an old man, who has dedicated his life to a dream...but there, is one thing that we might yet be able to do. It is something that I had decided never to share with anyone...but now I believe the time has come for others especially you, to know and hopefully gain from it."

Gustav's eyes widened, when he heard this. He held his breath... after the crushing disappointment, just a few moments ago, his brain refused to allow any hope to creep in easily.

"There was something that the sage said, right towards the end of our conversation that told me that there was just a tiny glimmer of hope. The partially destroyed document I had seen at the monastery had originally come from Tibet. Although I did not have its exact location, it was safe to assume that somewhere out there was a complete copy of the Vimanika Shastra. When I mentioned this, I saw sage's face briefly light up and then immediately...darken with sorrow. He looked at me with those piercing brown eyes of his, and revealed that in Tibet...at a secret location, not far from one of the most sacred pilgrim spots, there lay a 'lost city'...one that held all the answers I desired!"

It was now past eleven...and the only sound that could be heard from outside, was the soft moan of a predatory owl.

CHAPTER NINE

"A lost city? ...*in Tibet?* What sacred spot is this and how does no one know about this?" Gustav screamed in excitement.

Haushofer took a long puff from his pipe, to calm his nerves. "The sacred pilgrim spot that the sage spoke of is in fact very well known in the Eastern World. About 600 miles west of the capital city of Lhasa, deep in what is known as Tibetan Autonomous Region is a location that is sacred to Hinduism, Buddhism, Jainism and Bon. It is a mystical lake called 'Manasarovar' and it is seen as the supreme 'personification of purity', by all four faiths. What is truly extraordinary is that it is a fresh water lake, located at an altitude of more than 15,000 feet above sea level, on a plateau that has mostly saline lakes. In fact right next to Lake 'Manasarovar' is another lake named 'Rakshasthal' that has salt water."

"Yes I vaguely remember some references to *ANOTHER* sacred spot near the lake – Mount Kailasha!" Gustav murmured.

"Yes...you are right! However, getting to Lake Manasarovar is just the start, for around these regions is a legend of a city, built by a single divine teacher, from a lost civilization...one so perfect that it was literally paradise on earth! It is rumored to contain all the divine knowledge of that forgotten culture...among them vehicles that can levitate with just the power of the human mind and artifacts that can grant one, the secrets of eternal life!!!"

"We have these very descriptions in the Vedic traditions about the earlier eras or 'Yugas' and we also know that on account of humanity's moral and spiritual corruption, we can no longer access these abilities. Now just for a moment, imagine, *if this is more than just a legend*, my dear boy...we would then have our link with the earlier...more spiritually enhanced 'Yugas' right here...through his lost city!!"

- In the city called Kapala in the northern direction
A place where spiritual heroes expanding their hearts,
Cycles of Time and so forth remain stable forever
And the hallowed measures are supremely widespread.
Just to behold them heralds the supreme actual attainment -

"But how could a city like this survive? ...if as you say, it is some kind of a relic from a bygone era, how did it survive corruption from the outside world? Moreover, these beliefs of 'Vimanas' and the 'Yuga' cycles are Indian, not Tibetan!" Gustav argued.

"I agree...and this is something that has bothered me as well. I do not claim to have an absolute and complete explanation myself... *merely a working hypothesis.*"

"Which is?"

"One of the key elements in the concept of the 'Yugas' is that each Yuga ends in a destructive cataclysm...what the Hindus refer to as 'Pralaya'. This is a world ending catastrophe that generally takes the form of a massive flood. Now this is quite similar to the Judeo-Christian myth of Noah, right down to the part, where God chooses one man and his family to put all their belongings into a boat and then helps it on to safer grounds...thus restarting the next age."

"Ok."

"Now if for a moment, we consider that the reason a lot of the cultures in the Middle-East and the Far-East, have such similar flood stories is that in the distant past, a catastrophic flood *did* indeed occur...one that would have seemed 'world ending' to the victims. In such an event, it's quite possible that some of their more enterprising members might have tried to escape the flood, in man-made vessels. Most would not have made it, but those that did survive, *might* have landed in different parts of Asia, thus percolating the myth of the great flood! Over time this story would have morphed into the collective consciousness of people, across the area and attained all of its current variations!!"

"Yes...all this is certainly possible, but what does this have to do with the legend of this lost city?"

"Think my friend…If such a flood myth survived and still does, could a survivor from the actual flood also not have done the same? Wouldn't an individual or maybe a group of such survivors have then sought to protect their knowledge…*for all time*? In such a scenario, the high mountains of the Himalayas would provide the perfect refuge, from the flood waters. So even if this civilization had once flourished somewhere in the Indian Sub-continent, following the flood, Tibet would seem to be the perfect choice for a safe haven!"

"Yes…" Gustav said with some hesitation, "I guess that *does* make sense…probably another reason they went to Tibet is that this is also the site of one of Hinduism's holiest pilgrim spots – 'Mount Kailasha.'"

"Or…it's possible that the spot *BECAME* sacred, since these survivors stayed there."

"True." Gustav conceded, "But then why do we not know anything about these people…this city? Surely a city, established by survivors of a previous cosmic cycle and possessing divine technologies, would not have escaped the attention of the world!"

"Yes, absolutely…unless…it is a city, lost in the sands of time… completely hidden from the outside world, through means, we currently do not understand…a city that is accessible only during certain very specific times…a literal Paradise on Earth…known in legend as 'Shambhala'!"

"However…it is a magical city that appears on Earth *only* when certain celestial bodies line up. It is this alignment that is key to accessing the power and knowledge of this ethereal paradise. I have spent years trying to scrape together every last fragment of information I could lay my hands on, regarding these cosmic patterns…and now finally, I believe I have cracked its code!"

"Unbelievable…" Gustav whispered in awe, "If what you say is true, then all we need to do is find this mystical land and the secrets of the universe, will be ours for the taking!!! If Shambhala *did* somehow manage to escape the ravages and corruptions of time, it could be our access point into the Golden Age. Based on the legends of the Yuga

Cycles, who knows, we might be able to unearth far more than just a new source of energy...we could once and for all learn the long sought after secrets of immortality!!"

"Or...it could be...a trap!" Haushofer replied softly.

CHAPTER TEN

The crackling of the logs in the fireplace, seemed to share Haushofer's apprehensions, even as he spoke, "I have spent years trying to decode the mysteries of this Tibetan legend and its connections to esoteric powers…and along the way, I came across numerous sources…both eastern and western, which speak of similar quests that have motivated man, since the dawn of time…quests that have led heroic figures from antiquity, to seek out the secrets of absolute power and immortality… and that have *always* ended in disaster!"

"Most of these now serve as cautionary tales…and believe me, these aren't just isolated examples…I have found legends that echo the same basic principle, all the way from ancient Sumerian narratives such as the 'Epic of Gilgamesh'…all the way to unnamed folk tales, from around the Black Sea. So numerous were these tales and so consistent was their message that even as I delved deep into the mysteries of Shambhala, I found myself wondering, whether certain secrets were best not unearthed! Maybe…this was History's way of protecting its own!!"

"Bah…where is your sense of adventure, man? In your years of bookish pursuits, you have allowed yourself to be dissuaded by bed-time fables and old wives' yarns. The way I look at it is the very fact these tales exist, proves there is definitely substance to these legends… and *if* that is true, I am determined to seek them out." Gustav spat out contemptuously.

If the older man felt angered or pained by this rebuke, he hid it well. After a long and uncomfortable silence, he spoke again, "Do you even *know* of the 'Epic of Gilgamesh'? It is possibly the oldest recorded story that we have today and it is dated by most scholars to around 2000 B.C…*at least!* In spite of its incredible age, the epic contains amazing wisdom that helps one understand the inner workings of the human spirit. I would sincerely recommend that before you commit yourself to some asinine attempt at trying to uncover an ancient secret, you equip yourself with the requisite tools…and in a quest such as this…what better tool to have than knowledge." This last bit Haushofer added, with a touch of cynicism.

Stung by the sudden change in his mentor's tone, Gustav relented. He realized that he had let his emotions get the better of him. After all, the fact that Haushofer was sharing his life's work with him was only because he saw something in him. Gustav knew that without Haushofer's knowledge and research, the search for the alternate source of power, the quest for immortality and the Golden Age, would be just dreams.

He spoke again…this time, his voice, softer and full of respect, "Sir, you mentioned the Epic of Gilgamesh, being one of those allegorical stories that could help me understand the nature of this quest. Unfortunately, I, at best, have only a superficial understanding of this tale and even that is mainly from encyclopedic references."

The academician in Haushofer beamed with satisfaction, "I shall gladly give you a basic run down of the essence of the story, and while we are at it, you can look through some pamphlets, I picked up, which offer a more detailed perspective into the central character of the story – King Gilgamesh himself."

Gustav flipped through the pamphlet that his mentor handed him, and noticed that it contained a brief 'history lesson' about the mythical king Gilgamesh of Uruk - a city in the ancient land of Sumeria, along with a few illustrations of what looked like temples and monuments, built in his honor. *Why was this figure and his story, so important to the quest at hand?*

Gustav was intrigued, "From what I can discern from these notes is that for the Sumerians, the hero of the epic was not just the stuff of legend. The relief carvings on these Sumerian temples record his heroic deeds and suggest that he reigned as King over the city of Uruk sometime…around 2700 B.C. If that is true, he certainly must have been an important ruler, for he built these strong city walls and imposing temples that still stand today."

"Oh, he was far more than just an illustrious ruler! One of the things that are truly remarkable is that the Epic of Gilgamesh is older than Homer's Illiad and the Mahabharata. Till less than a hundred years ago, numerous fragments of this epic, containing many different versions of the same story, used to routinely turn up, all over the Middle-East. It was only by the middle of the last century, that compete parts of the epic were discovered at Nineveh – the site of the famous 'library of the Assyrian king - Assurbanipal'. This version of the legend is probably from around the 7th century A.D. and was written on 12 clay tablets. Incidentally, this version also contains the story of a great flood, *the Babylonian version of the Biblical flood!*"

Gustav's curiosity was piqued further...if the epic of Gilgamesh centered around a flood-myth, then it was very possible that the narrative might be *another* corrupted version of the original cataclysm that had brought to an end, one of the earlier cosmic cycles! It was then equally possible, as Haushofer had earlier suggested that there could have been a small contingent of survivors, who might have escaped the disaster and survived in a hidden city. This story might offer valuable clues towards their fate.

Haushofer, aware of its significance, continued in his monotone, "It is known that in Mesopotamian literature, the son of the Goddess Ninsum, a boy named Gilgamesh became a supernatural being. But in spite of his Demi-God status, he came to realize that he was mortal, after all! The narrative even portrays his character and weaknesses as more 'human' than 'godlike'."

"So even though Gilgamesh is the Hero of the Epic, he is described as a tyrannical ruler, whose subjects groan under his heavy-handed tactics and his many wars. The epic goes onto describe, how in order to get rid of their king, the people tried to get him to fight a being named 'Enkidu'- who was half savage and half man, and whom the Gods had created as a worthy opponent for Gilgamesh. But even this tactic failed!"

"After a single epic combat that ended in a stalemate, the two men became inseparable. Their friendship enabled them to perform superhuman deeds that became the stuff of legend, much to the angst of the Gods, who then decided to separate the friends by letting Enkidu die of an illness. This is probably the most significant part of the epic, for when Gilgamesh saw the corpse of his friend, he was devastated. He suddenly realized the existential nature of his own reality and went in search of eternal life."

"The epic describes this search in an extremely poetic way; as Gilgamesh literally crosses over to the other side of the river of death and meets a man named 'Utnapishtim', who happens to be a survivor of the great world-destroying flood and to whom the Gods have granted immortality."

"Could this be an early archetype of the Biblical Noah?" Gustav interjected.

"Yes…it's very possible that the stories in the Bible, since they were originally composed out of Sumeria, might borrow into some of these older myths. In this version however, Utnapishtim's advice to the king was to remain awake for seven days and seven nights in preparation for immortality…a test in which the king failed. Out of pity, Utnapishtim showed him the plant of eternal life, called *'The old man becomes young again'*. But just as Gilgamesh found the plant, it was stolen by a snake, forcing him to remain mortal!"

*"A plant offering immortality…the forbidden fruit…a snake in paradise…*there are so many similarities to this story and the Biblical story of the 'Garden of Eden' and Adam and Eve." Gustav breathed out.

"Yes…you are correct…In fact the word 'Eden' itself is Sumerian in origin…but you are missing the most important connection between the two narratives. In both the stories, immortality is *DENIED* to mankind!! Since the dawn of time, human beings have dreamt of heroes, who could grasp the mysteries of the spirit-world and uncover the secrets of eternal life. Gilgamesh was probably the first of those, who tried to actually find answers to these questions."

"The epic of Gilgamesh enjoys such widespread interest among historians in part because it seeks to address mankind's most important concerns: the relationship with the Gods, the power of friendship, pride and fury, life and death. The *SNAKE* in this story… or the one in the garden of paradise, seems to act as a cautionary reminder of the 'frailties of human existence'…and a warning against stepping too far out of line." Haushofer concluded.

"No…we cannot allow these ancient stories to dissuade us from our goal. The way *I* see it is *that* these stories even exist is proof…that somewhere out there, lies the lost power of the ancient world…a power that could make us – Germans, absolute masters of the human race…I will not back down from this quest…It is now only a matter of time, before I get what I want!"

Haushofer shook his head, "I cannot stop you, my boy, from doing what you think is right…but I will leave you to your fate with a final warning" …

"In Nietzsche's immortal words –

If you stare long enough into the abyss, the ABYSS starts to stare back at you!!!"

CHAPTER ELEVEN

After Gustav left, Haushofer thought of him, with a tinge of sadness and regret. He had tried his best to educate and warn the young fool… but ultimately, to each, his own. It was a lesson, Haushofer had learnt well in his life.

However, there was something else…that he just hadn't been able to tell Gustav…and not for the lack of trying! Throughout their conversation, Haushofer had felt an invisible force reach out to him… and prevent him from sharing one of the most astounding details about the saint, he had met in India. It was something that kept him awake, even now, after all these years!

Of course, he had told Gustav how the saint had known him 'in and out' and answered all his questions. But the thing that was most troubling…something he hadn't managed to share…was that the man, he met in a holy city on the Ganges, had spoken to him…and answered all his queries…*in GERMAN!!!*

Somewhere near the star named Aldebaran, the cosmic entity known as Chronux, smiled…it knew that its salvation was now, not too far away! The trap it had so carefully laid, so many millennia ago, was now reaching fruition!

The bait had been taken by a man, who it knew would stop at nothing, while trying to satiate his delusions of grandeur…in short…*a perfect candidate*…

…Hook…Line and Sinker!!!

EPISODE FOUR

CHAPTER ONE

Throughout his many discussions with Haushofer, in the early 1920s, Gustav always retained a sense of the magnitude of the task, in front of him. Regardless of the benefits finding a 'Golden Age Kingdom', would have for the Third Reich; he knew that this was not going to be simple!

Haushofer had made it clear that filtering through the numerous references to 'Shambhala' in Hindu and Tibetan sources and deciphering their true meaning was no easy task. Even after a decade spent in Asia; he had been nowhere close to uncovering its secrets. This had of course caused him great frustration, and he described his experiences to Gustav, warning him of the pain, such an obsession could bring…every *time you sought a closer look, the mystery seemed to pull away*…it was the ultimate 'forbidden fruit'!

And yet Gustav was unperturbed. He was sure that through his own talent and commitment, he would unravel the mystery…he *would* find Shambhala! Of course, this would mean preparing himself, both mentally and physically…for the many challenges that lay ahead.

And although, he did not yet possess the necessary financial resources, required for an expedition of this sort, he was firm in the conviction that one day the Nazis *would* come to rule the world…It was just a matter of time…the resources of all of humanity would soon be at his disposal!

February 1925: The first President of the Weimar Republic, Friedrich Ebert died, leaving Germany leaderless and in turmoil. For Hitler and the Nazis, this was the moment to begin their political comeback. No longer were the Nazis outlawed, as they were not considered a threat anymore. They once again began the process of galvanizing all the different Far-Right groups, under Hitler.

Meanwhile, following Ebert's death, Germany chose Marshall Von Hindenburg, a legendary war veteran, to lead the country. However, what soon became clear to everyone in Germany was that the Nazis were slowly spreading their tentacles all across society. Their membership increased to well over two hundred thousand! Most of them still financed themselves and were now organized according to rank and designated roles. Hitler organized the S.S. and the S.A. units as his Storm troopers, with separate units focusing on research and ideology.

For Gustav, being a member of the party, meant access to the huge financial and educational resources...resources, he used masterfully to further his dream. He began to hone himself, body and mind, through extensive mental and physical training, alongside the S.S. He also tried to learn the basics of languages and scripts from the Far-East.

As the years went by, his studies into the mysteries of Shambhala, would lead him down some very interesting...*and disturbing avenues!* He had of course read all of Haushofer's notes...*many times over* and reached his own conclusions...some which were in variance with his predecessor's. For him, finding Shambhala was more than merely finding the remains of a lost race. It was an opportunity to tap into hitherto unknown divine and mystical powers!

To Gustav, Haushofer seemed like someone, who had developed a fascination for a legend...but managed to acquire only a superficial understanding of it...one that lacked the conviction needed, to unlock its secrets.

He knew that to go further, he would need the support of his party...*and the rest of Germany.* For this the Nazis would have to emerge as the 'de facto' government of Germany...a possibility that seemed pretty remote, in the mid-1920s. Gustav knew that regardless of what was being said, the Nazis were far from being the big favorites. The mainstream population still looked at Hitler as a charlatan and a bully. For them, the Social Democrats, with their more tolerant approach, were still the favored choice.

Something would have to be done...and soon!

CHAPTER TWO

Leading up to the 1928 elections, the S.S. and the S.A. Storm troopers engaged in unprecedented acts of brutality and aggression, particularly against their political rivals - the Communists. The S.S. would patrol the streets and rough up any one, they saw as an opposition. Jewish shops and neighborhoods came under attacks, the most. These were tactics designed to scare the opposition into submission.

Unfortunately for Hitler and the Nazis, the terror and intimidation produced scarce results, as the Nazis secured less than 2% of the total ballot.

The immediate reaction that followed, involved a party-wide crackdown, directed at all those, who were considered expendable. Thousands of Nazi Party members now found themselves evicted from the organization, for failing to produce the results, expected of them. The departments that came under most scrutiny were the ones linked to the 'Thule Society', as these were considered defunct... *especially in such politically charged times!* As a lead researcher and theoretician, Gustav found himself in the crossfire. He barely managed to hold on to his position, as a result largely, of his dedication to his beliefs...and *repeated* promises to deliver on them.

Realizing that time was fast running out, he began to frequent all the old libraries across Munich, Vienna and Berlin, in search of books that spoke of Eastern/Oriental 'Occultism'. He began to follow up on *any* lead that suggested answers. Often, his search led him to obscure places, such as flea markets and old-book collectors, specializing in these kinds of resources. He would even visit 'psychics' and 'mystics' ,like his old acquaintance Maria Orsitch, with the hope of gaining new insights, through 'mystical séances'!

These séances were spiritual gatherings, where people attempted to make contact with the dead, especially through the agency of a medium. With nothing else working, Gustav looked to the 'afterlife' for answers...to the mysteries of the past!

He spent all his free time preparing his own notes, and carried a diary with him, at all times...one that he closely guarded! He often met Haushofer, whom he still considered his mentor...though one, who had largely served his purpose. Such was his conviction towards his beliefs that he held on to the wild hope of ushering in the Golden Age, even during the peak of the 'Great Financial Depression' that hit Europe, by the end of the 1920s!

CHAPTER THREE

Rise of Adolf Hitler

1929 marked the beginning of the rise of Adolf Hitler! The devastating economic crisis that began in the United States and snowballed over into Europe, affected Germany the most. Already reeling from years of mismanagement by the Weimar Republic and the economic devastation caused by the 'Treaty of Versailles', the Stock Market Crash of 1929 in the U.S. came as a body-blow to Germany. One by one, German factories began to close their doors and the number of unemployed soon crossed six million. The price of basic commodities escalated and starvation became a reality for millions!

It was in this climate of economic turmoil that any group representing order was looked upon as a savior. A lot of people turned to the Nazis or the Communists. *Anything...was preferable to this suffering!*

Faced with such a desperate struggle to gather the bigger 'vote bank', Communists and Nazis clashed violently, leading up to every major election campaign that followed. Often these clashes would begin as street fights and progressively...turn ugly! A number of deaths were reported on both sides.

Unfortunately for the Communists, for all their visible support in the mainstream public, they did not have a leader like Adolf Hitler. Hitler knew this well and exploited it to the hilt, by first provoking disorder and then claiming to be the only one, capable of stopping it!

These terror tactics worked...after a series of bitter struggles with the Communists, at the start of the 1930s, Hitler emerged as the head of the second largest political party in Germany...next only to the Social Democrats, who were still in power.

Gustav, now an important member of the 'Research and Propaganda' wing of the party, played a vital role in these successes. He worked closely with Rudolf Hess, Heinrich Himmler and Joseph Goebbels to keep up the Nazis public image, amidst all the chaos.

Often, this proved to be a huge challenge, as Hitler's instructions were very clear – the party *would not* apologize for any perceived 'hurt' that they caused to any individual or group. It was important that the people saw them not as 'moral messiahs', but as a tough, uncompromising and intolerant unit that was Germany's only salvation!

As time went by, Joseph Goebbels began to distinguish himself more and more, as an absolute 'master' of Public Relations. Hitler's attention leading up to the 1932 elections, was primarily focused on the German Parliament. The repeated losses, in spite of the massive amounts of funds the Nazis were pumping in, were a bitter pill to swallow.

Year after year, the Nazis were increasing their membership and standing in the German Parliament, but they were still not the official government! And now the massive funding and intimidation were becoming difficult to sustain. The wealthy supporters, including the 'Thule Society', were beginning to have second thoughts about Hitler... and even the public was reeling under an onslaught of propaganda. Goebbels realized he had to make the next campaign count... *somehow!*

With the help of the owner of 'Lufthansa Airlines', he designed an ultra-modern election campaign, with the use of airplanes, which involved Hitler descending from the clouds to his ardent supporters! This was to create a 'Cult of Personality' around Hitler, by making him a demi-god and forging the myth of 'The Führer'. Goebbels even coined the phrase – *'Der Führer über Deutschland'* - *The Führer above Germany!*

Racked by years of unemployment, for millions, these outlandish slogans seemed to be the only glimmer of hope, on an otherwise bleak horizon. In spite of this, not everyone in Germany was taken in by the Nazis. The parties in the Far-Left, still supported the ageing President, Marshal Hindenburg and the Social Democrats.

Finally on the 10ᵗʰ of April 1932, the results were out. Even though millions had voted for Hitler, he would still not be the President. Thanks to the unflinching support of the Social Democrats, Marshall Hindenburg was re-elected...*albeit, by a much smaller margin, this time.* It seemed that the Nazis' best efforts were not good enough. Hitler was crushed...or so it seemed.

With Germany still in political turmoil, Hitler began to campaign, once again! With all the mainstreams forms of propaganda, already in play, he began to look for new alternatives. The S.S. and the S.A. storm troopers would once again be given the charge of creating discord on the streets and provoking fights. There was an even greater attempt at giving the movement a decidedly racial tone, by deliberately attacking Jewish neighborhoods. This was to create a sense of 'pseudo-nationalism' particularly amongst the German youth, who would ultimately lend their support to the Nazi Party.

But Hitler realized that he needed something more...something that would convince the Germans that his warped world-view was ultimately the right one. During the many frenetic briefings he had with his closest associates, he was reminded once again of the work of Karl Haushofer and Friedrich Gustav...work that promised to unearth the lost links of Germany's 'Aryan Ancestry'. And suddenly, those who had seemingly fallen from grace were back in the limelight! Along with Haushofer and Gustav, hundreds of others, who could best be classified as the 'lunatic fringe', now found themselves in demand.

Once again, there were clandestine conferences organized for members of the Thule Society and ideas such as, finding Shambhala... were discussed with renewed vigor, after almost a decade. For those like Gustav, this new found interest and support of their cause, was like a new lease of life...for with it, came the promise of research grants...funds without which, it had proved impossible to verify any of their theories!

May 1932: More good-news was on the horizon, as a noted German hunter and biologist, named Ernst Schaffer, returned from an expedition to Tibet. While his exploration had mainly been for sport and zoological research, Schaffer's foray into that part of the world, was a source of great fascination for those all who believed that it was in Tibet that the ultimate secrets of paradise, lay waiting to be tapped!

What was even more significant was that in his very first interaction, Schaffer managed to make such a powerful impression on Hitler, with tales of 'pristine lands' and a 'race of pure, uncorrupted people', that the Nazi leader promised him full support for future expeditions into Tibet...*if* and when the Nazi came to power. For Hitler, Schaffer's hand-drawn sketches of Tibetan society and the numerous depictions of the 'Swastika' that he saw, seemed to confirm that the Tibetans were *indeed* related to the long lost Aryans. Schaffer, delighted to have his future expeditions sponsored by the state, seemed content to play along with this hypothesis.

Meanwhile, on the political front, the brutal tactics of the S.S. and the S.A. appeared to be paying off. In the months leading up to the July elections, the Communists lost more than a hundred of their members, to street fights with the S.S. A state of extreme paranoia was unleashed across Germany!

Curiously though, instead of creating a sense of mass hysteria about the Nazis, these tactics had the opposite effect on the people. Tired of the constant fighting, the public simply wanted peace. They supported the Nazis wholeheartedly, believing that Hitler could indeed put an end to the violence, in a way that the current government could not. By July 1932, over two hundred and thirty Nazis had been elected to the German parliament and were given important ministerial roles. Hitler, even though not the President, was now the head of the most powerful political party in Germany. However, for all the power that he held, the ageing President Hindenburg still refused to appoint him the 'Chancellor of Germany'!

The wolf however…was now within sniffing distance of the sheep's pen!

Under the command of Hitler's head of propaganda – Joseph Goebbels, the Nazis managed to prove that Hindenburg did not have a clear majority and thereby justify the call for re-elections, in November of 1932…*the third in the same year.* Believing that victory was his, Hitler even refused to take the ministerial role that Hindenburg offered him!

But this tactic *again* backfired. The voters loyal to the Nazis could not understand why Hitler had refused to enter the government. Believing him no longer to be the man, they had thought him to be, two million of them voted *AGAINST* him in the November elections. This would be the Nazis' third successive defeat in the same year!

Hindenburg's victory though had come at a cost. Even though he had secured his own position, he still found it impossible to form a clear majority and, by the start of 1933, was forced to name Hitler the 'Chancellor of Germany'. Hitler's first act as Chancellor was to force the 'Ministry of Internal Affairs' to come under the Nazis, with his right hand man – the bulky and diabolical, Herman Goring, taking over as the head of security. From this point on, it was only a matter of time before Hitler seized absolute power, bringing German democracy to its knees!

In February of 1933, the historic 'Reichstag' building...the German Parliament was burnt down in the dead of the night, under mysterious circumstances. In the aftermath of the disaster, accusations flew from all corners, but for the Germans, the fall of the last symbol of German Democracy, would be the start of the long road to disaster.

The investigations of the arson were carried out under the watchful eye of Herman Goring and implicated a young Dutch Communist, who was quickly executed. Hitler and the Nazis used the destruction of the Reichstag, to reignite fears that there was a nationwide 'Communist Conspiracy' to overthrow the government. Hitler also accused the Jews for being hand in hand with the Communists, and used this to justify massive crackdowns on both these groups. Thousands were arrested and imprisoned, without a trial...Jewish neighborhoods were blacklisted and their shops were stoned!

With all major opposition now silenced, the Nazis were able to form a clear majority, by March of 1933, making Hitler the absolute leader – the 'Führer'. That even in this election, the Communists won twelve percent of the ballot, did not stop Hitler. He had all their members arrested and sent to the first of the concentration camps, the Nazis would set up, to hold political prisoners...a camp at Dachau, near Berlin. Thus the year 1933, would mark the beginning of the 'great terror'.

Europe was headed... for the Holocaust!

CHAPTER FOUR

By the end of 1934, with political power firmly in their grasp, Hitler and the 'Third Reich' turned their attention to more 'esoteric' pursuits. One of the main reasons behind this was that the Occult Societies, who had supported Nazism, through the tumult of the 1920s, were now demanding *their* 'pound of flesh'. Among the most vocal were of course, Karl Haushofer and Friedrich Gustav. Moreover, even Hitler seemed convinced that these pursuits would further the mystique of 'Aryan Supremacy'!

Under Haushofer's influence, Hitler authorized Frederick Hielscher, to establish the 'Bureau for the Study of Ancestral Heritage' or the 'Ahnenerbe'. The primary objective of which, was to locate the original source of the Aryan Race...believed to be somewhere in the Far-East. This was strengthened by the fact that the Swastika...one of Hitler's long time obsessions and now adopted by the Nazis as their official emblem...was a part of most eastern schools of thought!

The members of the Ahnenerbe were also tasked with researching the religions and cultures of the Far-North, especially the 'Nordic' culture, and trying to decipher the 'Magic of the Runes'. It would often recruit corrupt and unscrupulous scientists, from all across Europe... men, who would then proceed to ravage German history, for *anything* that seemed to lend credence to the outlandish claim that the Germans were descended from a 'Master Race'. In doing so, the Ahnenerbe scientists often based their theories on half-truths...pseudoscience... *and outright lies!*

According to Nazi Chief, Heinrich Himmler, just like the great civilizations of the past, the German state needed to create its own 'mythology' and the Ahnenerbe was tasked with dissecting every accepted scientific discipline and scrape together the means of achieving this. One of the places that they were instructed to focus their energies, was Tibet.

Frederick Hielscher, the head of the Ahnenerbe, was close friends with the noted Swedish explorer, Swen Hedin. Hedin had made a series of journeys to Tibet and Inner Mongolia, throughout the early part of the twentieth century and was a popular favorite among the Nazis. He often spoke extensively about his experiences in Tibet, and gave the researchers in the Ahnenerbe, invaluable insights. Hitler was so impressed with Hedin that he even had him deliver the opening address, at the 1936 Berlin Olympics.

By 1937, Himmler made the Ahnenerbe, an official organization that was attached to the S.S. and appointed Professor Walther Wüst, chairman of the 'Sanskrit Department' at Ludwig-Maximilians University, in Munich, as its new director. This move was the icing on the cake, for those like Haushofer, who now felt certain that their decades-long struggle would finally attain fruition! Himmler even authorized the establishment of a 'Special Tibet Institute', under the auspices of the Ahnenerbe, named the 'Sven Hedin Institute for Inner Asia and Expeditions'.

Tibet had long been considered a place *closed* to Westerners. Getting permits meant navigating between India, Britain, China and Tibet *itself*...a task that became all the more difficult, if you were German! So, for the Nazis, the establishment of the 'Tibet Institute' was crucial!

Tibet was in the midst of trying to renegotiate its contracts with the Japanese. Long harassed by the Chinese and fed up of the British in India, using its soil for their opium trade, Tibetan authorities wanted to develop cordial and balanced ties with the Japanese...and their allies-the Germans! Under such circumstances, getting access into this secretive world was becoming more and more plausible for the Nazis. *'Paradise' finally seemed within reach!*

For Gustav however, the mystery of Shambhala wasn't simply about *where* it was, but also in trying to decipher '*WHAT*' it was. With his research now being regularly funded by the Ahnenerbe, he was beginning to believe that he could be the one for the task. The key was trying to unearth the origins of the name – Shambhala!

But as he delved deep into the damp and foggy wisps of history, he realized, much to his amazement that although the term had many different romantic interpretations, including as Haushofer had suggested - an ice age myth, it was by historical standards, a fairly recent one!

The earliest recorded reference to this term came from a Hindu text the 'Vishnu Purana', of the 4th Century A.D. This was something Gustav was familiar with, as it spoke of the 'Yuga' cycles and especially the fourth age – the 'Kali Yuga'...*the age of sorrows!* It spoke of how during this extremely bleak period that brings with it a complete collapse of human morality; the last 'Avatar of Vishnu' will descend on Earth, in a city called Shambhala, to cleanse mankind of all its evils! This source named Vishnu's last Avatar as 'Kalki' and described how he would ride out of this city and destroy an invading group, who were bent on destruction...thus bringing about the end of the 'Kali Yuga' and ushering in the 'New Golden Age'!

Unfortunately for Gustav, this was not particularly useful. It seemed to treat Shambhala as an allegory...*rather than an actual place.* According to this source, Shambhala would simply be the place, where Vishnu's last Avatar would take birth...not much to go on with.

The only part of this narrative that really bothered him was the description of Kalki riding out from his city, and destroying an 'invading force'. *What invading group was this?* ...Even his mentor Karl Haushofer had been troubled by something *he* had come across in his researches...something that had prevented him from exploring this further. Could this prophecy be the reason? Had Haushofer somehow made the connection between this invading force and the German Reich? *Could this be a prophecy about the Nazis?*

No...! Gustav pushed further. He wasn't going to follow in his mentor's footsteps and allow some age old superstition, deter him from his goals.

Relentlessly...with single-minded dedication, he kept up his studies, never missing out on following through any scrap of information that appeared promising. This constant obsession gradually began to take a toll on both his physical health and his psyche. His colleagues in the Nazi Party now began to take note of his increasingly frenzied behavior. It seemed the slightest of provocations was enough to set him off!

It was sometime in the summer of 1936, in a dusty, forgotten corner of Vienna, that Gustav got his first major breakthrough! Having spent every waking moment, thinking, researching and dreaming about Shambhala, he had been on the verge of giving up, when an old acquaintance happened to mention a strange collection of books, owned by an obscure Turkish book-dealer...based on the outskirts of Vienna.

After much searching, Gustav managed to track down the address and fix up a meeting with the man, who much to his surprise wasn't really a book-dealer at all, but rather just an old and partly senile emigrant, who had spent most of his youth in Asia.

It took some amount of communication with the locals, before Gustav could get the right address. When he finally found it, he realized that it was a structure he had in fact already walked past a few times, during his search. It was also located in the oldest part of the suburbs, a section that was largely abandoned and not easy to navigate.

Most of the locals could not even remember the home owner's name. They simply knew him as the 'eccentric bibliophile', who rarely came out and when upset, cursed loudly in Arabic! Those, whom Gustav spoke to, were reluctant to introduce him, for the old man was known to have a fierce temper.

By the time Gustav was finally able to convince one of them to *at least* lead him to the spot, it had gotten quite dark and the setting sun cast a dull haze all around...*the entire area seemed to emanate a strange hypnotic charm, drawing the exhausted Gustav towards it.*

From the outside, the man's house did not seem like much...a relatively small brick enclosure...not very creatively built, and having only one level...*possibly two.*

With his 'guide' unwilling to walk him to the gate, Gustav found himself staring across the narrow street, at this rundown place that he had walked past, earlier in the day! As he stood, wondering what to do next, his mind went back to his quest. It was probably the emptiness and the silence of the street, at this time of the day that made him reflect on Tibet and *how* it might connect to the lost city of 'Shambhala'!

Haushofer's theory, linking Shambhala with Mount Kailasha, in Tibet, seemed to echo in his mind...he had seen pictures of the place...a beautiful, pristine mountain, flanked by four smaller ones and a magnificent valley with two large lakes in it...he could visualize it perfectly, right now...a location sacred to the followers of four faiths...a line of pilgrims, steadfast in their faith, making their way up the valley...the sun in all its glory, reflecting off the snow covered landscape...so bright!...so, so bright...*BLINDINGLY BRIGHT!*

Gustav was suddenly forced to shield his eyes...against the glare... he squinted...*barely able to keep his eyes open!* He saw a faint outline in the background...an outline of a beautiful, floating city...an ethereal city with golden gates and sacred prayer bells...from which, drifted the most melodious and divine sounds, he had ever heard... the sounds themselves appeared to carry with them, perfumed winds from this magical land...and all of a sudden, he realized what he was witnessing...*Shambhala!*

WHAT!!!! He forced his eyes open and looked...he was still standing on the narrow street, opposite the house, he was to visit. Everything seemed to be the same as before. The setting sun still cast the same orange hue, only now; *it seemed a little dimmer somehow!*

He shook his head...what *HAD* he just seen? Surely, it was a trick...a hallucination...apparitions caused by an overworked mind... nothing more.

As he crossed over though, Gustav couldn't help but feel that it was also an omen!

CHAPTER FIVE

It had taken Gustav almost an hour, to introduce himself to the book-dealer and explain to him, his reasons for being there. The old man, who had initially seemed perplexed, gradually relented and allowed Gustav to enter his house, through an extremely low hanging corridor that led up to a central staircase.

Once inside, it quickly became clear that the house itself was a fairly large one...*much larger than it had seemed from the outside!* This was probably because of way it had been constructed. There didn't seem to be any definite plan or pattern to it.

But as large as the house was, it was completely overrun with books, scraps of paper and broken bits of unrecognizable material, from who knew where! The entire place looked like a scrap heap of curios, from all over the world, and yet Gustav couldn't help but notice that amidst the mountains of waste, were age-old, crumbling documents that possibly had some intrinsic value. The only *other* resident in this crumbling place was a much younger woman, who seemed to be the caretaker, cook and assistant...all in one!

The old man gingerly led him to what looked like an extremely crowded, yet nicely built, study area and offered him a seat, on a low lying cot. Tea was served as soon as the two had settled, and without a word, the old man pointed to a series of pamphlets, kept on a table between them. Gustav was about to say something, but something in the man's demeanor, caused him to change his mind.

This was...surprising...after a lifetime of bullying others, the feeling of being intimidated...was discomforting...to say the least! He quietly picked up the leaflets and began to skim through them.

Suddenly, something caught his eye. These pamphlets contained a Tibetan version of the same story, he had read earlier...the legend of 'Shambhala and Kalki'...but this one was a Buddhist variation of that tale. Gustav noticed that its source seemed to be a few centuries 'younger' than the one, he had read in the Vishnu Purana, and it was cited as being from Buddhist literary material called the 'Kalachakra Texts'.

"Kalachakra"...*where had he heard this term?*

Almost echoing his thoughts, the old man said softly, "Kalachakra means the 'Wheels of Time'."

"What?" How did you...?"

"Read" the man said simply.

Gustav looked at him, in mute amazement...and then read on. This was indeed a variation of the 'Shambhala myth'. Here however, Shambhala was described as much more than just a city...it was an entire land...*an entire continent!*

According to this version, a king would come to India, from this mythic kingdom and gain the knowledge of the 'Kalachakra', from the Buddha himself. He would then travel back to his kingdom and establish a dynasty of rulers, based on these principles.

Seven generations would follow, and then the 'Eighth King' would unify the people of all castes and communities, into one brotherhood and crown himself, under the title of 'Kalki'. The story also detailed how it would be during this phase that an invading army bent on destruction would arrive and all the righteous in the world would have to unite under the flag of Kalki to fight it off!

This last part was very similar to what he had read earlier. The *'repelling of the invaders'*...had an ominous feel about it! Gustav looked up in surprise and saw the old man staring at him; with a sly look in his eyes...*a disorienting look*...clearly, there was something going on over here...something the old man wasn't telling him! It was too much to assume that even as Gustav had searched this man out, this text, with a variation of the myth that had been such a burning obsession in his life, had just *happened* to be lying here!!! 'Who' or '*What*' was he dealing with over here?

"What do you know about this?" Gustav asked cautiously.

The old man simply smiled and looked on.

Gustav tried again, "Please...help me understand that which I look for. I have searched far and wide for answers to my quest and never have I felt more certain of finding them...than I do now! Please, help me get what I have come for. You clearly know much more than you are willing to share. I look into your eyes and see the wisdom of all your years, sparkle through. I *need* your guidance now."

"You search for the lost city of Shambhala." The old man said plainly.

"Yes!" Gustav replied in awe, "I have spent years looking up every possible reference to it and I am yet to unearth anything substantial. I know the secrets of Shambhala lie in Tibet, but I need something more than that to convince my superiors, to sponsor an expedition into the unknown...anything that you might have...anything that you can tell me...that you think will be of assistance."

"Drink" The man replied again in the same tone...his eyelids almost shut. There was a curious soporific taste to the drink that he offered Gustav. *'Tea'*? Gustav couldn't say for sure...but nonetheless... he drank.

"That what you seek has proved to be so challenging, for you haven't quite fully managed to understand it."

Gustav said nothing...*he was suddenly having a hard time keeping his eyes open.*

"My boy, while it is true that your journey *must* begin in Tibet, Shambhala is more than just a physical place...more than just a location one can travel to...It is a realm both internal and external! One that can be reached *only* when one has achieved the perfect balance between body and mind."

"But I thought that the lost city was the abode of an ancient culture that had managed to escape the destruction of an earlier cycle." Gustav said...his mind unnaturally calm...his thoughts much slower...his voice slurring!

"All legends have a grain of truth in them...it is for seekers such as ourselves to find that grain and decipher its meaning, from the chaos that surrounds it. The destruction you speak of...a great cataclysmic flood...survivors escaping to higher ground...are you certain that these legends refer to actual events? Or are they a metaphor for man's escape from the darkness of approaching ignorance...towards the higher ground of enlightenment?"

Gustav was silent…he couldn't be sure if his eyes were still open. But what the old man was saying was clearly coming alive in front of his eyes!

"If one *does* look at the 'Kalachakra' simply as a geography text, it would be easy to find the physical descriptions and the latitudes that mark Shambhala. In both Hinduism and versions of Buddhism, the center of the cosmos is believed to be a still point in the heavens, around which the entire universe revolves. The Earthly representation of which is 'Mount Meru', one of the most sacred spots, in the mythologies of both faiths."

"Mount Meru is described as being a high central peak, surrounded by four slightly smaller peaks and washed by the 'waters of purity' itself! If one were to compare the astronomical measurements given in the 'Kalachakra' to the geographical co-ordinates on Earth, the location of the Meru corresponds pretty closely with the location of Mount Kailasha, in Northern Tibet. This makes sense, considering how Kailasha is sacred to both Hindus and Buddhists."

Gustav nodded slowly…his mind felt heavy…and he still found it impossible to open his eyes…yet what this man was saying in every way matched his own research and talks with his mentor.

The old man continued, "If we look at the geography that surrounds Mount Kailasha, we can see that even the texts describe Shambhala, as a beautiful, pristine valley, with two lakes in it…and a narrow body of land that connects them. This is exactly what we see around Kailasha."

"I have studied this already." Gustav wanted to say…instead he found himself only able to incoherently mumble.

"And now, my child, now that your mind is finally at peace, I reveal to you the secrets of actually entering paradise!"

Gustav tensed…unable to move. *He could barely feel his own breath anymore.*

"The secret is in the name itself…for 'Shambhala' literally means 'a place of bliss'. The reason why it is associated with Kailasha is that according to Hinduism, one of the supreme deities, Shiva, lives on this sacred mountain and Shiva literally signifies bliss! For devout Hindus, a pilgrimage to Mount Kailasha is nothing short of a physical journey to a land of bliss. But your quest must take you much further. Once you reach this sacred spot, you must undertake the second part of your journey...*one that is internal!*"

"What do you mean?"

"In Hindu and Buddhist meditative practices, one of the most important principles is a focus on the 'Chakras' or 'Energy whorls' that exist within all living things. According to mystics, who practise this form of meditation, these energy whorls are linked to the 'Spiritual Self' *within* the 'Physical one' and generally lie dormant within a person. Hence most people live a life that is *purely physical* in nature. Only someone, who has mastered the techniques of 'Chakra meditation', can begin to harness his/her power and truly unify body and mind. These centers of energy are believed to be located along the spine in the human body, starting with the tail bone and going up to the crown of the head."

"Chakra meditation demands different techniques for activating each individual energy center. In this context, 'Shambhala' represents the 'Heart Chakra'...a place that can be accessed *only* if your heart is truly cleansed of all forms of 'Karma', including greed, anger, jealousy and hatred. Only by regulating these *Internal Karmic winds* can one truly ascend into Shambhala!"

Gustav found himself floating in a void...no longer corporeal, he felt absolutely weightless...the old man's voice seemed to echo from a far off location. He felt frightened...like an abandoned child...*cut off from the very tethers of reality!*

Slowly...gradually, from the very edges of perception...he felt clarity. *It felt like waking up, from a dreamless sleep, in an unknown place and not recognizing yourself!*

He found himself floating above a wind-swept, ice-covered landscape...a barren, austere, yet strangely enchanting landscape! ... One that he had never seen before...and yet one that felt...*strangely familiar*. A central mountain towering over four smaller ones...two milk white lakes separated by a narrow ridge of land...a vision straight out of an eccentric artist's wildest imagination...tortured beauty...an ethereal paradise...*Shambhala!*

"Yes…this is indeed the land of your dreams…now listen carefully my child, for I now reveal to you, that which has long been forbidden to others…the long lost secrets of entering paradise! Listen carefully, for one day; it could well be the difference between life and death."

Gustav said nothing.

"However, you shall remember my words only, if and when, you *actually* complete the physical half of the journey to Tibet and prove yourself worthy of the spiritual half. Till such a time…my words will simply remain a haunting mnemonic in the dark depths of your mind…a place that you know exists…but one that is forever…*just out of reach!*"

"How do you know all of this?" Gustav croaked…his words swallowed by the winds of the mystical land, he felt himself floating above.

"I know this…and guard it so carefully, for I was the last person to enter…*Paradise!*"

CHAPTER SIX

"To unlock the doors to Shambhala, one needs to approach the riddle of its location, both physically and *spiritually*...at the same time!"

"Travel past 'Nanga Parbhat'...the naked mountain that forces one to shed all desires...down to one's very soul. Free of inhibitions and cleansed of your sins, you may proceed to 'Mount Kailasha'...the entrance into paradise. You will then have to unlock the ancient seal that prevents the unworthy from entering!"

"What seal?" the question barely managed to breach Gustav's lips. The mystical vision he was witnessing...an astral vision of the sacred land around 'Mount Kailasha', was burning itself into his subconscious...*calling out to him!*

"Seven men you shall need...seven loyal brave hearts, who will act together for the greater good...each representing a different energy source, located inside a human being...the Seven 'Chakras'!"

The words seemed to echo throughout the sacred land Gustav was experiencing...their wisdom reverberating through his mind! The energy centers, the old man spoke of...appeared to dance in front of his eyes...a dazzling vision...*incomparable!*

He felt an energy spike move up the length of his own spine...the bottom of his tail bone...then the region of his genitals... then the naval...then the heart...throat...the spiritual 'third eye of enlightenment'...and finally the crown of the head...the 'Seven Chakras' that form one's life-force!

The voice continued...now much softer, "To enter the city of heaven, needs the perfect union of *all* 'Seven Chakras'! Together they form an energy grid that the ancients referred to as 'Kundalini'. The seven of you shall form the energy grid...together accomplishing, what is otherwise impossible! And you my son, you shall represent the most important 'Chakra' of all...the one that unlocks the gates of Shambhala... '*Anahata*' - the Heart Chakra"

Gustav strained to listen to the words, as the old man's voice dropped to a whisper. He was beginning to mumble the secret ritual intended to unlock the gates of paradise...then...*Gustav's mind went completely blank!*

CHAPTER SEVEN

Darkness...it is not just the absence of light, but the unspoken threat of being able to immutably *extinguish* it! It is humanity's perpetual... ubiquitous fear...one that invokes terror not through the horror of what it contains...but through what it *might* contain! Swimming through a sea of darkness, can be a scary proposition, especially when one does *NOT* remember having entered it!

Light...!! Almost always, it acts as the harbinger of hope...its ultimate manifestation...the Sun! But as Icarus found out to his peril...fly too close to it...*and it can burn your wings!*

But light also helps dispel the dark...clear one's perception...and vision...

...and as his vision gradually cleared, Gustav found himself lying on a low bed, in what looked like a poor run-down house. His mind was still filled with a haze that prevented him from thinking clearly. For one horrifying moment, he could not even remember who *he* was! As his memory slowly came back, a cold sweat broke out all over him. He sat up with a start and...instantly regretted it, feeling a wave of nausea, enshroud him.

"Hold still sir, you are still very weak." He looked to see where the voice had come from, and saw a young girl standing near him, holding a glass of water. He reached out gingerly, suddenly realizing that his throat was dry. His hands trembled, as he held the glass. "Where am I? What day is it?" He asked...slightly choking on the water.

"It is Tuesday, the 3rd of March. You have been sleeping for the last three days. We found you near the old market...in a terrible state... delirious, speaking incoherently! We would have dismissed you as a lunatic, but for your Nazi insignia. My father and I were barely able to get you home and you have been here since then. Tell me good sir, how came you in such dire straits?"

How indeed? Gustav shook his head trying to remember what had happened. He had been at the house of the old Turkish book lover and then...the situation had gotten completely out of hand. *The old man had done something impossible!*

Gustav had searched him out, hoping to learn more about Tibet's connection with Shambhala, and yet the man had done much more than that. He had somehow...in an inexplicable manner...actually taken Gustav to the very gates of the lost city! What had followed, he had no memory of...and yet, there was no way he was going to share all of that with this girl, however kind she had been!

"Tell me Fraulein, at the place you and your father found me, there was an old, oddly shaped house, belonging to an old man...a very strange old man, who the townspeople say is slightly eccentric. What can you tell me about him?"

The girl seemed stunned by his question. Her face filled with confusion, obscuring her pretty features. "What old man do you speak of sir and which townspeople? There is an oddly shaped beige-colored house at the place that you describe...but it has been abandoned since the time my father moved in over here...*and that was 30 years ago!* What is more, ours is the only house in the entire region that is still occupied! The others have all moved out...long ago. As you must know, this region of the suburbs has been marked for redevelopment. For all practical purposes this is a ghost town. So what townspeople do you speak of?"

Gustav left the house in a daze. There was no rational explanation for what he had gone through. Even after being asleep for over three days, his body still felt exhausted. He checked his pockets and found he still had all his belongings, including his money. As he hailed a taxi to take him back to his hotel room in Vienna, the old man's words rang out with startling clarity in his head.

"You shall remember my words only, if and when, you actually complete the physical half of the journey to Tibet and prove yourself worthy of the spiritual half. Till such a time...my words will simply remain a haunting mnemonic in the dark depths of your mind...a place that you know exists...but one that is forever...just out of reach!"

EPISODE FIVE

CHAPTER ONE

The year 1938 saw an audacious expedition launched into a land that was seen by many, as the *'living embodiment of spirituality'*…Tibet. The expedition was headed by one of German's top researchers – Ernst Schaffer and a team of Nazi scientists, with the purpose of finding concrete evidence in this most austere of lands…evidence that linked the 'Aryan Super Race' to the lost super-civilization of Atlantis!

The roots of this mission lay in a secret meeting Nazi Chief, Heinrich Himmler, had with the promising young natural scientist, Ernst Schaffer. For, it was in early 1936 that Schaffer, already a rising star in Germany's scientific community, found himself suddenly summoned to Nazi Headquarters…for undisclosed reasons!

On arrival, he underwent an extremely thorough safety-check, before being led down to a secret underground conference room. The meticulousness of the safety regulations and the sheer number of personnel present convinced him that his appointment was with none other than the 'Führer' – Adolf Hitler!

This realization had done nothing to ease Schaffer's mind. *Yes…it was indeed a privilege to be invited by Hitler to Nazi headquarters!* … but the suddenness of the summons, the veneer of secrecy surrounding it and the extent of security…were all deeply troubling…*Surely, something was not quite right!*

Even as he was offered a seat, Schaffer noticed that all the sentries carried assault rifles. This was becoming more and more worrisome… he tried to find out why he had been summoned, but got nothing from the guards. *They even refused to make eye contact.* As soon as he was seated, rather awkwardly at one end of a large oval conference table, they exited the room, with military precision. Left all alone, Schaffer felt like a man on a death-row!

...Throughout the 1930s, there was no one in the scientific community in Germany, more well-known and glamorous than Dr. Ernst Schaffer. Young, good looking and dynamic, he cut a dashing figure, whether in the field or on stage. He had been part of two American led expeditions to Tibet and his lectures and talks, about his adventures in remote and largely unknown lands, were loved by one and all.

Even though, his scientific expertise lay in the field of Zoology, Schaffer wasn't shy of using a gun. He fancied himself an ace hunter and claimed that 'he liked to study mammals and birds *after* he had shot them'. For a Germany that had been brought up on a regular dose of 'Alpha-Male' stereotypes, this image of Schaffer seemed to symbolize Germanic spirit! He was also well respected among the Nazi Elite... and as far as he could tell, he had done *nothing* to tarnish this image.

So why then had he been summoned so suddenly and whom was he supposed to meet?

Slowly, the thick, oaken doors of the conference room opened, and flanked by three others, in walked a figure that sent a cold shiver down Schaffer's spine. On the face of it, there was nothing imposing about the short, bespectacled man, who walked in with a slight stoop...*it was his feared reputation that made him so formidable!* Schaffer knew that this man was the head of all the police and para-military units across Germany...the absolute leader of more than a million armed troops. A man whose reputation for extreme cruelty, was already legend and who was the most feared man in Germany...*arguably even more so than Adolf Hitler!* With a sinking feeling, Schaffer realized he had been summoned by Heinrich Himmler...he also realized...he was most likely going to die!

Himmler's beady eyes hidden behind thick glasses, displayed no emotions. *Cold stones floating in a sea of black*! Schaffer half expected Himmler to simply shoot him right there...he was certainly known to do that...without the 'hassles' of an explanation!

Instead, Himmler simply nodded and the two armed officers spun about and marched out of the room... *'Like well-trained dogs'*, thought Schaffer. This left only Himmler and a much younger man, who looked like an academician, in the room with him. With no more guns in the room, Schaffer breathed a little easier...maybe this wasn't going to be as bad as it had seemed...maybe the 'Reich' wanted something *from him!*

Himmler did not waste time with pleasantries...one did not need to, if one held the power of life and death in one's hands. He introduced the younger man as, Captain Friedrich Gustav, and then got right to the point, "Dr. Schaffer, we have a proposal for you...one that we think you might find fascinating." *His voice could have cut glass.*

Schaffer breathed more easily now...his curiosity was piqued. *Interesting...the Reich had a proposal for him? They needed HIS help?* He waited for Himmler to go on.

"We have followed your work quite closely and your many sojourns in the Far-East are what most interest us. We know you have been to Tibet...*twice*...with the Americans." Himmler said the word 'Americans' with undeniable causticity.

Schaffer felt a trickle of sweat assault his brow...Shit! ...Was this what had irked the Nazis? *The room suddenly seemed colder!*

Schaffer did not consider himself, a Nazi sympathizer, but a lot had changed since Hitler came to power. Opposition from all walks of life had been persecuted. *This was deeply disturbing!*

"We would however like you to lead a third expedition to Tibet... for Germany...for *us*."

What? Schaffer's breath caught in his throat...another expedition to Tibet? This sounded interesting...more opportunities to explore that exotic land ...*one financed by the Nazis*...meaning this one would have none of the 'normal' limitations and shortages in supplies, he had encountered on his previous expeditions!

But surely...this was too good to be true! ...He was sure there was a catch somewhere...*there had to be!* It was unlike the second most powerful man in Germany, to just randomly call up an explorer, even a German one, and offer to finance his next expedition!

"I would love to, sir!" Schaffer replied, cautiously. "Nothing would give me greater happiness than leading an expedition under the German Flag."

Himmler looked across to the younger man; he had previously introduced as Gustav...and exchanged a wry smile!

"I am glad you think that way Dr. Schaffer." Himmler said...*his voice displayed none of that pleasure.* Here was a man clearly used to having his way around things. One did not say '*no*' to Heinrich Himmler. Schaffer had even heard reports of extra-custodial deaths, beatings and summary executions of those, who had dared to displease this man.

"You see Dr. Schaffer..." the younger man – Gustav now took over, "While you have graciously agreed to the expedition itself, it will have to be carried out on our terms."

'Here it comes' thought Schaffer...this was the '*catch*'. He wondered if he had been a little too eager, in agreeing to it, in the first place.

The man continued, "We have gone through your research and while it is largely fascinating, we believe that you like countless others, have been deceived by some very incorrect and Un-Germanic science."

'*Un-Germanic*'? *What did that even mean?* "What scientific lapse do you speak of sir?" Schaffer inquired hesitatingly.

Gustav looked over towards Himmler, who once again nodded. "You see Dr. Schaffer there are a few things that concern us. You have mentioned in your reports that these expeditions to Tibet were of a purely 'scientific character'...that the primary objective of these expeditions, was the creation of a complete scientific record of Tibet, through a synthesis of Geology, Botany, Zoology, and Ethnology."

"Yes." Schaffer replied, not really clear where this was going, "I did bring back valuable samples...both flora and fauna that have since increased our understanding of the planet's ecosystem."

"Yes, but this alone will not get you the benefits of a fully funded expedition to Tibet, under the German Flag. There is something else that we need...something more...much, *much* more!"

This was what Schaffer had been dreading...this was surely going to be something politically motivated. He decided to put all his cards on the table, *before* matters came to a head. "As both of you gentlemen are well aware, I am not a politically oriented man...I am a scientist...I will be honored to lead a scientific expedition to Tibet...or anywhere else that you want, under the banner of the Third Reich, but I will *NOT* be a part of a political mission!"

An awkward silence followed...*Damn*...Schaffer wondered whether he had spoken too soon...crossed the line...looking at Himmler's glassy expression, it was impossible to say. If Himmler thought him too head-strong and thus expendable, there was no telling what he might do. Maybe, he should just apologize to the man and hear what he had to say.

But before he could utter another word, the Nazi Chief spoke again, "Dr. Schaffer, I am sure you have heard of Atlantis." The voice seemed to come from nowhere!

"The Myth of the Lost City of Atlantis...?" Schaffer asked, surprised, at the abrupt change in context.

"Believe me Doctor, it is no mere myth. Atlantis was a very real place and we believe, we know where to find it. It is why, we need your assistance." Himmler said bluntly.

"You think Atlantis is in Tibet?" Schaffer asked incredulously. He had never *ever* heard a theory like this...and he had heard a few weird ones about Atlantis.

"No...not Atlantis itself...but we do believe that Tibet might be where the *Atlanteans* escaped to and settled! If this is true, in Tibet, we might find their descendants alive, today. In your own travels you have documented how austere and impenetrable some of the regions in Tibet are and how the natural terrain provides the perfect protection against any dilution of the gene pool."

"The way Plato describes Atlantis in his works, makes it clear that such an advanced culture could have existed *only if* its population was a Super-Race...probably the original Super-Race. The legend then tells us that this island Utopia was destroyed in one day and one night, as a result of a catastrophic flood, earthquake or volcano. We believe however, even with such a disaster, a Super-Race would have found some way of escaping. At least some of the Atlanteans would have survived the destruction and then made their way to different parts of the planet. We think that it is they who helped establish some of the earliest recorded cultures, such as the Egyptians, the Greeks and the Romans."

Schaffer wanted to shake his head in disbelief. This was not even a plausible theory. This was an absolute mockery of everything he had studied in his life. Himmler had given him a hypothesis that was straight out of the 'lunatic-fringe' textbook.

"But where is the evidence to support such a theory? *He wanted to say such a wild theory.* And how does this connect to an expedition to Tibet?" Schaffer asked, cautiously. He felt like an idiot...*surely no better theory could be expected of the Nazis.*

Himmler was quiet for a moment...perhaps unused to being challenged thus. "We believe...*I* strongly believe that some of the survivors of Atlantis ended up in Tibet. There the natural fortification and the sheer remoteness of the place kept them from intermixing with other races, thus ensuring a 'pure lineage'. These pure blooded people might even be related to the Aryan Super-Culture that we Germans descend from. It is paramount that we find this culture in Tibet and quickly at that! Tensions in Europe are simmering and might reach a fever-pitch any time. If war were to break out between Germany and Britain or France, we might find it impossible to enter Tibet. The British and the Chinese might simply block access to these parts, for any one of German origin."

'Ahhh'...finally the *'cat was out of the bag'.* This is the reason the Nazis wanted him to lead a mission to Tibet. Schaffer realized that if he did go ahead with this, the expedition would involve none of the old goals of trying to map out a relatively uncharted land. Himmler and the Nazis were not interested in the discovery of new species of plants and animals. The obsession with 'racial purity' had led them to concoct this wild theory that Tibet was the final resting place of a race of 'Super-beings' from the legendary lost world of Atlantis!

The fact that there was absolutely no evidence for Atlantis itself, *much less that its survivors had travelled to Tibet and settled there,* did not seem to bother Himmler. To Schaffer, Himmler seemed to be the kind of person, who did not let facts get in the way of a good theory.

But Schaffer also noticed that the younger man, Gustav, had seemed less convinced with Himmler's wild assertions. So maybe, not all Nazis were as delusional about Tibet...and yet Gustav seemed *just* as keen on the expedition...this was interesting...*maybe there were other hidden agendas.* Schaffer made a mental note to talk to Gustav separately...if possible.

His train of thought was suddenly interrupted, "So what do you say doctor…will you do us the honor of heading this expedition? Would you do your country this *one small service*?" Himmler's tone making it clear, that however polite the question…it was a purely rhetorical one!

"Yes…chief…I shall be honored to…however, I do have some requests of my own…things I would need, to make this mission a success."

"State them." Himmler said sardonically.

"Tibet is not a place that one can take 'new comers' or 'first-timers'. My two expeditions have shown me the sheer difficulty and innumerable obstacles one encounters, in a region so remote that none of the conventional rules of exploration apply! I would want that the crew, which accompanies me be made of only those who have been with me before. We can hire local porters to do the 'heavy lifting', but I do not want to endanger German lives, any more than absolutely necessary." Schaffer emphasized the last bit, to try and convince Himmler, of what he was saying.

"Unacceptable." Himmler said, flatly refusing to even discuss this further. "As noble as your motives might be, we have no intention of sponsoring an expedition to Tibet, for any purpose, but the one I mentioned earlier. This *cannot* become simply another one of your 'scientific explorations'. We have hand-picked a special team of rock climbers, mountaineers and researchers, who will be led by Capt. Gustav over here…that will accompany you into Tibet. The team has already been briefed about the purpose of the visit and will take every precaution to ensure its success. Your task doctor will be to guide them in and out of Tibet safely."

So that was it…he was meant to serve as a *lackey*…a tour guide. This was what it all boiled down to. Schaffer did not know if he could still refuse. It would appear that he had already made a commitment and…you did not break promises made to Heinrich Himmler!

"The entire expedition will happen under the auspices of the 'Ahnenerbe' - the 'S.S. Ancestral Heritage Society' and we ask you to perform research, based on Hanns Horgiger's studies and not what you consider 'mainstream science.'"

"You mean his theories about 'Glacial Cosmogony'?" Schaffer wanted to say *'bogus theories'* but held himself back...just in time.

"Yes." Himmler replied.

This last bit came as a complete shock. Schaffer had read some of the papers published by the Ahnenerbe...papers written by Horgiger and found them to be a complete waste of time! The theory that Himmler had just confirmed - 'Glacial Cosmogony' - was one of Horgiger's most famous propositions.

According to this, 'ice' was the basic substance of all cosmic processes and ice moons, ice planets and the global ether also made of ice had determined the entire development of the universe. Hence through this theory, it was believed possible to accurately predict the weather and achieve a body of physics, fundamentally different to what had been accepted since Newton and Einstein.

For Schaffer, what made this particularly *'unscientific'* was that Horgiger had not arrived at this theory through any kind of research or study but had allegedly "received it" in a "vision". By his own admission, Horgiger had been observing the moon...in a dream and had been struck by the notion that the brightness and roughness of the moon was due to its surface being made of ice.

And this was the theory that Himmler wanted him to follow, to locate Atlanteans in Tibet!

Schaffer knew that arguing was out of question, at this point. No matter how illogical these theories, the Nazis were intent on promoting them, for they supposedly represented a 'German' alternative to the physics based on Einstein's theory of Relativity that the rest of the world accepted.

CHAPTER TWO

Over the next several weeks, there were a series of clandestine meetings Schaffer had to attend at Nazi Headquarters, where he regularly met Himmler and Gustav. These were to discuss the various terms and conditions, as well as requirements, of the Tibetan Expedition. It was clear that this journey would take place under the patronage of the 'Ahnenerbe' and include individuals shortlisted by Himmler…individuals who were dedicated to keeping alive the pseudo-scientific theories, so fancied by the Nazis.

Schaffer, still keen on maintaining a degree of autonomy for himself…and not compromising the scientific temper of the expedition, refused to include Edmund Kiss in his team. Kiss was the Ahnenerbe's best adept of pseudo-science and his exclusion angered other members of the group. There was even the chance that the Ahnenerbe might *refuse* to issue funds, putting the entire expedition in jeopardy!

For Schaffer, Himmler's 'quasi-historical' description of Atlantis was a baseless fantasy…regardless of how the Ahnenerbe scientists sugar-coated it. What made it even worse was that according to Himmler, even conventional physics was somehow 'Jewish' since a large part of it was based on Einstein's work and so shouldn't be used in Nazi research. Instead he was expected to use the Ahnenerbe's pseudoscience…something he had no time for!

With neither of the parties willing to budge from their positions, Himmler resolved the deadlock, by proposing the following condition: Schaffer's demands would be accepted and the visit would continue as planned…*if* Schaffer and all his associates would become S.S. members!

In order to succeed in his mission, Schaffer had to compromise and agree. As a result, all the members who eventually undertook the long and perilous journey to Tibet *were S.S. members!*

CHAPTER THREE

Through his many briefings at Nazis Headquarters, Schaffer tried his best to speak with Gustav...*privately*. Since his very first interaction with the man, he had suspected that there was more to Gustav than what met the eye.

While on the surface, Gustav came across as a loyal, dedicated Nazi, it had seemed that he was unsure of some of Himmler's wild rants. Certainly, when the discussion had centered on the possibility of finding Atlanteans in Tibet, Gustav had looked extremely skeptical. And yet this was the same person, who desperately wanted to be a part of the expedition. Did he then have his own reasons for making this journey? Schaffer wasn't sure and each time the two spoke, Gustav would cleverly avoid taking the discussion towards those murky waters.

Schaffer's real concern was that in an expedition such as this, being able to trust those with you could well prove to be the difference between life and death. Having someone on board who had an agenda of his own was dangerous...*to say the least!* But Gustav assured him, that the success of the mission meant just as much to him as anyone else and promised to have Schaffer's back.

Having agreed to Himmler's conditions, Schaffer was allowed to recruit his own team. He chose to recruit young, fit men, who would be well suited to such an arduous journey. At age 24, Karl Wienert was the team's Geologist. Also age 24, Edmund Geer was selected as the Technical Leader, to organize the expedition. A relatively old teammate at the age of 38 was Ernst Krause, who was to double up as a Filmmaker and Entomologist and Bruno Beger was the team's 26-year-old Anthropologist.

Along with this team, Gustav would lead another group of six members, who had been chosen from *within* the Nazi ranks...but as to who they were and what their qualifications and accomplishments were, was anyone's guess. Schaffer just hoped that the expedition to Tibet…and specifically his own part in it…was not meant to serve as a cover for something more sinister. Ever since he had heard Himmler profess interest in Tibet, he had felt extremely uneasy. By giving these men access to such an innocent and uncorrupted land, he felt like someone deliberately leading a tiger…*straight into the sheep's pen!*

Nonetheless, the die had already been cast and the team began preparations for what the Germans hoped would be a historic expedition. Schaffer, the only one in the group, who had previously been to the Far-East, knew how dangerous expeditions into the Himalayan Mountain Ranges were…the weather itself could overturn even the best laid plans. The relentless climbs…extreme temperature conditions…the unceasing winds…and the extreme loneliness, could affect even the best explorers. Only those who were physically and mentally equipped to survive such extremes would have a shot at succeeding. This was why, those accompanying him, were asked to undergo a rigorous three-month long training camp with the 'Wehrmacht' – the Armed forces of Nazi Germany.

It was at these camps that Schaffer learnt more about the enigmatic Capt. Gustav, who was scheduled to accompany him to Tibet. Schaffer always had his suspicions, but soon one thing became clear: Gustav was a man, who kept to himself and the only person Schaffer saw him speak to, was an older man, who frequented Nazi Headquarters.

Schaffer was told this man was Karl Haushofer, a Nazi military advisor, who had served as the 'German Liaison Officer' to the Japanese, during their battle against the Russians, at the start of the century. Haushofer, Schaffer learnt, had spent years in Asia and claimed to have a lot of information about Chinese and Indian culture. It was clear Gustav looked up to him as a mentor.

Schaffer wondered why Haushofer hadn't offered more help to the expedition. Certainly, someone with his knowledge could be an invaluable source of information…even if he was himself too old to undertake such a journey.

The original plan was that the team would travel to China either via the Pacific or over land through Central Asia…which ever proved easier. Since Tibet was such an isolated region, getting there would mean going through a whole slew of permissions, formalities and bureaucratic red-tapism. Both the British and the Chinese, considered Tibet very much their responsibility and it was clear that getting in, would mean currying the favor of at least *one* of these powers. With German diplomatic relations with Great Britain already at an all-time low, China clearly seemed like the more viable option.

Schaffer himself recommended that the team use the Pacific route, so as to avoid raising too many eyebrows. Political tension had gripped the whole of Europe and now was certainly not the time to be disturbing the fragile peace Germany had with the Central Asian and Baltic republics. A lot of these countries had supported Germany during World War I and had ended up on the losing side. Their relationship with the German Empire since could at best be described as 'frosty'. Moreover, with the 'Bolsheviks' taking over Russia, a lot of these countries were now under the Soviet Union's 'sphere of influence'.

However, in July 1937 the team suffered a setback, when Japan invaded China's North-Eastern region of Manchuria. The unrest and carnage that followed the Japanese occupation, coupled with the fact that Japan was an ally of Germany, meant that Chinese cooperation in this matter was now virtually impossible. China had till this point maintained a neutral relationship with Germany and gaining *its* consent for the expedition had been considered difficult…but doable. However, after the Japanese invasion, the plan of using the 'Yangtze River' in China to reach Tibet was effectively ruined.

Schaffer then flew to London to seek permission to travel through India, but was turned down by the British government, who feared an imminent war with Germany. This was a second blow…and the expedition seemed doomed, before it had even begun!

With things already looking bleak, Schaffer experienced great personal tragedy. He and his wife, of just four months, were in the middle of a duck-hunting trip, when disaster struck. While on the hunt, a sudden wave caused Schaffer to drop his gun. The fall caused the gun to break in two and discharge its explosive contents, fatally wounding his wife. In spite of the best medical assistance, she passed away, soon after. For the first time in his young and adventure filled life, Ernst Schaffer found himself confronting the terrible specter of death!

This episode could have easily sounded the 'death knell' of what now seemed like a jinxed mission, but after weeks of dealing with his emotional turmoil, Schaffer got back to work on the expedition. Those, who knew him, stated that they had never seen him so focused...or driven. The hurdles that had been thrown his way only seemed to have strengthened his resolve towards the expedition. The ghost of his wife seemed to constantly egg him on...or maybe...just maybe...*it was something far darker...*

CHAPTER FOUR

There was more trouble on the horizon. By the spring of 1938, the German War Machine, re-armed under the 'tender' care of Reich's Marshall - Herman Goring was on the move. Since coming to power, Hitler had repeatedly mocked the 'Treaty of Versailles'. Now, in direct violation of it, the 'Wehrmacht' was mobilized to occupy and re-unite all German speaking provinces.

With brutal efficiency, the Nazis occupied the 'Rhineland'...a German speaking province that had been separated from Germany, following World War I and then quickly turned their attention towards Austria. These were steps towards creating a greater 'Germanic Empire'. Europe looked on with growing apprehension. Its worst fears...*those the Treaty of Versailles had tried to mitigate*, were coming true!

In spite of all of this, the Schaffer expedition set off from Berlin, on April the 19th, 1938. Along with Schaffer's handpicked team of researchers, was a second smaller group led by Capt. Gustav...its exact motivations still suspect. What was clear was that none in Gustav's team was a scientist!

Schaffer's biggest concern was that if the expedition was stopped and questioned at any stage during its travels through Asia, by the British, those under Gustav could raise suspicions that the expedition was simply a cover for a Nazi 'espionage' operation in Asia. Schaffer himself half suspected this.

The war in Asia meant that the only way they could get into Tibet was through India. And this would mean, interacting *directly* with the British Empire.

Schaffer knew there were major problems in negotiating with the British. Even though technically, Tibet was an autonomous country ruled by the 'Dalai Lama' and a 'Council of Ruling Elite', Great Britain maintained a strong presence in this region. Over the years, the British had gained the trust of the Tibetans and were the only Western Power, to be allowed access into the region. Schaffer knew that even without a European War on the horizon, the British would have been unwilling to grant him access into Tibet.

With the odds stacked against him, Schaffer decided on a dangerous gamble. As he and his crew set sail for India, they would have to cross the Suez Canal and enter the Persian Gulf. This region was under British control and Schaffer knew a German expedition would surely raise eyebrows. To avoid any kind of political connotation, he would try and emphasis the scientific nature of the expedition, while downplaying its 'Nazi Patronage'. Schaffer knew this move could anger the 'Ahnenerbe' and probably cost him their support.

Unfortunately for him, even as he and his team left Europe the racist Nazi newspaper 'Völkischer Beobachter' published a detailed article commemorating the expedition and celebrating its glorious S.S. connections.

By the time the expedition landed in British controlled Ceylon on the way to India; Indian newspapers were rife with articles titled - *'Gestapo Agents in India'*. Schaffer's worst fears had come true. He and his team were accused of being members of the German Secret Police – 'The Gestapo' - on an espionage mission in India!!

The British refused to allow the expedition even landing rights in India! In such a politically charged environment, Britain was taking no chances. Schaffer was aghast! The expedition that he had dreamt of undertaking… one he had borne so many hardships for…seemed to be over…before it even began! Suddenly, access into Tibet seemed beyond reach. He knew the only hope at this point was…if Himmler could somehow intervene and get the British to consent.

However, there was an unexpected surprise in store for him. Capt. Gustav, the secretive Nazi officer, who had accompanied the Schaffer mission with six of his own men, now proved his mettle. While in Ceylon, he managed to get in touch with Himmler and apprise him of Britain's refusal.

What followed was beyond Schaffer's wildest expectations. Himmler wrote a bitter letter addressed directly to the British Prime

Minister, Neville Chamberlain, mentioning how up to this point, the Germans had always welcomed British visitors to Germany...and treated them as close allies...and how he could not understand why the British were preventing this expeditions from entering India. He expressed his exasperation at how the British were suspecting the esteemed Dr. Schaffer, someone personally dispatched by the Reich, of being a spy!

The letter did have the desired result. Despite the Nazi war preparations, the ultra-conservative and reactionary Prime Minister Chamberlain did not want to upset relations with Germany and allowed the expedition to continue through India. Even so close to World War II, most of Western Europe was still keen on practising 'appeasement' towards Germany.

The British authorities eventually gave the Schaffer mission permission to land at Calcutta, and then travel and explore the northern province of Sikkim. Sikkim was the last Indian bastion, before crossing over into Tibet.

The British however, *DID NOT* grant him permission to enter Tibet. Apparently even 'appeasement policies' had their limitations. Schaffer would be allowed to carry out research on the tribes and communities, living around the Indian border, but to cross over into Tibet; he would need the consent of the Tibetan authorities. Even though this wasn't ideal, Schaffer decided that at *this* stage, he would have to take what he got!

As the expedition reached the northern province of Sikkim, he conducted regular briefing sessions with his associates, to once again outline the objectives of this mission. Throughout these discussions, he noticed that Gustav and his group of loyalists, kept to themselves. While none of them challenged Schaffer's goals, if they *did* have any special objectives of their own, they hid them well! Schaffer even began to suspect that except for Gustav, who clearly had his own reasons for being here, the others had very little idea. They were simply following their commanding officer...*like loyal soldiers!*

CHAPTER FIVE

On arrival, the team spent the first few days in Sikkim, acclimatizing themselves to the terrain and the weather. For all the conditioning work they had done with the S.S. they knew that each one of them would *have* to be at their absolute physical peak, in order to navigate the terrain that lay ahead. Letting the body get used to the temperature and the low levels of oxygen at these altitudes, was one way of ensuring this.

Meanwhile, Schaffer also tried to gather as much data about Tibet as possible, from local sources. He wanted to know if there was some other way of entering Tibet…one that did not involve Great Britain.

But as the days slowly crept by; the restrictions imposed by the British, began to seem more and more stifling. The only person, who seemed largely unconcerned about these limitations, was Capt. Gustav. Schaffer often got the feeling that the man knew more about this part of the world…than he let out. Gustav would often venture out on his own, and for long hours at a time…search for something… but what exactly…he always refused to disclose!

Schaffer even wondered if Gustav had been to India before…or… if he had some clandestine source of information, he wasn't willing to share. Could his entire reason for wanting to be part of this mission, actually be what the British had accused them of? Maybe Gustav wasn't a researcher at all…*but a spy*, dispatched by Himmler on a mission to gather vital data, on British forces stationed in Asia. Schaffer knew that knowing Himmler, this was a very real possibility. The German sponsored 'Tibetan Expedition' and Schaffer's unquestionable reputation, could all then be just a cover for an espionage mission!

However, what struck Schaffer as ever more remarkable was that just a few days after they had arrived in Sikkim, Gustav insisted that they start buying all the supplies needed for a journey into Tibet. This would include large quantities of food, winter-wear...as well as donkeys or mules that could transport the supplies across the staggeringly high mountain passes. All this seemed unnecessary at this point, as the expedition did not have permission to enter Tibet. But Gustav seemed adamant. 'Maybe', Schaffer suspected, 'He did know something that the rest didn't'. After all, hadn't Gustav been the man, who had managed to get them into India? If he could manage the next stage as well, Schaffer would more than welcome such assistance.

Meanwhile, true to Schaffer's suspicions, Gustav had been on a quest of his own. Unlike the others, he had in fact been overjoyed that the expedition would have to approach Tibet through Sikkim rather than through China. He had a special task awaiting him in Sikkim... something he felt he *had* to accomplish, before getting into Tibet. He wanted to locate the monastery, his mentor, Karl Haushofer had spoken of...the one containing the copy of the 'Vimanika Shastra'... the document that had started it all.

Before he left Germany, Gustav had met Haushofer numerous times, in his Berlin apartment. Apart from reminiscing about old times, he had gathered as much information about the monastery from his mentor as possible. The older man had of course been only too willing to help, knowing full well that he himself would never be able to undertake such an expedition. He had long since realized that for him to witness the end of his lifelong quest, he would require someone younger and fitter to undertake the journey to Tibet.

But even as they had gone over all the details of the expedition and discussed what they collectively knew about 'Shambhala', they had both realized that the first step of locating the monastery in Sikkim would not be quite so easy. Haushofer had last been to the place more than twenty five years ago...and undoubtedly, a lot would have changed since then. What was even more frustrating for Gustav was the fact that apart from offering a very loose and rough description of the place, Haushofer's memory seemed full of gaps. There were entire periods of time, he had no memory for...*It was almost as if someone had taken an 'eraser' and selectively deleted parts of this narrative!*

Now that he was himself in India, Gustav realized that the task of finding the monastery was even tougher than they had anticipated. His plan was to visit all the monasteries around the area of Sikkim, Haushofer had described and try and identify the one containing the precious document. What he would do if and when he did find the place in question, was something he hadn't given much thought to. He hoped the monks would allow him to *borrow* the text...or at the very least, make detailed copies of it.

But soon after he began his search, he realized that there were hundreds of monasteries in the region and searching all of them, was nearly impossible. It would take him months, if not years...and already his associates were beginning to wonder, where he kept disappearing every day. For Gustav, keeping the real purpose of his mission a secret was paramount. Both he and Haushofer had agreed that the technology and power they might find in Shambhala, was best first thoroughly understood...and only then revealed to the rest of the world!

Of course, Gustav knew that by keeping his associates in the dark, he was in-a-sense acting *AGAINST* Nazi interests, but he justified his actions by telling himself that *if* his quest were to succeed; its benefits would after all be for the German People. After all, Himmler and the 'Ahnenerbe' were also trying to locate proof of an Atlantis like super-culture in Tibet. Gustav simply had some more viable data with him. But for this he needed physical proof of the 'Vimanika Shastra'... which meant locating the monastery.

His biggest concern was that the scientist leading this expedition – Ernst Schaffer had some very different and mediocre objectives that included creating a complete listing of Tibetan 'flora and fauna'. As a result, Schaffer had been the most suspicious of his behavior, after arriving in Sikkim. Gustav had managed to divert some of the attention away from his own activities, by asking Schaffer to start preparations for entering Tibet...even though the team had no official permission to do so. Schaffer, believing Gustav would once again use his influence with Himmler to get the needed consent...just as he had done in Ceylon...agreed.

From Gangtok, the capital of Sikkim, the crew purchased food and other essential supplies, along with hiring porters and guides, who spoke Tibetan...*and a wee bit of English.* These would serve as their translators. Soon a massive fifty-mule caravan of supplies was formed, all in anticipation of the permission, Gustav was expected to secure. The British officials, who observed these preparations, with a mix of indignity and apprehension, described Schaffer as "interesting, forceful, volatile, scholarly, vain to the point of childishness, disregardful of social convention," and noted that he seemed determined to enter Tibet regardless of permission!

Now based as close to the Tibetan border as possible, Gustav asked Schaffer to begin his research, by documenting the evidence from the tribes inhabiting these regions...evidence that Himmler believed, would link the Tibetans to the Atlantean Super-Race. Gustav hoped that this would in turn allow him *more* time for his own search...of the elusive monastery.

The team began their research from the 21st of June 1938, traveling through the 'Teesta River' valley, before heading north. The Teesta is a three hundred kilometer long river that flows through the Indian state of Sikkim. It carves out verdant Himalayan temperate and tropical river valleys and forms the border between Sikkim and West Bengal, before joining the 'Jamuna', a distributary channel of the 'Brahmaputra' in what is now Bangladesh. For most of the research team, the opportunity to witness and document these incredible sights and sounds was *almost* enough to compensate for not being allowed to enter Tibet!

The 38 year old Entomologist, Ernst Krause, worked light traps to capture insects, Karl Wienert, the team's Geologist, toured the hills making measurements, Edmund Geer, the Technical Expert, collected bird species and the Anthropologist, Bruno Beger, offered the locals medical help in exchange for allowing him to take their measurements. These measurements included detailed calculations of the size and width of the skull, the distance between and position of the eyes, with regards to the face and also comparing relative skin tones.

For Beger, the realization that many of the races living in Sikkim were descended from Tibet meant his studies could proceed even *without* the permit. As the weeks rolled by, his calculations became even more detailed. He brought out charts that had different shades of eye-color, documented on it and compared this to the eye-colors of the different tribesmen from the region. Even Schaffer, who still hoped that somehow Gustav would be able to get them across the border, couldn't help but commend Beger's zeal!

He noted that Beger's initial research seemed to confirm at least *one* of Himmler's suspicions. Regardless of whether these races had descended from the mythical Atlanteans, what was clear was that even over here on the Indian side of the Tibetan border, the secretive nature and near complete isolation of these tribes, had enabled them to avoid racial contamination. These races, through a strict adherence to inbreeding, had ensured racial purity…something that had become an obsession for the Nazis!

Beger was most interested in finding if these tribes displayed a long, narrow angular-head. This would indicate North European ancestry. But the more he researched, the more it became evident that the team would struggle to find evidence of blond, blue-eyed Aryan descendents…in Sikkim. And if these races were in fact related to the Tibetans, then that would mean finding Himmler's fantasy Aryans in Tibet was also a pipe dream!

Those in the team that had come along on the recommendations of the 'Ahnenerbe', now clung to one last desperate hope!

Himmler wanted proof of a dominant race of Super-Humans, in this part of the world. The team held on to the belief that if such a race did exist here, they would naturally have formed the 'Upper Classes'. So the only way of actually finding them would mean reaching out to the Tibetan Elite…for which access into Tibet was vital.

The onus was once again on Gustav to provide the necessary means!

CHAPTER SIX

The British had condemned the German Expedition, to the borders of Tibet and it seemed impossible to get them to change their minds. Schaffer even wrote of his frustrations in his diary, mentioning how his destination was just meters away!...on the other side of the border...a border that did not even have any armed guards...just a series of prayer-flags, fluttering in the winds! He described how as each evening went by, he would look across the border to the land of his dreams...and feel a strong urge to sneak across...*without waiting for the permit!*

The only thing that stopped him from actually doing so was the knowledge that *if* he and his crew were discovered by the British, it would undoubtedly lead to an international 'incident'. The British already had their suspicions about the Schaffer Mission...calling it a network of spies. Gustav's relentless search and inquiries about monasteries across Sikkim had done little to ease the tension. The last thing Schaffer needed was to generate *even more* Anti-Nazi propaganda.

Gustav meanwhile was on the verge of giving up his search. No matter how many locations he visited and how many people he spoke with, the monastery that Haushofer claimed to have visited seemed to elude him. What was also disconcerting was that of all those he met, who claimed knowledge of Hindu and Buddhist traditions, none seemed to have ever seen an *actual* copy of the 'Vimanika Shastra'.

His only solace was the confirmation he got from the locals, that such a text was indeed said to have existed. According to local tradition, an ancient Indian saint referred to in legend as 'Maharishi Bharadwaja' was believed to be the author of the text...a text that contained over three thousand hymns, arranged over eight chapters.

The saint, whose accomplishments were detailed even in the 'Puranas', was one of the 'Seven great sages' or 'Satparishi', revered in Hinduism.

But beyond these scraps of information, it seemed that for all practical purposes, Haushofer's monastery *had never existed at all!* After months of extensive searching, Gustav realized there was no other option, but to turn his attention back towards Tibet. *There* hopefully, he thought, he might find something that could further his quest.

This was of course easier said than done. Gustav knew that Schaffer and the rest were relying on him to get the permits sorted out. His role in securing the landing rights in India had convinced the team that *he* was the man for the task! But the truth was that even Himmler's influence would not be enough to get into Tibet. Unlike the British, Germany had absolutely no diplomatic relations with the Tibetan Elite!

The Tibetans had historically always been wary of letting in outsiders, especially Westerners. It had taken Great Britain nearly a century to gain their trust...and Gustav knew that now the British actively discouraged others from entering Tibet.

It was clear that for this mission to succeed they would require 'Divine Intervention'...*and for once the answer literally seemed to come from above!*

CHAPTER SEVEN

As July turned to August, the Himalayan peaks that had towered over the team like an impenetrable barrier, began to turn back the rain clouds…and the occasional light drizzle soon turned into a regular downpour. The whole team now found themselves confined to their tents for long periods of time, unable to carry out even the most basic studies. Their mission seemed to have hit another roadblock and yet…none wanted to go back, having failed. To do so, would be to face the wrath of Himmler! Moreover, if their mission were to fail, the British would undoubtedly derive a huge sense of pleasure! Unanimously, the team decided that they would hunker down and withstand nature's bombardment!

It was during one such dreary, wet day in late August, that Beger the team's resident Anthropologist, observed a well dressed and regal looking Tibetan walk past their tents. His first impulse was to take his measurements, but one of the locals, who doubled up as a translator, warned him against doing so. This was no ordinary Tibetan…but a 'High Official' to the Ruling Elite!

When Schaffer heard this news, he was ecstatic! He and the others had long been awaiting some sort of official permit to cross over, but exactly *what would constitute such a permit* had never been defined by the British. Schaffer now believed that if they could somehow befriend this advisor to the Tibetan nobility, *his* consent might enable them to 'legally' cross the border. In doing so, they would still keep their promise to the British and thus avoid an international incident.

He had the High Official invited into his tent and through the translators, introduced himself and his associates. The official unused to seeing so many Westerners was initially reticent, but Schaffer soon gained his trust when he lavishly gifted the man, a mule-load of gifts!

It turned out that the man was an official advisor to the 'Tering Rajah' - one of the ruling princes of the 'forbidden land'.

During their interaction, Schaffer and his men followed all of the protocol expected of someone wanting to enter Tibet. *The official was duly impressed.* After the obligatory exchange of gifts and goodwill, Schaffer carefully brought out a sealed letter written in Tibetan, requesting the 'Tering Rajah' permission to enter Tibet. While he did not know to what extent the Rajah's influence, extended among Tibet's 'Council of Ruling Elite', he nonetheless hoped that he might somehow be able to influence their decision.

Initially, their guest seemed taken aback by the audacious request. He stood up with a shocked expression on his face and began mumbling a prayer...sweat pouring from his brow. Schaffer realized that in his desperation to get access into Tibet, he had scared this man. It was vital that they get back his confidence...*quickly!*

Then Gustav, who hadn't spoken a word till that point, decided to try an even more outrageous stunt. From within his backpack, he brought out a neatly folded flag...the Red Nazi Flag with the Black Swastika on it! The move had an immediate impact on the official. He stared at the flag and then, with great reverence, reached out to touch the symbol.

The team heaved a sigh of relief. Gustav's gamble seemed to have paid off. The 'Swastika' was a much revered, sacred symbol across the sub-continent...both in Hindu and Buddhist traditions, it symbolized the 'perpetual motion of time'...but the fact that it was being used for something very different in Western Europe, was unknown in this remote corner of the world. For the Tibetan Official, the symbol signified an instant bond with these Westerners.

But would this one commonality be enough to get the Schaffer Mission into Tibet? This was a slim hope...and all that the entire team could do, was wait and hope.

It took a further agonizing five months before Schaffer received any reply to his letter. During these months, the weather conditions at these altitudes progressively worsened. As winter approached, the temperature plummeted to twenty degrees below Zero, and nearly fifty-kilometer winds swept across the region, making any research impossible.

As the crew grew increasingly frustrated at its own condition, Schaffer had to grudgingly accept that the British were winning. They had prevented him from accessing his 'dream destination' and thereby reduced this entire expedition to a farce. Even the enigmatic and secretive Capt. Gustav's morale had begun to falter. After his initial quest for an unknown monastery in Sikkim had failed, it had become clear that he was just as keen as the others to get into Tibet. It seemed to Schaffer that whatever Gustav was searching for, *did after all lie in Tibet!*

However, throughout this entire period, the team remained in regular contact with Germany. This was mainly through mail and the 'Chinese Legation' radio. Schaffer knew that while this was a way of keeping Himmler up to date with the situation at hand, it could also prove disastrous, should the expedition not succeed. Heinrich Himmler was not a man you wanted to offend.

His only solace was in the fact that up to this point, Himmler had supported the expedition enthusiastically, in spite of the numerous setbacks...and even wished them well for the upcoming Christmas festivities!

CHAPTER EIGHT

December 1938: The team's long wait was finally over! Lhasa had at long last, responded to Schaffer's request. With great anticipation, the crew gathered around the translator, as he read and explained the contents of their letter.

It started on an ominous note, declaring that 'Tibet and its capital-Lhasa were forbidden to *any* outsiders.' 'However' the letter went on, 'Dr. Schaffer's letter had made it clear that he and his team were interested in visiting Lhasa for purely academic reasons and for studying its religious and spiritual institutions. For this reason Lhasa was willing to consider their invitation of mutual friendship'.

And then the letter mentioned what the crew had been desperately hoping for...the Council Elite of Lhasa were granting all four scientists, under Dr. Schaffer, permission to visit Lhasa for two weeks!

The absolute sense of elation the team felt, was beyond description. This was far, far better than they had dared to hope...*the British would not even be involved!*

But even as they hugged and congratulated each other, the realization slowly dawned on them that the letter had granted permission to *ONLY* five researchers, including Schaffer...it did not include Capt. Gustav and those under him! *How could this be?*

The Translator was made to read the letter again...yes...it clearly specified that only five scientists were being granted access into Tibet. Was this an oversight on Lhasa's part? Or had the British somehow intervened and once again changed the rules of the game...making sure that only those they were absolutely sure were scientists, could go through. Whatever the case, one thing was certain...reapplying for permission was completely out of question. There was no telling what the Tibetans would do, if another appeal was made. Schaffer knew that in a forbidden place such as Lhasa, being granted access...*even a temporary one*...was the most one could hope for!

The only person, who seemed completely unconcerned, was Capt. Gustav. Even as the rest of the crew was involved in a highly animated discussion, on how to interpret the letter, Schaffer observed that Gustav had seated himself on one of the tent pegs...and was calmly smoking a pipe. Was this simply his way of coping with the disappointment or was there more to this than met the eye?

Schaffer approached him...cautiously...hoping to find out, "Captain...I know things have been a little awkward between us... primarily because our objectives for this mission haven't always matched. But I am as disappointed as you are that things haven't worked out for *ALL* of us. But as you know very well, we need to honor this invitation from Lhasa, regardless of its terms and conditions. *If* we back out now...or apply for a change in the invite, we risk the wrath of the Tibetan Ruling Elite. We might never get a better chance of getting in."

Gustav puffed on his pipe a little longer, before looking up at Schaffer. When his eyes did meet Schaffer's, there was a cunning glint in them. "Dr. Schaffer you misunderstand me. I am perfectly alright with the invite from Lhasa. In fact I couldn't be more thrilled."

"But the invitation to visit Lhasa is only for five people. You heard it yourself...we cannot afford to take our entire unit into the holy city or the Tibetans might think of this as a violation of the terms of the agreement and refuse us access into the city!"

"Let that not trouble you...for, I and my team *Do Not* plan to enter Lhasa at all...in fact once we cross over into Tibet, you shall no longer have to worry about us!" It was difficult to gauge, whether he was smiling.

"What do you plan to do then?" Schaffer asked...shocked by what he had just heard. It seemed that his silent fears about Gustav really being an undercover agent for Himmler were coming true!

"What I and my crew do once we cross over, is our business. We never planned to complete this journey with you. As you yourself said, your objectives quite substantially differ from mine. We both serve the 'Third Reich' though...each in our own way."

"I and my team accompanied you simply to avoid any suspicion, and your 'glowing reputation' as a scientist, paved the way for us. The letter from Lhasa is an invitation that is no doubt meant only for your team. But the fact that we did receive a reply at all means that even without breaking our promise to the British, I and my team can also cross over into Tibet...if not enter the Holy City! So tomorrow morning as our teams move across the border, I and my loyal crew shall make our own way. Needless to say Dr. Schaffer that our very best wishes shall always be with you. I do sincerely hope that you find the evidence, you are searching for." The sly smile was now undeniable.

"Do the rest of your crew members know of these...'objectives' you pursue Captain?" Schaffer asked...his mind still ablaze with what he had heard.

"They are loyal soldiers Dr. Schaffer...loyal to the 'Third Reich' and their 'Führer'. And as soldiers they will follow me to the ends of the earth...if I so choose, since I am here by the orders of my Führer. What about you though, Doctor? Are you a loyal Nazi?"

The last bit was said with such cynicism that its implications weren't lost on Schaffer. He knew Gustav was testing him...probing him. "Yes." He mumbled softly. "Yes I am loyal...loyal to Germany!"

The deep purple haze that filled the late evening skyline was matched only by the crackling of the campfire and the haunting notes emanating from the flute, played by one of the local Sherpa.

CHAPTER NINE

At dawn the next day, a long line of men, mules and equipment, trundled across the Indo-Tibetan border and into the 'Forbidden Land'. For Schaffer, these steps marked the culmination of a lifelong dream. Getting into Lhasa would for him crown the pinnacle of a glorious career. He personally could care less about Himmler's wild theories!

Based on his own research and observations, Schaffer was sure that Tibet would not have any evidence of the 'Atlanteans' that the 'Ahnenerbe' hoped to find. For him, getting to Lhasa was an opportunity to document a habitat that was home to a seemingly endless number of plants and animals...*the ultimate dream of any natural scientist!*

Before crossing the border, Schaffer had sent his final radio transmission over to Germany...one meant only for Himmler's ears. When Himmler heard of the team's success in gaining access into Lhasa, he promoted all its members. Schaffer was elevated to the rank of 'Hauptsturm-Führer' or 'Captain' in the S.S. There was serious conviction among the Nazis that of all the Western Powers, Germans by virtue of their superior ancestry were best suited at dealing with Non-Europeans. For Himmler, the invitation from Lhasa...one that had come against all odds...was the ultimate proof of this!

While the promotions and honors bestowed upon the team, was obviously a good sign, what continued to bother Schaffer was that even though they were now authorized to visit the holy city, the invitation to enter Tibet wasn't for *all of them*. Captain Gustav and his six associates were technically 'stowaways'...and this was not even counting the porters, guides and translators, the crew had along with them. Schaffer had no idea how the Tibetan Elite would respond to these 'uninvited guests'. The Council might very easily take offense at this blatant violation of rules.

But his biggest concern was that since the British already had diplomatic relations with Lhasa, it was very conceivable that news of this invitation had reached them. There were probably British envoys already present at Lhasa. Schaffer was sure that these envoys would do everything within their power to sabotage his mission. The presence of Captain Gustav's 'uninvited band of followers'…could make matters very, very difficult.

Schaffer's only hope lay in what he had learnt the night before… before crossing the Indian border. The fact that Gustav and his associates were in Tibet on an altogether different mission…and that they would split from the main team, after entering Tibet. Schaffer, who had once been extremely curious about Gustav's 'secret mission' now wanted to have nothing to do with him. Gustav and his band of fanatics could go to hell, for all he cared…all he wanted was that Gustav keep his promise, of not entering Lhasa!

After weeks of travelling through some of the most difficult terrain on Earth, on January the 19th, 1939, just as the cold winter Sun broke through a thick blanket of clouds, the weary members of the Schaffer expedition were finally able to cast their eyes on the 'Patala Palace'… the ancestral home of the 'Dalai Lama'. After nearly a full month of near non-stop hiking, they had finally reached their destination. Just past a small valley, stood the magnificent 'Forbidden City of 'Lhasa'… the very epicenter of Tibetan Buddhism!

Even as the men from the civilized world gazed at this vision from another world, they realized that soon, they would be the first Germans to enter Lhasa. For Ernst Schaffer, this was arguably the finest moment of his life. As he turned around to congratulate his fellow comrades, he noticed that only the five scientists, who were officially invited by Lhasa, remained. Captain Gustav and his six loyalists were nowhere to be seen!

I take refuge in the Buddha, Dharma and Sangha
Until I attain Enlightenment.
By merit accumulations from practising generosity and the other perfections
May I attain Enlightenment, for the benefit of all sentient beings! -

CHAPTER TEN

Captain Gustav had been true to his word. He and his team had quietly split from the main expedition, just before reaching Lhasa, and made their own way westward, towards a region that was largely uncharted…even for the Tibetans…the area the British referred to as – Tibetan Autonomous Region.

Gustav's plan was to hire a couple of local guides, other than the ones accompanying Schaffer, and use their knowledge to navigate the extremely tough terrain that he knew, lay ahead. They would attempt to stay as close to the border that India and Nepal shared with Tibet as possible, while gradually making their way towards Mount Kailasha…a sacred spot, deep in Tibet's Western Desert.

For Gustav, the absence of an invitation to visit Lhasa had never really been a deterrent. He had conferred with Himmler, using a secure radio channel, on the same day Schaffer and his team received the invite from Lhasa. Himmler of course knew very well that the Schaffer mission was only a *cover* to enter Tibet…a safe way of ensuring the British did not suspect the Nazis' real objective…a 'sleight of hand'… *misdirection!* The naïve and simple Tibetans would surely fall for Dr. Schaffer's charms. In fact during their initial briefings, both Himmler and Gustav had tried to convince Schaffer of the expedition's real objectives, but the natural scientist in him had refused to accept something as bizarre as finding a mythical lost city in Tibet.

Now, following their split with the Schaffer mission, Gustav had given his team a brief idea of what they were really here for. This he believed was important, for even though all six men under him were Germans dedicated to the Nazi cause, it was only Gustav, who truly knew of their real objective. The rest till this point, at best had only a sketchy idea…and even *that* was mainly from hints and unintended clues, accidentally dropped during Top-Secret briefings.

Those briefings had happened in Germany, in the 'Fatherland'...in the comforts of magnificent underground offices...where the prospect of accompanying the noted S.S. Captain Friedrich Gustav – a dynamic and dashing army officer, and also a member of the infamous 'Thule Society', on an unknown and possibly future-changing expedition deep into Tibet, had seemed utterly intoxicating!

But as they began their journey, the team quickly discovered that as is so often the case, reality proves to be a very different ball-game, indeed!

Yes, it was true that Captain Gustav was a remarkably able explorer, even on his own, and his mountaineering skills were absolutely top notch. But the journey that led them into the region known as the 'Tibetan Autonomous Region,' would offer massive challenges, both physical and psychological!

They had picked up two local guides along the way, who would prove their worth and loyalty many times over, as the team journeyed deep into unexplored territory. Initially, Gustav had seemed reluctant to involve any more individuals than were absolutely necessary and hence the decision to hire local porters and guides...had been a difficult one...one involving countless arguments and disputes!

Even though his accomplices did not know this, the real reason behind Gustav's reluctance, was the mystical nature of the lost city itself. From what he had gathered through his studies, it was clear that only the 'worthy'...those who were absolutely pure of heart, could enter the gates of 'Shambhala'.

The megalomaniac in Gustav had no doubts about the 'worthiness' of the Nazis. After all, they were the only people in all of human history, who had dared to meet human destiny head on! Moreover, the unquestioned 'racial superiority' of the Germans meant that there was no one better suited to embrace this lost knowledge of the ancient world. The same couldn't be said about the Tibetans, though. These were people, who had lived for centuries...probably millennia, around these regions and had still not managed to crack the code of this mystery. Regardless of what Himmler thought about them, to Gustav, their inability to reach Shambhala on their own meant only one thing – this was a race that was *FAR from worthy!*

However, in spite of his concerns, the practical limitations the terrain imposed on them meant that the team *did* end up hiring two local porters, who would double up as translators and guides.

Under Gustav's instructions, the guides were asked to select routes that avoided most of Tibet's important cities, west of Lhasa. Gustav, aware that they were 'unwelcomed' and 'uninvited' guests in this land, was keen on avoiding any contact with the locals, unless absolutely necessary.

This would mean, often making use of roads that were far away from civilization and hence poorly maintained. Even though, back in Germany, the German team had trained extensively for an expedition such as this, the relentless climbs and treks through the wilderness would no doubt test them, to their very limits!

CHAPTER ELEVEN

On the second day of their westward journey, the team had to cross Tibet's second most important city – Shigatse – the ancestral home of the 'Panchan Lamas'. As always, Gustav had his guides find paths that would lead them away from the city and thus keep their presence a secret. This meant travelling some forty miles south, almost to the Nepalese border and then pushing westwards...a journey that would take the team through some of the most bizarre, yet hauntingly beautiful landscapes in the world.

No maps existed for these regions and in some of these places, even the local Sherpa were reluctant to continue. There were dark legends enshrouding these regions...legends that spoke of how these places were the abode of spirits...a *'middle-ground'*...where the spirits of the dead rest during their passage to the afterlife. As the days went by, Gustav noticed that the fears and superstitions of their Tibetan guides were starting to rub off, even on to the Germans.

This became palpably clear on the twelfth day of their journey. The team had trekked an average of thirty miles a day...difficult by any standards...but specifically so, in these conditions. Added to this was Gustav's insistence of avoiding any and all forms of habitation. This meant that even the rugged Tibetans, used to long hikes in high altitudes, were beginning to show signs of fatigue.

It was late evening on the twelfth day, and just as the sun began its daily descent from the heavens, the team managed to complete a particularly tough climb that had required the use of special climbing equipment. The extraordinary altitude, the extremely thin mountain air and the weight of their supplies, had more than once threatened to halt their climb. But Captain Gustav had been adamant. Come what may, they needed to get to Mount Kailasha quickly. To the others, it seemed like Gustav was a man possessed...driven by a 'dark force'... becoming more and more manic, as time went by!

Battered by unceasing winds and on the verge of exhaustion, the team reached a flat land that was flanked by high cliffs on one side, where Gustav *finally* agreed to halt for the night. As they searched for a natural rocky outcrop that would buffer their tents against the fury of the winds, one of the Germans named Baur, suddenly gave a loud shout to the others.

As the others looked to see what he was pointing to, the sight that met their eyes half convinced them that they were dreaming...either that or simply delirious from exhaustion! For half-way up the side of a cliff that rose like an imposing overseer in this otherwise flat region, stood what looked like a deserted monastery...incredibly ancient and built right into the mountain at an impossible height! ...it was as if the normally constricting *tethers of gravity*, held no sway over it!

The only thing more incredible than the monastery was the effect it had on the guides. The Tibetans abruptly fell to their knees and began to crawl up the road...towards the monastery, in what seemed to be a bizarre display of servitude. They repeated this several times... in front of the monastery! Even the Germans, who had seen many astounding sights through the course of this journey, were stunned into a horrified silence...by this spectacle!

When Gustav demanded to know the reason for their behavior, he was met with silence. Whether it was High-altitude Pulmonary Edema or sheer exhaustion that was causing his blood to boil, he pulled out a gun, screaming that he would shoot them all!

It was only then that one of the guides replied in a fearful whisper... "Maha-Kala...Maha- Kala". He repeated it over and over again... seemingly more afraid of the term, than the 9 mm semi-automatic pistol pointed at him.

'Maha-Kala'...Gustav vaguely recalled the name from some of his earliest forays into Indo-Tibetan cultures. From what he recounted, this was a demonic entity...a 'dark-force', whose very name meant 'Time-less' or 'Beyond Time.' Almost every source spoke of this being, in hushed whispers...It was revered as the terrifyingly fierce spouse of the Earth Goddess–Kali! Maha-Kala was always depicted with four arms and three eyes and his 'dark halo' was described as the sum brilliance of 10 million 'black fires of dissolution'. Seated on human corpses and holding in his hands, a trident, a sword, a scythe and a drum, Maha-Kala was said to dwell in the midst of eight cremation grounds and adorned himself with a necklace of skulls! The most horrific depictions also had him laced with ashes of the cremation ground and surrounded by a number of wildly shrieking vultures and jackals.

Maha-Kala and his consort Kali together were said to represent the ultimate destructive power of Brahman...a power not bound by *any* rules! They had the power to dissolve even time and space into themselves and exist simply as the 'Void'! In certain schools of Tantric Buddhism, this dark entity was responsible for the dissolution of the universe at the end of each great cycle...along with the annihilation of great evil demons, when the other gods failed to do so!

Maha-Kala

While these myriad sources differed wildly, in scope and significance, they all agreed on one chilling truth...and it was that Maha-Kala and his consort annihilated men, women, children, animals, the world and the entire universe without mercy, because they were 'Kala' or 'Time' itself personified, and 'Time' is not bound by anyone or anything...*nor does it ever show mercy!*

Slowly the realization dawned on Gustav. Through an elaborate series of allegorical legends, the ancient cultures were trying to understand the flow of time... *'Time'*...there was that word again...somehow all of this...his quest...his very life...seemed connected to 'Time.' It was almost as if 'Time' itself was manipulating him...Gustav suddenly felt extremely uncomfortable and nauseous.

CHAPTER TWELVE

– Mahakala, you wear a tiger-skin loincloth
Fully adorned with snake-ornaments on your six arms.
You wear a great necklace of fifty men's heads, dripping blood.
On your crown, you're adorned with five dry, jeweled skulls.
You come from your tree and accept our torma offering,
Glorious Six-Armed – homage and praise to you!
Sternly protect the Doctrine of the Buddha!
Sternly praise the height of power of the Jewels!
For us – teachers, disciples and entourage –
Please quell all bad conditions and obstructions,
And grant us quickly whatever siddhis we wish! –

The pragmatic researcher in Gustav would normally have scoffed at such stories, but of late, he had heard, seen and experienced far too many strange things to simply rubbish these claims. Ever since he had been first introduced to the occult, and had his first discussions with his mentor Karl Haushofer, Gustav had subliminally felt an unknown, unseen force, urging him on.

For a while, he had simply shrugged it off as a figment of his imagination…after all, for someone so involved in studying the mysteries of life, to gradually become delusional, wasn't completely unusual! But over time, he had realized that there was more to it than just that.

Now, as he trekked up the snow covered rocky outcrop on his way towards the monastery, he thought of the series of strange and inexplicable events that had occurred, since he began his research into Shambhala. He thought of his mentor Haushofer, finding the document –the Vimanika Shastra, in a forgotten monastery in India… of his talks with a mysterious holy man in India, who possessed god-like knowledge...and of his own bizarre experience, at the house of the old Turkish book dealer outside Vienna...a man who supposedly *did not even exist!* Every time, he had been on the verge of giving up, he had been shown the right path...by an unseen force!

This was deeply unsettling. Gustav realized that such 'Help' generally came at a cost. As to what that cost might be...was anyone's guess. If a force was indeed capable of such intricate and delicate manipulations, how much worse might it get, if he was unable to repay it for its assistance?

As he neared the monastery, he noticed one of the local guides, speak in hushed tones about the Statue of the Guardian Deity, carved out of black stone.

"Maha- Kala is always black in color. Just as all colors are absorbed and dissolved by black, all names and forms melt into 'Maha-Kala'. He is thus all-embracing and all comprehensive in nature. Since 'Black' is also the total absence of color, it perfectly symbolizes the truth about Maha-Kala...he is the ultimate...the absolute reality...known in Sanskrit as *"Nirguna"*...'beyond all quality and form'!"

Just as the guide finished his fearsome description and explained why the rest should also perform the ritual of humility and subservience, while crossing this spot...violent winds broke out across the entire region...screaming like banshees, with unearthly fury and threatening to rend all of them apart. It was only the sheer weight of their equipment that kept them from being blown away. *It seemed like the fury of this dark entity was taunting them!*

For Gustav, it was unclear what was more disturbing...the furious winds that could well become their deaths...or the piteous heart-wrenching wail that could be heard over it!

"That's the sound of weeping...the weeping of the dead." One of the guides whispered...his eyes wide, "They weep...for Maha-Kala refuses to allow unfulfilled souls from entering the afterlife. Only those who manage to complete their 'Karma' during their life are able to cross the 'Gates of Death'. This is why the search for enlightenment and the journey towards one's own salvation, is so central to our culture. Those wretched souls that do not achieve this in life, are denied entry into the afterlife by Maha-Kala...it is *their* cries that we now hear!"

Shocked and speechless for the first time in his life, Gustav heard the heart-wrenching cries of the damned...screaming outside the hallowed *Gates of the Afterlife*...denied from entering, by this dark entity. It was clear that these souls were trapped here...forever!!

In spite of his years of military training...Gustav felt pure, unadulterated terror. Whether it was simply the setting Sun that was playing tricks against the stark, white backdrop...or something more...he couldn't say, but he dimly perceived an absolutely gigantic, coal black outline standing against the horizon!

A disturbing sound closer to him, caused him to turn around and look towards his companions...he saw all six Germans soldiers, who had accompanied him...fall to their knees and weep piteously!

Only the damned weep outside the Gates of Maha-Kala!!!! Were all of them damned forever in this hellish place?

Maha-Kala was watching... *'Time' itself was watching them!*

CHAPTER THIRTEEN

As the days turned to weeks and weeks turned to months, the German team realized that their stuttering radio signals were no longer going through...*at all!* Their travels had taken them deep into Tibetan Autonomous Territory...and too far away from the Chinese controlled regions, for the radio signals to get the required strength.

For Gustav, this meant that for the first time since the start of this expedition, he was beyond Himmler's supervision. And although he didn't voice his feelings to the rest, he quite welcomed this development. He could now pursue his own quest with aplomb...the quest that had consumed most of his adult life and one that he believed, he was on the verge of completing.

Unlike Himmler, Gustav never had any illusions of finding a superior Master Race, in Tibet. That was now Dr. Schaffer's lookout. Gustav would lead his carefully hand-picked team of loyalists to a lost city hidden in these wastelands!!

The relentless hikes and the unforgiving terrain however, was having an impact on the team and although each morning they pushed themselves on, after listening to inspirational speeches from Gustav, the lack of oxygen coupled with almost no knowledge of their destination, meant their morale was slipping quickly. From an initial average of thirty miles a day, the team was now down to fifteen...and even that was sometimes not possible, if the weather chose to play spoilsport.

For Gustav, these delays were almost criminal...*unforgivable*...and he made no bones about it. He would regularly lambast his group, on their lack of dedication and will power. But as time went by, his loyalists began to grow increasingly restive and uncertain. With tempers starting to fray, in these high altitudes, Gustav began to suspect a 'Coup' in the making. He realized, he had to do something fast. For the expedition to go awry, when he was so close to his destination would be a terrible disaster!

Against his wishes, Gustav decided to indulge the group and give them some details of the nature of this quest. He hoped this would ease the tension and lessen some of their simmering distrust.

He would however give out details very sparingly...carefully choosing which parts to reveal and which to hold back. This would create the perception among the listeners, of having succeeded...of having got what they had asked for...while actually allowing him to retain the upper hand... *'Selective dissemination of information'*... It was a tactic Gustav had learnt from the master himself...Adolf Hitler. It was how Hitler and the Nazis had come to power, through the twenties and thirties!

The briefings that Gustav conducted each night, when the team rested, often saw him describe his own research in great detail...the strange, haunting beauty of this region, allowing him to fully exploit his storytelling abilities. Like a magician, he conjured up the mythic imagery of Paradise, through his words, masterfully manipulating the emotions of the listeners...and yet *always* holding back the most critical details of their quest...ensuring that *his* position as the head of this expedition, would remain unchallenged!

Over the weeks, the team that had so far been skeptical about the expedition began to appreciate and even glorify Gustav's efforts and dedication. The allure of finding the 'lost city of Shambhala' was a tantalizing prize indeed...one that fit perfectly with their own megalomania! No longer was there any dissension or signs of bickering... the men were now as motivated as their leader to see this through!

It was also during these briefings that their local Tibetan guides opened up, often adding valuable insights to some of Gustav's theories. Growing up near Lhasa had taught these rugged outdoorsmen all about the legends, surrounding these regions. The best example of this came when, sometime during their third month in Tibet, the team, having continually travelled west, reached the town of 'Saga', not far from Tibet's southern border with Nepal.

Gustav's guides informed him that the town was an important stop-over for travelers, travelling to and from Mount Kailasha and served as a destination for picking up supplies. The town also straddled the 'Dargye Tsangpo River' above its junction with the 'Brahmaputra' and was strategically located at the junction of three roads - the 'Lhartse' road coming from the east, the 'Dzongka' road from the south and the 'Purang' and 'Drongpa' roads from the west. The Tibetans seemed eager to stop at this town and interact with other human beings, for the first time in months, but Gustav's resolve was inflexible. He insisted that the team once again skirt the town, by taking a cumbersome and much longer circular route, so as to avoid detection.

After all, even though the Tibetans were an extremely friendly and hospitable people, news of 'White' Europeans in this little town would travel quickly. And if, as the guides said, this town was an important junction for travelers and tourists, it was very conceivable that there was the odd British officer here. Gustav and his band of Germans were by all rights not even supposed to *be* in Tibet. Unlike the Schaffer mission, theirs was an unauthorized one and being detected now could at the very least mean instant deportation…and possibly even lead to an international incident over illegal espionage! The British had already shown their true colors, when it came to trusting Germans.

As the team sordidly made its way into the hills once more, to circumvent the town of 'Saga', they came across something utterly bewildering. On the outskirts of the town, the team observed a group of ten Buddhist monks wearing what appeared to be 'Ceremonial' face masks, performing a ritualistic dance sequence. Even though Gustav encouraged his accomplices to remain hidden and observe the ritual from afar, it was clear from the reactions of his Tibetan porters that what they were witnessing was no ordinary ritual!

When asked what the ritual meant, one of the guides explained that this was the 'Kalachakra Initiation Ceremony' and that it was an important aspect of Tibetan Buddhism…a ceremony in which ten monks dress up as the 'Ten World Deities' and perform a dance of consecrating the location of the 'Mandala' in preparation for the initiation ritual, after asking the 'earth goddess' for permission to erect it at a particular site.

In one of his briefings Gustav had spoken of the concept of the 'Kalachakra' or the 'Eternal Wheel of Time'. This belief was an important part of 'Tibetan' and 'Tantric Buddhism' and was normally used to refer to a very complex and advanced practice.

That night around the tents, the guides explained its full significance. Much like the dark guardian deity, they had crossed on their way over here, 'Kalachakra' referred both to a patron tantric deity of 'Vajrayana Buddhism' and to the philosophies and meditation practices contained within the 'Kalachakra Tantra' and its many commentaries.

The 'Kalachakra' tradition revolved around the concept of time – 'Kala' and cycles – 'Chakra'. These included cycles of planets, as well as, cycles of human breathing. The teachings included a series of meditative practices that involved working with the most subtle energies, *within* one's body...on the path to enlightenment.

The 'Kalachakra deity' represented 'Time' and as 'Time' was always aware of everything, 'Kalachakra' represented omniscience. 'Kalachakri', his spiritual consort and complement, on the other hand was aware of everything that is 'timeless', not time-bound or out of the 'realm of time'. Together, the two deities represented all that there was, is and will be as well as all that never was, is and never will be.

The classic representation of this principle was the 'Kalachakra Wheel'. The wheel is without beginning or end and thus acts as a perfect metaphor for the union of 'Time and Timeless'.

The guide explained that while this ritual was distinctly Tibetan, the concept of the 'Kalachakra' was also accepted in Hinduism and Jainism.

He then showed the team a small cloth he carried with him...a ritual cloth. In the extremely poor light of a flickering campfire, the team huddled around to see what it contained. Against a dark background, the cloth had on it a representation of the 'Circular wheel of Time'. The guide explained that the diagram was called the 'Mandala'. The Kalachakra deity resided in the center of this 'Mandala' in his palace...one that consisted of four Mandalas, each within the other. Each had a special significance: the Mandalas of body, speech, and mind, and in the very center, wisdom and great bliss.

The 'Kalachakra' and 'Mandala' were dedicated to both individual and world peace and physical balance. Only someone who truly understood this could be considered an adept. As the rest of his exhausted colleagues slept the sleep of the wicked, Captain Gustav wondered if he would indeed be able to unlock the mysteries of time… mysteries that would allow him entry into 'Shambhala'.

The anguished howl of the winds, cascading across the mountain peaks provided him with scarce solace and certainly no answers.

CHAPTER FOURTEEN

By the end of March, the team was closing in on its destination. After skillfully avoiding detection, thanks to the expertise and knowhow of their Tibetan guides, they were now in the final quarter of their journey…one that would lead them to Lake Manasarovar and Mount Kailasha!

The near complete isolation and absence of human contact, had imposed a strange silence on the group. The Germans had become withdrawn and reticent, refusing to communicate, except when absolutely necessary. When not hiking, Gustav spent all his free time speaking with the Tibetan guides and studying a series of diagrams, from a tattered note book, he carried around. The team noticed that even now after all this time together, Gustav *refused* to share the contents of the book…not even with the Tibetans. Its secrets, it seemed for now, were only for the Captain's eyes.

The Germans however had some far more pressing concerns. Regardless of their personal convictions about finding Shambhala in these barren mountains, they had some extremely pertinent questions, regarding their own departure. The last they had seen or heard of, from the Schaffer mission was at the start of the year…and that was outside the gates of Lhasa!

Ernst Schaffer's group of scientists had been granted a two-week stay in the holy city…unless things had dramatically changed, that two-week stay was long over. Undoubtedly, following their stay in Lhasa, Schaffer's team of scientists would have left Tibet via Sikkim, India, as per their agreement with the British.

This automatically created a huge problem for Gustav and his associates. If the Schaffer expedition had already left Tibet, then they would have no way of explaining their own presence in this region. There was no way that they could leave through Sikkim now, without raising British suspicions. Compounding this were the fears of their Tibetan guides, who insisted that going back the same way they had come, was out of question. In their view, by venturing past the lands of the dark entity 'Maha-Kala', they had doomed themselves, through their own ignorance!

The only one, who seemed completely unconcerned, was Capt. Gustav. Whether it was his obsession with Shambhala that was preventing him from acknowledging this problem...or if as the team feared, he was viewing this journey as a one-way road to paradise!... wasn't clear.

And yet, no matter how much they quizzed their leader and reminded him of the impossibility of going back the way they had come, Gustav remained steadfastly resolute and refused to divulge his plans. The only solace that he offered was the assurance that once they got to Shambhala, they would no longer need to worry about conventional means of departure. Why this would be so...he gave no reasons. Needless to say, the relationship between Gustav and his companions were never quite the same again.

The final leg of their journey took the team up to the town of 'Paryang' and beyond. Located at an elevation around 4,700m, Paryang was known as the *'World's highest town'*. It was also the last village on the way to Mount Kailasha, and from what the Germans had heard; it was largely deserted.

As they reached the outskirts of Paryang, the Tibetan guides went up to Gustav and requested permission to enter the town. The reason they offered was that the supplies the team was carrying, were getting dangerously low...and regardless of *how* Gustav planned to make the return journey, there was no way these would last much longer. Even the climbing equipment, the team was using, had become heavily frayed and needed replenishing.

Gustav privately suspected that the real reason the Tibetans wanted to visit the town was that *this* would provide them a way to reunite with their brethren. Even the German soldiers seemed quite taken in by this idea. At this point, after months of being on the road, any prospect of human contact seemed welcome!

Gustav, however, would have none of it. He once again reminded his team of the dangers of being discovered and the importance of their mission. He conceded however that the equipment needed to be upgraded and allowed the two Tibetans to briefly visit the town, under oath that come what may, they *would not* reveal their real objectives. He gave them a maximum of five hours to procure all the requisite supplies.

He countered their protests that this was an impossibly small window of time, by again assuring the group that they did not need to worry about food supplies... at least for the return leg of their journey. The 'City of Heaven' would provide all the necessary means of getting back...*instantaneously!!*

Grudgingly, the Tibetans left for the town, a journey that would require them to descend into the valley below, while the Nazis moved into the shadows to avoid detection. It is here that Gustav made an attempt to improve the strained relations with his accomplices.

"My fellow countrymen..." he began, "We face probably the most crucial phase of our expedition...and all of what we have accomplished would amount to nothing, if we fail over here."

The men simply stared...They had heard speeches like these before...speeches used by the Nazis, to galvanize the population... speeches that so far away from their homeland didn't seem to matter at all.

"You have questioned some of my decisions during the course of our journey, but never once have you directly opposed me...for that I commend you. For my part however, I do think your dedication deserves greater honesty...greater openness! The two local fools, who accompany us, cannot be trusted. They are neither 'fit' enough nor 'worthy' enough to enter paradise with us. You might have wondered how was it that *I* allowed them to visit this township. It is because one way or another, we will *have* to abandon them to their fates, very shortly!"

"What?" Abandon them? After all that they have done for us? All they have borne with us?"

"Yes...difficult as it might seem the success of the 'Third Reich' depends not on the decisions of weak-kneed men, but on the efforts of those who have the strength and courage to do the right thing...no matter *how ruthless* it might seem to others. We were born to be leaders of men...and you want me to be bothered with societal morals? No!!...I shall prove myself a worthy son of my Fatherland, and enter Shambhala with...or without you!"

"Apologies, my leader..." Baur the youngest of the team said meekly, "We meant it not as an insult or a challenge but as a question that we genuinely thought was important. If we do abandon the Tibetans now, how shall we get to the lost city and back? They are the only ones, who know these paths so well...and even if, as you have mentioned before, we will leave by a different path to the one we have taken so far, surely there is no one better suited to guide us through it, than those, who have spent a lifetime in these mountains!"

"Again you underestimate me." Gustav replied...his voice a little softer now, "For these Tibetans, Shambhala is simply 'Paradise on Earth'...a 'Utopia'...one that is ultimately unattainable! They have founded an entire religion around it, over the last thousand years, without ever realizing the true significance of what they had in their backyard. For decades historians and mythologists have gone back and forth in their interpretations and poetic renditions of this place. But I...Capt. Friedrich Gustav have finally cracked its code...and you shall have the glorious opportunity of joining me, as we unearth this treasure for Germany."

The men now sat up straighter...for the first time since they had begun this journey, they felt like they were going to be given the full disclosure...*no more secrets*...no longer would they be expected to risk their lives in these white wastelands, for an unknown glory.

"You see my friends...the years, I spent back in the Fatherland researching Shambhala, taught me something very important. It is that *this* is no mere myth but a very real place that remains invisible and inaccessible to the rest of the world, through the use of ancient technology, now lost to mankind...but one that formed a big part of a lot of pre-historic cultures."

Gustav then gave them a brief overview of the technologies described in the Great Epics of the Eastern World, including the Mahabharata. He also explained to them the Indian concept of the

'Yuga Cycles' which speak of a gradual decay from the 'Satya Yuga' to the 'Kali Yuga'.

"This lost technology works on an energy source that we call 'Vril' and it exists in all life forms on the planet. The 'Vril' has been referred to by different names throughout human history, but one thing remains consistent...it can only be harnessed by someone, who is an absolute master of mind and body. Unfortunately, such mastery is no longer possible in today's highly corrupted society. So, the only option we have to once again access this energy, is to reach a place which *has* retained its purity...a place so perfect that it enables one to literally *be* a part of the 'Satya Yuga'...a virtual paradise on Earth... Shambhala!"

The wind seemed to drop a few decibels...listening...whispering!

A wave of understanding spread among the Nazis...even though there was still so much that wasn't clear; each one of them felt a sense of unbridled awe. They now knew that they could be a part of something truly special...the dawn of a New Age!

"But my leader, you said that once we get to Shambhala, we would no longer need to worry about transportation...so much so, that we could afford to abandon our Tibetan guides. What did you mean by that...what exactly do we expect to find in this land...and more specifically how do we get to it?"

"Questions...questions..." Gustav laughed softly.

He looked around...and took a deep breath, before continuing, "The knowledge of how to access the lost city was revealed to me by a man, who was its living resident...*the last living resident!*"

"A living resident???" A collective gasp went around!

"Yes...and he spoke to me, words of wisdom...*secret words*, whose meaning will become clear, only when we complete the first half of this journey...up to Mount Kailasha. The keys to unlocking the Gates of Heaven lie in the same energy source, I referred to earlier – 'Vril'... in Hinduism, this energy is known as the 'Kundalini' and Hindu mystics believe that it exists in the form of 'Seven Energy Circles' called 'Chakras', inside each human being."

As Gustav spoke, his voice trailed...his eyes had the hazy look of one, who was trying to recall forbidden knowledge, "Only if we are at the right place…at the right time, can we hope to unlock the power of the Seven Chakras!"

He paused dramatically…before dropping the bombshell, "Do you think it is any coincidence that there are exactly *seven* of us over here?"

The team was speechless…what they had considered a suicidal and impractical expedition into the unknown, was turning out to be something so much bigger!

"You asked me why soon we would no longer need our Tibetan friends…it is because, once we reach Shambhala, we shall no longer need to walk out of this land…we shall FLY out…*like gods!*"

The stunned look on the faces of his accomplices was matched only by the tortured beauty of the land that surrounded them.

"My friends…" Gustav continued, his voice now almost a whisper, "My research revealed to me that Shambhala is a place full of secret and forbidden technologies…technologies that were once used by mankind to establish a deeper connection with the Gods… technologies that have been repeatedly described in the great epics of the past…my friends it's time you learnt the secrets of the 'Vimanas'!"

The gently setting sun cast its fading amber hue over the entire valley…the sounds of Buddhist prayer bells, ringing rhythmically in the distance, echoed softly across the valley…the town of Paryang was turning in for the night…

…it was time to head to Paradise!

CHAPTER FIFTEEN

Journey across Tibet

More than a hundred days, after having crossed over into Tibet, Gustav and his team reached the sacred spot, they had travelled so far for...holy Mount Kailasha, a majestic peak flanked by four smaller peaks...and one that also towered over two other sacred fresh water lakes – 'Lake Manasarovar' and 'Rakshasthal'.

The arduous journey across the Tibetan Plateau had taken its toll on the group. Even the two Tibetans were at the very end of their endurance. The team had covered more miles than they cared to count, and along the way, experienced sights and sounds, forbidden to any ordinary mortal! Yet, the sheer beauty of the sacred mountain, alongside the two sacred fresh water lakes, took their breath away. The fabulous vistas and the serene landscape of Lake Manasarovar instantly lifted their spirits. Whether they really could reach Shambhala from here, remained to be seen, but for the team, one thing was clear...*this was as close to an 'earthly paradise', as one could possibly get!*

After all the efforts the team had taken to keep their presence a secret, it was clear that doing so any longer was going to be impossible. The entire area around the sacred mountain was full of pilgrims... Hindus...Buddhists...Bon...Jains...even the odd Westerner ...all hoping for a little bit of spiritual salvation!

The Tibetan guides seemed particularly overwhelmed by the breathtaking majesty and supreme tranquility of the place. Kailasha was a destination that they had hoped to visit, at least once during their lifetimes, and even though ideally, they would have hoped to visit it in a more relaxed fashion...actually being here, was still special!

All eyes turned to Gustav. If what he had said was true, the first part of their journey...the 'Physical half', was done...from here on, would begin the second phase...the 'Spiritual half'. Somewhere, around this sacred region, lay the secret entrance to Shambhala!

But where?

Was it somehow hidden in these mountains? ...a mystical portal?...a gateway shrouded, using exotic technology?...Gustav had expected the clues for locating the entrance, to reveal themselves, once he had completed the physical journey...after all, hadn't he studied every possible document pertaining to this mystery? Hadn't he proven himself *worthy* of this challenge?

The possibility that he *might NOT* actually be able to locate the entrance, had never crossed his mind...and yet, now that he was actually here, the sight of hundreds of pilgrims, devotedly making their way around the sacred area, did not fill him with hope. With just a tinge of nervousness building up within him, he looked towards his team members...however skeptical they might have been, they *HAD* come to respect and believe in him. Certainly, they were banking on him to find the path!

With the weather closing in, Gustav decided the best thing to do, was to rest for the night and re-evaluate his options the next morning... and for this they would have to find accommodation...and for that, they would *have* to interact with the locals. As the German team made its way towards the pilgrims, they realized that their anonymity in this mystical land would soon be a thing of the past.

Initial enquiries revealed that the only place, which could offer accommodation for the entire group, was 'Darchen' – a small village located directly in front of the sacred mountain. Resting at an altitude of over 15,000 feet, Darchen, which had previously been a sheep station for nomads and their flocks, now served as the starting point for all the major pilgrimages.

As the team approached the hamlet, they noticed that not many of the locals paid much attention to them. Probably, the sight of seven rag-tag Westerners, trying to seek solace away from civilization, wasn't so uncommon in these regions! Gustav had instructed his team to keep up the façade of being here on pilgrimage. This would mean, doing all the things regular pilgrims did, while simultaneously keeping their eyes and ears open, for any scrap of information that might prove valuable. They needed some clue...*any clue*...on how to proceed!

The team was offered a small shed, where they could keep the bulk of their gear and another one, where they could spend the night. If their host, a wiry man in his sixties, was in any way suspicious of their true agenda, he did not show it. The team was given a warm meal of Cabbage and Yak milk that was tasteless, yet refreshing. After being on the road for so long, the sight of *any* freshly cooked meal was a Godsend!

After hastily consuming their supper, the group huddled around a small campfire, trying to garner warmth and strength from its dying embers. Their host arrived to ensure that all was well with them and even pointed out a couple of extremely filthy and badly made toilets, they could use the next morning. The Germans were appalled! They could not believe their eyes...*or the stench that reached their nose!* Even after spending months cut off from civilization, the prospect of using 'facilities' like these...was horrifying!

Their host's toothy smile, said it all...this wasn't the first time a group of foreigners had reacted this way to what passed as "Washrooms" in these regions. This pilgrimage of course was supposed to put one through the most extreme challenges and help attain *Nirvana*...after all, the need for hygiene was just another 'attachment' that one had to forgo, on the path to liberation!

As the heat from the campfire began to die down, one by one the Germans retreated to the warm, welcoming embrace of their shed. Only Gustav remained seated around the fire, along with the two Tibetan guides and their host. The bitterly cold winds that howled through the valley seemed to pose no new challenges to the German Captain. For him nothing mattered more than his quest. *The still waters of Lake Rakshasthal seemed to reflect his somber mood.*

As he stared into the fire, his mind dwelt on the terrible possibility that his mission might *not* succeed! By now, the path ahead should have revealed itself. Even though he hadn't confessed this to his team, he had no idea how to proceed! He had always assumed that his mission had been 'Divinely Inspired'...and that guidance would eventually come. What if Shambhala had judged him...and found him wanting? All his efforts till this point would mean nothing! ...No! This was too terrible an option to even consider.

"Sometimes what we need exists right in front of our eyes...and yet we search the world for it."

Gustav looked up suddenly...Were his ears playing tricks on him? The words seemed to resonate directly inside his head...rather than from an external source! He looked around himself and saw no reactions from the two Tibetans, who looked half asleep. But the old man – their host, had a sly smile on his face. "Old Tibetan Proverb, Herr Gustav!" He replied softly...in flawless German!!

Gustav sat up with a start. "*Who* are you? How do you know me? And what is your interest in all of this?" he demanded, his heart pounding in his ears.

"You know exactly who I am...I have been with you since the very start of your quest." The old man replied tantalizingly. "In fact, it would be right to say that the quest you have undertaken...is actually MINE! So, I have every reason to be interested in your fate."

Gustav was too shocked to reply. As his mind desperately sought answers...he suddenly noticed something odd...not only was the man's face no longer clearly visible...it seemed to be in a constant state of flux...ebbing and flowing, as if its very molecules were unstable...but what was even more disturbing was that each time the man spoke, the wind, the sound of the water and every other sound of the night...seemed to STOP...*It seemed like Time itself was holding its breath!*

Gustav felt a wave of terror spread all over him. He desperately looked around for help. Nothing moved around him...the two Tibetans seemed to be frozen in place...petrified...he even observed the frozen breath that had escaped their nostrils...suspended in midair...like some grotesque abstract artwork! He tried to scream for help...someone...*anyone*...but no words escaped his mouth. He turned back towards his tormentor...hoping to avoid direct eye contact, and heard a soft chuckle.

"Ironic isn't it? All your life you searched for Paradise and now that you are on the verge of finding it...you feel like escaping...but let me assure you, there is no escaping your fate...no one...absolutely no one can come to your rescue now...just as you chose Shambhala as your goal, *Shambhala chose YOU as its!*"

Gustav's found it hard to breathe...he had never felt terror like this before. He knew he had to do something...ANYTHING! "What can you tell me about Shambhala?" he screamed...forcing the words out, still unable to make eye contact. He felt that if he looked this being in the eye, he would lose everything!

"Why do you still ask, when not so long ago, I actually showed it to you?" The man said with a sly smile.

Gustav gasped...*showed him before?* How could that be possible unless... "Are you...are you the same person, whom I met in Vienna? The old Turkish dealer, who knew so much and took me on that mystical journey...I searched for you long and hard after that...you just disappeared...who are you really and how do you know all of this?"

"As I have told you before, I am the last person to travel through the Gates of Shambhala...and return to tell the tale...making me the only person, who can truly assist you in your quest. All you need to do is trust me...and follow my instructions...unconditionally! The road to paradise is difficult and fraught with hidden dangers...it has no time for those not completely committed to the cause. Any half-hearted attempts on your part...or any acts of betrayal, will instantly result in a fate that shall make death seem like a good option."

An ominous silence followed. Gustav offered no response...he *HAD* none to offer. He simply let the man's words sink in. It was absolutely clear to him now that the being he was seeing in the light of this flickering fire, was no ordinary local, but the same dark influence he had felt...probing him and urging him on...throughout this journey!

No longer invisible and certainly no longer just an ambiguous feeling, this entity that had now assumed the shape of a man, clearly had its own agenda...one that it was very keen on achieving...that much was certain. Gustav also realized that opposing it...or trying in any way to counter it wasn't a good idea...even if such a thing were possible!

As to how far back in his life the entity's manipulations went, Gustav could only guess. Had it been the silent force behind his interest in the occult?...a decision that had led him to join the 'Thule Society' and ultimately to this expedition?

If so, then why had it specifically chosen *him* for this task? Or had the entity become interested in him, *AFTER* he began his forays into these areas? Had it been his desperate search for forbidden knowledge, which had introduced him to this shadowy force? With a sinking feeling, Gustav realized he had only himself to blame for his current fate...trapped within its iron clutches!

His thoughts went back to the famous quote by his own countryman - Friedrich Nietzsche – 'Whoever fights monsters should see to it that in the process he does not become a monster, for if you gaze long enough into an abyss, the abyss will gaze back into you!' ...a sobering thought...a disturbing thought.

"What do I have to do?" Gustav asked simply...painfully aware that all the cards now lay squarely with this being...there was no option, but to do what *it* wanted him to do and see if he could complete this journey. It seemed like he would *be* entering paradise...whether he wished to or not!

The being smiled… "To begin with, you will have to perform the 'Parikrama'…and then…"

The soft sounds of the waters of the two sacred lakes, gently lapping against their shores could once again be heard.

CHAPTER SIXTEEN

Early the next morning, the crew got up with massive head and body aches. The first proper rest in months, had caused their bodies to act up, as muscles and bones they never knew existed, were now screaming in protest. Amid groans and moans, they readied themselves for what promised to be the last phase of their expedition.

Gustav had already informed them that they would be undertaking the 'Parikrama'...or the circular pilgrimage around Mount Kailasha. The team noticed that their leader spoke in a monotone and his eyes were red...he clearly hadn't slept much the previous night...*if at all!*

For pious Hindus, the 'Parikrama' generally performed in a temple, meant repetitively walking around the deity, in a clockwise direction... it was a ritual meant to prompt introspection and humility within oneself. This could be performed at *any* sacred pilgrim spot.

Since Kailasha was of course one of the most sacred spots in Hinduism, a complete journey around its base...a 'Parikrama'...was certain to bring one, eternal salvation! The start of this ritual was generally marked with a dip in Lake Manasarovar...*a cleansing ritual,* meant to purify oneself of all evils, before starting the arduous journey around the mountain. As the Nazis immersed themselves in the freezing cold waters of the sacred lake, they noticed a number of other people of different faiths join them. For these pilgrims, unlike the Germans, the ritual was not just a means to an end...but an end in itself!

As they emerged from the waters, the Germans observed their leader in intense conversation with their host, from the previous night...the old man...who in the light of the morning sun, looked even older and frailer. Whatever the content of the conversation, the old man looked visibly confused, while Gustav's face showed signs of extreme distress!

The Germans wondered if it was simply a consequence of the enormous physical toll, their journey had taken...or something more. Of course none of them knew what their leader had gone through the night before. Nor could they suspect that what was really bothering Gustav, was that their host – the old man, who had revealed himself to be so much more the previous night, was now seeming very, very *confused* indeed! In fact the more Gustav quizzed him, the more disoriented, he became. It was almost as if this was a completely different person to the *presence* that had confronted Gustav the night before.

After a while, the Nazi Captain gave up. There was clearly something strange going on here...here was an entity ... 'a dark force' ...that had been responsible for a succession of extraordinary events that had guided and sometimes manipulated him throughout this journey...it had shown that it was capable of manifesting itself in various ways, seemingly whenever it wanted to...but now it seemed it had even developed the power to *POSSESS* others! This was the only explanation Gustav had for the events from the previous night...maybe the old man really *did* have no memory of the night before...maybe...*he was just another pawn in this dark entity's clandestine 'war' against Gustav!*

With this realization weighing heavily on him, Gustav ordered his team to ready itself for the 'Parikrama' – the circular journey that lay ahead. From their host, they had learnt some important details about it. The 'Parikrama' involved walking around the entire mountain. This would take the Germans three full days, during which, they would have to trek over some extremely rough terrain, cross streams, climb steep trails, jump from boulder to boulder and traverse a pass high in the mountains, all at 19,000 feet. The weather being the way it was, even at this time of the year, they could expect rain or snow, at different points during the journey.

For most pilgrims, who came to Kailasha, the 'Parikrama' was the greatest challenge and hundreds failed to complete it. In fact, the Germans observed the locals segregating the new arrivals into different groups...some who were considered totally unfit to perform the Parikrama and had to satisfy themselves, with merely a dip in one of the two sacred lakes...some who were allowed to participate, but only on the back of a Yak...and some who were declared fit enough... and able enough to undertake the whole journey on foot!

A worthiness test!

Having spent so much time in Tibet trekking all the way from Lhasa to Manasarovar, this final phase of their expedition seemed to hold no surprises for the Germans. For them the prospect of camping outdoors...on the sides of a mountain...was now par for course. They had after all been at it for months.

They knew that this time however... judging by the frenzied activity among the other pilgrims...they were sure to have a lot of company! It was clear that for all who came here, the 'Parikrama' held special significance. Occasionally, one of the pilgrims would wave out to the Germans...or shout out a greeting, in the name of Lord Shiva!

The team wondered *how* their leader hoped to be a part of this circus AND still try and find the entrance to 'Shambhala'. Surely the entrance...if at all it lay somewhere around the sacred mountain, would not reveal itself, if they simply went around the mountain like the others! This pilgrimage had been undertaken for more than a thousand years...and apart from a sense of 'spiritual salvation', the thousands of pilgrims, who visited Kailasha each year, had nothing else to show for.

Whatever Capt. Gustav thought of this, he remained withdrawn and quiet. The team had by now realized that even though their leader was prone to the occasional mood swing, he was a dedicated Nazi and was giving his absolute all, for the cause. For the team who had sworn an oath of loyalty to Hitler and Germany, this was enough!

And so amidst a cacophony of shouts and prayer chants, the Germans began the journey around Mount Kailasha. Unlike some of their more pious counterparts, they carried none of the prayer beads or sacred offerings, and for that, they received quite a few condescending stares.

The Parikrama began in a dismal valley that seemed totally devoid of life. The only sign of human presence was a narrow trail made entirely of pebbles. This was the path all pilgrims were supposed to take. As the more boisterous devotees raced each other to the trail, Gustav quietly signaled to his team to fall back...The Germans would proceed at a more leisurely pace, as compared to the main body of pilgrims. Doing so, would allow them to split from the main group of pilgrims and maintain at least a semblance of privacy and tranquility. Moreover, they were in no hurry to complete the 'Parikrama', for they would have to carefully and minutely scan the entire route…*if* they ever hoped to find the entrance to the lost city!

But much as Gustav hated to admit it, their biggest problem was that even *HE* really had no idea what it was that they were looking for. Since the start of this expedition, he had relied on intuition and guidance from some external para-normal force, to choose the course of action. Even now, they were undertaking this journey, under similar "guidance". But at some point he felt, they were going to need more than just that.

As vociferous chants of "Om Namah Shivai"…prayer chants glorifying the name of Lord Shiva, rent the air, the team came up to a spot, where a small mound of stone tablets was constructed, with inscriptions on them. Taking a leaf out of their former companion - Ernst Schaffer's book, Gustav took out a notebook and began to carefully document what the tablets said. Their local Tibetan guides read the inscriptions as "Om Mani Padme Hum"…a Buddhist chant… They explained that the stones had been placed by devotees, from previous expeditions…*from earlier eras*…as a sign of goodwill for future travelers. If so, this was certainly an auspicious start!

But even as the team felt its morale lift, the skies darkened and the weather began to cast an ominous shadow over the entire valley. It began with fierce winds striking the mountain, dismissive of its sanctity and creating a moaning sound…*like banshees wailing for the dead!* As the team scurried along the path looking for cover, they knew full well by now that in these altitudes, fierce winds were generally followed by heavy rains. It was important that they find a rocky outcrop, where they could resist the imminent onslaught…and then suddenly…abruptly…they came across another curious monument…a little archway that one of their guides described as "Yama Dwar" or 'Yama's Doorway'.

Gustav recalled from his own studies that 'Yama' was the Hindu God associated with death…and so an archway named after him, didn't seem very pleasant. Their guides explained that the region at the base of Mount Kailasha was considered to be 'Yama's domain'. To perform the Parikrama, one had to be *absolutely* pure in body and mind. Tradition dictated that one, who performs the Parikrama, must go through this narrow archway...symbolically, going through the 'House of Death'...and be 'Reborn', having been cleansed of all sins. The Germans couldn't help but note that for a journey that hadn't even begun yet, there certainly seemed to be a lot of 'worthiness' tests!

Gustav was the last to enter the archway symbolizing death and rebirth. As he paused briefly right underneath the archway, he heard a thin...tortured sound...behind him...*like fingernails scratching a slate*...it made the hairs on the back of his neck, stand up! Grimacing, he turned and looked around. In the haze that seemed to permanently hang in this freezing mountain air, he felt, he saw the shadowy silhouette of a figure that appeared to be following them!

Gustav blinked...he was certain that he and his team were the last...they had deliberately allowed all the other pilgrims to move ahead, so that they would face no obstacles in their search...so who was this shadowy figure?

Gustav strained his eyes to see...the silhouette seemed vaguely familiar...it looked very much like that of...their host from 'Darchen'... the old man...but that was impossible!! ...even though he was a local, this journey was clearly well beyond his capacity to perform...so why was he following them? ...*Had the dark entity once again taken control of him?*

The narrow archway greatly restricted his field of vision. Gustav exited the archway and then looked back once more...a barren and austere, white landscape stared back at him...*empty!* He blinked... trying to clear his eyes...he was sure he had seen something...this could not possibly have been a figment of his imagination...and almost on cue, the skies opened up!

CHAPTER SEVENTEEN

That night, as the team set up camp beside the trail, the Nazis seemed unusually withdrawn and quiet. Whether it was the supreme sanctity of the mountain…or the overwhelming sense of fatigue that engulfed them all, most seemed resigned to doing their own stuff. Their loyal Tibetan guides – Tenzin and Tashi, who had accompanied them all the way from Lhasa, tried their best to incite some banter, but to no avail. After a while, even *they* gave up.

Alone…in one corner, Gustav sat brooding over the course their travels had taken and what the future might hold in store for them. His mind kept going back to the mirage he had seen, while underneath the 'Archway of Death'. Had it been the dark entity? Was it following them for its own purposes or…was it trying to send some kind of a message? If so, why hadn't *he* been able to understand it?

As his mind vexed over these matters, his eyes turned towards one of his crew members, the twenty eight year old Hans Muller, from Vienna. Muller was a curious one, even by Nazi standards. A devout follower of Hitler, he had proved his loyalty, by protecting the Führer from the anger of the crowds with his own body, when a political rally in 1931 had turned sour. But in spite of his complete dedication to Nazi philosophy, Muller was a devout Catholic, who refused to give up his Christian faith. This had been the cause of many an altercation with Himmler, who had repeatedly told the young man of the ills of following what the Nazis referred to as a 'decadent faith'.

Nonetheless, Muller carried his Bible around with him all the time, and regularly read from it. Gustav had observed that at numerous points through this expedition, Muller would bring out a tattered and much used copy of the holy book and diligently read from it.

Now, he saw the young man seated with his back against the mountain wall, his eyes partly closed from exhaustion, slowly thumbing through the pages of the book, as it rested on his lap.

The repetitiveness of the man's actions and the slow pace, at which he was leafing through the pages, had a very comforting feel about it. Gustav had never begrudged the young man his religion. He had always believed that so long as an individual was loyal to the cause, he could be trusted, regardless of his religion. Now as he watched the young man seek some solace from scripture, his own mind went back to the dark presence that was plaguing him. Every time he was confronted by this entity, he was left with more questions than answers...and each of these experiences had been necessarily frightful. *How long would he have to live with this?*

Suddenly, he heard a thud. He saw that the Bible had fallen from Muller's lap and landed...still open...near the dying campfire! The young man had fallen fast asleep and was clearly unaware of what had happened. Gustav reached over and reverently picked up the book, by its thick binding. He flipped it over to see if the open pages had in any way been damaged by the fall. In the eerie half-light, his eyes fell on a specific section of the page that was open. Gustav was stunned!

He had just been wondering how long this dark force would remain with him and...how it always found different ways of reaching out to him...and now this...!!!!! One specific verse on the open page seemed to glow with a light of its own! It was Matthew 28:20... *"I will be with you even unto the end of the age."*

"Shit!"

As Gustav turned in for the night, he made a silent prayer to any God that was listening...for he now realized that he was well and truly 'damned'!

CHAPTER EIGHTEEN

Over the next two days, the pilgrims performing the 'Parikrama' were subjected to every conceivable assault, by the weather. The skies never completely cleared and the rains every now and then turned into a hail storm, savaging those seeking salvation. For Gustav's team, even after months in Tibet, these two days were easily the most trying. They huddled together each night, to keep the cold away, as much as possible.

Gustav had insisted that the team maintain a safe distance from the other pilgrims to avoid any kind of interaction that might raise suspicions about their real objectives. From the start, the team had allowed the others to take the lead and followed them at a considerable distance.

But the one problem they repeatedly encountered was that the pilgrims performing the Parikrama, for all their initial enthusiasm, were not trained mountaineers and belonged to all age groups. As a result, each time they had to cross a narrow mountain pass or leap over a few high rise boulders, some of the weaker ones would end up invariably slowing down the rest. This meant that every now and then, the German team had to slow down and stop, to avoid running into them.

Gustav however didn't seem to be too perturbed by this. Each time the team was forced to halt; he would pull out his notebook and try to document all the details they had seen, along the way. He believed any one of them could offer a vital clue into the mystery of Shambhala.

For the rest of the crew, this felt like the supreme test of their loyalty towards their leader. They had followed him diligently…all the way across the world, on the belief that he possessed forbidden knowledge…knowledge that would lead them to a lost city. To see him now join a pilgrimage...a particularly arduous one at that...and desperately search for clues, was a pitiful sight!

Surely, if any clues to the location of the lost city *did* lie on this route, the hundreds of thousands of pilgrims, who had walked these paths, year after year, would have stumbled upon them. What *did* their leader hope to accomplish by once again undertaking the same journey? Gustav's plight seemed to most echo the sufferings of a Tibetan woman, probably in her sixties, whom the team came across on the second day...a woman, who was performing the entire Parikrama in an extraordinary fashion!

Normally, the team had tried hard to avoid any and all contact with the pilgrims, but what this one pilgrim was doing, demanded their complete attention. On the rocky trail of the Parikrama, the old woman would prostrate completely...lying flat on her belly in devotion...then get up...take one step forward and lie down again in prayer! When a shocked Gustav asked Tashi, the team's Tibetan translator/guide, about the woman's actions, he quietly explained that this was the *Ultimate Form* of the Parikrama ritual, where a devotee performs the entire journey around the sacred mountain...by prostrating every step of the way!!! He said that completing the Parikrama *this* way would take her anywhere between twenty five days and a month!

The team was stunned...here they had been complaining about the difficulties of crossing this barren, inhospitable terrain on foot, even though they had some of the best mountaineering equipment available...and this woman, who was well past her prime, was planning to perform the entire journey pretty much on her knees!

Gustav saw that the woman wore a sort of leather vest on the front of her dress that served as basic protection against the harsh trail. She also wore some sort of wooden clappers on her palms, with which she prostrated on the ground...clappers that rang out with startling clarity, each time they made contact with the ground...*a stirring tribute to the holiness that was Mount Kailasha!*

Such dedication was truly astonishing! Gustav remembered the words of the 'dark entity' that the team needed to perform the Parikrama to be judged worthy by the mountain...for entering

Shambhala. Would the team have to show such extreme dedication in order to gain access? Did the team members have it in them to show such conviction?

That night as the team once again prepared to camp, Gustav found his thoughts being drawn back to the old woman and her astonishing display of faith. He sat outside the tents, going through all the notes he had prepared through their journey and tried once again, to see if he had overlooked anything.

The dim light of the campfire did not seem to offer much hope.

Tomorrow would mark the final day of the Parikrama. They would have finished one complete circle around the sacred mountain. If Gustav wasn't able to discover some clue…some way ahead, the entire expedition would have proved futile. Even though, as leader, he wasn't exactly answerable to his team members, Gustav wondered how long he would be able to bank on their unquestioning co-operation… should their mission fail!

From a distance, a couple of miles further north of where they were camped, trickled the sounds of the other pilgrim groups…sounds of chanting…uttering the name of Shiva. *It was so much simpler for them,* Gustav thought…*no external agenda to worry about…simply perform the ritual and be blessed for it!* As he felt his eyes grow heavy from fatigue, he knew that unlike the blessed pilgrims, he would have to sleep the 'sleep of the damned'.

Suddenly, he heard a sound that seemed to come from somewhere further south of where he was. He strained to see in the dark…was it an animal?…or a bird?

Strange…since they had not seen either along the way! But there it was again…a sharp thud…a sound like a wooden object of some sort…striking against the hard ground. What could it be? …the sound seemed to be coming closer. Gustav had a torch in his haversack, but that was still inside the tent. He strained to see in the direction of the sound.

Damn this fog…each time the sound travelled through it…it seemed like the fog dispersed…just that little bit…but surely…this was an illusion…*there was no way something like could happen…* Could it???

In the hazy darkness, he finally saw its source…a frail, hunched figure that was making its way up towards their camp…a figure that kept performing a strange ritual…of prostrating every step of the way on the harsh terrain…It was the old woman, they had passed along the way!!!

What was she doing here at this time??? How could she have gotten here so quickly…surely the way she was performing the Parikrama, it should have taken her days to reach this spot!

But no…it was indeed her…in the freezing cold darkness…all alone on this forsaken path; she was clawing her way over to the German camp! Something was very, very wrong over here!! A cold sweat broke out all over Gustav…he knew this feeling all too well. In the recent past, many were the times, he had encountered this sickening sensation…fear boiled alongside extreme panic. And each time, it had been followed by a visitation of the dark entity!

Surely…the woman was another manifestation of this being…but was it here to taunt him…or guide him? Gustav knew it usually did both. The figure was now very, very close…the woman still kept up her ritual…bending down…prostrating flat on the ground…standing up again and then bending down once more…Clap…Clap…Clap…sounded the clappers on the hard floor…the sound, a haunting reminder of the entity's presence.

The flickering light of the campfire caught on her dress. Gustav noticed that much of her face could not be seen, even though she was so close. He couldn't even be sure if it was the same woman, they had seen earlier in the day…but certainly, her dress and décor seemed familiar.

He found he couldn't breathe, as the macabre apparition came up to where he sat frozen. He closed his eyes tightly, silently… desperately…mouthing a prayer. He hoped that whatever this thing was, it would simply keep going. The prayer seemed to WORK!!! The apparition slowly…excruciatingly…WENT *PAST* the German Camp…but then…it stopped and turned!

Shit…shit…shit…shit…shit!!!!

Gustav almost choked on his own fear. Even in his panic, he knew it was going to come back…for him!! Why was it that it tormented only him? Why was no one else ever around when it decided to make contact?

"So, you are the fool, who plans on entering Paradise?" an eerie voice suddenly cut through the darkness, followed by a sadistic chuckle. Gustav gasped...he hadn't expected that it would speak to him...definitely not so brazenly!

"Who are you? Why do you keep tormenting me so?" He croaked. One thing seemed clear now...the apparition, he had seen on the first day...from below the archway of death, was no mere illusion...this dark entity *had* been following them!

"I am what you shall one day become." The reply sounded ominously prophetic...the figure no longer resembled an old woman on a pilgrimage...it barely even looked humanoid. Had it possessed and completely *consumed* the old woman?...or had there never been a woman at all?

The voice continued... "Tomorrow you and your cohorts complete the Parikrama...the sacred pilgrimage that is a tribute to this place and its inherent sanctity. But your journey doesn't end there. To reach your destination, you must do something more...something that will prove to be the ultimate test of your endurance and fortitude... something that will cause even your most ardent followers to question you...You must climb the sacred mountain itself!...Kailasha is believed to be the abode of Shiva...and after performing the Parikrama in honor of the deity, to enter the sacred city, one must climb the mountain and sit with Shiva himself!"

Gustav was shocked, "How would that lead me to my destination? Is this another one of your traps? You have deceived me and manipulated me for so long that I no longer trust even myself! Stop speaking in riddles and for once tell me honestly what I need to do... my followers already doubt me...they don't say it, but I see it in their eyes...I cannot aimlessly drag them around this forsaken place when I myself lack clarity!"

The fear that he felt towards this entity was slowly...irrationally... transforming into anger, "I came here looking for ancient technology... technology that according to my research must exist in this mythical place...flying machines that allow for near instantaneous travel...the

'Vimanas'...instead I find myself being manipulated and deceived by you...through this seemingly endless journey and now you want me to scale this peak???"

"Even assuming I agree to do so, the Tibetans would never grant me the permission to scale it from the side that faces the valley...we would need to instead scale it, in secret, from the rear, probably after dark...a feat that would be near impossible, even if we were fresh and rested...but now my men are on the verge of exhaustion."

The being said nothing...it merely looked at him with resignation. Then in a voice that could cut glass, it continued, "This is paradise that we speak of my boy...nobody ever said it was going to be easy...if you do indeed crave the sacred knowledge of the past that has been denied to humankind for thousands of years, you must prove yourself truly worthy of the prize. Shambhala contains much more than mere flying machines...don't set your sights so low...the city possesses knowledge that can make you the master of all space and time...but be warned... you are not the first person to try and reach for the heavens. However, you *could* become the first one to succeed."

"There have been others before me? Germans?" Gustav asked in surprise.

"Yes...many others...not necessarily from your homeland."

"So what happened to them? How is it that in all my researches, I never stumbled on any evidence of this sort of a quest being undertaken before? Where are those people now?"

Silence...the being just looked at him...the complete absence of an answer...was in a way, the most bone-chilling of replies. It was clear that this quest had no time...or mercy for those, who played and lost...if the destination was 'everything'...the price one paid for not getting to it was also absolute!

Gustav realized he would need to plan the final phase of this journey with great precision. There could be no errors whatsoever... tomorrow he would need to galvanize his team to give it one last superhuman effort, with absolutely no second thoughts and no room for doubts...the entry into paradise would need their complete conviction.

But before he took this final plunge, he needed to clarify one crucial point, "What happens once we get to the top? How do we know what to do next?"

"Complete your journey...the physical half of it first and I shall guide you through the spiritual half...once you and your team reach the top of the peak, you will have to perform a ritual that I shall mentor you through...a ritual that shall elevate seven sacred energy spheres inside your body...the 'Seven Chakras' to the levels needed to transcend the physical realm...The Gates of Shambhala can be breached *only* by someone, who is both physical and transcendental... this is the reason why during one of our previous interactions, I insisted that you form a team of seven for this quest...each one will be responsible for one energy chakra within the rest...only when all seven chakras are channelized in this way, will the city allow *YOU* access. All of your team will have to work in perfect synchronicity for *YOU* to unlock the Gates of Paradise."

Gustav was dumbfounded...he said nothing...he felt he couldn't understand himself anymore. There were still so many questions he had...especially troubling was the description of the ritual needed to enter Shambhala...the dark force had just mentioned how his entire team would need to perform the ritual together...but then specifically stressed on how only he – Gustav, would gain access...just 'he'...*so what would happen to the rest?*

"If we perform the ritual correctly, we shall ALL be allowed access into the city?" he quizzed...half dreading the answer... "If not, what happens to my team?"

The entity said nothing...buffered by the winds that tore through this valley, Gustav could barely make out its face...he couldn't tell if it was smiling, "Your team will have to perform the ritual for YOU to gain access."

"So what happens to them then? Do they...?" Gustav started in horror.

"The price of gaining 'Everything'...is 'Everything.'" The entity said almost in a whisper.

"I leave you now to rest and plan your strategy carefully...for when you finish the Parikrama late in the day tomorrow, you shall have to make this terrible choice...will you be content with simply completing this pilgrimage like so many thousands of others...or will you still crave more...just keep one thing in mind...once you do make your choice, there will be no turning back!"

"Wait..." Gustav almost screamed, "I need to know more...what happens after we enter Shambhala? How do we exit it? How do we go back to our homeland? ...we cannot travel back through Tibet again."

"You speak of 'exiting paradise' without having entered it yet? Ha ha ha...I hope you don't feel the need to regret these words...as far as going back is concerned, all I can offer you is a phrase that is used around these parts, a phrase about Kailasha –

'Only a man entirely free of sin could climb Kailash. And he wouldn't have to actually scale the sheer walls of ice to do it – he'd just turn himself into a bird and fly to the summit.' –

"The sacred mountain is a lot bigger than what it seems...the physical structure you now see is only a small part of it...open up your mind's eye Captain Gustav...elevate your 'Chakras'...and you shall see Kailasha in all its glory...you shall see Shambhala!"

The wind howled through the valley...Gustav suddenly found himself looking out at...absolutely nothing...he was all alone standing beside the trail...he suddenly felt very lonely.

As he made his way back towards the tents, he thought about what the entity had said...the journey and the climb that they would have to make the following night...and especially the enigmatic phrase about Kailasha...

- 'Only a man entirely free of sin could climb Kailash. And he wouldn't have to actually scale the sheer walls of ice to do it – he'd just turn himself into a bird and fly to the summit.' –

He realized he had been right about at least one thing...whatever happened; they certainly wouldn't need to travel back through Tibet...

on foot… '*Just turn himself into a bird and fly to the summit*'…this part of the phrase…was very clearly a metaphor…for Vimanas!

Just before he entered his tent for the night, Gustav cast his eyes one last time on his goal…the majestic Mount Kailasha, rose imposingly over the valley, dwarfing the four smaller mountains surrounding it. In Hindu mythology, Kailasha was the home of Shiva, since its location and its geography perfectly matched the mythical mount 'Mandera' – a mountain that was thought to exist at the very center of the cosmos and one that was also surrounded by four smaller peaks!

Mount Kailasha was thus the physical image of its cosmic counterpart…however, if what the entity had said was true, Gustav would need to see Kailasha…in its true form…physical and meta-physical.

Safely ensconced in his tent, he closed his eyes, in a moment of sudden reverence and then slowly opened them to get a final glimpse of the sacred mountain…and saw for the first time a sight that would last him an eternity…Mount Kailasha standing silently against the horizon…but now buffered and enshrouded, by an even larger mountain…one that perfectly mirrored Kailasha in all its shapes and contours…but one that was at least twice as massive!

Gustav stared…unable to believe his own eyes…the larger mountain he was witnessing seemed to simmer in the wind…almost as if it lacked any solid physical moorings…and on the very top of it he saw, a glowing monastery, full of divine prayer bells and flags… whose sacred sounds flowed down into the valley…reaching his mind rather than his ears. A divine perfume wafted down through the whole region, as if it were carried by the very sound of these bells… ethereal and abstract, he realized that what he was witnessing was a mere reflection…an ethereal echo…from another world…a more spiritual world…one that he would *have* to enter tomorrow…even at the cost of his loyal team-mates!

The entity had told him to open his mind's eye…and now as a reward, *Shambhala was giving him a glimpse of paradise!!!*

Even though he tried his best to hold back, Gustav's eyes filled with tears.

Shambhala

CHAPTER NINETEEN

The next day, amid more rain and snowfall, the team completed the final leg of the Parikrama, around the sacred mountain. Gustav had spoken to them about the encounter from the night before and explained the revelations he had received from the entity. Keeping any secrets at this point did not seem wise. He knew for what remained of their quest, he would need the complete trust and dedication of his team. However, his declaration that they would need to climb the sacred mountain, was met with mixed reactions. Silence from his German colleagues…shock from the two Tibetans!

For the Germans, this journey had already taken so much out of them that they were keen to get it over with, as soon as possible…if that meant scaling what was arguably a near vertical cliff after dark, so be it! For the two Tibetans, Tenzin and Tashi, Mount Kailasha had always been a hallowed shrine. Growing up as Tibetan Buddhists, they had heard countless stories of this peak and its inherent sanctity. To actually set foot on its sacred rocks and attempt to scale it, without the permission of the local authorities, seemed just too blasphemous!

They had been nothing but loyal to their guests – the Nazis, since their arrival in their land. They had even ignored the fact that Gustav and his group, unlike Schaffer, were 'uninvited visitors' to Tibet. They had borne the same risks and hardships that the Germans had, throughout this journey. But surely, this was going too far! If the Nazis felt like desecrating a sacred shrine, the Tibetans would certainly have no part in it. They jointly declared that as soon as the Parikrama was complete, they would take their leave and head back to the village of 'Darchen'. The Germans could then tempt the Gods all they wanted… on their own!

This greatly angered Gustav and he questioned the guides' sense of loyalty. How could they abandon their guests at this critical phase, when the journey was nearing its completion? But the Tibetans were adamant. They would accompany Gustav to the ends of the Earth and beyond, but they would NOT be a part of this heretical venture. They even tried to dissuade him out of it. They reminded him of 'Maha-Kala' the dark guardian and how he haunted these lands and preyed upon those who violated its sanctity!!

But *nothing* could persuade Gustav to give up the quest now. He scoffed at the Tibetans…his frustration giving him more anger than was called for…deeming them cowards and arrogantly boasting that he no longer needed their services.

And so it was that a group that had begun this epic journey together in silence because of a language barrier…ended it in silence having reached an ideological barrier!

The plan now was that as the team would near the end of the Parikrama and close in on the trail that took them back to their starting point, the Germans would pull back a little to avoid being detected by the other pilgrims, while the two Tibetans would head back to the village and replenish the supplies. They would then head back to the German team and hand over these supplies to them… these would include food, dry clothes and fresh water. The team would then wait for nightfall, resting their battered limbs, still protected from view by the mountain they hoped to climb.

Come nightfall, the two Tibetans would take their leave and once again head back to 'Darchen', having agreed to keep mum about the German plan of action, while Gustav's team would begin the process of scaling the mountain…a journey that Gustav calculated would take them around eight hours. Even taking into account the enormous risks that were involved in scaling such a peak in the dark, he estimated that they would reach the summit at first light. From then on of course, it was a matter of faith and fate!

That evening, just as per the plan, the team took a halt at the final bend of the Parikrama…over the last three days, they had done what pilgrims had been doing for thousands of years and had earned many a bruise and sore limb for their efforts! Tashi and Tenzin, their Tibetan guides, silently left to complete *their* part of the commitment and bring back fresh supplies. The rest of the team members mentally prepared themselves, for the climb ahead...flashlights were checked and re-checked...the climbing gear was pulled out of the haversacks and made ready...once the Tibetans returned and darkness fell, there would be no time to lose!

They knew, if they were discovered now...*even accidentally*, there would certainly be trouble. Gustav was the only one who didn't participate in this build-up. He kept thumbing through his notebook, occasionally re-reading certain notes he had made. For the team this wasn't unusual. They knew their leader was uncharacteristically quiet for a German...but as loyal Nazis they were sworn to follow his directions ...What they *did* worry about was whether *he* himself knew what he was doing!

Their Tibetan friends returned within three hours, carrying with them all that they had been asked to bring...and some more! Apart from the food and fresh supplies needed for the climb, the Tibetans carried with them 'prayer pendants', for each member to wear around the neck. These were symbols of goodwill and a plea to all the mountain deities to keep the travelers safe. This simple, yet touching gesture of love, brought tears to the eyes of even these battle hardened Nazis. Even Capt. Gustav affectionately embraced both of them, as all the harsh words from earlier, were forgotten. The months of togetherness, amidst the harsh wilderness of this land, had created bonds of friendship and camaraderie much stronger than blood ties!

And now it was time to say goodbye...*perhaps for the last time!* Whether they succeeded or failed, it was unlikely that these men would ever meet each other again. Amidst tears he could no longer hold back, Tashi embraced each of the Germans, as they took their leave and said, "I hope you find your paradise brothers and when you do, reserve a place for me...for I shall one day want to meet you there!"

The Germans watched their Tibetan brothers walk away...all the way, till they were mere specks on the horizon, and then somberly turned their attention to the task at hand. The sun had just about set and the climb up to Shambhala beckoned!

With heavy hearts, the team slowly turned to the mountain. All their efforts had led up to this point...and then...like gentle summer dewdrops wetting the mystical sands of time, lost, sacred words began to resonate…hauntingly…across the valley, *"Gar firdaus bar-rue zamin ast, hami asto, hamin asto, hamin asto!"* …the famous Persian quote, prophetically summing up what lay in store. "If there is paradise on Earth…this is it…this is it…this is it…" Gustav couldn't help but wonder, if this would be 'Paradise lost' or 'Paradise found!'

CHAPTER TWENTY

Dhuk...Dhuk...Dhuk...listening to the beat of your own heart can be both exhilarating and terrifying. On one hand, the sound is steady and rhythmic much like the precious gift of life; On the other hand, it serves as a reminder of just how fragile that gift really is!

For Captain Friedrich Gustav, leader of the Nazi S.S. expedition to Tibet, the sound was causing all the strength in his body, to fade away. He knew he had failed in his mission...albeit an impossible one to begin with! He had failed to find the mythical city of Shambhala...he had failed his Führer...and he had failed the German people...but above all else, he had failed himself!

It is said that in your dying moments, your entire life flashes before your eyes. Yet for Gustav, his mind's eye saw nothing. His brain seemed incapable of anything beyond its most basic functions...all he could think of was the sheer vertical cliff face, he found himself trapped on.

This was a death-trap!

The icy cold terrain and the over 30 miles an hour winds that tore at his battered body, accentuating this point. Lying precariously some 17,000 feet above sea level on a narrow rocky ledge, halfway up Tibet's holy Mount Kailasha and supported only by his nylon harness, Gustav took a deep breath and tried to reassess the situation.

When he and his team had begun their ascent, they had calculated that the peak would be an eight-hour climb. Using 'state of the art' rock climbing equipment, they had scaled most of the mountain, without much difficulty. Even though, they had done it under the cover of darkness, the lack of illumination had not proved to be a deterrent. Astonishingly...*the very mountain had seemed to emanate an inner light*...illuminating the path to the top. The Germans had been too exhausted to investigate this phenomenon and merely focused on completing the trek.

The climb had proceeded smoothly, till the last bit, where the angle of incline had suddenly changed! From an already steep 80 degrees, the trajectory had altered itself to almost sheer vertical. It was here that their troubles had begun.

One of the two grappling hooks the team used to scale these cliffs, had given way and fallen some five hundred feet below, onto a narrow ledge. This presented a massive problem. The particular mountaineering technique the German team had perfected and used so effectively to scale all the peaks they had crossed so far, required the use of both hooks in synch. The loss of one of these, at such a critical juncture, could severely compromise their ability to continue.

The team had faced a difficult choice...one or more of the climbers could pull back a few hundred feet and retrieve the fallen hook. This would mean the loss of precious time and energy, both of which the team had in short supply. Gustav had insisted from the start that they complete the journey before day break...a proposition that seemed more and more difficult with each passing moment.

Alternately, the team could attempt the remaining part of the climb with only one hook and rope apparatus...a far, far riskier approach. At such altitudes, one slip and it would be all over. However, this was their only shot at getting to the top on time. Even as they stood debating, disaster had once again raised its ugly head.

Johann Baur the young twenty year old Bavarian, whom Gustav had come to look upon as a younger brother, missed a snow covered gap between two footholds...and plummeted straight down through it to his death, before anyone could react!!! The shocking speed of the young man's demise had a profound impact on the Germans. One second, they were a tightly knit group of seven, and the next...one of them lay at the bottom of a crevasse!

It had been Baur alone in the entire group, who had the most belief in Gustav's vision and had been one of the main reasons the group had managed to keep its spirits high, throughout this arduous journey. Now, his sudden death was a stark reminder to the rest...of the true nature of the land, they were in. *The beast was finally revealing itself...* nobody had spoken a word!

However, this also seemed like the last straw. The group had been together for months now...and had come to look upon each other as family. They had never once openly contested Gustav's orders, regardless of their personal feelings, and had followed him even when he had asked for the impossible!

But with Baur's death, that morale seemed to finally snap. What began as an argument, quickly threatened to turn into an all-out mutiny. The crew insisted that the exact nature of this climb be revealed...immediately!! They wanted to know what Gustav hoped to accomplish at the summit. Why was he so convinced that the entrance to Shambhala lay somewhere on top of this mountain? It was clear that his lack of full disclosure had been a contentious issue with the team for a while now. And now...*détente it seemed...was finally over!*

With no options left, Gustav had decided to play for time. Without a word, he pointed out a natural alcove just past the narrow ridge they were on, and proceeded to lead the team towards it. Here the group could rest and recuperate their shattered nerves, while taking stock of the situation. It would also allow him some time to plan his next move...clearly the plan of reaching the summit together as a team by day break, would have to be altered. Shocked and dazed from the death of one of their own, the others silently followed him into the alcove.

Once inside the small opening, Gustav had insisted that they all eat and rest...before any further decisions. The team had grudgingly agreed...for the prospect of eating so soon after Baur's death left them all feeling sick in the stomach. The meal and the rest had nevertheless served their purpose, leaving the team exhausted and delirious...the massive emotional and physical fatigue, finally taking its toll!

Gustav had made it a point to eat sparsely. Even after Baur's horrifying fall, his mind had been working overtime. Whether it was the adrenaline pumping through his veins...at the prospect of being so close to his lifelong goal...or the manipulative influence of an external force, he couldn't say, but he knew that as soon as the others were asleep in this death-defying alcove thousands of feet above ground, he would need to make his terrible decision.

Taking only the barest of supplies and just enough food to last him half a day, Gustav had set off alone to complete the journey to the summit. Somehow, he knew that the dark entity manipulating him, had plans for him. What those were, he neither knew...nor cared...for him all that mattered was that, the being possessed knowledge of paradise. The price it charged in exchange would have to be paid... *regardless of what it was!*

At the back of his mind, he knew that one of the things the entity had repeatedly insisted on, was that entering Shambhala, would need a team of seven...where each member would play a role in the channeling of certain energy sources, within the human body...the 'Seven Chakras'.

That he was now headed to the summit...alone...left him with mixed feelings. On one hand, he knew this could severely compromise his attempts at reaching paradise, but on the other hand, he felt a quiet sense of peace. The entity had heavily implied that the ritual to unlock the gates of the lost city would almost certainly end up destroying his teammates!!

So far, Gustav had kept this last bit...absolutely secret, from the others. He had been mentally steeling himself for the ruthlessness he would need to show, while sacrificing his teammates on the altar of German Glory. It would be for a greater cause, was how he had tried to justify the choice. But after Baur's death, he no longer felt up to it. Alone he felt, he would confront this entity and alone he would pay the price...whatever it was. If he did succeed, he would attribute it to the glory of the Reich, if not, so be it.

He had followed a natural ridge that stuck out from the face of the mountain, with the hope that it would lead him to the top. He estimated that the journey wouldn't take him more than three hours... enough time to still reach the top as per schedule.

But that hope quickly turned sour. What had promised to be a natural ridge strong enough to support the weight of a human being had turned out to be an optical illusion! This was brought about by a phenomenon that the Germans referred to as 'Ice-eyes'. The monochromatic nature of the surroundings and the constant exposure to the elements could cause a mountaineer to 'see' shapes and forms that don't actually exist. The brain, devoid of any of the regular visual inputs it is used to receiving…normally in three-dimensions and colors, begins to construe a two-dimensional monochromatic surface…in additional layers!

This phenomenon had been particularly heightened in the case of the Germans, as they had been in this terrain, for months. Now, it was clear that the constant presence of the icy landscape and days of solitude, was taking its toll on Gustav. He was starting to see shapes and pathways that did not exist…especially dangerous so close to the summit. Worse yet, Gustav was carrying the only set of rope and hook mechanism that the team still possessed. One false step and he would not only end up killing himself, but also leave his team, with absolutely no hope of escaping their mountainous alcove!!

This had always been an all or nothing venture!

To make matters even worse, the terrain was such that once he had made up his mind to continue on his own, there was no going back. No place to rest…no place to re-assess. He knew full well that if he did take a break and stop, there was always the chance his exhausted muscles would simply give in…and freeze. In spite of it all, he had clawed his way up to almost the top of the cliff, scaling over a hundred meters of sheer ice. Only his superb mountaineering skills and years of military training had allowed him to do what for most would have proved a step too far.

Half an hour into his solitary sojourn, and Gustav had been forced to keep himself from falling asleep…on his feet. One hour into the journey and his physical condition got much worse. He was wheezing and gasping for breath and each step seemed to require a superhuman effort. By the time, his addled brain finally pieced together that the ridge he had been banking on to make his final assent, was nothing more than a 'light and shadow' effect, his body had long been ready to give up.

Now listening to the sound of his own heart beat, Gustav felt his strength fade away. He was still some meters away from the top but it might as well have been a hundred miles. The rock climber's icicle and the harness were the only things that prevented him from tumbling into the ravine. It would be so simple…to simply let go. The valley beckoned lovingly…death beckoned lovingly…eager to take him into its warm embrace…all the pain…physical…mental…emotional, would simply disappear…sweet sweet oblivion…all encompassing… eternal…perfect…*even this way, he could still get to Paradise!*

"No!" he screamed…his mind suddenly jolted back into sanity…he broke into a cold sweat…he had come so, so close to succumbing…so close to giving up…to losing it all…this would simply not do. He *HAD* to reach the summit. He realized this was Shambhala's ultimate test…one he needed to pass, in order to prove himself worthy!

He once again heard a dull thud…it sounded much like his own heart beat…but this time, from beyond…footsteps…*FOOTSTEPS??* How could anyone be possibly walking here? Surely, he was dreaming…hallucinating…then he heard it again…a sound…the unbelievable, unmistakable sound of a voice…a human voice…He scarcely dared to breathe…lest his very breath, scared the voice away. But no…he heard it again…it was speaking to him…saying something…a word… "Chronux"

Gustav listened in amazement…he hadn't heard the word before… but it seemed oddly familiar. He had to know what was going on…he couldn't give up at this stage!

With one final superhuman effort, he tried to hurl himself to the summit. He knew full well the distance between where he had been perched and the summit was a good four to five meters…a vertical distance too far to cover in a single bound! Still, he tried, giving it his all…his body arched like an athlete…striving for maximum distance… his left hand holding the icicle, high over his head. He hoped that with the force of his leap, he would at least be able to find the strength to lodge the icicle somewhere close to the top, even if he wasn't himself able to make the distance. Then with the tether still fastened to it, he could drag himself the last few feet…*in theory.*

The slender rays of the rising sun caught the tip of the icicle, as it slowly, dramatically descended from the heavens, towards its rocky destination. Gustav felt an agonizing jerk, as it made contact with top of the peak…and then slipped!

With no strength left in his own body, the violence of the impact caused him to hit his head against the other end of the icicle, his entire body reverberating from the impact. As he looked up...the misfiring synapses in his brain trying to process what was happening...he saw... very briefly...the top of the mountain, he had so desperately sought to scale...the very summit of the holy mountain... Kailasha ...and then he saw it...beyond Kailasha itself...floating silently like an ethereal paradise...simmering against the morning sky...another sight...the Golden Gates of Paradise... *Shambhala!*

Then slowly...almost sadistically...the divine view was snatched away, as gravity once again began to assert its non-partisan influence on him...and he began to fall silently into the ravine below.

In Hindu mythology, 'Yama' the God of Death, is always depicted as an impartial judge of men...neither favoring the good nor specifically targeting the evil...perhaps this is why at the foot of the mountain, there is a sanctuary dedicated to him...the 'Yama Dwar'...the Gates of Yama!

The ancients probably understood this irony, all too well...you might climb the sacred mountain, in all your virility, seeking the glories of Paradise, but a single slip-up and Yama greets you with the same impartiality, he reserves for everyone – 'Gravity'!

So close...and yet so far away were Gustav's last thoughts, as he tumbled into the darkness.

CHAPTER TWENTY ONE

The world seemed to be deep crimson and full of pain...pain that refused to go away. Then all of a sudden, it turned bright...*so bright that his eyes hurt*...he tried to shield against this unnatural light...but found he couldn't...was this how death felt? He tried to move...and screamed in pain. Wait a minute...why would he still feel pain, if he was dead?

The brightness now reduced in intensity...ever so slightly and he could make out just the hint of color. Something was very wrong here...this didn't feel like the afterlife. He tried to move once again, and this time had a tad more success. He felt a warm re-assuring presence, on his right arm...someone was holding on to it.

Gradually, as his vision cleared a little...he was able to dimly perceive his surroundings. Rather than lying dead at the bottom of the mountain, he found much to his surprise, that he was lying face down on top of it...very much alive! *How had this happened?* He tried to see more, but pain quickly forced him to close his eyes once again.

He still felt the warm comforting presence close by. Someone...or *something* had saved him...the dark entity!!! There was no other explanation...after all, *it* had been the one that had wanted him to succeed! .Whatever its own agenda, it had repeatedly assisted him through this journey...and now it had saved his life!

But there was something different this time around...Gustav could sense it even with his eyes closed. Yes...it was now morning and the rays of the rising sun were certainly doing their best to dispel the dark and moody clouds...but the presence he felt near him, was unlike anything he had felt before.

Each of his previous encounters with the dark entity had been confusing and terrifying to say the least...this one however, seemed different. In spite of his extreme exhaustion, he felt like a child, in the warm, loving arms of its mother. There was something about this encounter that promised much more than before. Maybe, at long last, he *HAD* been judged worthy!

As he felt himself once again slip into an exhausted, yet relaxed slumber, he heard the voice speak to him. He couldn't quite understand the language and yet somehow, it made perfect sense...it was just a soft whisper... "My son... I couldn't simply let you pass...there are big things in store for you...after all *in Chronux lies your destiny!*"

Then everything once again...went dark.

CHAPTER TWENTY TWO

"The Entrance to Shambhala lies within your grasp...all you have to do is reach out for it!" The voice of the dark entity resonated all over scared Mount Kailasha. Capt. Gustav of the Third Reich found himself finally facing his destiny!

After he had regained consciousness and some of his strength, Gustav had dragged himself over to where this being stood. He noticed that the entity now looked far more physical...and coherent than during any of its previous visitations.

He saw that it was in the guise of an old man...not dissimilar to their Tibetan host, from the village of Darchen. However, the costume it wore looked far more ancient than what even the Tibetans wore... it looked almost Indian!

The being spoke to him in a voice that sounded almost musical... the words floating in the rarified air, on the mountain top. It had told him that in order to enter the sacred city, a lot of external factors needed to fall in place...as to what those were, it hadn't elaborated... yet!

Gustav knew that he would have almost certainly died, had it not been for this being, "What do I need to do? You mentioned a ritual... tell me what needs to be done...I am ready." he said simply...there were so many questions he still had, but those would have to wait.

"You see, my son, the Gates of Shambhala open *only* during certain select periods...under a series of very specific astronomical alignments. What these alignments are, is of no consequence to you right now...its sufficient to say that you completed your journey at just the right time...as I knew you would...for as we speak, the celestial bodies I spoke of, move into the necessary positions!"

"But we had so many obstacles during our journey...so many times we questioned our decision to embark on such a journey...if the final part of this quest can be accomplished only under certain very specific conditions, how could you have known that I would succeed in time?" Gustav asked stunned, "Unless…"

"Ha ha …you catch on quick my boy…how could I know for certain…unless *I* was in some way responsible for all those situations!"

"My God! …You caused all of it to happen! All the troubles we faced with the British! …the problems we faced while crossing Tibet! …even Baur's death!" Gustav screamed in anger.

"My boy, you have and still continue to underestimate me…by the time we are done, you will know just how far my manipulations run… but let's not squabble about bygones…all of what you have gone through, will pale in the face of what is to come." the being replied, coldly.

"What do you mean?"

"To unlock the Gates of Shambhala, you will need to perform a 'Ritual of Purity'…the process whereby you first unlock the power that exists within each human being…you know it by various names… 'Chi'…'Ki'…'Kundalini'…'Vril'…However, I had specifically instructed you to complete the journey with a seven member team…with each member performing a part of the ritual…however, one of those members now lies dead at the bottom of this cliff…and the others lie trapped, without equipment, half way up this peak…You have *not* been able to keep up your end of the bargain…I am really beginning to wonder, whether I overestimated YOUR potential…it seems to me that you after all, aren't worthy of reaping the fruits of your labor!" The voice was filled with causticity.

"No" screamed Gustav… "I *am* worthy…I have proven myself enough through this journey…Surely…any lesser man would have failed…let me take up the challenge and I shall prove myself equal to seven men!!! Tell me what I need to do!"

There was a long silence and then…the entity smiled…and even though the fury of the rising sun, reflecting against this stark and austere mountain top, made it impossible for Gustav to see his tormentor's face clearly, what little he saw, sent shivers up and down his spine!

"Are you sure you are up to it? This requires great sacrifices…much greater than what you seem capable of!"

"Yes…I am ready…I was born ready…tell me what needs to be done!"

"What you seek from Shambhala…is the lost technology of the ancient world…the divine technology…but…without your team members, there is absolutely no way for you to enter the city… unfortunately…that window has closed." The entity responded with a sense of finality.

"But…But…" Gustav stammered, his mind refusing to accept what was being said.

"Yes…that is the non-partisan truth…I would know…I am, after all the Gatekeeper of Paradise! Only someone, who has his internal energies…all seven chakras active…can hope to enter the city…and unfortunately, this is a feat no longer possible for any one person! However, on account of the astronomical alignments that I spoke of, *I* can very briefly open the portal to the city, on your behalf…this will allow you to reach into Shambhala, and salvage the secret document – the Vimanika Shastra that you so desperately crave. Using it, I am sure you and your researchers would find a way of reverse engineering the devices, back in your homeland. Moreover, as a gesture of goodwill, I will also provide you with the means of activating these devices!"

Gustav stared…he had dreamt all these years of entering this lost city of Tibetan myth…one that for thousands of years had been inaccessible to the outside world…and now as he stood on the brink of success, he was being told that it was forever out of his reach! All his efforts…his research…the trials and tribulations…the frustration and the grief that he and his team had gone through…was going to amount to nothing!

Tibet had for long been considered the 'Roof of the World'…a land so high up and pure, that it could literally support the heavens.

The full weight of those heavens now seemed to bear down on Gustav's shoulders. He had to decide what to do…something was better than nothing. Maybe…just maybe, if he did access the sacred text…the blueprints for divine technology…he might even be able to return to this place again…in the future!

"I am prepared...unlock the portal and grant me what access you can!" He replied, his voice trembling.

"I warn you once again...once the process begins, there will be no going back...no backing out from it... Remember! ...Paradise does not forgive and forget...easily! Even what little access you ask for, will take a lot out of you...you shall be reaching into a realm that no mortal is destined to traverse in life! To do so, one must be prepared to sacrifice everything...after all; the price of 'everything' is 'Everything!!!'"

"I am ready." Gustav reaffirmed...albeit, much more softly.

"Perfect." Said the being...and turned its back on the German.

For Capt. Gustav, what followed seemed handpicked straight out of his worst nightmares. The entire top of the mountain was suddenly blanketed by a mysterious swirling ball of energy. Powerful shockwaves emanating from within began to physically assault his person. It felt like being inside a maelstrom...tentacles of fluid, viscous energy raked across his face...his darkest dreams seemed to take on life and rape and pillage his psyche!

Desperately, he tried to hold on for dear life, as the very rules of physics began to fall apart. 'Up' now meant 'down' and the four cardinal directions started to superimpose themselves on each other. Light was being bent so far out of proportion...that briefly...*very briefly*...he was able to see the back of his own head!!! How long, before his own corporeal structure came apart?

He could no longer 'see' the entity but sensed its role in this mayhem.

And then...just as he felt, he could no longer hold on, he heard a voice...the words, reverberating against this chaos... "Quickly, reach out and grab what lies just beyond this mystical barrier...time is of the essence!"

Gustav reached out blindly and felt a sudden powerful pull... forcing him towards an opening...Was this the portal?...the hallowed 'Gates of Shambhala'?

There was no way of knowing. But as his hands breached the opening, he felt a dramatic shift in activity...that part of his hand inside the portal, experienced unbelievable tranquility...the perfect harmony between the physical world and the spiritual...body... mind...soul...*Paradise!*

The rest of his hand, much like his body, still suffered the full assault of the unearthly maelstrom. Oh...how he wished he could witness...however briefly...the sights and sounds of Shambhala! ... to walk this magical land...the things that he might learn from it! But one moment of supreme bliss...was all that he was being offered!

"Grab what you find over there...quickly and pull back, lest this vortex pulls the entire mountain apart." The entity's voice once again cut through the blizzard.

Gustav clasped his hands around whatever he could hold on to... on the other side of the portal. But horror of horrors...that what he held seemed to suddenly grow impossibly heavy...resisting him...he realized, he could not pull it out!!!

"Quickly...quickly...the portal will close any moment now and you need to recover whatever you have found...or risk losing your hand." The entity's voice again...now filled with real panic.

Gustav lunged desperately, throwing his weight against the object on the other side, hoping this might tip the scales in his favor. What kind of a document was this? He felt the object he was holding on to, slowly begin to rise! Yes!...he was succeeding! ...but then it began to get hot...really, really hot! His entire hand felt like it was on fire, and he screamed in pure agony. Dimly...through his pain, he could hear the entity's voice, screaming at him to pull back...and pull back he did...empty handed! And the next moment, the turbulence ended its withering assault, just as mysteriously as it had begun!

Gustav fell to his knees, crying in pain and anger! After all this effort ...his reward? – Nothing!!!

As he lay weeping, he heard the voice of the entity...calm... soothing. "You did much better than I hoped Capt. Gustav, much better than almost anyone else would have...in your position. Unfortunately, the wonders of Shambhala are not meant for you... or your people. However, you shall not return entirely empty handed."

"What do you mean?" Gustav asked, pathetically.

"Look at your hand…the hand that tried to hold on to the treasures of Paradise…it certainly carries more than just a reminder of the pain, you felt. Look Capt. Gustav…look!"

Gustav stared at his hands, wondering what the entity meant. At first, he saw nothing, except a dark burned area, on his left hand that stretched all the way to his palm…the scars of his failed attempt! Then he suddenly gasped…within the large burn marks, he noticed what appeared to be writings…and drawings…the entire text of a book, seemed to have literally infused itself onto his arm! *What the hell was going on here?* He had reached out through the portal for not more than a minute…How could all of this content have inscribed itself on his arm so quickly…What had *that* kind of power?

"That's the very text you came for, isn't it? – The Vimanika Shastra… the 'Science of Aeronautics'…sacred knowledge of the ancient world… knowledge that for millennia has remained beyond the covetous reach of man…and now you, Capt. Gustav, have finally managed to possess it…one way or another!!" The voice was deliberately provocative… taunting!

"How did this happen? What am I supposed to do with it?" Gustav moaned, the pain of the burns, only seemed to escalate, with the dark entity's words!

"Oh, I am sure when you calm down a little, you will know exactly what to do with it. This, my dear, is the full version of the Vimanika Shastra and it is now absolutely, inalienably yours…you always said you wanted to possess this knowledge…now *IT* has possessed you! Ha ha ha…"

Gustav felt the energy drain from his body, and he fell to the hard ground. The world seemed to spin around him…after all his extraordinary efforts at accessing this lost wisdom; it had finally come his way, in a way he could never have imagined.

He had been tattooed by Paradise!!!

CHAPTER TWENTY THREE

It is said that for all the sins one commits and all the goodwill one generates, there will come a day...one final and inescapable 'Day of Judgment', where all of it will be weighed on a divine 'Scale of Balance'! Only those judged righteous and worthy, shall be welcomed into Paradise, while the wretched shall face their destiny, in the harrowing pits of Hell!

But while the 'Fates' speak of the 'just' and the 'unjust'...the 'worthy' and the 'unworthy'...the 'pious' and the 'sinner'...even they shy away from describing the plight of him...who had the chance of reaching out to 'Paradise', and yet...only succeeded in pushing it away!! Yes...even the 'Fates' tremble when they speak of Captain Friedrich Gustav of the Third Reich, who sought the ultimate prize of eternal life...and ended up with everlasting grief!

"What do I do now?" The despair in Gustav's voice was palpable. "I no longer possess the means...or the strength to leave this place. Help me rescue my trapped comrades and go back to my homeland... Shambhala was going to be my refuge...its mystical Vimanas, my escape out of here! But...now, I find myself hopelessly trapped!"

His plea was met with an eerie silence, during which time; he felt the dark entity sizing him up. When finally it did speak, its voice was but a whisper, "Let not the fate of your comrades, weigh down on your conscience...suffice to say that they have served their purpose!"

"No!" Gustav screamed...the ruthlessness in the words, was shocking. "I came on this journey...with my comrades and I shall leave this infernal place with them...they stood by me through thick and thin and I shall not go down in history, as the one who deserted those loyal to him...Tell me how to get them out!"

"You misunderstand me...you cannot rescue them now...since you, yourself condemned them to hell!"

"What? I did what?" Gustav stammered, stunned… "Yes I did take the only piece of climbing equipment we had, but I always planned to go back for them!"

"That you did…but you then made the choice of unlocking the portal on your own…a feat that should never have been attempted, without all seven individuals…for the life force it requires, far exceeds that of any one individual! And yet…even as you climbed, you lost one of your comrades, severely compromising your mission…to make matters even worse, you alone were able to make it to the top."

Gustav felt like he couldn't breathe anymore…he was frozen with horror…slowly…excruciatingly…he was beginning to sense where this was going!

"I did ask you, if you would indeed be willing to do what it takes to unlock the portal, all by yourself…to sacrifice 'everything' in order to gain 'everything'…and you agreed!"

Gustav closed his eyes in pain…he could not believe what he was hearing…he did not *WANT* to believe what he was hearing… "What did you do?" He screamed at the being, in front of him.

"What did I do?…Ha ha…the real question is what did *YOU* do… and the terrible answer to that is that with your consent, I tapped into the combined life forces of your five loyal comrades…and used that energy, to open the portal to heaven…through which you managed to get what you came for. As you already know, this requires seven individuals…and we had only six!"

"No…no…no!"

"Yes…unfortunately, the results I fear were less than pleasant for your comrades!"

"Where are they now?" Gustav shouted into the wind.

"Oh, I do not claim to possess knowledge of the afterlife…but depending on which religion you personally subscribe to…you can console yourself with the cliché that *'they are in a better place'!!!*"

"They are dead? All of them?" Gustav howled…the pain was almost physical. These men had been like brothers to him!

"Well considering it was *their* life energies that you saw swirling around, as you were reaching through the portal…Yes…they are dead…as 'dead' as dead can be…their bodies currently lie, dried and shriveled, in the mountain cave that you left them in…sapped of their life forces…*poor souls*…they never even realized what hit them, never had a chance to respond…their very souls taken away by their 'beloved leader'!"

"Oh no no no no…What have I done…Oh God! What have I done!" Gustav moaned piteously, the information refusing to sink in. "You…you caused me to do this…you kept inciting me…provoking me…manipulating me…I will send you to hell, if it's the last thing I do." Maddened with rage, he launched at the being, intent of murder… but much to his amazement, his battered body flew through the air… straight *through* the entity!…and landed with a bone crunching thud, some four meters away.

"Ha ha ha ha!" The entity smirked, "Do you really want to compromise your *only* means of escaping this freezing mountain top? And speaking of 'damning me to hell'…you shall one day come to realize that I am already 'damned'. Now…let's talk about your future… calmly!"

Gustav said nothing…his entire body burned with agony from the harsh landing. With bloodshot eyes, he simply stared at the entity.

"I can get you off this peak…and back to your homeland…although I am under no obligation to do so…after all, I did keep up *my* end of the bargain, by helping you reach your goal…it isn't my fault that your ineptness caused you to be such a disappointment!"

Gustav still said nothing.

"Nonetheless, over our long association, I have grown quite fond of you and I wouldn't want you to come to any harm. So…I will help you get off this mountain and get back to Germany, without any further problems…for a price of course!"

"More conditions…more complications…more manipulations." Gustav felt sick to the core.

"Ha ha ha, well when you play beyond your 'station'…you must be prepared for the consequences. Nevertheless, the consequences of using my help will prove beneficial to you…in the long run."

"What price do you speak of? Tell me plainly…no more secrets… what long term benefits?" Gustav demanded.

"You see, the information you acquired from the lost city...the blueprints of the 'Vimanas'...will allow you to reverse engineer the ancient flying machines, but by itself, this is worthless, since these devices would still lack a power source...one that exists only *within* Shambhala. But...fortunately for you, I do possess a device that if placed within one such Vimana, can recreate that mystical power source!"

As he spoke, the being held out a small crystalline device, shaped like an un-blossomed flower, in the palm of his hand. "Using my powers as the Guardian of Shambhala, I can transport you back to Germany, in the blink of an eye...provided you agree to have me accompany you!"

"Why would you want to accompany me? If the device does what you claim it does, why not simply hand it over to me?" Gustav wondered aloud, knowing full well that his question was meaningless. *The entity always got what it wanted.*

"Ha ha ha, you are a smart one aren't you? No...I cannot simply hand it over to you...since the mechanisms, we shall use, to achieve instantaneous travel are so disorienting that by the time we get to Germany, you will lose most...if not all memories...of your interaction with me. Certainly, your memories will become heavily corrupted, through the process. That will of course, leave you with no knowledge of the function of this device...and no way of *ever* using it! This entire expedition would then have proved futile...no...you will need me one way or the other!"

Gustav grimaced...there was always a hidden cost...always some subtle manipulation...it angered him to know that once again he found himself pushed against the wall...if he refused the entity's help, he would face certain death, on this frigid mountain top...he had already lost all of his comrades, and his mission would end in complete disaster!

If he did compromise, at least there was a chance he could salvage SOMETHING from this mess. But there was something else that bothered him...even though the entity claimed to be assisting him... purely out of goodwill, it almost seemed like even *IT* had wanted him to succeed...like it had its own stakes in all of this!

If this was the case, then with careful planning, he might one day be able to somehow use this *against* the being...but for now; he would *have* to bite the bullet. "How much of my memory will I lose?" He asked slowly.

"Ah! The great Capt. Gustav finally sees the light." The entity beamed, "Don't worry I'll try to ensure that you remember most of this journey...*albeit with a few mythic embellishments*...for instance, you will not remember the trauma of sucking the life-blood out of your comrades...nor will you remember this, or any other 'traumatic' conversation, you have had with me...instead, in your mind, you will have successfully completed your mission, along with all your comrades...alive!"

"In this new version, you shall recall uncovering the secrets of Shambhala, *entirely* on your own...a version that should fit very comfortably with your German ego! Further...according to these 'new'...'revamped' memories, the quest to unearth the lost city, will lead you to overcome challenge after supernatural challenge, eventually bringing you face to face with an eccentric old man, who shall pose as Shambhala's guardian. In all of your righteous might, you will overpower him and enter Paradise. Eventually, after sacking Shambhala of all its power and knowledge, you along with your teammates will march out of Tibet in triumph, along with a captive...the old guardian, who refuses to say a word, but carries a crystalline device with him. Needless to say, this wretch, you bring back to Germany, will be me...thus allowing me to retain my secrets...and be of assistance to you, come the right hour...This is my offer Capt. Gustav...accept it or reject it...as always *it's YOUR call to make!*"

Captain Friedrich Gustav took a long, deep breath...he knew that any one of these choices, he was constantly being manipulated into, could well prove to be his last. But for now, he saw no other recourse. Refuse the offer of assistance and even if he somehow did manage to make his way back to Germany, he would be left with just the blueprints and no powering device. Accept the entity's offer and he would lose most of his real memories and be left with fake recollections, meant only to assuage his ego...but at least, he *WOULD* have access to the powering device. After having come so far, the final choice was a no-brainer!

"Let's get this over with." He whispered…his voice, cold as a stone.

"Certainly my boy…Certainly!" A broad smile broke out all over the entity's face.

EPISODE SIX

CHAPTER ONE

Between 1939 and 1945, while most of Europe found itself embroiled in World War II, a team of scientists from the Third Reich went to work on a mysterious project so secret that its very existence was known only to a select few in the Nazi Party. It was code named 'Die Glocke' or 'The Bell', and was considered the ultimate frontier of knowledge and power.

The project was headed by Captain Friedrich Gustav, of the S.S. who along with the noted biologist, Ernst Schaffer, had captured German imagination, with his heroic expedition to Tibet in 1939. Of course, when the expedition was first launched, Gustav's role in it had been kept secret by the Nazis. The expedition had to travel through British occupied India and the Germans knew that a team of scientists under the renowned Dr. Schaffer were far more likely to secure permission, than a group of S.S soldiers.

And yet...against all odds...Gustav had managed to 'piggy-back' along with the Schaffer mission, and smuggle himself into Tibet, to undertake an outrageous quest of his own...the quest to find the lost city of Shambhala!

For months, he and his team had gone missing, and were feared dead. But astonishingly, nearly a year after his departure, the S.S. Captain had resurfaced alive...*in bizarre circumstances!* In broad daylight, late in August of 1939...in front of hundreds of onlookers, Gustav, along with an extremely old and frail looking Asian, had suddenly materialized out of thin air!!! ...right outside Nazi Headquarters, in Nuremberg!

This shocking and some might say, *para-normal phenomenon*, in the streets of Nuremberg, had threatened to cause mass public hysteria...but had quickly been silenced through a combination of a hastily put out German 'disinformation campaign', which claimed that

Gustav's miraculous appearance was merely the result of a play of light and shadows...and a persecution drive carried out by the S.S. against anyone who thought differently!

Of course, the Nazis themselves had been extremely curious to know where one of their leaders had been for almost a year...and how he had managed to 'teleport' right into the middle of one of Germany's busiest cities. Unfortunately...there were no easy answers to be had, as Gustav claimed to have very garbled memories of his time in Tibet and the only real clue on offer, was the presence of the old Asian man, who had materialized alongside him. This mysterious stranger looked at least seventy, and spoke a tongue, no one understood. After months of unsuccessfully trying to elicit information from him, the Nazis had eventually lost patience and locked him up. Gustav meanwhile, was taken to Nazi Headquarters, for a special de-briefing, with the Führer - Adolf Hitler.

Slowly...as Gustav's memories returned, it had become apparent that he and his team had managed the impossible...they had not only tracked down a mythical lost city, but actually secured access into it! Their expedition had taken them all the way to the holy site of Mount Kailasha, deep in Western Tibet, and at every stage, the team had to decipher a series of allegories clues and reinterpret local legends. All through this epic journey, the team had been guided only by the inflexible, iron-will of their Captain, and managed to overcome forces beyond human comprehension, thus proving themselves worthy...of the ultimate prize!

Of course, the exact nature of events at Kailasha, still remained a mystery, but the presence of Gustav's mysterious 'fellow traveler'...and the tattooed inscriptions, on his arm suggested that the team had indeed managed to enter Shambhala! This...in addition to Gustav's mysterious return convinced the Nazis that only a magical land like 'Shambhala' could possess such powers! The fact that Gustav seemed to have no memories of his time in Shambhala...or that the rest of his team could still not be traced...did not seem to cause great concern. *After all, who really understood the workings of 'magic'!*

His confirmation that the symbols on his arm were details of the technology from the lost city...technology that allowed for near instantaneous travel...anywhere in the world, was itself a huge bonus…and further proof of Germany's ultimate victory over humanity! *Surely, with otherworldly knowledge like this, they would be truly unstoppable!*

The Nazis had quickly got to work, gathering the resources needed to fulfill their grand ambitions. Gustav once again found himself reunited with his old mentor, Karl Haushofer…and together, the two were tasked with decoding and deciphering the symbols, recovered from Gustav's arm. Haushofer's knowledge of Eastern languages, particularly Sanskrit, would prove vital, as a team of scientists and engineers began work on a project intended to push the boundaries of human ingenuity.

The site chosen for this was an S.S. facility, located deep in Poland, in the 'Owl Mountains' not far from the Czech border. Known as 'Der Riese' or 'the Giant' it was a massive complex, mostly underground, near the Wenceslaus mine.

Here the Nazis would construct a series of underground chambers that resembled bomb shelters, predominantly using slave labor. These were mainly captured prisoners of war, from Hitler's attack on Poland…*an attack that heralded the start of World War II!* Within these underground facilities were a series of laboratories, factories and living quarters, all dedicated to the construction of the German 'Wunder-Waffe' or 'Wonder Weapon'…intended to give the Nazis, an unbeatable edge.

This 'Wonder Weapon' was going to be based on the text they had managed to recover from Gustav's arm…text that appeared to carry detailed descriptions of flying machines! But what really disturbed the scientists working on it was the layout and the shape of these designs… none of them seemed in any way…aerodynamic!

The most detailed of the blueprints…the one the Nazis had eventually decided to duplicate…in fact seemed to depict a craft that very much resembled a large bell, roughly 9 feet in diameter and over 15 feet in height…thus giving the project its code name – 'Die Glocke' or 'the Bell'. While some in the scientific community harboured doubts about its true nature and purpose, Gustav and Haushofer remained convinced that what they had here, was indeed one of the lost weapons of another era…a 'Golden' era!

CHAPTER TWO

1944: Five long and frustrating years had passed...and the Nazis seemed no closer to success than they had been, when they started. From the details elicited from the 'Vimanika Shastra', a team of German scientists had managed to reproduce numerous 'prototypes' of the device they referred to as 'Die Glocke'. Each of these was roughly the same size...approximately 9 feet wide and 12 to 15 feet high. Each constructed of extremely hard metals, just as the text specified...some speculated that the hardness of the metal would allow the craft to deal with the stresses of near instantaneous travel, without any side effects!

Fully constructed, the craft would contain two counter-rotating cylinders, which were to be filled with a violet color, mercury-like substance. This metallic liquid was code-named "Xerum 525" by the Germans and was normally stored in a tall, thin thermos flask, encased in lead...its exact nature, a closely guarded secret! They also employed additional substances referred to as 'Leichtmetall' or 'light metal', which included substances such as Thorium and Beryllium peroxides.

The Nazis had employed a team of slaves to construct a large metal framework, directly above the underground facility...to serve as a test rig, if and when, their craft became fully operational. This framework was the only outwardly visible sign of their work...everything else, including the tests, was underground.

One of the team's earliest and probably most significant observations was that 'Die Glocke' seemed to emit an extremely powerful form of radiation when activated...one that had caused the deaths of several researchers, as well as various plant and animal test subjects. It was quickly becoming clear, that whatever the internal dynamics of this device were, they were far from normal!

Die Glocke

So top-secret were these tests, that by the summer of 1944, the Nazis had executed 60 scientists, who had been working on 'Project Die Glocke' for breach of protocol. However, in spite of all these precautions...the craft they were trying to reverse engineer from Capt. Gustav's blueprints, continued to frustrate the researchers. And now, Himmler and the 'Ahnenerbe' were beginning to ask some very uncomfortable questions...*questions that even challenged the legitimacy of Gustav's research and expedition!*

During the early 1930s, Gustav and Haushofer had stuck their respective necks out on the hypothesis that the 'Eastern World'...and specifically Tibet...was a font of lost, esoteric knowledge...knowledge that had always been sought, by groups such as the 'Ahnenerbe' and the 'Thule Society'. But the situation in Europe had changed much since then.

Over the years, following a succession of treaties and military alliances, the atmosphere in Europe had become decidedly more political...and especially after the start of World War II, the Nazi mindset had changed significantly. The reversals faced by the 'Wehrmacht' – the Armed forces of Nazi Germany, in Russia in 1941 and 1942, and the problems posed by the displacement of millions of people across Europe, had left no space for exotic ideas such as 'Vril' energy and 'Golden Ages'.

For the Nazis, all secret experiments still being conducted at the start of 1944, were now to be completed with military urgency, keeping in mind the demands of the German Army. If any project did not *directly* correspond to the needs of the army, it was scrapped. The Nazis were even getting rid of projects, such as examinations and dissections conducted to achieve new medical breakthroughs and others like 'Project Eugenics', which were aimed at perfecting the human race, because they offered no direct, short-term military application. Each project from here on would undergo intense scrutiny by the S.S. and those not operating at maximum potential would face Himmler's wrath!

Funds were now being released on an extremely tight leash…most of the money diverted towards project facilities, involving experimental weapon systems such as those under Dr. Von Braun in Peenemunde, Northern Germany. Here the Nazis were perfecting a top-secret weapon called the 'V-2'…this would be the world's first ballistic missile that could carry a one-ton explosive warhead. This missile, capable of a vertical take-off and designed to travel faster than the speed of sound, could bypass the best Radar systems in the world. After the defeat of the German forces in Stalingrad, Russia and the stalled offensives in North Africa, Hitler needed a weapon that could once again instill terror in the hearts and minds of his enemies!

Many speculated that the 'V' in the V-2, stood for Vengeance!

Like so many others, even Gustav felt the effect of this change in focus. No longer were the Nazis simply interested in a new energy source. Now, 'Die Glocke' was being looked at as the weapon destined to win Hitler, his war! Unless, this project succeeded…*and quickly at that*…Gustav realized his status as the 'favorite explorer-soldier' would soon be over. And by the start of 1944, the writing was pretty much on the wall. Gustav and his team, based in Poland, received a notification from Nazi Headquarters. Signed by Himmler, the note made it clear that the team was being granted a limited amount of time and money to complete the project. Failure was *not* an option… under any circumstance!

As he read the note, Gustav realized that however imperfect their understanding of this device, his team would have to initiate final-testing, as soon as possible. He pressed those under him to work even harder, as 'round the clock' experimentation began to take place on the craft. He and Haushofer repeatedly went through what little data they had about the device...information they had put together, from the images on Gustav's arm.

They both agreed that the images and descriptions were indeed from the 'Vimanika Shastra'...the text matched perfectly with Haushofer's own incomplete version. The document also made it clear that once completed, the craft was capable of easily transporting between nine and twelve people, at undefined speeds, by using a mysterious energy source called 'Laghima'. Haushofer of course recognized this term from his own research and its presence merely confirmed the authenticity of the text. For him, as well as Gustav, this detail was of vital importance, as it ruled out the one outcome both of them had secretly dreaded...the possibility that all of this was just be an elaborate hoax!

Now, all they had to do was crack its code and figure out how it worked. And yet, something about this mysterious...'Laghima', bothered Gustav...something that seemed to gnaw at the very edges of his consciousness...just beyond reach...for some reason, he felt very strongly that it had something to do with the old man, he had brought back from Tibet...the one, currently languishing in a German prison. Was this some kind of a warning?...an ominous premonition? It was impossible to say!

For now, he decided to allow the feeling to pass. For now...*there were more immediate concerns!*

CHAPTER THREE

With Himmler's deadline fast approaching, Gustav began to ready his men for the first major field-test of the craft that they had worked on for over five years! The frenzied effort saw the scientists and soldiers in the underground facility scream and shout at each other, as they prepared for the most important day of their lives. Everyone knew, they would have only *one* shot at this…failure was not an option. But the real danger stemmed from the fact that some of the substances the scientists were using to fuel the device, were highly radioactive and had already caused deaths. There was no telling what their effects would be, once the device was fully activated!

In true Nazi fashion, it was decided that the first test subjects…the "guinea pigs" for this grand experiment, would be five unfortunate Polish prisoners of war. They had been hand-picked for their slight build, from among the two thousands slaves, who had helped construct most of this facility. The prisoners were of course told nothing of what was about to happen…or about the nature of this experiment. If they survived, and that was a big 'if'…then the Nazis would be able to confirm the effects of this experiment on their bodies.

Someone with less 'steel' and more of a conscience, would surely have balked at the sight of five helpless bound men, blindfolded and led up to a device that was going to be fueled with some of the most radioactive substances known to man! But Gustav had seen it all before. Even though he had never fought in the War, he had seen *his* fair share of combat, alongside the S.S. The ruthlessness displayed by some of the hardened S.S. members in their fanatical drive towards achieving a racially pure society, had initially left him shocked and shaken. He had also heard horror stories of what took place inside

German concentration camps, where most of the P.O.Ws were sent. Some that had emerged from camps like 'Auschwitz' and 'Treblinka'... were scarcely believable!

Over the years, however, he had justified this level of violence with the comforting cliché that the *'end always justifies the means'*...and he and the Nazis were simply trying to create a *'better society'*. So now, the plight of these five 'volunteers' did not greatly disturb him. After all, it was imperative that the Nazis once and for all figure out, what this craft was capable of.

Gustav already had ordered all the units, safeguarding the premises, to secure the outer perimeter. In addition, he had asked of his superiors, a very special favor...the mysterious stranger, whom he had brought back from Tibet. For reasons he couldn't quite explain, Gustav felt that the stranger's presence at the site of the first field test of 'Die Glocke' was absolutely essential!

It was a strange request...one that had been met with a fair amount of skepticism. The Nazis were certainly not keen on having an unknown foreigner granted access into a top-secret German base, especially when *such* an experiment was under way. However, after a lot of 'hand wringing' and grumbling, they had finally relented and granted Gustav, his request.

And so it was that those at the secret underground facility saw the extraordinary spectacle of an old frail Tibetan man, handcuffed and dragged over to the site, by four burly S.S. guardsmen. The guards confirmed that during the last five years of solitary confinement, the man hadn't spoken a word and the only reason they had kept him alive was that there was still the unresolved mystery of how he and Gustav had arrived in Germany.

Now as the stranger looked at Gustav for the first time in years, he smiled softly...*it was a knowing smile!* Gustav noticed that in these five years in spite of being a prisoner, astonishingly, the stranger seemed not to have aged at all!

With everything finally in place, the grand experiment began. The five prisoners were marched towards the craft and their blindfolds were taken off. The men took one look at the strange 'bell shaped' object before them, and visibly paled. Whatever the nature of this experiment; the thought that this bloated, ugly contraption, could well become their tomb was not a happy one!

At gunpoint the five were herded inside the device. The Nazis treated them with the same amount of respect and dignity that one reserves for lab rats...*to the Germans that is precisely what they were.*

Once inside, the door of the strange contraption was closed and locked from the outside. The prisoners held each other's hands tightly...whatever happened from this point on, they knew their fates were interlinked. They heard the faint sounds of frenzied activity...of scientists and soldiers running around screaming instructions and activating protocols. Something big, was definitely about to happen... the craft they were in, suddenly began to light up...a dull, bluish hue seemed to rise upwards, from the floor and gradually make its way to the roof. One of the prisoners reached out to feel this unknown vapor like substance...and immediately screamed...pulling his hand back in pain! The others groaned...was this some sadistic new killing tool that the Germans had invented?

As the pale blue light began to spread through the interiors of the strange craft, the men felt their vigor and vitality, start to gradually fade. Within moments, the very act of standing upright became a struggle. Even as all five prisoners fell to the floor, they felt the walls of the craft slowly becoming translucent...they could now *almost* see the activity happening outside...the shocked look on some of the German scientists' faces...a look of anticipation on the face of their leader, Gustav...*could the scientists see them as well?*

The entire scene resembled some kind of a dream...a hallucination! But only one image shone through clearly...one that seemed to burn itself deep into their psyche...the image of a mysterious handcuffed old man, looking at them with startlingly clear eyes...and as they stared back, they felt his eyes twinkle. Then all went dark!

For Gustav and the Nazis, the experiment appeared to take place in slow-motion. After their experimental craft, Die Glocke, had been infused with the top secret liquid metal...one they had prepared based on the 'Vimanika Shastra', they had activated it, with the five Polish prisoners locked inside. Since nobody really knew what the device

was capable of, the Nazis had secured it to the ground with thick metal chains. In the event the craft was successful in achieving flight, they did not want their *only* working prototype to take off...with the prisoners inside!

All those concerns were tossed aside, as the device they referred to as 'the Bell' suddenly came alive, and began to pulse with mysterious bluish-white energy. The sudden charge sent the scientists scrambling for cover, and for a few moments, it seemed that the device would simply explode. Only Gustav stayed, where he was...there was something eerily familiar about this bluish white energy...something he couldn't quite place.

He looked over to his Tibetan prisoner and saw the old man looking straight back at him...*his eyes glowing!* This was troubling...something about this man wasn't quite right. Even though he was in handcuffs, it felt like *he* was the only person in the entire facility, who was in control of *anything* at all. *Damn...maybe...he should have never brought him here!*

The strange energy pulse lasted all of a minute, during which time, most of those whose initial fear had given way to curiosity, swore that the device was slightly...very, very slightly...levitating! And then it happened...as the onlookers stared in amazement, the walls of the device stared to become translucent...allowing those outside to glimpse the tortured and terrified expressions of those trapped inside!

Then...after what seemed like an eternity, the pale blue energy pulse subsided, and the device once again settled. Astonishingly, the thick, powerful metal chains, used to hold 'Die Glocke' in place, now lay completely melted. Regardless of whether this experiment could be deemed a success, the forces unleashed were clearly destructive on an unprecedented scale!

With bated breath the Nazis gathered around the smoking device, to inspect it. Clearly, even if *had* actually levitated, the device had failed to achieve controlled flight...and now the scientists wanted to know what had happened to those inside!

Were the prisoners still alive? Had the scientists simply imagined seeing their terrified expressions through the walls of the craft? What the hell had that mysterious bluish energy done to the craft?

As the thick reinforced doors of the device slowly opened, a stunned silence fell over the entire complex...the hollow chamber of 'Die Glocke'...was completely and absolutely...*empty!!* Nothing...No traces of the five prisoners existed. It seemed as if their very existence had been nullified!!

The cold horror that everyone in this underground facility suddenly felt, was broken only by a haunting voice...their old Tibetan prisoner was speaking for the first time...addressing Capt. Gustav...in flawless German!

"What you know my son is like a drop in the ocean and what you don't could fill the infinite void!"

CHAPTER FOUR

'The sage awakens to light in the night of all creatures. That which the world calls day is the night of ignorance to the wise' – the Bhagvata Gita

Shock and awe...this is how the Nazis felt...Throughout his long stay in a German prison, the stranger had never displayed the ability... or willingness to speak any language...let alone German!

Yes...there was something very strange about this old man...after all, this was the same being who, along with their leader Gustav, had magically appeared in Germany, following their clandestine adventures in Tibet, in 1939. Back then, with Gustav unable to explain the stranger's presence and the man himself, unwilling to speak, even under torture, it had been decided that he would be transferred to a high security prison and held in solitary confinement...the only concession was that the facility was to be located close to the site of project 'Die Glocke'!

But as the years went by, and work on their top secret 'Wonder Weapon' progressed, the Nazis had grown more and more indifferent to the old man, almost reluctant to believe the circumstances surrounding his arrival. Those in the security team, who looked after him, were taught to think of him as nothing more than a relic...a token reminder of another era...*a fossil!*

When Gustav had ordered the old man to be brought over to the facility; nobody knew what to expect...Gustav had decided to have the stranger present during the experiment...purely on a hunch. Somehow...the two seemed connected...although how exactly, he couldn't say. And now...after their bizarre experiment, their mysterious 'guest' had finally decided to speak directly...in German!

Gustav looked at the man intently...old...bent...frail and yet... there was something about the almost lyrical sing-a-song way he had spoken that reminded Gustav of someone else...or *something* else! He was sure he had heard this voice before...it somehow seemed to be connected to his time in Tibet. But...like so much of that trip, this memory too seemed blurry and broken!

Mildly cursing under his breath, Gustav turned his attention back towards Die Glocke. Five years of non-stop toil, and the scientists working in this underground facility, had managed the impossible... this device was now operational! Of course, how it exactly worked, wasn't quite clear...there were still many unanswered questions. For years, the Nazis had been operating on the hypothesis that the device was a 'flying craft', and that through a combination of wind currents and radioactive liquid metals, it would propel itself and those within, through the air.

But much to their surprise...the device they called 'Die Glocke' had proved capable of much more...Yes...it had levitated only very briefly, but astonishingly...it had managed to transport the five prisoners locked inside, to an unknown destination...through unknown means...a form of teleportation, not too dissimilar to Gustav's own arrival in Germany!!!

The old man smiled...slyly!

Gustav's blood boiled...In the light of what had just happened, the implications of the stranger's comments...were utterly damning! Yes...the Nazis would have to perform more tests to properly understand this device. But given Himmler's deadline, what had occurred, was already a monumental success!

He pulled out his pistol, pointed it straight at the old wretch and growled, "What do you mean? I represent the highest echelons of scientific progress on earth. I am a son of the Germanic people... righteous in my might and incapable of failure...and you...you have the courage, nay audacity, to tell me that I am wrong?"

The prisoner was quiet for a moment. Gustav couldn't be sure if the sight of the gun had robbed him of his courage. But when he finally did reply, it was in a softer voice...*again in faultless German*, "My boy, you play with forces far beyond your station. This is no mere 'flight simulation'…this device, you have created, threatens the very fabric of space and time!"

"Seek not to intimidate me, old man." Gustav hollered, "We have come very close to solving the mysteries of space and time. We know the two are connected…Einstein's 'General Theory of Relativity' confirms it. Very soon we shall tear the mask off the face of God, and lay bare the universe! If…what you say is true, then this experiment will only help us better understand Space and Time…and give our Führer, the ultimate victory!"

"Half knowledge is a dangerous thing, my child…and in this case you have absolutely no knowledge!"

Gustav felt his fingers tighten around the trigger.

"You view 'Time' as something that 'flows', something that can be 'harnessed', and 'bent' to your will. You speak of theoretical equations formed by people, who only worked in laboratories. But there is a lot that these 'equations' do not reveal! Listen to me carefully boy…do not disguise your ignorance with arrogance…this experiment is a dangerous descent into madness!!!"

"Stop talking in riddles, old man! …I see through your pathetic ruse…You are biding for time… Why exactly, I do not know. You challenge concepts, proposed and verified, by some of the finest scientific minds of this century, and instead expect me to fall for your delusional ranting?"

"Your theories and equations mean nothing…your scientists will *NEVER* be able to see the truth…because they are all working within the same conditions that veil this truth from us!"

"What conditions? What truth do you speak of?" Gustav's voice rose with frustration.

"My son…my son…" The stranger spoke shaking his head, "One day you will know of how the universe truly functions…and the insignificance of our role in it! Let me tell you about the scope of the 'infinite'…let me tell you about 'Chronux'!"

'For the senses wander, and when one lets the mind follow them, it carries wisdom away like a windblown ship on the waters.' - The Bhagvata Gita

"What we perceive as Time is merely an 'illusion'...created partly, by our own cognitive faculty and partly by a unique subatomic particle...one that in the far flung future, shall come to be known as 'Chronux.' Don't look surprised...your physicists will not be able to confirm its existence...neither now, nor anytime during your lifetime! The technology to do so cannot even be conceptualized at this point in time! It will only be discovered in the 31st century...and the day of its discovery, will forever be remembered as a 'black day', in humanity's long and sordid history!"

Gustav stared at the stranger...unable to believe his own ears...*31st century? 'Chronux'? 'Space-Time' relationships that even Einstein didn't know of?* It all sounded bizarre...coming from the mouth of an old Tibetan man, whom he barely knew and...who yet somehow seemed so familiar!

Most sane individuals would baulk at such outlandish claims. But Gustav had spent a lifetime studying ancient oriental epics...epics that spoke of a magical age, full of godlike beings and divine weapons. His mentor, Karl Haushofer, had certainly fueled his interest in the esoteric...and it was this fascination that had propelled him to join the 'Thule society' and risk everything, in trying to uncover a fairytale - the legendary 'lost city of Shambhala'!

To the uninitiated, these descriptions might sound like fables... moral allegories. And yet, in spite of the spartan memories he had of his journey to Shambhala, he knew they were true! Moreover, their experiments with Die Glocke...the mysterious disappearance of the five Polish prisoners did seem to support the stranger's words!

Gustav still couldn't bring himself to completely trust him, "How do you know all this? Surely you are delusional...I should have my head examined for even *contemplating* what you are saying!"

The stranger smiled, "And yet you feel drawn to listen to me...to what I have to say...such is the 'Curse of Chronux'...*no one* is safe from it...I fear my boy, that even in saying so much, I have already doomed you!"

"What do you mean?" Gustav said, his voice betraying the slightest trace of concern, "Tell me more about this particle... Who discovered it? Tell me now!"

The stranger was quiet for a moment. Then he continued, "The exact event that will lead to its discovery must remain a secret…at least for now." Before Gustav could protest, he added, "Remember… everything I say right now, has a direct impact on the world your descendants will inherit. Trust me; if you were there to witness what I have, you would also be very careful about your actions in the past!"

"Humanity's discovery of the particle was the result of a tragic mistake by an individual…not too dissimilar to you. A man obsessed with perfecting human knowledge…too caught up in his own hubris, to fathom the madness he would unleash on mankind…a man, who arrogantly put himself above humanity, only to prove just as fallible to temptation…as the rest."

"Stop talking in riddles…speak clearly what you know…"

"Be quiet you fool…and listen carefully! Somewhere within these words, lies your salvation…or your doom." As he spoke, the stranger's eyes lit up with a strange unearthly glow that seemed to strip Gustav of all his strength and courage. He felt he had no choice but to mutely listen to what was being said…*a helpless babe in front of a predator.*

Then…the stranger's voice softened ever so slightly, taking on a more paternal tone, "To understand the power of 'Chronux', one has to understand how the cosmos actually functions. You must know that the universe we see around us follows certain patterns and cycles that are repetitive and predictable. This is why; planetary movements, as well as the movement of the stars, have *always* been a source of fascination for civilizations."

"Their balance and cyclical nature meant that civilizations could map their own brief and transient lives against this grand tapestry. The repetitive patterns also proved to be a source of great comfort in the otherwise uncertain life of early man. This is how all societies and cultures have evolved. Studies like Astrology and Astronomy were developed to try and find a meaning to the struggle of everyday existence. And so, till the start of the 20th Century, there had always been one constant and comforting factor."

"And what was that?" Gustav inquired softly.

"It's the fact that we seemed to live in a universe, which was *NOT* chaotic! We might not be able to decode all its mysteries, but for believers and atheists alike, this consistency was proof that the universe had certain basic rules...*regardless of whether there was or wasn't a supreme creator!*"

"But all that changed with the invention of the first electron microscopes and the first forays into the world of the atom. It was here that scientists including one of your own greats – Einstein, were appalled to discover that while objects in the macro universe follow definite rules and patterns, those in the sub atomic realm seemingly don't! One of the great paradoxes of the sub-atomic world is that not only does an electron – one of the building blocks of matter - exist both as a particle and a wave, but it seems to exist in any one of the two states, *ONLY* when observed...Astonishingly, *the mere 'act of observation' seems to change the 'outcome' of the observed!*"

"This extremely chaotic nature was disturbing to say the least and still is. In fact, the subatomic world will continue to baffle scientists and physicists, for generations to come. *How do you uncover the truth behind a phenomenon...when the mere act of observing the phenomenon causes it to change?*"

"Why are you telling me all of this? How do *you* know all of this?" Gustav asked helplessly.

"Think...you idiot...if you plan to understand the mysteries of 'Chronux'...much less harness its wondrous power, you will have to first understand the universe, in which you live. We have always wondered about our purpose here on Earth...the scientists, who first uncovered the truth of the micro universe, asked themselves the same questions. Could it mean that *we* as a sentient species were responsible for more than just contemplating our own existence... maybe we were responsible for *observing* the universe into existence!!! Maybe...*this* was our true purpose!"

Gustav stared open mouthed. He had known this old man since his capture, outside a mythical city in Tibet...or so, he remembered - a capture that Gustav was now beginning to suspect had just been a ruse to get into the German Camp. However, never once had the stranger attempted to share his secrets or even appeared capable of such wisdom!

Seemingly unconcerned with the impact he was having, the stranger went on, "Over time, humanity will come up with a series of explanations to explain this 'scientific anomaly', but none will prove satisfactory. Each time physicists start to believe that they have finally figured out the true nature of space and time, a new paradox shall emerge, prompting a new line of enquiry."

"If you were but a little smarter, you would have observed the same with your own scientists...men, whom you have worked to a breaking point. If I were you, I would be a little less harsh with them. They are not unique in their inability to understand the forces we deal with... for the scientific community will continue to dabble in this mystery... without success, till the late 31st century!"

The stranger's voice trailed off...but something what he had just said, bothered Gustav more than just the depth of his knowledge.

"But why? Why is that the case? Why are all efforts to understand the true nature of the universe doomed to fail? You talk of developments in the 31st century, like you know the future...even assuming there is a semblance of truth in that...why would modern science need more than a thousand years to understand something that we are already on the threshold of uncovering? ... *This is madness!*"

The stranger looked at him intently, "My son...my son...you remind me of...never mind...so promising...so keen to gain knowledge...so keen to study the universe like it is some kind of a 'science experiment'...have you ever considered the possibility that...

...*the universe could also be studying you?*"

CHAPTER FIVE

"Insanity!" Gustav felt like he had been struck by a thunder bolt. "How can that be? …clearly, bringing you over here was a colossal mistake…I should have just left you to freeze in the snow, outside your precious Shambhala."

"But you didn't…you knew that you needed me then…and you know it even now…without me, you can bid your precious 'Wunder Waffe' goodbye…even your 'elite' scientists fumble in the dark like idiots. Who is to say that I was even your captive, all these years? Maybe, I was…maybe I wasn't…*You* certainly weren't observing me throughout, were you? Maybe, when you sent for me…the very act of observing me…*CAUSED* me to exist!!!" The stranger replied mockingly.

"ENOUGH!!! I have had enough of your nonsense…you will either talk clearly, or I'll shoot you myself, and be done with it." Gustav's anger was reaching a fever pitch.

The stranger looked at the furious Nazi soldier-scientist, half mad through sleep deprivation, and spoke calmly, "I am afraid, you find that more and more difficult to accomplish, as we go further…but you are right about one thing…I *have* been using delaying tactics and buying 'time'…a commodity that *you* will find in short supply, very soon! You see this device that you think will win Germany her war, is not actually a weapon, but a trap…one that was designed…or more specifically, will be designed, more than a thousand years from now! In case you still doubt my words, you will begin to see the effects of it all around us!"

Gustav was about to respond, when the mysterious 'bell shaped device' suddenly came back to life. As he looked over to where the scientists and slaves were working, Gustav saw something strange. Even though this entire set up was in an underground reinforced bunker, there had been sufficient arrangements made, to keep the area well lit, day and night. In spite of this, the immediate vicinity of the device and the aisle leading up to it seemed unusually hazy. Even the scientists working on it, seemed to be moving in slow motion. How was this possible…was it Die Glocke that was doing this? *Was it even supposed to act like this?*

There were so many things regarding this project, no one understood. After all, this was technology that was not even supposed to exist. Even when Gustav had actually recovered the 'Vimanika Shastra' from the lost city, he had been skeptical about it. So outlandish was the prize!

Gustav remembered a specific verse from the ancient Indian epic 'The Ramayana' that described these 'Vimanas' or flying crafts.

'The Pushpaka Vimana that resembles the Sun and belongs to my brother was brought by the powerful Ravana; that aerial and excellent Vimana going everywhere at will … that chariot resembling a bright cloud in the sky … and the King Rama got in, and the excellent chariot at the command of the Raghira, rose up into the higher atmosphere.' -

Through their own research, Gustav and Haushofer knew that the epics had accounts of great aerial combats in antiquity, fought using unbelievable weapons of mass destruction. Their dream had always been to recreate these doomsday weapons, for the 'Third Reich'. The fate and future of the German empire was resting on it. The Western Allies would have nothing comparable!

Now…after their initial tests, Gustav had begun to suspect that the true scope of their 'Wonder Weapon' was much greater. Yes…this craft did seem capable of carrying people, but it was not going to transport its passengers…through space! Its aerodynamics clearly made it useless, for conventional air travel. Rather, the craft seemed to use some kind of 'spatial displacement' to move its passengers from point 'A' to point 'B', which centered on harnessing certain exotic subatomic particles and strange new, radioactive elements. And yet, this mysterious stranger, who claimed to possess otherworldly knowledge, was speaking of the 'true' nature of space-time, and calling the device, *a mistake!*

Could it be that everything they knew about the 'Wonder Weapon' was wrong? Could the stranger's warning of this being a trap, be true? Myriad thoughts passed through Gustav's mind, as his attention was drawn to a flash of bluish light, emerging from inside the device.

The others saw this as well…and instinctively tried to move out of the way! One physicist in particular, a Swiss scientist, named Higgins, tried to shield his eyes, against the unnatural glow, just as the light completely enveloped him. For those witnessing this, it seemed like *time* was slowing down…to a crawl!

The man caught in this unnatural maelstrom, opened his mouth to scream, but unbelievably…even as he did so, a rift…a hole in the empty space, right next to his head, opened up! *What the hell was going on???* Gustav gasped, as he saw the rift grow bigger. Higgins was still trying to scream…but words steadfastly refused to come out… seemingly swallowed up by this monstrosity!

Then…slowly…almost *prophetically*…the rift in empty space, seemed to settle…and time once again appeared to 'flow'.

As the others rushed towards their fallen colleague, the man's body twitched…once…twice…and went still. It was only then that the shocked onlookers finally realized the full horror of what had happened. Paul Higgins, the Swiss researcher, lay on the ground, features twisted in agony…his body sliced vertically, from head to toe…with one half…completely missing!!!

'And now I am become Death…the destroyer of Worlds!'

CHAPTER SIX

As stunned scientists stared at their former colleague, who lay cut in half, with perfect symmetry, the entire underground chamber erupted, in a dull bluish haze! A wave of nausea and delirium spread throughout the room, sending everyone into a state of semi-consciousness.

During the course of this brutal war, Captain Gustav had heard of men, dying in their thousands, in ways too horrible to describe. He had also been privy to the full horror of the Nazi death-camps at 'Auschwitz' and 'Dachau', where Jews were being murdered in the millions. And yet, even as he now witnessed this otherworldly horror, he felt that the worst was still to come!

From within the deafening calm, came an eerie chuckle. Gustav turned and looked over to the stranger, still tied to his chair. The man seemed to be shaking his head, in mock sympathy, at the unbelievable scenes playing out before them! Amazingly...even as he tried to take stock of the situation, Gustav noticed that within the rift in space at the center of the chamber, was what seemed like the night sky...the stars and constellations clearly visible in all their glory!

Gustav struggled for answers...his brain desperately trying to make sense of this madness. And then...suddenly...inexplicably...images from stories and myths from across the world, began to appear in his mind...with startling clarity...stories he had heard, during his childhood...stories of heroism and great courage!

He saw the Norse myths of Odin - the 'All-father' and his son - the legendary 'god of thunder', Thorr...of the great battles Thorr fought with the World-Serpent 'Jörmungandr', of the day of all ending –'Ragnarok' when one of Loki's sons - the monstrous wolf 'Fafnir', swallows Odin, the moon and the sun, thereby ushering in the end of the current cycle!

These were now replaced, with elements of the Greek Creation Myths...the Earth-Goddess 'Gaea' giving birth to 'Uranus' of the heavens...together the two produce the 'Gods', the 'Titans' and the 'Cyclopses'...

As Uranus begins imprisoning his own off springs, Gaea gives the youngest Titan 'Cronus', a flint sickle to castrate his father and exile him. Cronus becomes the next ruler, but begins to consume his own children, as soon as they are born. His consort 'Rhea' becomes angry at the treatment of her children and plots against Cronus. When it is time to give birth to her sixth child, Rhea hides herself and then leaves the child to be raised by 'nymphs'. To conceal her act she wraps a stone in swaddling clothes and passes it off as the baby to Cronus, who swallows it.

This child was 'Zeus'. He grows into a handsome youth on Crete. He consults 'Metis' on how to defeat Cronus. She prepares a drink for Cronus designed to make him vomit up the other children. This plan works and the other five children are vomited up. Being gods they are unharmed. Forever indebted to Zeus, they make him their leader.

Gustav's mind seemed to travel from there to the other great epic that had been such a vital influence on his life - the great Indian epic – The Mahabharata.

The epic speaks of two sets of cousins – the evil and greedy 'Kauravas' and the kind and noble 'Pandavas'. The God, Krishna, fights on the side of the just against the forces of evil, greed and avarice, in a great battle that would be remembered through the ages, much like the war, Gustav and his comrades were fighting in...*wait a minute... Why was he remembering all of this, now?* In fact, so vivid were they that they seemed *more* than just memories!

Gustav shook his head, trying to clear his vision...and shake off this sense of disequilibrium. *This was like a nightmare that you just couldn't wake up from!*

There was no way to rationalize what he was seeing! This was sheer insanity! Had his lifelong obsession with 'Pagan' cultures, finally come to a head? He had sacrificed so much energy, time and effort chasing supernatural legends that his mind had probably gone overboard! Maybe that's why these memories seemed so real.

As Gustav stood spellbound, he suddenly realized that the old man was his prisoner no longer! He looked across and saw him standing tall...and surveying the ensuing chaos! Unbelievably...the walls of this underground bunker seemed to have somehow mysteriously melted away...completely! This did not even seem like the insides of the bunker anymore! A cold sweat broke out all over him...for reasons he didn't understand, this phenomenon was stirring up some extremely unpleasant memories!

As he once again turned his disbelieving eyes towards the stranger, he saw a Godly, red bearded figure attack and fight off a gigantic serpent that was coiled around the entire planet. The figure carried a mighty mystical hammer that spewed lightning, as he twirled it around!

"Thorr"...gasped Gustav and the old man merely nodded. Abruptly the scene changed to a city built atop an acropolis, where a swarthy figure, wearing magnificent white robes, sat on an imperial throne, as music and dance were being played in the courtyard. "And that my dear friend, is the Greek imperial camp from legend, presided over by *their* 'All-father', Zeus", whispered the stranger.

Gustav could not believe his senses...surely this was an illusion... it *HAD* to be...maybe, activating of the device had released certain toxic fumes in the air that were causing him to hallucinate, bringing his fantasies to life...surely this would pass... *Wouldn't it?*

Oh, how he wished he hadn't brought this deceitful old man back from Tibet!

The images continued unabated...the scene now was of an open battle field, for which Gustav required no introduction. The size of the battle field and the sheer number of combatants, made it clear that this was the legendary battle of 'Kurukshetra', as described in the 'Mahabharata'.

Two thoughts rushed through his fevered brain – One: He could no longer see *any* of his colleagues...or the S.S. Guardsmen. Two: the fact that the stranger could also witness these images, seemed to suggest that Gustav wasn't losing his mind. He had to put an end to this! ... somehow...*anyhow!* Years of military training began to kick in, as he dragged himself to his feet and tried to grab hold of the stranger... with the intention of questioning him.

Horror of horrors, Gustav's hand went straight through the old man's body...like it was a hologram! He tried again...the result the same...The stranger merely smiled. "My time on this plane of existence is almost up and *if* I must tell you about what is happening, you must refrain from any more nonsense. Your future...and the future of humanity, now hinges on how much you are able to comprehend of what is about to be revealed. Fail to understand me, and you doom yourself forever. I can see that you have many questions, but they must wait for now...because as you shall soon discover, either to your eternal satisfaction or everlasting grief that *'Knowledge is the key'*. Prepare yourself Captain Gustav, I am about to reveal to you that what you have spent a lifetime trying to understand...the secrets of Chronux!"

The stranger took a long breath, before he spoke again, "One of the great ironies with human existence has been that what we consider 'History' is just an incomplete recollection of events, we believe took place, in the past. It is this recollection that we believe forms the basis of our identity. However such a 'History' is at best a very fickle standard on which to rest our entire understanding of the universe!"

"Of course not" scoffed Gustav, "You seem to imply that history is entirely unreliable...but that is not correct...while it is true that our knowledge about the past is far from complete, it is also true that history provides us with a platform to evaluate our deeds against those of others. Just imagine, if there was no history, what would we have told our grandchildren?...our descendants? That what we leave behind for future generations needs to carry our mark on it...of the time we spent on Earth!"

"Unfortunately...your knowledge about what you refer to as 'Time' is extremely one-dimensional. You look at time as a back-drop, a kind of universal canvas, on which all human achievements can be displayed and measured, but that's where you have it wrong. The 'Time' you fathom of is merely an illusion...and has always been so!"

"What?" a stunned Gustav asked, "*Time is an illusion?*"

The stranger looked around what had once been an underground bunker...searching for a way to better underscore his point. The entire arena was bathed in an eerie half-light, making everything appear ghostly and surreal. Gustav followed the old man's gaze...like a deer trapped in the headlights, his mind ablaze!

"Tell me something Captain...you look like a man, in the prime of his life...probably in your thirties...a soldier, by profession...an explorer...a scientist and seeker of knowledge, at heart...tell me...do you remember each and every event that has happened, in your thirty-odd years on this planet?"

"Of course not" Gustav replied, "My memory...Human memory... is not perfect...events that have had a greater impact on our lives leave behind more prominent scars on our subconscious...as against those that are more mundane. Like anyone else, I do have gaps in my memory!"

"But are you sure..." the stranger pressed, "Are you sure that those 'gaps' you refer to...*ACTUALLY* contain events?"

"Of cour..." began Gustav...and then suddenly stopped...the implication of the stranger's words, hitting him like a sledgehammer. "What do you mean?" he gasped, "Events that I don't remember...*did not actually happen?* ...is that what you are saying? ...most of my past has been a lie?"

"Ha ha ha...my child..." the stranger said...shaking his head... "Your past...my past...the future...we can't quite be sure of anything... the only thing, we can be sure of is the 'here' and 'now.'"

"What does that even mean? ...are you trying to say that existence itself is a lie...what would the purpose of life be then?" Gustav asked disbelievingly.

"Look my boy, I am not here to discuss existential dilemmas with you... 'Time' by any reckoning grows short...I am merely trying to introduce you to a concept that will be discovered, some thousand years from now. The physical universe we see, perpetually exists in a non-changing state i.e. to say that the 'physical matter' of all that 'has been', all that 'is' and all that ever 'will be', is always present in the universe. In laymen's terms all the 'events' from the 'big-bang' to the 'big-crunch' are always in existence...physically!!!"

"Impossible...!" exclaimed Gustav... "If what you say is true, we should be able to see our futures as well!"

"That's true, but to understand the nature of this paradox, you need to understand the nature of a sub-atomic particle, so fundamental to the universe that *nothing* can exist without it. This particle - 'Chronux' for want of a better name, can simply be understood as the 'Time particle'. It is responsible for literally CREATING 'time' or should I say *'the illusion of time'* all across the cosmos." declared the stranger.

Captain Gustav felt the knot in his stomach tighten.

Thunder rolled in the background, as the Hindu God of thunder 'Indra' countered his Norse counterpart – 'Thorr' by calling down fire from the skies. Apparently the different myths were now capable of overlapping!

Gustav tried to ignore these utterly bizarre scenes, "If what you are saying is true…this particle would need to be EVERYWHERE…at the same time…a physical impossibility!!!"

"You are correct about that" the stranger answered, his voice almost a whisper, "This particle keeps 'REVERBERATING' – in a sense bouncing back and forth, between all the other sub-atomic particles in the universe, at an unbelievable speed, one that borders on…but is not quite INFINITE!!!"

"As a result, there is a miniscule 'GAP' between when Chronux makes contact with a particular particle the first time and the next. For each particle in the universe, this 'gap' constitutes the *'PASSAGE OF TIME'*. Quite literally 'Entropy' – the single most destructive force in the universe, responsible for the decay of all matter and energy, sets in, as a result of the collisions Chronux has, causing all matter in the universe, to constantly regress to a simpler state…a process we refer to as 'deterioration' or 'degradation'."

Gustav stared open mouthed.

"But what is important to understand over here is that had the particle not been present in the universe, matter and energy across the cosmos, would forever exist in a non-changing state! It is only Chronux that makes change possible."

"You, I, we all exist only *WHEN* the particle hits us. On contact Chronux creates what we can describe as the 'HERE AND NOW' essentially the 'PRESENT TENSE'."

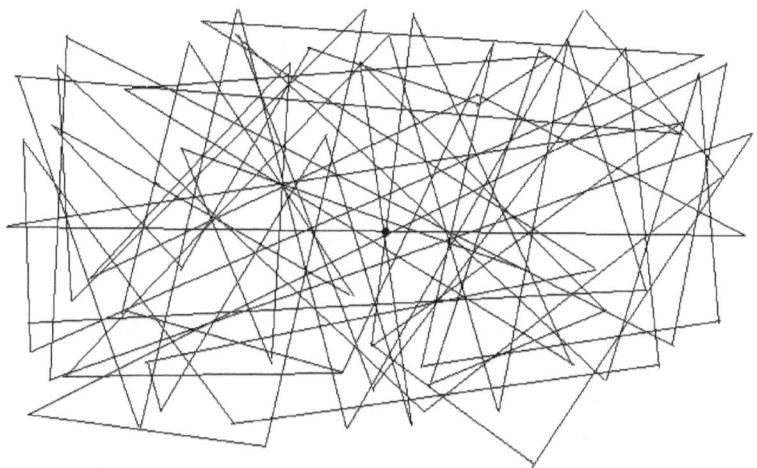

Chronux reverberating through the cosmos

"However, apart from creating 'Time' at the point of contact, Chronux also leaves behind its imprint, on every bit of matter, by creating a *'field of illusion'*...one that is perceived by all sentient beings as the 'flow of time'...in a sense...past...present...and future..."

Gustav could barely speak, "Holy mother of God!...If true...we always exist only in the 'present'...and we only 'think' that we have had a 'past' and a 'future'!"

The stranger quietly nodded, "You finally begin to grasp the true nature of time...it is the ultimate paradox...the ultimate mystery...the ultimate prize...the ultimate illusion and for those, who have sought immortality ...the ultimate trap!"

The wind bellowed, in the background...the unearthly scenes from mythologies that had all but surrounded them, now seemed more tangible than before. Utterly bizarre, utterly unexplainable...Gustav stared mutely at the unfolding chaos...and yet nothing seemed quite as shocking...as the stranger's words!

CHAPTER SEVEN

Time is an illusion! ...time is not what we believe it to be...we only THINK Time exists...in reality it is all an illusion...created by this infernal particle...all the so called 'established scientific theories' were wrong! ...Gustav felt the comforting safety blanket, of conventional wisdom; slip away...All this seemed like a cruel joke...at mankind's expense. Panic filled his thoughts, making him lash out blindly and topple the chair that had once held his captive.

So much was still not clear...so much that just did not fit. "What about this...insanity?" screamed Gustav, "What is this device doing? ...What the hell is happening around us? Why are the stories and myths I heard as a child coming to life? Why can't I see the rest of my team?"

For a brief moment, something akin to sympathy flared in the stranger's eyes. The once proud S.S. Captain was now a broken man. The roles of 'captive' and 'captor' had been reversed!

He spoke softly and carefully, like one would to a child. "My son... You blame a sub-atomic particle for what is happening...but rather it is the result of man's insane attempt at trying to control that which *cannot* be controlled! The device you have foolishly constructed... your 'Wonder Weapon'...is a blueprint for disaster...a colossal mistake, from the far flung future!"

"What do you mean?"

"You see my son, there will come a time...a thousand years from now, when humanity will attain unbridled scientific progress...when man will finally put his warring ways behind and embrace the spirit of cooperation...when all things will seem within reach...no problem, without solution... It is then that we will once again fall prey to two age old hubris – curiosity and temptation."

"What you say makes no sense...why would man fall prey to temptation? Isn't everything attainable in this Utopia like future?" Gustav debated.

"Yes...everything that is *meant* to be attained will be...but there will always be frontiers...that we are not meant to breach...the quest for immortality, for instance...imagine what it would be like to live forever!!!"

"But surely this is madness...not even the most deluded of persons would think such a thing possible...even if, one were to envision a future, where there exist remedies for all human ailments, this would only increase our average lifespan...but Immortality? That's a biological impossibility!" scoffed Gustav.

"My boy, you still seem intent on limiting your vision...now that you do know a little bit about 'Chronux'...about how time really works...imagine what mankind could do with such knowledge." replied the stranger quietly.

Gustav froze, "...You mean...we can actually manipulate this particle? Harness it? *Bend* it to our purposes?"

A sly look came into the old man's eyes, "What do you think your misinformed scientists were doing...or at least attempting to do?"

"What?" Gustav exclaimed in shock, "Die Glocke is a 'TIME MACHINE? ...Are you trying to tell me that this device harnesses the power of the particle you just described? It can manipulate *TIME*?"

The old man looked out towards the device that was now making a dull humming sound and spoke, "The blueprints for this device will be first conceived in year 3067 A.D. under some of the most trying conditions, ever faced by humanity! For in that year, mankind will suffer an invasion, the likes of which it has never faced...an all-out, epic Solar System spanning war. The casualties during this 'mother of all conflicts' will be astronomical! Oh...the losses that we suffered..." There was a slight tremor in the stranger's voice.

"Forgive me for saying so" Gustav interjected, "But you don't look much like a soldier...and what war is it that you speak of...would the Germanic Reich have to prove its unquestionable superiority...even in the future?"

A sudden burst of energy hurled both of them to the floor. An unnamed Norse demigod called his weapon back to him. Gustav could feel his hair standing on end…there was intense static in the air and part of his uniform…near his chest, had caught fire! He had trouble breathing. "What just happened…why are we seeing this?" he screamed over the demigod's bellow of triumph.

The stranger looked him in the eye and spoke, "I am sure you would agree with me now, considering the state of your uniform, that these are much more than mere 'optical illusions'. What we are witnessing is the harrowing echoes of a 'death-trap', whose only outcome…will be end of all there is!"

There was a sudden chill in the air!

"This is Die Glocke right? It is the dammed device that is doing these things, isn't it? Help me shut it down!" gasped Gustav.

The stranger shook his head, "The device is merely a tool…it was designed to harness forces…well beyond man's station."

"What does that mean? Why do you keep describing this as some sort of forbidden knowledge?"

"My child," the stranger began, with a touch of exasperation, "What I say next will be vital to your own future. Fail to understand me… *interrupt me*…and you doom not only yourself, but also your entire civilization."

Gustav was about to respond with customary Nazi bombast, but decided to shut up. Too much had happened today…*so much he did not feel in control of!* Mutely, he nodded.

The old man looked at him carefully…and began, "Today, when we speak of terms like 'civilization' or 'progress'…we are reminded that these are problematic terms with many shades of meaning. However, by any yardstick, 'civilization' ultimately boils down to moving towards a society, based on an increasing access to information. It is this desire that has always propelled our march towards the unknown."

"We have gone from enclosing tombs within simple mud brick structures to building devices, capable of navigating the cosmic winds…in a matter of millennia…and all this, for what?…What has been the silent, subtle motivator behind all these endeavors? It is the insatiable appetite for knowledge and the undying curiosity and desire to understand, to tap into and eventually to control the uncontrollable!"

Gustav nodded. He felt compelled to listen...and also a curious sense of *déjà vu*...memories of another time threatened to claw their way into his mind...memories of him, at the house of an eccentric Turkish book dealer...of him, floating over a magical land in Tibet... sitting around a campfire, in a small village called Darchen...of a night spent at the foot of Mount Kailasha...watching an eerie figure perform the Parikrama!...of a dark force that had dogged his footsteps...ever since he began this infernal quest!!!!

With a sinking feeling, Gustav felt he now recognized the voice, addressing him...

CHAPTER EIGHT

"Since time immemorial, travelers have held a special position in society. These were individuals, who had access to knowledge and ideas, from far-away lands and forbidden kingdoms. They were the bearers of ideas and philosophies, both exciting and controversial... and always seemed to stimulate this most basic of human qualities – curiosity! A lot of the 'History' that you Germans keep emphasizing on has also come down through these story tellers!"

"In primitive societies, travelers were often patronized by their rulers, since during the course of their travels; they acted as *absorbers* and *transmitters* of information, so vital to any society...for the stories they brought back, were often the only source of contact people had, with an unknown and sometimes frightening outside world!"

"Over time these stories took on a life of their own...and the 'facts' behind them...or their 'purposes' were forgotten...and gradually, with the passage of time, the focus shifted more towards *how* these stories were gathered, rather than the stories themselves...but ultimately, information has always been all that ever really mattered!"

"Even the current war that you Germans wage is more of an 'information war' than anything else. You call it as a 'war of expansion', but that subtly disguises the real purpose...in truth, it's an 'ideological war' that you wage. Above all you want the world to accept your belief system...your way of life. You have your 'intelligence officers' all across the world...your S.S. and 'Gestapo' strong arm their way through the private lives of ordinary citizens...always alert for any scrap of information that might come their way. In spite of all this, you have still been found wanting!"

"So as you can see, the desire for information is always at the forefront of all our endeavors...the better the means of gathering it; the more progressive our society!"

"Today, because of an increasingly scientific outlook, there is intense speculation over how many of these storylines can be classified as 'History' and how many, as 'Mythology'. Some old-world romantics like me, might argue that this kills the story of its most important function - that is to inspire awe, while at the same time, stimulate further thought. But our over emphasis on 'Scientific research' and 'Facts', often destroys the essence of a story."

"Make no mistake…even you Germans have been guilty of it. You journeyed all the way to a forgotten corner of the world, pursuing a legend that promised untold power…but in trying to uncover the facts behind it; you failed to consider one crucial detail!"

"What?" Gustav asked, now truly concerned.

"In your arrogance, you simply assumed that there would have to be some basis to every legend…that the purpose of each story, is to ultimately *reveal* the truth. Did you ever consider…even for even a moment…that the purpose of some legends…could be to *HIDE* the truth?"

Gustav felt his body go cold…even as the wind howled in the unearthly background. He felt the first pangs of real panic…much like he had, in Darchen…*like the cold, slippery body of a reptile…slowly slithering its way up his body!*

"Why are you telling me all of this? What does any of this have to do with Die Glocke?" he screamed, over the roar in the background!

The stranger took a deep breath…letting it sink in…before he answered, "Think…my boy, if we have always been aware of the importance of information…just for a moment…imagine tapping into a force that exists almost simultaneously, in every part of the universe…at the same time! Imagine what kind of knowledge, *such a* force would possess!!!"

Gustav's mind froze… "What do you mean?"

"The 'physical matter' of all the events that *have happened…are happening* and *will happen*, already exists in the universe…and has existed since the first such event – what your physicists refer to as the 'Big Bang'. According to this theory, in the beginning, all matter was compressed into one super-dense particle, which then exploded outwards, to form our universe. However, this theory doesn't quite explain what it was that *caused* it to explode? Why was that super-dense particle *unstable* in the first place?"

Gustav felt his stomach curl. From his years of research, he knew that science could not answer this question...What came *before* the Big Bang? Who orchestrated it? Religion, of course, had a simple answer – GOD! - *One omnipotent, omniscient being...that had neither a beginning...nor an end!!*

Science had always been a little more reluctant to accept this answer, right away...and therein lay the problem. Scientists could speculate about the Big Bang itself...discuss what it led to...but would typically squirm, when asked about its cause. Scientific enquiry had always focused on what *followed* the Big Bang rather than on what came *before*!

The stranger allowed this to simmer for a moment, before going on, "At the very beginning, the 'Big-Bang particle' was indeed stable...and by itself, would *never* have exploded. But in that tiny microcosm of time that existed around this particle, it was bombarded by 'Chronux'. It is this impact that made it unstable, causing it to explode...and setting into motion, the chain of events that ultimately resulted in the known universe."

Gustav stared open mouthed!

"Imagine stacking cards, one on top of the other. They will remain in formation...as long as there is no external disturbance. But if you hit this stack, with another object, the whole house comes down! This is exactly what happened, at the birth of our universe. - *'Chronux' was the disturbance that caused the Big Bang!"*

"Even as the Big-Bang particle exploded outwards, Chronux began to reverberate back and forth, between all the newly formed bits of matter and energy...modifying its own trajectory to accommodate each new variable that emerged in the new universe. Thus...by locking on to the energy signature of each and every sub-atomic particle, Chronux has ensured that all matter across the cosmos, forever remains in its 'sphere of influence'...its own extraordinary speed, creating the illusion that 'Time' is flowing and continuous...rather than existing in discreet bits!"

Gustav's mind reeled at this deluge of information…struggling to grasp the sheer magnitude of this revelation, "If what you say is true… the fact that this force…this particle - 'Chronux' exists ALMOST simultaneously across the universe, would make it the holder of an unbelievable amount of knowledge. Through it, we would be able to know every event that takes place *EVERWHERE* in the universe…*at the same time!!! …My God!!!* "

"Exactly…" the stranger replied… "…it is the closest that humanity…or any other life form, has ever come to the concept of God!"

Every fiber in Gustav's being, wanted to reject this thought…there was no way, any of this could *possibly* be true…and yet, he felt compelled to know more, "Even if we are able to tap into it, how could anyone process that kind of information? No instrument on earth will ever be able to store all of it."

"You miss the point; my boy…while it's true that any man-made device will find it impossible to retain all this data, the beauty of Chronux, is much more than just knowledge. Its ultimate secret, is that if properly tamed, Chronux allows us to break one of the most fundamental laws of the universe…a law, which normally all matter in the universe *must* follow, without exception…the law of Entropy!"

"You mean this device we have built can tap the power of this particle…and actually allow for immortality?" Gustav gasped incredulously. "How is this possible? …cheating death…is a scientific impossibility!!!"

"You see my dear…as I described earlier, for any particle in the cosmos, 'Time' exists only when Chronux strikes it…and it is this impact that causes the particle to change…to decay…a process, which when seen over a period of time, appears to us as an 'Event'. None of us are exempt from this, since Chronux constantly bombards our physical structures, as well! As a result, we age…so to say…we go through changes. When this change reaches a point, where matter can no longer retain coherence, it deconstructs to a simpler form…a process that in the case of structures like mountains or rocks, we call 'Erosion'…and in the case of complex sentient beings…we refer to as 'Death'!!!"

Gustav fell to his knees, as the full implication of the stranger's disclosure, suddenly hit him, "My God…since we only age, when this particle hits us…if we somehow ensure Chronux doesn't connect with our physical structures…we would never age at all!!!… *Immortality!*"

CHAPTER NINE

The 'Germanic Empire'...the 'Third Reich'...the quest for 'Victory' in World War II, all now seemed very trivial! Gustav felt like he was standing on the edge of a precipice...one that separated that which he knew from that which he did not...And the void beyond seemed to call out to him!!

One thought in particular...a worrying thought...crept into his sub-conscious, "If this particle is as ubiquitous as you say, how *can* we ever avoid its influence? Any device or technology, we design will also automatically come under its influence...making the experiment futile!"

"Yes...you are correct...that is precisely the problem that scientists in the future grappled with, for decades. How does one design an 'objective' experiment to measure or observe something, when any tool used is automatically compromised by the 'subject' of the experiment?"

"I would know...one of my many predecessors...*a being not from this world*...was one of those who slaved for years, to find a solution to this problem. 'Project Chronux' became his life obsession. The exact circumstances through which he achieved the breakthrough, must for now remain a secret. However, like most epiphanies, the solution came out of nowhere. He realized that the solution lay in the problem itself."

"And that is?" Gustav wondered, "And wait a minute...one of your predecessors...*at what exactly?*"

"Ha...that you shall soon find out...but to go back to your initial question...you are right in judging that to correctly observe and tap into this particle, would require a tool made of matter that was somehow *outside* the influence of Chronux! But no such matter exists anywhere in the universe. What we need is a form of matter that follows none of the conventional rules of space and time. It would have to be absolutely unique...an anomaly! Now...we knew of only one particle that defies all the laws of the universe and has rules only unto itself."

"Chronux...!" Gustav completed, in stunned awe..."We use the particle to study itself...that's absolute genius..."

And then his voice suddenly caught in his throat, "But...but...how *can* we actually do that though? Wouldn't we again be caught in the same paradox? Whatever tools we use, would immediately be compromised!"

The frustrating realization felt like a physical blow!

"If only the particle would do this on its own!...but of course... that's wishful thinking...an 'inanimate' particle...no matter how unique...would *never* do something, just because *we* want it to. It would never even *know*, we want it to..."

"Unless..." the stranger concluded in a hushed whisper..."Unless... the particle is now...'Alive' and 'Sentient'!!!"

The wind screamed against the night...in protest!

CHAPTER TEN

The unearthly scenes from mythologies had now all but ceased. Gustav looked over to where the bodies of his comrades lay, and noticed a strange kind of energy...like a 'Null Field'...covering the area, just around the 'Wonder Weapon'.

And shockingly, the entire area seemed devoid of anything...as if matter itself, had ceased to exist...a dead zone...no matter ...no sound...*no time?*

As his mind struggled with the implications of what he had learnt, the stranger's voice cut through harshly... "The forces you have so unwittingly released through your half-baked experiments, now enter their final stage!"

"What does that mean?" Gustav choked... "And what do you mean when you said, Chronux has achieved sentience?"

The old man looked off into the distance, as he spoke, "Have you ever wondered how 'life'...especially what we refer to as 'Sentient life'...evolved in this universe...from an earlier state of 'non-life'? Think about it...if the early universe was only made up of non-living matter, where *did* the ingredients for such 'sentience' come from? Don't you think this a little odd? If we look within our own cells and genes, we find, we are all carbon based organisms, made up of matter that is abundantly available in the cosmos. So, in that sense we are not all that different from our surroundings, which are all also made up of the same basic elements. I am sure you, who have studied the Eastern philosophies, are aware of this."

Gustav nodded, slowly. Words and texts he had studied in what seemed like another era seemed to ring out. Core Hindu philosophies stressed on the significance of the "Pancha Maha Bhoota" - five basic elements - Earth, Fire, Wind, Water and Ether - that formed the basis of everything, even life itself! This is why, at its heart, Indian mysticism had always been an elemental one, focusing on the need to balance man's ambitions with nature's purposes. *We are all individual components of a greater sum.*

Seemingly aware of Gustav's thoughts, the stranger smiled and continued, "Yet, we differentiate ourselves from the rocks and mountains that we see around us, by classifying ourselves as 'Alive'. So I ask you again, how do you think 'life' particularly 'sentient life', first evolved in the universe?"

Gustav began to answer...but hesitated...the question seemed to take on new weight.

The stranger went on, "It was possible for 'sentience' to evolve... because what we define as 'sentient life' is merely matter, in a super-complex state! As the early universe expanded, matter began to arrange itself in ways that were purely random...think of it like a game of billiards, in which a player simply focuses on striking the balls... randomly and without any skill or objective in mind. You will find that after a few such strikes, the balls get dispersed all over the table... in formations, which are purely arbitrary!"

"True." Gustav conceded...his mind finally reaching out to grasp the stranger's words.

"However, if one were to repeat this experiment...say over billions of years, mathematical probability would dictate that somewhere down the line, we will get patterns that are complex enough to be recognizable and meaningful. This is exactly how 'life' emerged in our universe!"

"So, you are saying that 'sentient life' is just a super-complex arrangement of particles...that has emerged purely by chance? But if that is the case...then this chance...these patterns...might not exist only on Earth...but elsewhere as well!" Gustav concluded in awe.

A smile appeared on the old man's face, "At last...you begin to comprehend the real scope of what we are dealing with. As the early universe began to get increasingly complex, 'Chronux'...the reason for this complexity, now found itself reverberating between these new increasingly complex bits of matter."

"Every time, it strikes another particle, the impact creates 'time' around that particle...however this works both ways. During the collision, each bit of matter...in turn *also* influences Chronux, by transferring a little of its own information over to it. This is the reason every bit of matter 'ages' or 'decays', after a collision...it has essentially *given up* some of its own data. Eventually, when a particular bit of matter has given up enough of its information; it can no longer exist in its original state, and begins to reduce to a lower...or simpler state! We call this process... 'Death' or 'Decay'."

"And that is also why Chronux carries knowledge, from across the cosmos!" a stunned Gustav concluded.

"Yes...Chronux is the one true 'God Particle'!!!"

"Was this the reason my childhood memories were being brought to life, when we turned on 'Die Glocke'?" Gustav asked, a new realization dawning upon him.

"The answer to your question is both 'yes' and 'no'." declared the stranger emphatically, "For Chronux, 'fact' and 'legend' are indistinguishable. It is all just *information*. Chronux treats any and all kinds of information, in the same way."

"I however cannot say with certainty *why* those particular memories were being dragged up. Maybe...the bizarre nature of the experiment you undertook, might have led your subconscious to make connections with *other* bizarre stories! After all, you are a man of great paradoxes Captain - on one hand, you claim to be a man of science...one, who claims to rationalize the world and solve all its mysteries, and yet on the other hand, you deeply immerse yourself in the study of esoteric ideas and philosophies. So maybe, this was your rational side trying to make sense of the unfolding chaos...or maybe...just maybe...it was Chronux trying to communicate with you, even as you attempted to control it!"

"What?" Gustav gasped, terrified, "How can a particle communicate with me?"

"For billions of years...following the Big Bang, Chronux was simply a messenger, a carrier of information. But over time, as life emerged in the universe...and gradually evolved into 'sentient' life, Chronux began carrying information from such *'sentient matter'* as well. Ultimately, there would have come a time, when the amount of *sentient information,* it was carrying, crossed a certain threshold, causing Chronux to *itself* achieve sentience!!!"

"The messenger at last becoming aware of the message, he carries!!!" Gustav's voice was but a whisper.

"Yes my child…the universe is now 'alive'…and it studies us…even as we attempt to study it!"

CHAPTER ELEVEN

A stunned silence fell across the entire chamber. The dull hum of the electricity, powering the facility, could be heard emanating from the inlaid wirings. The wild scenes had stopped and the underground bunker seemed to be back the way it had been...*if it ever had truly disappeared at all!*

"It still makes no sense...even if the device we built using your designs, somehow *does* tap into Chronux, why did my childhood fantasies and myths come to life?" Gustav asked, looking around.

"What is fantasy...what is reality? Who can say for sure...to the particle, it is just information...the fact that we know of these stories, means that the information of these stories, exists in the cosmos...and if that information exists, Chronux can and will act as its carrier. Think Captain Gustav, ultimately our interpretation of reality...is only based on our own limited perceptions. For instance, if a tree were to fall in an empty forest, when there is no one to hear it; *does it actually make a sound?* Who can truly say...Perhaps in the absence of an observer, such a question *itself* becomes meaningless...for in the absence of an observer, does the tree even *exist*...Much less fall?"

Gustav's jaw dropped...all his notions of reality were being challenged...*every fiber in his being, rebelled at this thought.* "No no no...this is madness...you are questioning the very nature of existence..."

"No...I am not...in fact, the question does not need to be answered, as it should not even be framed. Such speculations are completely meaningless...much like your own about *why* certain memories were brought to life."

A haunting mist swept the bunker. Gustav shook his head groggily, trying to make sense of this insanity. Had the Nazi's unwittingly let loose forces, far beyond the comprehension of man? Could such a force that had been active for billions of years, really *be* harnessed? What he had witnessed today was enough to drive a lesser man mad!

The Nazis had thought they were experimenting with 'esoteric propulsion systems' and 'anti-gravity devices', in the hope that they would get an edge in this most desperate of all conflicts! It had been this desire that had motivated the Tibetan expedition. Gustav's personal triumph had been, when on the verge of exhaustion and despair; he had managed to locate the entrance to the lost city of Shambhala. True, it had been achieved with the assistance of this mysterious old man, whom he had captured and brought back. After that, it was the sheer dedication of the German scientists and the blueprints from the 'Vimanika Shastra' that had enabled them to build this device – 'Die Glocke'.

"Here...this is something you will require, to *really* harness the power of your 'Wonder Weapon.'" Gustav looked up and saw the stranger holding a mysterious crystalline, egg shaped object. He simply stared at it. His hands seemed incapable of reaching out and accepting this 'gift'. It was as if, his entire body had been shut down!

The old man calmly continued to hold the device in front of him... *like offering candy to a dog.* Gustav saw that up close, the device was incredibly nuanced...finely detailed to resemble an un-blossomed lotus flower...*one made of crystal!*

He hesitated...there was still so much he did not understand. He remembered how during the experiment they had conducted a while ago; he and the other scientists had felt a sensation of being crushed by an invisible force, after the device had been activated with the five prisoners inside. It had felt like space itself was being twisted, violently! The sensation had lasted a good five to six minutes...until one of the German scientists had managed to turn off Die Glocke.

Did he really want to harness such power *again?*

The scariest part of the experiment was when the device had been opened...no trace of the prisoners could be found...whatsoever! The five men trapped inside had seemingly *vanished* from existence. It was only then that the stranger had begun to speak; admonishing the Nazis and revealing the device's shocking true function!

Gustav's mind suddenly jolted back to the present...the same being was now offering him a strange crystalline artifact and telling him that *this* was what was really needed to activate their 'Wonder Weapon'. Once activated properly, the device was allegedly capable of tapping into a primordial force...and controlling 'Time'. The real question was, could he really trust this being?

"How does Die Glocke work?" It was clear that Gustav was buying for time. Gone was his swagger and self-belief...He had always considered himself an adventurer...a seeker of truth...*capable of anything*, but during the last one hour, he had seen and heard things that had stretched his mind to the brink of insanity! "How can I use it to exploit the power of Time?"

The stranger looked at him with a mixture of pity and disgust...the once arrogant S.S. Captain, reduced to a bumbling wretch, desperately seeking answers.

"You cannot exploit time, you fool...this is not some mere third-world country that your 'Wehrmacht' can strong arm its way through...The device, your scientists have cobbled together, runs on technology that will not be invented...for a thousand years from now...technology that is ensconced within this crystalline artifact, I now give you. Only through its use, can your precious 'Die Glocke' truly come to life. Else, all you shall ever have, is a *smoke and light effect!*"

Gustav was silent. It would be so easy to simply reach out and accept this 'gift'...after all, what could possibly go wrong that hadn't *already* gone wrong? But for some reason he couldn't explain, he hesitated. He needed to know more!

"If, what you claim is true, and this is indeed technology from the future, then it proves that *YOU* have managed to exploit the power of 'Chronux'...meaning that the particle *can* be exploited." He spoke tentatively.

The stranger sighed...realizing the German still had a bit of spunk left in him. He had hoped the events leading up to this point would leave him a pitiful mess...ripe for manipulation. But it was clear that to buy Gustav's trust; he would have to indulge him some more...*more precious time would have to be spent!* Nonetheless, he had come too far now, to worry about this…the plan had been several millennia in the making and was only now reaching fruition. So, if that meant indulging a desperate German officer some more…*so be it!*

He looked scornfully at Gustav and spat out, "I offer you the secrets of immortality…a chance to gain ultimate power…and you insist on asking questions? Have it your way!" The room trembled.

"The origins of this device I hold, must for now remain a secret… if however, you are as smart as I suspect, and *do* manage to master it… Then all of space and time shall be yours to manipulate." This last bit was aimed at exploiting the German pride.

"It should suffice to say that the first experiments to successfully tap the power of Chronux…and harness its legendary power, were conducted *NOT* on this world, but on another one, which had its own share of 'egomaniacs' and 'power seekers'."

"Those otherworldly researchers faced the same problems that we spoke of…How do you manipulate something that is so ubiquitous? To harness the power of Chronux, they had to build a device using materials not touched by Chronux…an impossibility! For centuries, they experimented with all kinds of shielding technologies, but to no avail. Eventually, the breakthrough came in an unusual way…but that's a story for another time. They realized that since all matter in the universe was influenced by Chronux, the only substance, exempt from this influence, would be one *not yet* a part of the universe!!"

"What?" Gustav almost shouted… "A substance that is not yet a part of the universe? What the hell does that even mean? How does one procure something like that?"

"No, we cannot…and so, we create it on our own…from nothing!" replied the stranger calmly.

"Create 'matter' out of 'nothing'???"

"Yes… 'Sui generis'…'something out of nothing'! Isn't this how most Earth based religions explain the concept of the divine? *One, who has neither beginning nor end…one, who has emerged out of nothingness…*"

"Madness!!!" breathed Gustav.

He watched mutely, as the stranger walked over to the device the Germans had constructed so diligently…'Die Glocke'. He watched the being reach into the craft and gently place the small crystal he was carrying, into a small opening, near the control panel. The object seemed to embed itself tightly, with a satisfying 'THUNK'...as if it were made for the craft!

Then slowly...very deliberately, the stranger turned around. As the dull flickering half-light caught part of his face, Gustav couldn't help but feel that he knew this being...that he had shared a *long* association with him...and something also told him that this prior association hadn't ended well! An inner voice seemed to tear at his conscience... was it a warning? Damn his memory...he still remembered so little of what had happened to him in Tibet!

"Yes..." he heard the being speak again, "Create something out of nothing...that is exactly what this device does. More than the blueprints you stole from my sacred city, the miniature artifact, I have now placed at the heart of your "Wonder Weapon", is the key. It is *that* which shall ultimately power your device. The mercury mixture you have been using so far merely functions as a coolant!"

"Sweet holy mother of God..." Gustav groaned. "You are telling me now...after all these years...all this effort...that we have been on the wrong track...all this while?"

"Quite so" the stranger chuckled. "But don't let that get you down... you did the best you could...after all, without my help, this power source would be well beyond your capacity to even comprehend. The crystal contains a mixture of 'Beryllium' and a substance that in the future will be referred to as 'UnUnPentium'...yes, I know this surprises you, as this element hasn't been discovered in your time...and so, doesn't appear on any of your periodic tables!"

"UnUnPentium better known as 'Element 115', has some extraordinary properties, even though it is extremely radioactive... It has a half-life of only 220 milliseconds. When whipped around in a vortex, the mixture generates such intense energy fields...concentrated over an extremely small area, that for the merest fraction of a second, it is able to rip an opening...into the very fabric of space and time!!!"

"Your creation... 'Die Glocke'...the one your scientists reverse engineered from the 'Vimanika Shastra', merely provides the means of creating such a vortex...but ultimately, it is the materials present inside the small crystal artifact that do all the 'heavy lifting'! This is why, without this key ingredient, your machine was but a *pale shadow* of what it could have been. But now…with the addition of the final piece of the puzzle, 'Die Glocke' will finally be able to do, what it was meant to!"

"Mein Gott!!" Gustav could hardly believe his ears. "But if Die Glocke was in some way incomplete all this while, how do you explain what happened to the Polish Prisoners? …My memories being brought to life?"

"You forget that incomplete as it was…you had *ME* dragged over here, before you began your experiment…which meant that your craft was always in close proximity to the crystal, I was carrying. Once activated…like a good twin, 'Die Glocke' sensed my presence and reached out to complete the union…the results as you know were… spectacular to say the least!"

"Unbelievable!" Gustav whispered, under his breath, "So now that the device is finally complete, it will allow us to create that rift in space? Right here? …And then what?"

"Yes" the stranger continued, "Once the rift is created, the device allows a set of 'unique and exotic particles' from another dimension, to very briefly enter ours! However, these other-worldly particles can remain in 'our existence' for a very small interval of time…an interval so tiny that it would come up as *ABSOLUTE ZERO*, in any unit of measurement, you have today. In fact, so connected are they to their own dimension, that as soon as the rift in space begins to heal itself, these particles get sucked back, into their own universe!"

"The rift *heals* itself?" Gustav asked incredulously.

"Yes…that seems to be one of the fundamental principles of our cosmos…an ability to instantly and automatically correct any flaw that creeps in! When this experiment was first performed, the race conducting it, felt that with enough energy focused on a particular spot, they might keep the rift open, *indefinitely*. But what they soon realized was that once space-time began to heal, no amount of energy could keep the fault open, for long…it was as if, the universe was overcoming its 'injuries' and emerging stronger! This discovery was a seminal moment in the study of Chronux!"

"Wow!"

"But in spite of their very transient existence, these 'otherworldly' particles are very important. Since, they aren't native to our universe... and basically just 'blink in and out' of existence; Chronux is unable to compensate its own trajectory to accommodate them, during their brief stay in our universe! As a result, for one trillionth of a trillionth of a second, we have an area encompassed by these particles that Chronux cannot recognize and hence cannot influence...in essence creating a *NULL FIELD!!!*"

"Holy FU...!"

"Objects within this 'null field', are now *outside* the influence of Chronux and thus outside the debilitating effects of time! In this state of 'Timelessness' these objects/bits of matter are not exposed to Entropy and by definition..."

"...become immortal!!!" completed Gustav breathlessly.

'Time is not composed of indivisible 'nows' any more than any other magnitude is composed of indivisibles.' – Aristotle, Physics

CHAPTER TWELVE

One thing still troubled Gustav. "You said that the 'null field' lasts only very briefly…after that, we shall be back where we began…for, once the field collapses, the objects inside, would once again be exposed to Chronux!"

"Not really, you see…this effect is a little more serious, than just a 'passing phase'. By eliminating the influence of Chronux, objects inside the said field, in effect, briefly 'PHASE OUT OF REALITY'… so, even when the field decays, Chronux no longer recognizes them, as they are no longer on its new, slightly altered 'flight plan'! It is almost as if the null field causes Chronux to suffer from 'amnesia'…in a sense 'forget' …the matter it envelopes!!!"

"What you observed a while back, with your unfortunate comrade, who lies cut in half…was the result of him being partially inside…and partially outside the 'null field', generated by Die Glocke. As a result, half of him 'phased out of existence', while the other half did not! I imagine, it might have been quite painful." The stranger laughed ruthlessly.

"And remember, that was Die Glocke functioning at only half its capacity…without the aid of my crystal! For you to truly benefit from your invention, you will have to step inside the craft…like those Polish wretches, you forced to, albeit this time with my device, embedded inside. My crystal will kick things into action…and once the vortex engine reaches a critical speed, create the conditions required for the birthing of the exotic particles!"

"What if 'Die Glocke' once again causes the kind of destruction it did, when we first activated it…what if it again brings my memories to life?" Gustav asked, nervously.

The stranger sighed, "You really are obsessed with that, aren't you!!! I do not claim to know exactly, why your memories were brought to life…but, like I said earlier, the particle acts as a carrier of information…*all kinds of information.* It is also influenced by its sources, in this case YOU. Your entire life has been governed by the notion that you are supposedly descended, from some lost, superior race, with pagan origins!"

"Not supposedly," Gustav angrily retorted…his pride stung, "We ARE descended from the Aryan race - the true inheritors of earth… and after this war we will once again reign supreme!!"

"Be that as it may," the stranger continued nonchalantly, "You have been inducted into 'Pagan' philosophies and theologies all your life, not just German but Greek, Scandinavian and even Indo Aryan! Your insignia - the symbol of your organization that you bandy around so proudly, is a 'Swastika' – an Aryan design!"

Gustav remembered his mother reading out stories to him as a child, stories about the great myths of the ancient world - the 'Iliad' with its roots in Greek antiquity, the 'Mahabharata' that spoke of a great war fought between the righteous and the unjust…*that had always been his favorite*…the great 'Nordic legends' of Thorr, the Thunder God, and his epic adventures.

All these stories had connections to wars, much like the one Gustav and his compatriots were now fighting…*a war that had the potential to remake the world!* Was this why the particle had selected these memories from his subconscious? …or…was it sending him a message?

"The fact that we actually witnessed and physically experienced these scenes, would indicate that Chronux wasn't simply recreating my memories, but rather displaying information from 'real' events, not myths!" Gustav wondered out loud. "Does that mean all myths have a factual base? That all of them are actually part of history?"

"Your ignorance and lack of vision is staggering! You refuse to grasp the truth even when it stares you in the face. You hold on to archaic concepts, even after I have wasted so much time explaining them to you. You have proven to be a massive disappointment Captain Gustav. Maybe I have erred in selecting you. You have the desire and drive…but *not* the intellectual ability to back it up!"

"How dare you speak to me this way you pompous bastard? I have just about had enough of you…you have been nothing but trouble, since I first found you." Gustav pulled out his belt pistol and screamed, "You will now tell me what that effect was about…and you will do so in words I can understand!"

The old man merely looked over to the null field that Die Glocke had created, ignoring the rants of the confused and angry German officer. Then…he lowered his eyes…and slowly began to walk towards it.

"What do you think you are doing? Didn't you see what it did to the others? Come back now…I order you to come back right away…or I swear to God, I will shoot you!!!"

"God! Ha…" the stranger smirked…

Gustav's voice trailed off, as he saw the stranger's form become even more and more immaterial…translucent…hazy…*ghostly!* The utter futility of his threat, struck him, even as he stared dumbfounded. The old man walked ever closer to the null field…at the heart of the chamber. Unlike before, the field now seemed more passive and docile…*inviting even*…and the stranger seemed completely unaffected by it!!

Gustav saw him slowly enter the field, as if he had always been a part of it. A dull, bluish, grey aura once again enveloped the entire chamber. Time seemed to slow down…the stranger was now completely engulfed by the field!

Gustav gasped for words …Still, desperately trying to wave his prisoner, back…his mind refusing to accept what was happening!

Then something else occurred…something truly astonishing! The stranger reached the area around Die Glocke…an area that had been charred, by the experiment… and kept walking. As he neared the craft, he reached out with his hand, as if to feel the outer walls…and seemed to enter the device, straight through its metal casing…*like a wraith!*

Gustav stared openmouthed. No words could do justice to what he was going through!

Just before he completely disappeared into the device, the stranger, turned around and looked the S.S. Captain, straight in the eye …and smiled cunningly. The implication seemed obvious…it was a clear invitation to the German…daring him to follow!

Then in a blinding flash of light, the entire place…the underground bunker, returned to its former placid state. Gone was the body of the Swiss scientist, who had been sliced in half…gone were the charred remains of the other researchers…gone were any signs that the events of the last couple of hours had ever occurred! The only visible sign that the bunker had been used for any human endeavor was a strange bell-shaped contraption…and a shell-shocked S.S. officer…down on his knees!!

Not for the first time in his life, Capt. Friedrich Gustav felt like he was the last man on Earth.

'They say time heals all wounds, but that presumes the source of the grief is finite!' – Cassandra Clare, Clockwork Prince

CHAPTER THIRTEEN

To everything there is a season, and a time to every purpose under the heaven: A time to be born, and a time to die; a time to plant, and a time to pluck up that which is planted; A time to kill, and a time to heal; a time to break down, and a time to build up; A time to weep, and a time to laugh; a time to mourn, and a time to dance; A time to cast away stones, and a time to gather stones together; a time to embrace, and a time to refrain from embracing; A time to get, and a time to lose; a time to keep, and a time to cast away; A time to rend, and a time to sew; a time to keep silence, and a time to speak; A time to love, and a time to hate; a time of war, and a time of peace. - BIBLE, Ecclesiastes 3:1-8

Hours passed…

Finally…after what seemed like an eternity…Gustav felt the blood, slowly…return to his limbs. As he tried to regain what remained of his composure, an ominous sound began to roll across the chamber. A voice…*it sounded human…!!!*

To Gustav's feverish mind, it sounded like the stranger's voice…but heavily corrupted! Curiously, the voice seemed to emanate from everywhere in the room…and from nowhere! In no known language… and yet, containing words!

Even more astonishingly…the words were not in a linear order…it seemed as if…time *itself* was being corrupted…the future and the past being *superimposed* over the present! However…somehow…the words seemed to be directed straight at Gustav's subconscious!

"You still wonder whether the myths are 'real'! 'Fact', 'fiction', 'real', 'unreal'…these are just human concepts…to Chronux, it is all just information! Your life, your past, your future…are no more real, than these stories from your childhood, which hold just as much power, as events from your life!"

Gustav stared speechless...all his years of research...had been overturned, during this one conversation! His mind reeled under the weight of the possibilities. The German 'Wonder Weapon' was far more powerful than any one had ever imagined! If it could really tap into any story, any concept...and bring it into existence...*nothing* would be out of reach for Germany!! Victory in this war would be a formality!!!

It would no longer matter that they had lost millions in Russia, and that the Americans and the British were staging a counterattack in the West. None of it would matter, if he - Capt. Gustav, mastered this device. He could use the awesome power of the ancient legends, to smite the enemies of the Fatherland...and redeem his people!

He once again recalled the Mahabharata's descriptions of divine weapons, which could be unleashed with just a thought...*or a prayer*... and that could lay waste to an entire army! One such weapon was the 'Brahmasthra' or the weapon of Brahma, which was meant as a last resort and which even the epic spoke of in hushed tones!

Gustav knew that his own scientists were working on a weapon not too dissimilar to this. Though considered 'Above Top-Secret', certain Nazi officials knew of a project, which, using a metal called Uranium, was trying to split the atom and harness its nuclear fury. If successful, this technology could revolutionize wars in the future and give Germany the means of ending this one!

He had always wondered about the similarities between the descriptions of the 'Brahmasthra' and its effects, and what his own scientists were working on. Even though German nuclear research was still in its nascent stage, scientists had already experienced the hazards of nuclear-poisoning...and particularly, what it could do to human tissue. Disturbingly...these effects were eerily similar to those described in the epics!

Gustav remembered seeing a Jewish slave, who had been exposed to lethal radiation, while handling some of the by-products of the experiments. The man's health had rapidly deteriorated, eventually resulting in a torturously slow death! He also remembered a discussion he had, with one of Germany's top researchers, during a conference in the late 1930s. The conference had been organized to discuss new innovations that might assist Germany, during the then imminent war.

Gustav remembered how one of the researchers had prepared a presentation on the potential power of a new *atomic* weapon, they were working on. At the time of course, it had all been purely theoretical...but the implications of actually possessing such a weapon were clear. Everyone in the audience had applauded, and even Himmler had been impressed by the claims. But towards the end of the discussion, Gustav had made a comment that none of this was 'new' and was merely being 'rediscovered'!

This had created quite a stir. Regardless of his position in the S.S. it was unheard of for someone to so brazenly question a member of the scientific community...especially *during* a scientific convention!

But Gustav knew that he now stood on the threshold of doing just that. What he had witnessed here, was far more than just the power of an atom. With the power of the 'Wunder-Waffe', he was poised to become the first man to gain mastery over all that there was! ...*the power of God was at his fingertips!* He felt lightheaded and dizzy, and felt his knees buckle.

As he struggled to maintain composure, memories began to flood his system...forgotten memories...of a journey to Tibet! Driven by a cause, he and six of his accomplices, had put their faith and their lives on the line over a fairy tale! He *SEEMED* to remember how along the way, the locals had ridiculed their attempts, warning them of a fate far worse than death! And yet, against all odds, they had managed the impossible...they had found... The mythical lost city of Shambhala! ...and in the bargain, very nearly paid the ultimate price!

Again, he *seemed* to remember, how he and six of his accomplices, had been at death's doorsteps...from frostbite and starvation, when this mysterious stranger had rescued them and nursed them back to health, in his cave! Even though initially, he hadn't spoken a word, the old man had quickly mastered German, and demanded that the Nazis abandon their fanatical quest. Only when the Germans had threatened to shoot him, had he relented and revealed himself as the gatekeeper of the secret they were searching for – Shambhala.

According to legend, the city was the source of unlimited power and immortality! The stranger had told them that he had been guarding it for millennia, a claim they had rubbished as delusional! However, he had promised to lead Gustav and his comrades to the city, under oath that they would keep its location a secret from the rest of humanity.

Gustav's mind seemed to conjure up memories of numerous challenges and tests; he had *apparently* navigated along the way. But something about these memories bothered him...they seemed 'artificial' somehow...*manufactured even!* He also could not remember the names of all those, who had accompanied him on this expedition... or their eventual fate. How could this be possible? ...and why did he have no memory of what had happened at the end of the journey...or how he had managed to make his way back to Germany?

Damn it!

Surely...this is how the events in Tibet had occurred...

...Right?

CHAPTER FOURTEEN

'The habit of looking to the future and thinking that the whole meaning of the present lies in what it will bring forth is a pernicious one. There can be no value in the whole unless there is value in the parts'. - BERTRAND RUSSELL, Conquest of Happiness

Gustav knew that what he had witnessed over the last hour or so *hadn't* been an illusion. If...he could somehow manage to harness the power of this device, the power and knowledge of an entire universe... would be at his fingertips. Chronux would bestow unto him... Immortality!

As his megalomania grew the puny and petty affairs of the state... 'Disputes over territories'...began to seem trivial and insignificant. It was true that as a soldier and explorer for the S.S. he had sworn an oath of absolute loyalty to Adolf Hitler...and...had never once dared to challenge his authority...yet! The expedition he had undertaken, along with Ernst Schaffer, had been *with* the support and blessings of both Hitler and Himmler. But none of them had gone through what he had. He had sacrificed all...for the German Reich!

And now a different set of images seemed to dominate his mind... He seemed to remember the lukewarm reception he had received on his return to Germany...while news of the 'Schaffer mission' had been prominently displayed! There had been no gala dinners thrown in his honor...no medals of courage...no recognition! The only time his mission and its success were even discussed, was during an hour long de-briefing, with Hitler and Himmler, in the Führer-bunker.

These memories now seemed to take on a life of their own...he remembered Hitler showing little interest in the details of the perilous expedition, Gustav had undertaken, on his behalf. The Führer's only interests had been the blueprints, brought back from Tibet...for they represented some sort of advanced technology, which could be reverse-engineered and weaponized! Surely, Gustav thought, he and his team had deserved better. In fact, if he didn't know him so well, Gustav would have suspected Hitler of being envious!!

Nonetheless, he had been first deployed to a top secret military facility, at 'Peenemunde', near the Arctic Circle…and later to an even more secret one, known as 'Der Riese' – 'The Giant', near the Czech border. This entire bunker, constructed underground and heavily reinforced, was in fact part of a 10 kilometer-long structure, built to serve as a military base and armament factory! He was also given a seemingly unlimited number of slave laborers - most of them Polish Jews, to work with.

Years of back-breaking work, hundreds of sleepless nights and casualties numbering in the thousands, had all led to this point. Throughout this period, the only communication he had from either Hitler or Himmler, had been disinterested inquiries and curt reminders to speed things up.

Under such conditions, Gustav thought to himself, he could be forgiven for not harboring too many 'ultra-patriotic' thoughts. He was about to accomplish something that no one in history…*or mythology*… had accomplished! He was the only man on Earth, who truly understood how the universe functioned…and the real nature of time and reality! Not even a hundred years of research, would be able to match what he had learned.

So why was it that there was this nagging feeling of dread…at the back of his mind? Was it simply a case of nerves?

He had killed men without batting an eyelid…he had seen men bleed to death, in unimaginably brutal ways. He had fought enormous odds and done a hundred other things for the glory of the Third Reich, making him one of Hitler's most trusted accomplices.

So what was it about this infernal device that was troubling him so?

CHAPTER FIFTEEN

Slowly…stealthily…another thought began to clasp Gustav's frenzied mind… *'Leave this complex and escape with his family, to Eastern Europe'.* He had enough money saved from his earlier expeditions… plus unchecked access to the funding that 'Project Die Glocke' had received over the years. Moreover, he still had permits to travel back and forth across all the German occupied regions of Eastern Europe… he could escape this isolated facility, take his family, his wife and his beautiful three year old daughter…and never return!

There were of course no eye witnesses still alive, except for the few remaining Polish slaves, who could testify against him. It would be simple to line them up and shoot them…or gas them, as had *always* been the plan, once they had become expendable. The facility got its supplies only once a month and Gustav knew that the convoys, delivering those, weren't due for at least another fortnight!

Nobody would discover his escape, till he was well clear of the German borders…and the charred, twisted bodies of the scientists, would be evidence to suggest that a catastrophic accident had claimed the lives of *ALL* those involved. He could even live out his days with his family, on some remote sub-tropical island…probably in the South Pacific…or the Caribbean, under a new identity. His wife, Anna, had always wanted to visit the Bahamas!

A wave of tranquility swept over Gustav, as he found himself slipping more and more into this comforting fantasy.

"NO" he screamed…His mind suddenly aflame! He had come too far…sacrificed too much, to stop now. The Power of God was within reach…and only a fool would turn away now! *Damn the old man and his mysterious ways!* …why hadn't he been more forthcoming…all these years of wasted effort, when the Germans had believed 'Die Glocke' was a flying machine…never once suspecting its true purpose.

If, they had only known what it was capable of in 1939…the outcome of the war could have been very different!

But there was no point, thinking about that now…

He took a deep breath to still his nerves, and stood up gingerly. He felt his legs tremble, uncontrollably. A wave of rage swept over him at his own weakness. "Get it together!" he admonished himself…now was the time to act.

He tried to recall all he had learnt, by mentally going over his conversation with the stranger…*still, there was that nagging dread*… like a warning…but for the life of him, he couldn't put his finger on what was causing it. But…there was something more…something the stranger hadn't revealed…he was sure of it!

Beneath all the swagger and arrogance the stranger had displayed, were the undercurrents of a challenge…a challenge to Gustav's ego… daring him to achieve the impossible! Was that what was bothering him?

If so, he would not fall prey to such *womanly* fears. He was a German…an Aryan…descended from a race of pure bred…blue eyed…blonde inheritors of planet Earth. It was his destiny to embrace divinity! He had been taught that the 'strong' always dominate the 'weak'…and that the universe has no place for those who gave up!

Steeling his mind, Gustav gingerly got up and looked out towards where Die Glocke had been placed. The broken remains of the metal chains, securing it, now lay all over the floor. The device itself appeared to have calmed down, but there was still the smell of brimstone and burning metal, in the air.

He hobbled forward, tentatively.

As he crossed the massive reinforced bunker, he saw the full extent of the chaos. The bodies of his former associates lay strewn around the floor, amidst pieces of bent concrete and iron. Gustav felt his knees tremble and shake violently, as he saw some of the faces, contorted in their death throes. A few sparks mixed with a strange bluish energy, still danced in the air…and a barely perceivable humming sound, seemed to emanate from within the object.

Just as he was about to reach the craft, Gustav noticed a darkened area, at the base of the pedestal that supported Die Glocke. The concrete floor appeared to have been scorched and burned. This caused him to pause briefly...*again...he felt the nagging dread*...Was this, such a good idea, after all? How much did he or anyone else really know about this device? The stranger had spoken largely in riddles, and at no point been absolutely clear about its inner workings. How smart was it to reactivate the device without giving it the once over?

Carefully...he walked around the device...a slow deliberate walk all the way around the craft...a *'Parikrama'*...the act seemed to stir long forgotten memories, buried deep within him...of another pilgrimage, he seemed to have undertaken...*but where?*

As he studied the device up close, he noticed certain things about it that he hadn't seen before. The door that led into the device was partially open...and he could now see inside. Carefully, peering inside the chamber, Gustav spied the small crystal artifact that the stranger had declared the energy source of Die Glocke. If true, this tiny object could very well provide the means for his salvation...or his doom!

He climbed the steps; on one side of the pedestal...this was where he had seen the stranger...merge with the device. Hardening his mind, he reached out and let his fingers run along the smooth exterior of the craft. He wasn't sure whether it was his mind playing tricks or simply fatigue, but...he could swear the device seemed to pulse under his touch...like it was alive and beckoning to him!

This was it...this was *the* moment of truth...casting aside all doubts and misgivings, Capt. Gustav stepped into the 'Wonder Weapon'.

The device hummed softly...seemingly aware of his presence! *Was it really alive?* As he closed the main entrance to the bell shaped craft, Gustav experienced the unsettling feeling of being watched. He tried to shrug it off; he was after all about to embark on an experiment that would either make him the master of unlimited power...*or instantly kill him.* There was bound to be some apprehension!

He looked around the small chamber. Even though the craft was a large one, the shielding on the roof had caused the insides to cave in, allowing for just enough space for a grown man to stand fully erect. At the very center, was the flower shaped crystal object that the stranger had brought with him, resting on the engine core. *Strange…* he distinctly remembered the old man attaching it somewhere close to the entrance of the craft! So, how was it now…that the device seemed attached to the engine core?

As he mulled over this, he saw that around the core, were a series of cables…containing an extremely potent mixture of Beryllium and Mercury that the 'Vimanika Shastra' had spoken of. The original text of course, had been in Sanskrit…but with Karl Haushofer's support; Gustav had managed to crack its code…even though some of it had proved difficult to comprehend. The text had used phrases like 'Pancha Loha' which the Nazis understood as an 'alloy of five metals'…although which five, the text hadn't specified…they had eventually managed to reverse engineer most, if not all of the designs!

Now, standing inside the craft, Gustav knew that to activate the process, he would have to start the cylindrical turbines…that would then spin the radioactive mixture around at high speeds. As the mixture reached a critical speed, their latent energy would power the engine, bringing the stranger's crystal to life…one that supposedly contained the mysterious 'Element 115' or 'UnUnPentium', as the stranger had called it…thus launching the countdown that would ultimately allow him to harness the power of Chronux!

He also realized that *if* he now initiated the process, it would be the first time Die Glocke had been activated…twice…in the same day! Disturbingly…what that would do, there was no way of knowing!!!

He allowed himself a nervous smirk, as he began to grid himself for the final phase. Two voices seemed to echo in his head. One the voice of reason, telling him to check the device once more or have someone else try it out, the other that oddly sounded much like the voice of the stranger… Smirking…challenging…telling him to…continue. *To hell with all these fears!*

Silencing his troubled mind, Gustav took a deep breath and reached out for the levers. This was it!!!!…This was *THE* moment…the moment that man embraced his true destiny and became one with the divine. He felt a wave of sheer exhilaration, as a slew of indescribable emotions swept all over him. Clutching the levers firmly, Gustav pulled them back. There was no going back now...even if he wanted to; there was no way to stop the process!!!

'But at my back I always hear Time's winged chariot hurrying near'
- ANDREW MARVELL, To His Coy Mistress

CHAPTER SIXTEEN

The devious, otherworldly craft put together through a combination of Nazi ingenuity and esoteric eastern mysticism, sprang to life. Gustav saw circular bands of bluish-green energy, erupt all around the insides of 'Die Glocke' and move rapidly towards the top of the device! He knew from his research and his conversation with the stranger, that this was the effect of the radioactive mixture in the turbines and the *UnUnPentium,* within the Crystal artifact.

During their previous experiments, he had observed this effect from the outside, but to witness it *first-hand*…in all its glory, was still an awesome experience! The entire interior of Die Glocke was now enveloped, by a pale bluish hue…much like the aura that had surrounded the device, when the stranger entered it!!

If, what the stranger had said was true, when this energy built to a crescendo, the mysterious crystal at the center of the chamber…would tear open space and time, creating a temporary 'null field'… permanently phasing him and everything inside, *out* of Chronux' influence…thus making him immortal!!!!

He did not have long to wait. With a ruthless suddenness, the crystal jewel burst into life, flooding his perception and everything with it. He felt himself being bombarded with a maelstrom of wild energies as deranged and chaotic, as the darkest nightmares of a capricious surrealist! The forces began to burn the very core of his being, with an unspeakable fury. It felt like he was being burned physically…*and spiritually*…from within and from without! He had never believed such agony possible! He tried to scream, but no words came out. He knew…he was going to die…but then…just as suddenly as the pain had begun, it seized!

Gustav, now felt himself hurled forward, at incredible speeds, through a funnel shaped energy vortex…the boundaries of which, he seemed to perceive with his *mind* rather than his brain! He felt his senses and perception, simultaneously expand and…collapse! He was just one microscopic dust-mote, whipped around in a storm cloud… at fantastic speeds!

Desperately, he tried to hold himself together…he saw flashing lights and colors, never seen or named before, zoom past him. His sense of scale and proportions and directions, was completely distorted… 'Up' and 'Down' no longer held any meaning. He felt himself begin to come apart physically…bit by bit…and yet, felt no pain! The boundaries of the cosmos raced in to meet him, as his form and self, expanded beyond the physical. In this non-corporeal state, he felt himself becoming something much more than human!!!

No longer did the mortal tethers of his physical body hold any sway over him…he felt himself begin to fully integrate with the universe. He was Gustav no longer…he felt himself 'everywhere' and 'nowhere'… at the same time! As his mind struggled to understand what was happening, there was a tremendous explosion of light…an unbelievably beautiful sight, perceived directly by the soul…he marveled at its beauty…gazed at its wonder …and then eventually in awe, realized…that the explosion had been *HIM* all along!!!

He felt the euphoria of the universe rush out to meet him…and then…then he felt…nothing!

CHAPTER SEVENTEEN

In the beginning God created the heaven and the earth.

Now the earth was formless and empty, darkness was over the surface of the deep, and the Spirit of God was hovering over the waters.

And God said, "Let there be light," and there was light.

God saw that the light was good, and he separated the light from the darkness.

God called the light "day," and the darkness he called "night." And there was evening, and there was morning—the first day.

Genesis – The Bible

Initially there was nothing…from that nothing arose everything… 'Sui generis'…created on its own…this is the ultimate truth about the universe…The birth of existence!

Different cultures and traditions around the world all have their own interpretations of how the universe came into being and the notion of who or *what* the creator was – Sumerian…Egyptian… Mayan…Christian…Jewish…Hindu…Muslim…Pagan…all contemplating the same supreme mystery!!

First there was only darkness…from this primordial darkness arose the Zohardingo, the winged Ptredonton who would breathe life into the swirling mists of chaos and create a forge.
On this forge, would be formed a template for all life on Migazon. Zohardingo would further create the framework for all…

Wait…What????… 'Zohardingo'? … 'Migazon'? …the images that were now materializing were of an increasingly alien nature and yet… somehow…oddly familiar…at least they SEEMED to be getting more and more familiar!! Surely this was not from the earth that he knew so well…not in any language that he was familiar with! This version of a creation myth appeared to come from an *alien world*…but…even assuming there was such a thing…why was he seeing these images?

More importantly…who was *HE* again??

Softly…disturbingly…a chilling voice broke the deadlock…a voice that seemed to emanate, from everywhere, all at once!

It was a voice he had grown quite familiar with…and one he had hoped never to hear again…but now, he heard it laugh…

"Ha ha ha ha ha…" the stranger from the lost city of Shambhala, now stood in front of him…smirking…with an awesome sense of accomplishment!

"Look around you…you, who were once Capt. Friedrich Gustav… Look around you…See what your actions have wrought…See what your actions have helped *me* accomplish! Your greed and megalomania, have led you to the ultimate trap…and in doing so, liberated me from the 'Curse of Chronux'…Ha ha ha…you are indeed the ultimate fool… but one, I owe a great deal to!"

CHAPTER EIGHTEEN

He could no longer see…smell…touch…hear…or feel! No physical…corporeal shell to hold his essence…No way of communicating with the physical world! All he could perceive was a swirling maelstrom of dust, energy and tiny bits of matter, being tossed around at impossible speeds…some that were forming recognizable patterns…others that remained utterly bizarre!

And yet…somehow, he was still able to perceive his surroundings…'Observe' it, in some way! But disturbingly, as soon as he so much as "*looked at*" the patterns around him, they immediately started to lose coherence and fall apart …it was as if their very physical structure, was coming apart under his 'gaze'. He felt like the '*great destroyer*'!

This was extremely distressing!!

He also realized that with each passing moment…he was beginning to feel more and more distant from the man, he had once been…more distant, from the life he had led…more distant from everything! It was as if his entire life had been…from another lifetime…his entire existence, someone else's story. Only one thing seemed certain…he was gradually becoming something more than just human…*much, much more*…a force of nature…a universal force! …Madness!!

"Yes…you finally begin to realize what has happened." The voice rang out once again, "You realize the 'chasm' you have fallen into…in your fanatical quest for ultimate knowledge and power…you have allowed yourself to be manipulated and ended up literally *BECOMING* that which you sought!"

"What does that mean?" As terrifying as this thought was, there was no way to voice it!

He, who had once been Gustav, tried to reach out and *somehow* connect with the voice of the stranger that now appeared in the guise of a tormentor! Even *that* seemed almost impossible…he had already transformed into something much beyond human…and was still changing! The stranger seemed to sense what was happening. He stepped back and looked all around, as he replied, "Your questions are as clear to me, as the light of the day…but…before I answer you…try to look at me, in whatever way you can … and tell me how I appear to you?…look carefully!"

Surprised, Gustav the entity paused and did what was asked. It was difficult at first to 'See'…but within moments…it became easier! *Was it simply a matter of getting used to its new station?*

Even in all this ensuing madness, the stranger appeared just as before…tall, gaunt, standing erect…wait a minute…not really erect… the stranger appeared bent…ever so slightly…at the hip, like he were injured…or somehow *older*! How was that possible? How could this being, who had been fine, just a moment ago, age so suddenly? …And in the very act of voicing this mystery, Gustav the entity, reached out again towards the stranger!

And again…the act caused the stranger to stagger, like he had been physically struck! And…horror of horrors…he now seemed even older!!!

"Every time you reach out to me…to ask me something…you affect me, physically…I physically *age*…you are literally unleashing the dark and morbid forces of Entropy…and not just on me…look around… you are also doing it to everything around you!!"

This was true!! Shockingly, the swirling maelstrom of matter and energy also seemed to have slowed, appreciably…as if its very life energies were somehow being sucked dry!

Why was this happening? How was it happening? And yet…this phenomenon of ageing other matter…seemed oddly familiar! The entity had heard all of this before…in what now seemed like another lifetime…when it had still been a mortal named Friedrich Gustav!

Wasn't this what the mysterious, omnipresent particle Chronux did? Wasn't this *its* function in the universe? - To get events moving and allow 'Time' to 'Flow'. It was Chronux, the great anomaly, with its own unique rules that caused matter and energy to age, change and eventually fall apart!!!

So why was he – Gustav, now having the same effect on his surroundings? Absolutely terrified, he looked towards the stranger's voice for guidance.

"As unbelievable as all of this might seem right now, as much as you would want to deny the undeniable, you who were once Capt. Gustav, in your greed and arrogance, have committed the ultimate folly…and as a result, have damned yourself to an eternity of isolation, as the ultimate anomaly! You are now…and shall forever *remain* – CHRONUX!!! Ha ha ha!"

Impossible!!! The entity wanted to scream…*this was pure madness… how could something like this have happened?*

The stranger continued to laugh, "You never guessed, who I really was, did you? You and your pitiful 'Third Reich' were so obsessed with your quest for 'Ultimate Power' that you did not recognize it…even when it was staring *at* you all the time!"

A wave of nausea hit the entity. *'You lied to me…tricked me'*…it wanted to scream out.

"By now, you must realize that I was no mere guardian of some lost city. However, small parts of what I told you were in fact true. Like you, I too was once a warrior…a seeker of knowledge, and the technology, I gave you…the crystal device…*does* in fact come from roughly a thousand years in your future. That much is true!"

"What I *did not* tell you however is that *I* was never in that future. I was once a naïve, young man named Bhrataha, who lived in an obscure and primitive part of the world, thousands of years *BEFORE* your time! My people were visited by a mysterious 'teacher', who claimed to be from THAT future and who gave us the crystal device. Little did we realize that he would turn out to be the 'Great Deceiver'!"

"Like you, I too sought unlimited power and knowledge…power that would help me rise above my primitive world…and tragically like you, I too fell for the 'Chronux Trap'. It was only when I found myself in the situation that *you* currently find yourself in, that I realized how countless others before me had also fallen for its trap!!!"

The Chronux Trap? … Countless others?

"Yes...the 'Chronux Trap'...you shall soon learn that unlimited power is a curse! As the former bearer of this power, I learnt that universal sentience is a double edged sword!"

"I also realized that I wasn't the first...Ever since Chronux first attained sentience, it has known that it is an anomaly...unable to interact with the rest of the universe. Its every movement caused matter and energy to fall apart...just like you realize it now! By its very existence, it was killing the universe through entropy!"

"While it, itself was immortal, Chronux realized very early on that there would come a time, when it would find itself all alone in the universe! Immortality no longer seemed so appealing! The answer for Chronux was that since it could not abandon its unique role in the universe, it would lure, tempt and trick someone else, into taking its place."

The sickening horror that Gustav - the entity felt was mirrored by its surroundings. As it reacted in shock, ripples of fear spread across the cosmos...*like perverted memories of a pebble, dropped in a still, clear lake!*

CHAPTER NINETEEN

"All this while, we always thought *we* were manipulating Chronux, what none of us realized was that it was *Chronux* that was manipulating us, by creating this seed of desire within us…this thirst for immortality and ultimate power, in humanity! Chronux manipulated us into harnessing it!! All the efforts, all that unrelenting toil, all of civilization…manipulated by the damned particle! And…it was doing this not just on Earth…but across all the sentient corners of the universe…Simultaneously!!!"

"Chronux was laying its devious trap, across the cosmos…inviting any and every one to partake off its twisted offerings! All it needed was some power-hungry, deluded idiot to take the bait. We don't know *when* it happened or *how* it happened, the first time…but it did happen, setting into motion an endless cycle of deception!"

"The first being that fell for its trap, ended up replacing the particle and performing its role. But…by replacing Chronux, that unfortunate fool allowed Chronux to replace him, in the universe and thus be 'liberated'! That unnamed being would have soon realized his mistake and gone through the same turmoil, the original Chronux had suffered! He, in turn would have realized that the only way out, was to get someone *else* to take his place!"

Damn!

"But…all this is easier said than done. As Chronux, one has almost unlimited scope, in terms of what the universe has to offer, but as you now realize, it is *ALMOST* impossible to interact with anything physical. So, to con someone into replacing you, you will only have a tiny window of opportunity."

Meaning?

"You see my dear liberator, as Chronux, you can only interact with the universe, when certain planets and celestial objects, align in a particular way. These alignments last for anywhere from a year to a maximum of six. From Earth's perspective, these conditions occur, when the planet Mars also known as 'War', performs a 'retrograde motion' around the star – 'Antares'…and the planet Saturn is at the constellation of 'Aldebaran'!"

"Only under these conditions, can you physically materialize in the universe…and interact with other life forms… just like I did, outside the 'lost city' you were hunting. In truth, there was never any lost city!!"

What!!! How is that possible? …The Myth of Shambhala is legendary and it's been a part of Tibetan, Chinese and Indian societies…for millennia! How can you say, none of it is true?

"Ha ha ha, you forget my dear, that as Chronux, I had access to all of 'Time'. Inserting a 'legend of a lost city' into the collective consciousness of certain Asian societies was the least of my problems… for I was 'Time' itself… 'Sentient Time'! I have been laying this trap for a long, long time and…you are not the first person to attempt to find it! It is just that…no one else was stubborn enough to see it through."

"I always knew, I needed someone, who was a zealot, who could be tempted with the power of Chronux. *You* fit the bill perfectly!…Oh, and how I have coaxed and coerced you throughout your life!"

The entity said nothing…

"I knew my window was small…for even though you *did* have the desire and curiosity, you also had your moments of doubts… moments of hesitations! You never openly confessed it, but I know… deep down, there were times you contemplated giving all of it up… and joining your fellow Germans, on the war front. Imagine my anxiety - if you had given up half-way through, this painstakingly laid trap…nurtured so meticulously for so long…would have fallen apart. But credit to you, Capt. Gustav, you stuck it out and came through… ha ha ha!"

"Do not blame yourself too much though; you are not the first to fall thus. This cycle of 'trapping' and 'getting trapped' has continued for how long…only Chronux knows…and…it has led to some epic disasters and blunders, by individuals thirsting for immortality! I should know, I am the most recent of these fools, or should I say, I *WAS* the most recent, considering how you - Capt. Gustav have so kindly replaced me now, in this eternal role!"

The entity grimaced with pure frustration!

Still…one thing was not clear – *why was it that Chronux could interact with the universe…only under certain specific celestial alignments? What was so special about these alignments?*

Almost sensing its turmoil, the stranger remarked, "The celestial alignments are 'key'. They represent a pattern that first occurred more than a billion years ago…one that existed at that precise moment in the past, when Chronux first developed sentience! It was under these alignments that Chronux went from being a simple messenger…a mute and impartial carrier of information…to an entity aware of its own existence and status in the universe!!!"

"So, even though Chronux keeps reverberating throughout the cosmos, it finds this particular alignment very special. You could call it nostalgia…*akin to a birthday!*" chuckled the stranger. "It is only during these alignments that Chronux feels compelled to reach out and interact with the physical universe – a universe that gave it sentience! However, given that this is an unnatural act, this process is rarely peaceful."

"Throughout history, 'Saturn in Aldebaran' and 'Mars at Antares' has been considered extremely inauspicious…and you will notice that these periods have generally been scarred with great violence! Small wonder then, that the ancients made the connection between these 'celestial patterns' and 'periods of war and destruction'! What might interest you, is that the Ancient Greeks called Saturn by another name – 'Chronos' – 'The God of Time', and Mars…with 'Ares' or 'War'?"

"Saturn and Mars…when these two perform their cosmic dance, 'Time' and 'War' share a powerful connection!"

"Chronux' physical interaction with the universe causes extreme chaos – with effects ranging from the sub-atomic realm to the macro universe. What a lot of people do not realize is that when the interaction begins; it causes 'time dilations'…at the sub-atomic level. These 'dilations' are unknowingly perceived by all entities, across the cosmos. Different life forms respond to them differently - birds might use this as a 'cue to migrate' from one area to another, animals often respond to them by displaying 'extreme anxiety', but the human reaction is the most interesting!"

"They affect human emotions, often exaggerating our responses. For instance, we have an individual in power, who let's say, is on the verge of making a crucial decision, regarding the fate of a neighboring country. These 'time dilations' might cause him to react in an unduly aggressive manner, leading to grave lapses in judgment. Imagine the impact such lapses could have…tempers become frayed and emotions begin to crack! This is why these periods generally lead to war and violence!"

"Even if you consider your own scenario, my entry into the universe caused intense turmoil that it led to the event, humans call World War II. If you now look at the end of the war, what do you think caused the U.S. President Harry. S. Truman, to sanction the use of the Atom Bomb, knowing full well that history will never forgive him for it? It is the time dilations that my presence…*and now yours*, caused that led to these decisions!"

How long do they last?

"Well…they last for as long as Chronux remains in physical contact with the universe – essentially throughout the planetary alignment. As soon as the alignment passes, Chronux once again becomes an anomaly, bringing the effect to an end!"

The stranger sighed and continued, "I knew my time as Chronux, in the universe was limited. I needed to get you to do what you did, *WHILE* the planets were still aligned. If you had delayed any longer, we would have each been stuck in our respective roles - you as a German soldier seeking glory and I, an anomalous particle… immortal, and alone!"

Silence…an angry silence! …but one that could potentially cause great upheaval in the surroundings!!!

"Careful" warned the stranger, "As Chronux…every move you make; your every reaction…has an effect on your surroundings. You currently perceive things only at the sub-atomic level and are hence unable to observe the macro universe, but trust me, you disturb this structure too much and the universe could be irreparably damaged!"

You tricked me!!!. You promised me immortality; you promised me unlimited power…but you lied!!!

"I gave you exactly what you wished for. I also warned you…but your own arrogance and lust for power blinded you. Just like me before you, you, who were once Capt. Gustav of the Third Reich, are now a universal anomaly. But in taking over my curse, you have become my salvation!"

"I go now to take your place, within the universe, one that you so helpfully vacated. In your fanatical quest for immortality, you ignored one crucial fact: Only if you are mortal, do you truly exist, do you truly live! This is the undeniable law of the universe. By becoming immortal, you have trapped yourself in a state of perpetual 'non-existence'. This is the curse of immortality…the curse of Chronux! From now on, *I* will be Mortal. *I* will be alive and *I* will exist!!!"

As the stranger began to fade from perception, he turned around one final time.

"I leave you with one final piece of advice. If you have learnt anything at all, you will treat this with a little more respect. Every move you make from now on, your every reaction will have immediate impact on the rest of the universe. If you damage the cosmos too much, you run the risk of dooming *yourself* forever…*for there will be no one left to con!* You have already committed the single greatest mistake of your Earthly existence. If you want to have any chance of redemption, treat the universe kindly and maybe, just maybe, the universe will offer you a way out. Remember knowledge of the particle is the basis of the trap. Sharing the knowledge of Chronux will help you tempt and trap others…in theory!"

"I leave you now dear Chronux, to mull over your fate. Of course you need not worry; after all, you do have all of eternity. You are a particle with rules only unto yourself. You are the 'Alpha' and 'Omega'. You are immortal. But you are also completely alone! …for remember, '*In Chronux lies your destiny!*' Ha ha ha ha…"

Even as the fading echo of the stranger's laughter reverberated across the cosmos, the entity that had once been Gustav, felt the despair of the entire universe...as the full extent of its predicament finally became clear. It was 'Chronux'...

...and it was alone!

'One meets his destiny often on the road he takes to avoid it.' - French Proverb

CHAPTER TWENTY

The entity that had once been Gustav experienced anger and frustration, on a universal scale…and as it furiously reverberated across the cosmos, Chronux' rage was absorbed by every subatomic particle it struck, leading to tremendous disturbances in space and time. On Gustav's native planet, Earth, this translated into one of the most calamitous periods, in recent memory!

August 1945 – Earth: A series of disasters…some natural…others that appeared to be driven by the hand of man…racked up a huge toll in life and property.

Between the 1st and the 29th of August, earthquakes of magnitude 6 and above on the Richter scale, struck the east coast of Taiwan, Haida Gwaii in Canada, the Andaman Islands of India, Japan's Ryukyu Islands, the Pasco region of Peru and Vanuatu.

The 1945 flood of the 'Ohio River' was one of the worst in Louisville, Kentucky's history and caused the razing of the entire waterfront district of the neighborhood of Portland, while the 'Texas hurricane', a slow-moving tropical cyclone, caused extensive damage in late August.

Between the 3rd and the 9th of August, with the war in the Pacific reaching its climactic stages, 3 Japanese Cargo ships, 'Tencho Maru', 'Kotohirasan Maru' and 'Rashin Maru', were torpedoed and sunk in the South China Sea and the Sea of Japan, resulting in massive human casualties. While at the same time, the 'USS Bullhead, United States Navy' - a 'Balao-class submarine' was sunk off Bali, Indonesia by a Japanese Air Force Mitsubishi Ki-51 aircraft, killing everyone on board.

The 'El Teniente mining accident' was the biggest metallic mining accident in the history of Chile, in which 355 men died. Many of the miners died of carbon monoxide poisoning, due to a fire that broke out near the mine. Rescue workers spent 3 days trying to free the miners, but to no avail.

In August 1945, World War II: The United States dropped atomic bombs on the Japanese cities of 'Hiroshima' and 'Nagasaki'. A uranium gun-type atomic bomb - Little Boy was dropped on Hiroshima on the 6th of August, followed by a plutonium implosion-type bomb - Fat Man on the city of Nagasaki on the 9th. The two bombs instantly killed over 100,000 people and almost twice that number in the following months, through acute radiation poisoning. In both cities, most of the dead were civilians.

The catastrophic aftershocks of Chronux' fury, were not limited to Earth. Across the cosmos, a wave of entropy was unleashed, causing massive carnage!

In the 'Regilon Star System', 1 million light-years from earth, the life-giving red giant – 'Aldorius' suddenly and mysteriously went Supernova, almost instantly wiping out close to a trillion life forms, throughout the system. The energy output was so large that the explosion was clearly visible up to a billion miles away. The massive explosion finally ended with the star collapsing back on itself, eventually devolving into a Black Hole. This most destructive of all forces – 'The Singularity' – then began to devour all matter and energy, throughout the system.

The 'Verdian System', had long served as home to the super-intelligent Dwarfs of 'Gebe'. Its high tech space observatories had been observing an unusual meteorite-swarm headed towards their system, for close to a year. But…on the fateful day of August the 20th…*by our reckoning*…no one could explain how the substance of the meteorites suddenly changed into Anti-matter! The resulting 'Matter- Antimatter Collision' was equivalent to fifteen thousand, billion mega tons…and instantly annihilated billions of years of civilization and progress!!!

So terrible were these forces unleashed across space and time that they threatened to unravel the very fabric of the cosmos! Never since the Big Bang, had the universe felt such chaos! The fury of Chronux fed on to the surrounding antipathy and increased…geometrically! Such was the level of destruction, that the universe lost 3 percent of its total mass and energy, reducing its life-time by some 4.5 billion years.

Entire galaxies were ripped out of their 'adolescence' and artificially aged into 'adulthood'...Stars and Quasars appeared drained and exhausted.

It felt like 'Death's clandestine paramour' had finally awoken... and...now the universe would reach its ultimate demise...*just a little sooner than scheduled!*

CHAPTER TWENTY ONE

- 'krodhad bhavati sammohah
sammohat smrti-vibhramah
smrti-bhramsad buddhi-naso
buddhi-nasat pranasyati' -

'From anger, delusion arises, and from delusion bewilderment of memory. When memory is bewildered, intelligence is lost, and when intelligence is lost, one falls down again into the material pool.' – The Bhagawat Gita

As it always is...and always has been; all things...even the most violent of acts, must eventually wear down and come to an end! Slowly...painfully, the chaotic reverberations of the newly formed Chronux began to slow down. This was after all, not the Chronux of the past, but one still in its infancy...still barely aware of its scope and power. Like a child, it was prone to the occasional temper tantrum... but this was a child, with the power of God...*and it saw the universe as its plaything!*

Gradually, as the memories of a life as a German Officer began to recede, its feelings of betrayal, of being tricked, started to get replaced with a sense of curiosity...a sense of wonder! The infant particle suddenly became aware of the enormous amount of information; it was tapping from across the universe!

At speeds bordering infinity, Chronux bounced across the cosmos, keeping the universe in an ever-changing state. The wonder of all of this was awe-inspiring, and Chronux felt a sense of elation at its own glory. The last traces of Gustav buried deep within, wanted to scream, in absolute unbridled joy, as power over all that there ever was...and all that ever will be, was finally *his!* Gone was the feeling of being cheated…the feeling of being ostracized…*Chronux now felt like God!*

The particle hurled itself across the cosmos with unchecked exuberance! This would be a new age…a golden age…one where the universe would respond to it…bend to its every whim…or *BE* bent! A billion, billion galaxies…a trillion worlds…many of them sentient… all now and forever, under its withering touch!

The sights and sounds of the cosmos, raced out to greet their new master. In the 'Andromeda Galaxy'…seven worlds with sentience… dominated by the 'Hyprecean Race', had managed to colonize three successive Star Systems. This was a race for which warfare came as easily as progress…a race that had an unquenchable thirst for expansion. Chronux experienced this thirst…and learnt from them!

It marveled at the wonders of the 'Xygmanium Star System'…7 billion light years from the center of the universe, a race of plant like species that had evolved sentience over millennia, and were possibly the most peaceful life forms, in the whole universe!

It reverberated through the magnificent underwater kingdoms of 'Perrikis', with its impenetrable domed structures that were built to protect its inhabitants from the extremely high levels of nitrogen, in the oceans of this watery planet!

Chronux felt the pulse of a billion worlds…the soft, rhythmic beating of a trillion, trillion hearts…and found it overwhelming! The sights, sounds and knowledge of the cosmos were being laid bare before it. Not a single molecule in the universe could as much as tremble…without Chronux becoming aware of it. Truly, this was the greatest conquest of all…! Nothing else in the universe could do what it could…or match its power and influence…!

And yet…something seemed to trouble it…a feeling…just a stray thought…nothing more…one so vague, even Chronux couldn't tell if it was real. But like a bastardized fact gnawing on the delicate tethers of a beautiful myth…*it persisted!*

Chronux tried to still itself…to focus on the source of this feeling… try and isolate it. *Yes!* There it was again…at the farthest corners of its consciousness, was a memory, of another time…another place…

another lifetime! A place called Earth…a pale, blue marble of a planet…'Earth'…so fragile… so beautiful…*so hauntingly familiar!*

Chronux felt drawn towards it…for some reason, this place felt important…*but why?*

This was neither the only sentient world in the universe…nor the most progressive. Yet a feeling of great nostalgia…of remorse… seemed to well up within the particle. *Impossible!!!* For one so nearly omnipotent, such feelings should be inconceivable!

But no…it was true…these feelings…these longings…were undeniable!

As a curious Chronux probed this mystery, what began as stray thoughts, began to take the shape of memories of a life on this planet… a life as a soldier, an explorer…a life dedicated to a cause, under a famous leader.

What were these memories? Why did they seem so familiar? And more importantly, why was there a sense of great incompleteness to them? …it was as if that life had been ended, abruptly!

The memories…if that's what they truly were…intensified each time, Chronux reverberated towards Earth. Yes! …*Earth definitely was the source!*

Curiosity slowly began to give way to anxiety. With each reverberation, the images and memories of this life were becoming more and more distinct! A life as a German Captain, a soldier and explorer, a seeker of truth - who had been deceitfully tricked into taking over the ultimate responsibility of ensuring the flow of 'Time' across the universe - tricked by his own hubris and a desire for immortality, by the previous bearer of 'Time' – Bhrataha!

Chronux suddenly felt the full weight of the burden it carried. 'Godhood' and 'Immortality' no longer felt like they were worthy of envy. 'All powerful'…but 'all alone'…*no sentient being should ever have to shoulder such a burden!*

The true meaning of the great legends of Earth was at least clear! … the 'Epic of Gilgamesh' that spoke of the mythical king recognizing the 'futility of immortality'…the Mahabharata, with its cautionary tale of Ashwatthama, for whom immortality came not as a blessing but as a curse! These were the great lessons of the past.

It was natural that when faced with such an affliction, *any* being would react the way that Bhrataha had. *He* had probably been similarly tricked by *his* predecessor! God knows how long he had been trapped as Chronux! The reaction the new Chronux, felt towards Bhrataha's treachery was not one of anger or frustration...but of empathy!

But it now found itself at the same crossroads; its predecessor had found himself on! Unless it wished to forever remain the anomaly, it would have to find a replacement...someone...some wretched soul... somewhere in the cosmos...who could be lured into uncovering the universe's darkest secrets...and who would in turn fall for the Chronux Trap!

Of course, for that, a trap would have to be laid...and that of course would take time!

...as if *that* was ever a constraint!

CHAPTER TWENTY TWO

When the whole of time and space…from the birth of the universe to its fiery demise…is your plaything, the challenges isn't about what to pick…*but rather what to avoid!*

From its relentless journeys through the cosmos, Chronux knew that close to a billion different Star Systems held sentient life. Any one of which could serve as the basis of its trap…the only constraint being, the level of evolution of the sentient life, on these worlds!

Life had to have evolved enough for it to be manipulated, for unless a species had some concept of 'mortality' and 'death', it would not fall for the 'Chronux Trap'. It was after all this concept that bred the fear of 'Death' and 'Extinction', ultimately leading to aspirations of 'Immortality'…so vital to the success of the trap!

Moreover, merely identifying a victim was not enough. For an entity to even consider Chronux' offer, it would have to possess the potentially toxic combination of curiosity and desire!

The new Chronux, just like its predecessor - Bhrataha would have to lay the trap; deep in the remote 'Past' of any civilization that it chose. Over time, this quagmire would unfold and become an integral part of that civilization's culture…causing zealots to take on its challenges! Timing this first phase was crucial. The trap would have to be set at a point in history that was early enough to allow for large scale manipulations of culture, but also, when civilization had evolved enough to understand and appreciate the 'gift'!

Chronux knew it would also have to target multiple beings. *History was at best, a fickle friend!* The best, laid plans would amount to nothing, if a potential victim saw through them. So, over dependence on a single target was fraught with danger! The lure of 'Immortality' and 'Unlimited Power' would have to be offered freely, for someone to actually take the bait. And even then, Chronux would have to constantly stir the 'broth of betrayal' and coax and concoct its way to success!

This is exactly what Bhrataha had done. Even after Gustav had taken the bait he had 'needled' him and 'egged' him on...just enough to ensure that the German stayed on track. He had cleverly played Gustav's Nazi pride against him...and won!

Chronux seethed with fury at how easily his former-self had allowed himself to be manipulated. But lashing out in frustration would only worsen the situation. Its rage could imperil the entire universe. And if the universe were destroyed, Chronux would remain trapped for all time!

No...this was not the time for anger...this was the time for strategizing and planning...this was the time for *payback*! If not Bhrataha, some other fool could be lured into the trap...and then Chronux would reclaim its own life!

'For I know the plans I have for you," declares the Lord, "plans to prosper you and not to harm you, plans to give you hope and a future.'
- Jeremiah 29:11

But as it began the process of filtering through those civilizations and culture it deemed adequate, Chronux came to a sobering realization. While there were dozens of cultures that fit the bill, laying a trap would mean having detailed knowledge about *each* one of them...from the civilization's remote past all the way to its distant future! Only then would Chronux know for certain, whether its stratagem would succeed!

However, gathering such an epic amount of data and then planning a trap around it, would take millennia...millennia during which Chronux would remain stuck in its current state. Worse still, after all of that, the chosen culture could well prove unfit for the challenge!!!

But the greatest concern was that while Chronux *did* have all the time in the universe, the longer it remained an anomaly, the more used to, it would get to its station. *Given enough time, even the worst form of torture becomes mundane.* It would have to guard against such complacency!

Something its predecessor had said suddenly came back to it. According to Bhrataha, every time an individual was trapped as Chronux, he would try and get rid of it, by enticing someone *else* to take over the curse. But this raised a terrifying new possibility: If Chronux had indeed achieved sentience more than a billion years ago, why was it that there were only so few individuals, who had been trapped by it?

The only possible, gut-wrenching explanation was that sometime after it had trapped its first victim, one of the unfortunate bearers of the power had *NOT* acted soon enough! He might have forgotten his mortal life and in doing so, remained the God Particle for thousands, possibly millions of years!!!

This was not a comforting thought. No!!...it would not let this happen...it would find a host for this accursed burden and get rid of it, once and for all! If gathering knowledge about myriad civilizations, across the cosmos was too time-consuming and risky a venture, it would set the trap in the history of the one civilization, it had complete knowledge about!

There were probably other cultures on other planets that were more pliable and more amenable to manipulation...and in general, more conducive to this trap, but the stakes were simply too high! Chronux knew from its own experience that the planet it had in mind, had a history of making monumental blunders! It was almost as if there was something in the very DNA of its inhabitants that made them stare disaster in the face...and still keep walking... towards it!

Of course, it was not a quality to envy, but it was one that Chronux needed more than anything else. The civilization in question was based on a pale, blue almost inconsequential speck, in the outer-arms of the 'Milky Way' Galaxy. It was a planet that had given the previous bearer of the particle his freedom, and a planet that the late Capt. Friedrich Gustav had once called home. Chronux was headed towards Earth!

Bhrataha's final words seemed to echo indelibly, through the cosmos, "*Remember...sharing knowledge of the particle is the basis of the trap...it allows you to set the trap around your chosen victim. For ultimately remember... In Chronux lies your destiny!"*

Like the soulful, tear-stained reminders of long lost love, Chronux had an epiphany about how best to share this knowledge...how best to trap its *next* unsuspecting earthly victim...it was going to leave its story behind in the form of...a book!

Epilogue

- *'dhūmenāvriyate vahnir yathādarśho malena cha yatholbenāvṛito garbhas tathā tenedam āvṛitam'* -

'Just as a fire is covered by smoke, a mirror is masked by dust, and an embryo is concealed by the womb, similarly one's knowledge gets shrouded by desire.' – Bhagawat Gita

My dear, unfortunate savior, the unadulterated regret I feel for your plight, is matched only by the absolute sense of gratitude I have for you...for liberating me from this eternal nightmare!

Needless to say, I am responsible for a lot of the paranoia that you are now beginning to experience...the disconcerting 'gaps' in your memories...for instance, I am sure, you find yourself suddenly no longer able to recall all the incidents that have *supposedly* occurred, in your decades long existence...and are now starting to rely on comforting assumptions...by feverishly holding on to the notion that you DID exist, even *in* those 'gaps'.

But slowly...the sickening realization of your current predicament...a sense of utter hopelessness...shall begin to sink in... as my snare closes around you! You are...after all, beginning to change...to evolve...to transcend towards your true destiny!

As you know by now, sharing the knowledge of Chronux *is* the very basis of its trap...and in reading this book, you have unwittingly allowed the walls of that trap, to crystallize around yourself!

Unlike some of my predecessors, *I* did not feel it necessary to lure you onto some epic quest...and through it, shackle you within the *adamantine* bonds of Time. All of that happened...through your reading this text itself...for in doing so, you succumbed to the seductive lure of curiosity's quagmire!

But...already...I fear that the debilitating effects of the 'Chronux Trap' are making it difficult for you to comprehend me... *Already, Time begins to clasp you to its cold, withered bosom!*

So, I allow you to slowly embrace your new role, as the immortal but anomalous, 'Custodian of Time'...even as, I go once again, to drink from the bittersweet cup of 'mortality'!!!

You, my dear savior, shall forever have my eternal undying gratitude...for, after all, as you NOW know very well...

...*'In Chronux lies your destiny!'*

References

These were just a few of the many sources that I referred to, through the course of this work. Although this book does not necessarily agree with all the premises proposed in these sources, they still proved invaluable at various points.

1. The Nazi Connection with Shambhala and Tibet- by Alexander Berzin http://www.bibliotecapleyades.net/sociopolitica/sociopol_shambahla01.htm
2. http://studybuddhism.com/en/advanced-studies/vajrayana/kalachakra-advanced/overview-of-kalachakra
3. http://studybuddhism.com/web/en/archives/advanced/kalachakra/practice_texts/guru_yoga_prayers/prayer_shambhala.html
4. http://www.crystalinks.com/shambhala.html
5. http://www.crystalinks.com/vril.html
6. http://www.crystalinks.com/blacksun.html
7. http://www.crystalinks.com/thule.html
8. http://www.conspiracyarchive.com/NWO/Vril_Society.htm
9. https://sitsshow.blogspot.in/2015/03/the-black-sun-and-luminous-lodge-vril.html
10. http://nexusilluminati.blogspot.in/2015/03/the-black-sun-and-luminous-lodge.html
11. B. N. Narahari Achar, "A Note on the Five-year Yuga of VedAGga jyotiSa", EJVS, 3-4, (1997).
12. B. N. Narahari Achar, " On the meaning of AV XIX.53.3: Measurement of Time?" EJVS, 4-2, (1998).
13. B. N. Narahari Achar "Date of the Mahabharata War Based on Simulations using Planetarium Software" in The Date of the Mahabharata War Based on Astronomical Data Edited by

Suryakanth U. Kamath, The Mythic Society, Bangalore, India, (2004) pp. 65-115

14. B. N. Narahari Achar "Planetarium Software and the Date of the Mahabharata War" in The Mahabharata: What is not here is nowhere else, Edited by T. S. Rukmani, Munshiram Manoharlal Publishers, New Delhi, India (2005), Pp. 247-263
15. http://www.historyplace.com/worldwar2/riseofhitler/
16. http://www.bbc.co.uk/history/worldwars/wwtwo/hitler_01.shtml
17. http://www.history.com/topics/world-war-ii/battle-of-the-bulge
18. http://www.history.com/this-day-in-history/battle-of-the-bulge
19. https://www.army.mil/botb/
20. http://www.thranguhk.org/buddhism/en_mahakala.html
21. http://buddhism.lib.ntu.edu.tw/FULLTEXT/JR-BH/bh117515.htm
22. http://www.history.com/topics/world-war-ii/bombing-of-hiroshima-and-nagasaki
23. http://www.history.com/this-day-in-history/atomic-bomb-dropped-on-hiroshima
24. https://www.osti.gov/opennet/manhattan-project-history/Events/1945/hiroshima.htm
25. http://www.stephen-knapp.com/complete_review_of_vedic_literature.htm
26. The Secret Teachings of the Vedas. The Eastern Answers to the Mysteries of Life - by Stephen Knapp
27. http://www.bhagavad-gita.org/index-english.html
28. http://www.o-bible.com/kjv.html
29. http://info-buddhism.com/Tibet-1938-1939-Ernst-Schaefer-Expedition-Engelhardt.html
30. http://www.ancient-code.com/element-115-infamous-alien-element-mentioned-over-a-decade-ago-in-area-51-added-to-periodic-table/
31. http://www.rense.com/general96/dieglocke.html
32. http://www.crystalinks.com/nazibell.html
33. *Allen, Louis (1969). "The Nuclear Raids". In Hart, Basil Liddell. History of the Second World War. Volume 6. London: Purnell. pp. 2566–2576.*

34. https://web.archive.org/web/20060624185903/http://www.dtra.mil/toolbox/directorates/td/programs/nuclear_personnel/docs/DNATR805512F.pdf

35. http://www.rerf.or.jp/shared/ds02/pdf/chapter01/cha01-p42-61.pdf

36. https://www.trumanlibrary.org/whistlestop/study_collections/bomb/large/documents/index.php?pagenumber=42&documentid=65&documentdate=1946-06-19

37. Fire in the Sky: The Air War in the South Pacific- by Eric. M. Bergerud

38. http://www.ancient.eu/gilgamesh/

39. http://www.aina.org/books/eog/eog.pdf